Julie Miller is an award-winn[ing] author of breathtaking romantic [suspense.] Readers' Choice Award and a Daphne du Maurier Award, among other prizes. She has also earned an *RT* Career Achievement Award. For a complete list of her books, monthly newsletter and more, go to juliemiller.org

Bestselling author **Anna J. Stewart** honestly believes she was born with a book in her hand. After growing up devouring every story she could get her hands on, now she gets to make her living making up stories and fulfilling happily-ever-afters of her own. Her dreams have most definitely come true. Anna lives in Northern California (only a ninety-minute flight from Disneyland, her favourite place on earth) with two monstrous, devious, adorable cats named Sherlock and Rosie.

Discover more at millsandboon.co.uk

SHARP EVIDENCE

JULIE MILLER

A DETECTIVE'S DEADLY SECRETS

ANNA J. STEWART

MILLS & BOON

First Published in Great Britain 2023
by Mills & Boon, an imprint of HarperCollins*Publishers* Ltd
1 London Bridge Street, London, SE1 9GF

www.harpercollins.co.uk

HarperCollins*Publishers*
Macken House, 39/40 Mayor Street Upper,
Dublin 1, D01 C9W8, Ireland

Sharp Evidence © 2023 Julie Miller
A Detective's Deadly Secrets © 2023 Anna J. Stewart

ISBN: 978-0-263-30755-9

1223

SHARP EVIDENCE

JULIE MILLER

To the state of Missouri, which was celebrating its bicentennial (aka two hundredth birthday!) at the time this book was written (not when it is being published).

Thank you for being the state where I was born. And thank you for giving me so many wonderful places to visit and so many interesting places to set my books!

Chapter One

Jackson Dobbs left the Monday morning staff meeting at the Kansas City Police Department Crime Lab with his usual focus on the work he needed to accomplish. He rolled up the printouts with the notes he'd jotted from the meeting and stuffed them into the back pocket of his jeans before striding down the hallway toward his office, where he'd left his lab coat and safety goggles.

As a criminalist with the KCPD Crime Lab, he had a varied job. He was trained to report to crime scenes and collect evidence. Because of his inimitable patience and eye for detail, he was often called on to analyze reports and review tests conducted by other team members. But mostly, he was known as the Sharps Guy, the crime lab's resident expert on weaponry of all kinds, especially blades or other *sharp* weapons. He knew more about killing tools than the average criminalist, and he was sometimes requested to consult on investigations with other labs. He didn't have a kinky obsession with analyzing bloody wound tracks and gruesome crime scenes. But he was far too familiar with all the ways one person could kill another. His life had been profoundly impacted by violence since and including the murder of his parents when he was twelve.

The *unsolved* murder, which had irrevocably changed his life.

Even as a twelve-year-old, he'd vowed that if he could survive his uncle's home, he'd find a way to help others the way he wished someone had helped him. Always the biggest kid in his class, he'd taken down bullies in school—then been punished at home for getting suspended. He'd been picked on himself because he preferred books over sports despite his imposing physique, and he could be freaky quiet, which had earned him nicknames like Creeper, Stalker and Mutant.

He'd been fortunate in high school to find a teacher who encouraged him to try out for football, even though his heart wasn't in the game—mostly because Uncle Curtis was such a big fan of football—and recovering a fumble or allowing the defense to sack the quarterback could determine whether or not he was "loved" at home that week. He'd enlisted in the Army to escape Curtis Graham's house, and to pay for his college degree.

After basic training, he'd been recruited for the military's Golden Gloves boxing program. The damaged facade that sports had started was completed in the boxing ring, giving him the look of an MMA fighter with a nose that had been broken and reset more than once, a scar through his left eyebrow, and two misshapen fingers from broken metacarpals and phalanges. When his stint in the military was up, he'd skipped a homecoming with the family that hadn't wanted him and gone to college to major in science and criminal justice. Then he'd gone to work at the crime lab.

Marriage and family had never been in the cards for him.

Despite the loving example set by his parents in his early childhood, Jackson had too many strikes against him to develop a lasting relationship with a woman. Intimidating size. Ugly face. Working with crime and violence and death. Being an introvert. And an inability to process his emotions in a way most people understood.

But he had friends here at the lab. He had good memories from before and after his years at Uncle Curtis's house. And he was very, very good at his job.

He was assisting others by collecting and processing evidence that could help the police, local sheriff's department and district attorney solve cases, win trials and get criminals off the streets. One day, he'd solve the murders of Everett and Melora Dobbs. But for now, helping others was enough. His work at the crime lab gave him a reason to get up in the morning, and to use every skill he possessed to find the answers needed to solve a case. Because every crime he solved got one more bad guy off the streets and freed up the caseload of one more detective who might just reopen the investigation into his parents' deaths.

Jackson breathed out a heavy sigh that buzzed his lips. Helping others. Right. People were counting on him. Maybe just professionally—but they needed him to do his job. It was the only reason anyone had ever needed him—to get a job done. And he wasn't going to let *anyone* down.

The first thing on his to-do list today was to process a handgun that had been found in a dumpster behind the Yankee Hill Road homeless shelter. At the scene, he'd been able to determine the gun had been recently fired. But with no reported gunshot victim or shots fired in the area, it was most likely a dump site. It was up to him to run ballistics to see if the gun could be matched to any other crime scene, and if it could be traced to a registered gun owner who might have reported it stolen or who might be a viable suspect for the KCPD to pursue. He'd ID the gun first—the serial number had been filed off, but he knew the chemicals that could restore the missing identification, if it wasn't too degraded. Jackson opened his office door. Then he'd test-fire a round...

"Hey! Excuse me?"

Jackson turned in the doorway. A petite woman was hurrying toward him, the ample curves of her hips and breasts shimmying a little as she walked. She had a big purse slung over one shoulder of the denim jacket she wore, and a paper sack with handles on it hooked over her other arm. Automatically, he glanced over his shoulder to see whose attention she was trying to get, but he saw no one in the hallway behind him. Everyone was either lingering in the conference room to continue conversations, or they had headed into the memorial lounge to refill coffee mugs and grab whatever snack they wanted to fuel their morning.

"Hello? Sir?" Her cheerful contralto voice called out again and he turned. "Yeah. You."

Jackson faced the pint-size dynamo again. Good grief. She was talking to *him*. She was making a beeline straight toward him. Jackson felt the hackles at the back of his neck prick to attention and his muscles brace in anticipation.

Did he know this woman? Was she a cop or someone from the DA's office? She wasn't armed, and didn't wear that guarded air of wary alertness that the law enforcement personnel he knew did. She looked too young to be an attorney with her fitted jeans that were ripped at one knee, and her worn leather ankle boots. Maybe a law student?

Had she been involved in a case with him? It couldn't have been directly. He would have remembered her short bouncy hair, the color of copper burnished with gold. Or the violet-blue eyes. Or the freckles dotting her face and hands like cookie sprinkles. Or curves that were almost too much for her short height.

He knew he hadn't dated her. His relationship history was next to nil except for a few friends with benefits encounters over the years.

Such was the love life of a man who was six foot four, built like a defensive lineman, with the distorted features of a prize fighter and who had a damn hard time speaking to most people. Especially a pretty woman. And this one was pretty. In a cute, shapely, all-American sense of the word. Like a breath of fresh air.

Or a hurricane.

"Hello? Did you hear me?" She slapped her hand over her mouth as a blush flooded her cheeks and blended the freckles away. With her face tilted to his, she leaned to the left and then to the right, studying either side of his square-jawed face. "I'm sorry. You're not hard of hearing or on your phone, are you?" She twirled her finger up by her own ear. "I didn't see you wearing anything on your ear."

She thought he was deaf? Preoccupied? He'd heard her just fine. "No."

"You're not on the phone? Whew." She smiled, and the light coming in through the front hallway's floor-to-ceiling windows suddenly seemed to pale in comparison. She thumbed over her shoulder toward the reception desk. "There was no one at the front desk when I came in. I heard voices down this way and thought I'd see if I could find someone to help me, and here you are."

She smiled again. As if meeting him was a good thing.

"She's pregnant."

"Who?" The violet-blue eyes blinked as she processed his terse response. "Oh. The receptionist at the front desk? She's taking a bathroom break? I hear that's pretty common when you're having a baby."

Isn't that what he'd said? That was the explanation he'd meant to give. But Freckles here seemed to understand.

"I didn't realize she'd be coming back. Should I have waited?" She held up the sack she carried. "I can't stay too long. I have a class to teach this morning, and parking's a bear on campus. But I didn't want to risk anything happening to this. It already felt creepy keeping it in my apartment last night."

Now Jackson was genuinely curious about whatever was in the sack. As a rule, his team collected, labeled and processed evidence themselves to ensure the chain of custody. "What?"

She handed the sack over to him, and he was surprised to feel the weight of it. He opened it to look inside and saw a rolled-up piece of flowered material stiff with dried blood. Clearly, there was something else in the bag with the blouse. But if this was something legit, he couldn't reach inside until he gloved up. Jackson's eyes narrowed as he moved his gaze to hers, asking for more information.

Freckles leaned closer to peek inside the sack. "I found it at the theater on Williams University campus. I was going through boxes with a bunch of donations. I thought it was a prop at first. But the more I looked at the blouse it's wrapped in, the more I thought the blood might be real. Stage blood gets goopy and gelatinous after it sits for a while. This is different. I assumed I should turn it in to someone who knows what to do with it. To look at it. Analyze it. Frankly, it's a little disturbing." She rolled her eyes. "Actually, it's a lot disturbing."

Jackson nodded. Generally, a concerned citizen called the police when they discovered something like this. He wondered what had prompted this woman to deliver it to the crime lab herself. "Looks like blood."

She pulled back to clasp the strap of her small duffel bag of a purse and shrugged. "I'm certainly no expert. You are. I hope."

Actually, his friend Grayson Malone was the blood expert here. He should direct her to Gray's office. But his brain short-circuited for a moment when she reached out and briefly brushed her fingers against the bare skin of his forearm before latching on to her purse again.

"Sorry. I should back up. I'm Reese Atkinson."

Reese? Now why did that name sound familiar? He was going back to the idea that she might have been a witness or a suspect or even a victim on a case he'd worked. But wouldn't he have remembered all those freckles and red hair?

"I'm an assistant professor at the Williams University Theater."

Jackson's speculation ceased and his jaw clenched at the mention of the place where his parents had once worked—and where they'd been killed. Did she know about his parents? Did she think her find was related to a twenty-three-year-old case? But if this woman picked up on his distress, she didn't let on. Or maybe his discomfort was the reason she kept right on talking. He knew he could put off a scary vibe when he got upset. Maybe she thought that if she spit everything out as quickly as possible, the conversation would end sooner and she could leave. Maybe she was just as stressed out about making this report as he was hearing it.

"I'm directing a show there now, an Agatha Christie murder mystery. It's part of my doctoral work. At first, I thought this was someone's idea of another practical joke."

His radar pinged with the detail that slipped into her conversation. "*Another* joke?"

She shook her head, waving aside his query. "Long story. Someone has been playing games with me. I'm sure he or she thought it would be funny to hear me scream. Not that I did. It was more of a gasp and a couple of unladylike words. At any rate, if they truly wanted me to find it, why bury it in a pile of boxes behind the stage? Why not leave it in my office again?"

Again? What games was she referring to?

"Or onstage? Everyone knows I'm the first one to arrive and the last one to leave rehearsals." Shaking her head had loosened some of her hair so that it fell onto her face. She tucked her copper curls behind her ears. One of them sprang back onto the apple of her cheek and Jackson wanted to touch it.

He wanted to see if it was as soft as it looked, and if her skin was cool like porcelain or warm like the tiny spots that dotted her face. He carefully tightened his grip around the handles of the sack, willing the urge to leave his fingers.

"Dr. Diamant has been on my case about the backstage area being a mess—for Pete's sake, we're building sets and pulling costumes and running secondary rehearsals back there. Of course, it's going to be messy. But he wants to have a party at the theater and have everything look nice. So, yesterday I stayed late to carry the boxes of recent donations from one of our patrons upstairs to get those out of the way, at least, since they aren't related to my show. I started sorting through the boxes—I pitched a couple of 1970s prom dresses that would only fit someone who was a size zero, and I hung up some other things we might be able to use." She paused for a breath and shied away from the sack he now held, hugging her arms beneath her breasts. "Then I found those. The material was wrapped around it, so I brought both."

"Around what?"

"The knife."

Knife? Williams University Theater? Blood? A chill ran down from his head to the toes of his work boots. In the very next breath, the heat of grief, anger and frustration that he'd buried inside for twenty-three years poured through him. The memories of all he had lost, and couldn't yet understand, buffeted him on all sides.

Reese Atkinson pulled her bottom lip between her teeth in an unspoken apology before holding up the finger and thumb of her right hand. "FYI, if you find my fingerprints on it, it'll be just these two fingers on the tip of the handle. That's how I picked it up. That's when I realized it was too heavy to be a prop. The blade didn't retract, and I thought the blood looked real, so I rolled it back up in the blouse where I found it, and decided to show someone who dealt with, you know, evidence things."

"Evidence things?" He pushed aside his emotions to stay with the conversation.

She nodded. "Crime lab stuff. I know television isn't always accurate, but I've seen shows where they put things in a paper sack and try not to touch anything so you don't transfer your own DNA or trace from your body onto what may be a significant clue to help solve a crime." She gestured to Jackson. "Then it goes to you guys at the crime lab."

"Pretty accurate." Television gave an unrealistic view of the speed with which tests were run, and how quickly conclusive results could be verified. But she had the basic facts right. "A certified criminalist should collect the evidence."

"I don't know any. Well, except you now. You're a certified criminalist, right?"

Jackson nodded.

"You're thinking I should have called the police?" Her red-gold eyebrows arched with an apology, and she gnawed on that full bottom lip again.

Reese Atkinson had such an expressive face. He could read every emotion there, from her worries about the knife and bloody blouse being some kind of sick joke to the nervousness she was feeling right now. He even saw her shoulders lift and her facial muscles still as she calmed herself and took on a more detached, professional demeanor.

"I considered it for about two seconds. But it wasn't like there was a crime scene at the theater. And I really don't need any more trouble with my show or want to explain to Dr. Diamant why the police were at the theater so late last night."

Jackson shifted with a concern he didn't want to feel because it wasn't his place to do anything about it. But was Reese saying that she had been in the theater by herself in the middle of the night? Where was campus security? Where were the people who cared about her? "You were there late?"

"Last one to leave, remember?" She raked her fingers

through her hair, as if she was shaking off a bad memory. "I didn't think I should leave that lying around where someone might hurt themselves, or it could disappear."

"It's safer here." The situation wasn't ideal, as she might have inadvertently disturbed a secondary crime scene. Or, if she had nefarious intentions like covering up a crime that she or someone she knew had committed, then bringing the evidence to the crime lab herself might compromise any further investigation. "The police will want to talk to you."

She nodded. "I figured. I'm trying to do the right thing here, but I'm not sure exactly what that is. Like I said, I didn't want to make too much of a fuss. I don't need any more attention on me." She held out her hand in a friendly gesture. "Thanks for listening. I really do need to get to class."

She was still holding out her hand, so he shifted the sack to his left hand and swallowed hers up with his right. Although he intentionally made his touch as gentle as possible, she squeezed his hand in a firm grip that zapped frissons of electricity beneath his skin. Before he fully understood that little jolt of awareness, she was pulling away and pointing to the sack.

"I left my name and phone number in the bag, in case you need to follow up on anything. Or your police friends want to contact me."

He followed her gaze to where he heard footsteps behind him in the hallway, and saw his friends and coworkers Grayson Malone and Officer Aiden Murphy with his K-9 partner, Blue, strolling beside him.

"Looks like you've got company. It was nice to meet you, Mr... Um...?"

He swung his gaze back down to her violet-blue eyes. "Jackson Dobbs."

"Dobbs? Do I know you?" Her face squinched up into an adorable little frown. "Usually, I'm good with faces."

Since he didn't have an answer for her, he didn't say anything.

"Oh, well. It'll come to me."

Her pretty smile aimed up at him distracted him for a moment. But he was never distracted enough to forget the job. He reached behind him to pull out his wallet and handed her a business card with the crime lab logo and his contact information. "Here."

She skimmed the pertinent information before tucking the card into the bottomless pit of her purse. "Jackson—cool name. Thank you for your help."

With one last dazzling smile, she turned and hurried toward the front door, leaving Jackson standing there. She paused to introduce herself to Heather, the front desk receptionist, before looking back at Jackson and wiggling her fingers in a wave goodbye. Then she pushed open the glass doors and disappeared into the crisp autumn sunshine.

Feeling an urgent flare of curiosity, Jackson carried the sack into his office and set it on his desk before retrieving a pair of sterile gloves from the lab coat hanging on his closet door. By the time he had pulled on the gloves, Gray, Aiden and Blue had walked in behind him.

Blue, a Belgian Malinois, who considered the crime lab offices his second home, hopped up onto the small couch in Jackson's office. The dog pulled the blanket off the back of the couch, pawed it into a nest and plopped down to take a nap. Jackson heard the distinctive sound of Grayson's prosthetic legs and crutches as he came up on one side of him. Aiden turned and propped his backside against the desk on the other side.

The uniformed officer was grinning from ear to ear as he mimicked the wave Reese had given him on her way out. "You been holding out on us, big guy? Who's the redhead?"

Jackson pulled open the bag and snapped a picture of the contents with his cell phone. "Reese Atkinson from Williams University."

"Who's that?" Grayson asked, equally curious about Jackson's unexpected visitor.

"No idea."

Aiden chuffed him on the shoulder. "Man, you suck at giving us the scoop on your love life."

What love life? Aiden had married Jackson's team supervisor the previous Christmas, and Grayson was now engaged to the woman who had lived next door to him, and been his physical therapist. Jackson liked and admired both women, but he wasn't holding his breath that he was going to find the same sort of happily-ever-after for himself.

Once it became clear that Jackson was more focused on the contents of the sack than on answering their teasing questions, Grayson asked, "Other than the fact that she was cute enough that even you had to notice, what did she want?"

"Dropped this off." Jackson flattened the sack after he pulled out the rolled-up ball of clothing, and he carefully set it down on the clean brown paper.

With a long, low whistle, Aiden straightened when he saw all the blood. "What's that?"

"She thinks it's evidence."

"Of what?" Aiden asked.

Jackson carefully unwound the stiff bloodstained blouse. "You'll be sending that to me for analysis?" Gray asked.

Jackson nodded, studying the long steel item inside. Although it was caked with blood and tarnished with age, he could make out the basic details of a Bowie knife with an eight-to-nine-inch blade and a cross guard to protect the user's hands. "A collector's weapon," he surmised, knowing the design was too impractical to carry on a belt or in a boot. Military and hunting knives tended to be shorter, and might have a serrated edge. Plus, their handles were made of a polypropylene or other polymers rather than wood wrapped in leather like this one.

"An antique?" Grayson clarified. "Something old used for a more modern crime?"

A wave of something familiar prickled the nape of Jackson's neck. "Don't know."

Aiden voiced the concern Jackson probably should have. "That's not her blood, is it? Is she all right?"

"Said she found it." Jackson opened his closet to retrieve his crime scene kit. He pulled out a couple of evidence bags to stow and label the knife and blouse. "Saw no injury on her."

Just smiles and freckles. Soft curly hair and sweet womanly curves.

"She found it at the theater?" Gray's investigative mind seemed to be heading down the same path as Jackson's suspicions.

"Yeah."

Grayson swore. He knew the history of the Dobbses' unsolved murder. Over the years they'd worked together, he'd helped Jackson run a few off-the-books tests that had amounted to nothing. "That hasn't been in our chain of custody," Grayson pointed out. "You need to follow up on it. Get pictures of where it was found. Take statements from any witnesses."

"Just her. She found it."

"Hell, Jackson. Are you thinking...? Your parents?"

"That weapon was never found."

Aiden interrupted the back-and-forth volleys of the criminalists' suspicions. "What are you two talking about?"

"His parents were murdered in the parking lot outside the Williams University Theater," Grayson explained.

"I thought that happened years ago."

"Twenty-three." Jackson felt a little light-headed as he sealed the bags. A clue like this hadn't dropped into his lap before. Why would it show up now? If it even was connected to his parents' murders. "Stabbed to death. A few suspects were questioned, but no one was ever arrested. KCPD never did get their hands on the knife." He passed the bags over to Grayson. "Can you process the blood that's on the blade? See if it's a match to Mom or Dad? I can give you a sample of my blood if you need it for comparison."

"Murder cases remain open until they're solved. They'll be in the system." Grayson squeezed Jackson's shoulder, reminding him not to get his hopes up. "But you know it's a long shot."

"Reese found it in a box of clothing from the '70s. Older than the murders, I know, but who knows how many years the knife has been sitting in that box? Where did it come from?" Jackson peeled off his gloves and chucked them into the trash. "Or if someone recently hid it in there, then they have access to the theater."

"Chelsea could compile a list of names," Grayson suggested, referring to the lab's resident computer guru. "Students, faculty, staff."

"Does she know where the box came from?" Aiden asked. Like a good cop, he'd pulled out his notebook and was already jotting down information to generate a report.

"Donation." Jackson grabbed his leather jacket off the back of his chair.

Grayson followed him to the door. "Where are you going?"

"Williams University Theater."

"You think this is a lead?"

If not, it was a damn cruel coincidence. He was either going to find a lead toward solving his parents' murders, or rule out the possibility of hope.

Jackson had a feeling that, either way, Reese Atkinson was the key to determining which answer he'd find.

Chapter Two

"You have to break it during every show? That sucks."

Reese tried not to feel cornered by the younger man. He'd stopped her at the stairs leading up to the apron of the stage after she'd dismissed her Theater in Society class. But she was leaning back, and would have to sit on the middle step to avoid making physical contact if he came any closer.

She put up her hand to ask him to take a step back. "A little room, please, Zach."

"That's not fair."

She knew Zach Oliver was barely out of his teens, and that her show was his first Williams University assignment as property master, so he was still learning the ropes about doing a production that was more professional than those he'd worked on in high school. Yet it annoyed her that instead of making an appointment to discuss this during her office hours, or before or after rehearsal that evening, he'd started this conversation now. His fellow students hadn't even cleared the auditorium, and she hadn't had a chance to gather her bag and lecture notes. If she thought he was the conniving, dangerous sort, like the creeper who'd been leaving her cryptic messages and unwanted gifts, she might have suspected he was trying to catch her off guard and intimidate her into acquiescing to his demands. She also tried not to feel threatened by the way she had to crane her neck to look at him, since practically every adult male on the planet towered over her five feet, three inches of height.

Zach finally huffed a curse and propped his fists at his waist before taking one small step back. This was worth it, right? She worked the extra hours and dealt with all the egos surrounding her in theater academia so she could end up with the title of *Doctor*, and people would take her more seriously. Well, not everyone. Mostly her coworkers. And her more problematic students. All for a little respect. All to prove she was more than just a cute face or a child star who'd never reached her full potential.

Reese breathed in deeply, schooling her patience and remembering that she was the adult here—the teacher, an assistant professor of theater arts, a soon-to-be PhD if she could survive this semester and defend her dissertation next semester. Zach was the student, part of her backstage crew on her play—if an understandably upset student.

His short dreads bounced against his dark skin as he gestured to the three-foot-tall gargoyle sculpted out of two-by-fours and papier-mâché sitting on the edge of the stage. "Do you know how many hours I put into making that?" Zach whined. "I thought you'd like it."

"I'm sorry, Zach." There was no arguing that the young man had created a work of art that looked as if he'd pulled it off the surviving parapets at Notre-Dame Cathedral. "It's a beautiful piece. But the character is killed when a pediment from on top of the building is pushed off and it crushes him. We'll be dropping it from the fly space every show. That's why I asked you to make something that looked more like a piece of stone. Like this." She drew a quick sketch on her omnipresent notebook.

Zach snorted at her simplistic drawing. "You want me to build a cube?"

"Your gargoyle is stunning," she assured him, hoping to turn this misunderstanding into a teachable moment. "We can use it as a set-decoration piece. Or in the display window in the lobby where we advertise the show. But part of being the property master is that you find or create props that meet the needs of the show. What I need is something that looks like a carved piece of stone. One that doesn't have a delicate neck like your gargoyle that will break when we drop it."

"Why don't you just get a real rock or cinder block?"

"Think about it. I'm not going to endanger anyone in the cast or crew by dangling a real chunk of stone over their heads that could break loose, or be accidentally released and come crashing down and hurt someone."

Understanding sparked in his dark eyes. "It needs to be about function as much as design."

"Exactly." Reese smiled, relieved that he was finally getting the point.

Zach was nodding, and she could see the wheels of creativity turning again. "Back to the drawing board, I guess."

"Thank you. Study some of the architecture around the old campus if you want inspiration. And remember, I *will* find a place to use your gargoyle."

"Sure thing, Ms. A. I need to get to class." Now he was backing up the aisle, his temper cooled by her explanation. It was a small victory. But it was a victory. "Are you still up for knitting that scarf we need for the show?"

Reese reached into her bag and pulled out the knitting needles stuck inside a skein of marled gray wool. "Already working on it. I've got the matching wig done, too. Go. You'll be late."

Zach gave her a thumbs-up, grabbed his backpack and jogged up the aisle to the exit. As he pushed open the door to the lobby, the dean of the Fine Arts Department, her doctoral supervisor, Dr. Dean Diamant, entered the theater. He stopped to chat with a group of three female students who were laughing when he approached and drew him into the middle of their conversation.

"Dean Dean!" One of them greeted him before trading a light hug. Now they were laughing at his once charming but woefully overused joke about being called Dean Dean.

But when the dark-haired girl who'd hugged him glanced back at Reese, Reese couldn't help but wonder if Dr. Diamant was checking up on *her*. As dean of the School of Fine Arts, he had every right to sit in on any class in the theater, music, dance or art departments. But since he was the adviser for Reese's PhD program, as well as the senior professor on staff in the Theater Department, she was always conscious of his subtle evaluations of her performance—as a teacher, director of the current production at the theater and interim manager of the theater itself for this term.

Unfortunately, Reese needed to chat with the same young lady who'd glanced her way. Reese packed her knitting back into her bag and waited for the conversation to wane. When it looked like the three girls were about to head out the door, she called after them. "Maisey?" She waved the young woman down to join her at the front of the stage. "Do you have a few minutes?"

"Sure." Maisey flipped her long dark hair behind her shoulders, and waved goodbye to Dr. Diamant before coming down the aisle. Her friends followed right behind her, and sat down in the third row to wait for her. "What's up? Do you have some notes about Vera?"

Maisey mentioned the part she was playing in *And Then There Were None*, the Agatha Christie murder mystery Reese was staging. Maisey was a beautiful girl, and a talented actor, who hoped to make it big on Broadway or in Los Angeles one day. Just as Reese had once hoped to pursue that same dream.

Before fear and tragedy rewrote the journey of her life.

While Reese couldn't deny Maisey Sparks's onstage talent and enthusiasm for the theater, there were some real-life issues the twentysomething needed to deal with. "Did you get your paper done? I'm ready to hand the others back to the class, but I'm still waiting for yours."

The younger woman lifted one brow into a beautiful arch, and pressed her lips into a pout. "You gave me an extension to get it done and turned in."

Reese kept her voice low so that Maisey's friends couldn't eavesdrop on their private conversation. "Yes. But now it's a week past that extension."

"I'm focusing on learning my lines and creating my character for the show. I'm the star. The play ultimately rests on my shoulders."

No. A play was all about teamwork. Talent behind the scenes and onstage all had to do their part to make a show come to life. Even a one-woman show needed the expertise and support of a strong director and a dedicated tech crew. And this was no one-woman show.

Reese hated feeling like the bad guy here. She'd once had that same devotion to her theatrical career until the nightmare had started and she'd lost her parents in their fight to keep her safe. Afterward, she'd moved in with her newlywed older sister and brother-in-law and had been forced to rethink her priorities. She'd used her free time to work two jobs to help pay her way instead of participating in play after play. Still reeling from the tragedy of losing half her family on one wintry night, along with the sense of security she'd taken for granted growing up, Reese had given up her dream of treading the boards on Broadway in favor of sticking closer to home and what family she had left.

No longer a starry-eyed young teenager, Reese had gone back to school and rediscovered her love for theater in the world of academia. Now she had her hand in all elements of the theater, not just in onstage performance. She enjoyed working with young adults, and hopefully was inspiring their love for the arts now and for the rest of their lives. She could support herself on her modest university salary, and she was happy. Mostly. She still missed her parents. She worked for a capricious boss. She had a sister and two darling nephews she adored. She loved her job, if not all the people. But she could get along with pretty much anyone if she had to. The rest of her reimagined life would fall into place one day, too. Love. A family of her own.

A bone-deep sense of security that she would never doubt. One day.

Today, she needed Maisey to understand the reality of priorities in *her* life. "I appreciate your devotion to your craft, but you also are a student at WU. You told me you were struggling with your core classes—algebra and biology."

"I still don't see why I need to know those things if I'm going to be an actress." Maisey's shoulders lifted with a petulant sigh.

Reese repeated some of the advice she'd given when they spoke last week about the paper. "Anything you learn gives you a better understanding of the world around you. It helps you put yourself in the mindset of a character. What if you were cast as a mathematician or a scientist?"

"A boring part? I wouldn't take it."

She wasn't going to argue that there were many movies and plays that took something as mundane as calculating mathematical formulas or discovering a new element that had fabulously meaty parts for actresses. Maisey equated acting with glamour. "What about understanding numbers so you could manage your own paycheck and taxes, or make sense of any contract you might sign?"

"I'll have a lawyer and agent to take care of that."

Clenching her jaw at the young woman's sense of entitlement, Reese gave up on reasoning with Maisey, and laid out the truth that she *would* care about. "If you fail my class, and any other classes this semester, you'll be put on academic suspension. At that point you can't be in any plays here."

Maisey glared down her long, narrow nose at Reese. "Then don't fail me."

Reese opened her mouth to reply to the subtle threat, but was interrupted by one of Maisey's friends.

"You're not a real professor. Not yet, anyway. I've heard about tenure. You can be replaced, you know."

Maisey arched a trimmed dark eyebrow. "Maybe you should quit, and let someone who isn't jealous of my talent take over the show."

Jealous? Reese almost laughed out loud. Worried about her student's arrogant disregard for the dangers of the real world outside the theater? Yes. But never jealous.

Reese straightened to every bit of her five feet, three inches of height. "I'm not jealous. I'm a grown-up. I understand responsibility. I'm trying to teach you—"

"I know you quit the business when you were in high school," Maisey whispered in an unpleasant snarl. "You couldn't make it in New York and had to come back here and resort to being a teacher. You're jealous because you know I'm better than you ever were."

"You don't know my story, Maisey."

And she wasn't going to waste the cautionary tale on this young woman, either.

"Miss Atkinson?" Dr. Diamant strode down the aisle. The man was a striking silver fox with broad shoulders, salt-and-pepper hair and a neatly trimmed beard. She could admire the man's vast knowledge and expertise, but there was an air of self-importance he carried with him and hands that were a little too touchy-feely with some of the students that kept Reese from finding him attractive. He came up behind Maisey and squeezed the shoulders of the girl who was young enough to be his daughter, before asking her to wait with her friends while he spoke to Reese. "Is there a problem?"

Reese couldn't miss the smug smile that spread across Maisey's face as she plopped down in a seat beside her friends. Why did it feel like this conversation was now four against one? Instead of allowing herself to be bullied, Reese tilted her gaze up to Dr. Diamant's dark eyes and shook her head. "I'm taking care of classroom business."

"And upsetting one of our premiere students," he pointed out. "Do we need to make accommodations for Miss Sparks?" His tone said he was telling rather than asking. He glanced back at the three young women and winked before speaking to Reese again. "After all, her grandfather is Simon Lowry. He and his late wife are the theater's greatest benefactors."

"I'm aware." She was still sorting through the boxes of props and costumes that had been donated from Mrs. Lowry's estate. But more than physical items, she knew Dr. Diamant was talking about the endowment the theater was receiving from the woman's estate. "At the last staff meeting, we discussed renaming the theater after the Lowrys since they've been giving us generous donations for years. With her passing, we'll have the funds to remodel this whole facility."

He dropped his voice to a whisper. "Or build a whole new theater. If we want those donations to continue, I don't think failing Simon's granddaughter is a wise move."

"I'm not failing her. I'm reminding her to turn in a paper. I'm teaching her the importance of keeping her commitments. Every other student in this section has turned in his or her paper." She appealed to the bottom line her supervisor was so focused on. "Mr. Lowry is an extremely successful businessman. Don't you think he'd appreciate the university teaching his granddaughter that theater is more than acting or singing? It's a business. Directors and producers will appreciate her being professional and responsible."

His dark eyes studied her for so long, Reese clenched her hands into fists down at her sides to keep herself from squirming or looking away. Then he smiled, breaking the tension between them. "Of course. I'll talk to her. Maybe she needs help with her research. Or tutoring. She *is* more of a performer than a writer. You could allow her to give an oral report. I'll see what I can do to help." It sounded like support, but it didn't feel like it. "Make those accommodations."

Reese swallowed hard, pushing down the snark that wanted to creep into her voice. After all, she'd been an actress. She could play the role of a coolheaded professional, even with the subtle digs being aimed at her. "Are you making any accommodations for me? You put me in charge of managing the theater this semester on top of teaching two classes and directing this play, plus finishing up my dissertation. And it's *Professor* Atkinson, not *Miss*. I earned the title." Okay, so her emotions were getting the better of this performance. "And you can address me as *Doctor* Atkinson once I defend my dissertation next semester."

Dr. Diamant's handsome face lined with concern. "You assured me you could handle the pressure. Do I need to reassign your jobs to someone who doesn't lose her temper at the slightest provocation?"

"I *am* handling it," Reese insisted. "But it's not easy, especially if I don't have your support." She heard noises from the backstage area. Footsteps. Voices. A stack of boards being dumped into a pile. The testing whir of a drill or power saw. It must be time for Patrick Brown's stagecraft class to get to work on their set-building project. "And I didn't lose my temper. I was having a civil discussion—"

"Whoa. Who's that?" Joy Archer, one of Maisey's entourage of friends, punctuated her loud observation with the pop of her gum and pointed to the stage behind Reese. Maisey smirked while the blonde girl elbowed her. "We should be doing *Beauty and the Beast*. He wouldn't even need a costume."

"Then how would you turn him into a prince?"

"That totally would be a problem."

"Joy!" Reese chastised the catty comments before glancing up the steps to see Jackson Dobbs scowling down from the stage above her.

Okay, so he wasn't exactly a handsome prince, with a jaw that was a little too pronounced, a scar bisecting one eyebrow and a crooked nose that looked as if he'd been in one too many fights. Although that dour expression wasn't doing him any favors, he was hardly a monster, hardly deserving of that cruel teasing. And, despite the growing din of conversations and power tools backstage, thanks to theater acoustics, he had to have heard the girls' disparaging remarks.

"Hey," she greeted him. Once again, she was struck by the sense that he was somehow familiar to her, that they shared a connection she couldn't yet place. "What are you doing here?"

He answered with a grunt.

Jackson's gaze was locked on Dr. Diamant, not the snooty trio, not even Reese herself. The big man she'd met that morning set a squarish black briefcase with KCPD Crime Lab emblazoned in white beside him on the edge of the stage. That looked official. He shrugged off his worn leather jacket and draped it over the kit, all without taking his gaze off Dean. Why had he come through the backstage area instead of entering the building through the front lobby? Clearly, she wasn't the only one prone to paying surprise visits.

"Jackson?"

Before he could answer, the third girl of the group whispered none too softly, "Do you think he can sing?"

"Who cares? You see the guns on that guy? I bet he's big all over." Maisey said possibly the most provocative thing she could think of as she ushered her friends from their seats.

Reese couldn't help but let her gaze slide to the muscular, veined forearms revealed by the rolled-up sleeves of Jackson's gray canvas shirt. Her fingertips had been drawn to them that morning at the crime lab. Jackson's biceps and shoulders stretched the material above his elbows, just as his muscular thighs stretched the denim covering them. The man was built in so many fine ways. When her gaze drifted to the zipper of his jeans, her thoughts following Maisey's crude remarks, Reese grimaced and shifted to study the large booted feet that were at eye level. The man wasn't a piece of meat any more than she considered herself a freckle-faced cutie-pie. Although, she did find him...compelling. He was just so much more masculine than anyone she'd ever dated, or maybe had even met.

He made another grunting noise that could have been a sigh of embarrassment or a snort of derision, but the expressive sound drew her gaze up to his rugged face. She realized those cool gray eyes were studying her reaction and he was frowning. Reese pressed her lips together and gave her head a sharp shake, pushing away the errant hormones that, apparently, she hadn't indulged in in way too long. She was having such a visceral reaction to a man she barely knew.

Without an outlet, the sensual heat blossomed on her cheeks, and she remembered that she'd taken offense at the young women's objectifying conversation. "Ladies. Get to class," she ordered. "Or lunch. Wherever you're headed next."

The three young women oohed and laughed, their voices fading as they headed up the aisle in a flurry of giggles and whispers. "He's way too old…"

"I don't know…"

"Maybe if you turned out the lights…"

"Ladies!"

The fact that Reese felt attracted to the same magnetic pull of Jackson Dobbs that the girls were making fun of was a little discomfiting. She and Jackson might have met just that morning, but Reese felt curiously protective of him. Which made little sense, really, since the man had more than twelve inches and a hundred pounds on her, and could clearly take care of himself. But he'd been nice to her at the crime lab, even though she suspected halfway through their conversation that she'd skipped some kind of security protocol by approaching him directly. He'd listened to her nervous ramblings instead of sending her back to the waiting area. And since very few people besides him seemed to be truly listening to what she had to say today, yeah, she was feeling a bond with their taciturn, polite and unaccountably hot visitor.

"Sorry about that," she apologized. "They're barely more than teenagers. Don't always think before they speak. Are you here to see me…?"

"Everett…?"

Reese swiveled her gaze at hearing Dr. Diamant's odd, nearly voiceless question to find him studying Jackson with narrowed eyes. Dr. Egoist's skin had gone strangely pale beneath his tan.

"Who's Everett?" Reese asked. She touched his shoulder, concerned by the pain she saw etched in his expression. "Dr. Diamant? Are you all right?"

"My mistake." Responding to neither her question nor Jackson's unblinking glare, the older man shrugged off her touch, dismissing whatever thought had surfaced. Color returned to his cheeks, and he donned his more familiar I'm-the-boss demeanor—smiling and polite, but not overly friendly until he'd determined a person's status in his world. "The theater isn't open to the public except for show nights. Miss Atkinson and I were having a private conversation."

Jackson watched a young man jogging down the aisle and up the steps onto the far side of the stage, before he disappeared behind the scenery to join the noisy stagecraft class. Then he was looking down at Dr. Diamant again. "Not very private."

Reese was embarrassed, and feeling some of that temper her supervisor had mentioned, to realize that not only had her students overheard the dressing-down from her adviser, but Jackson had, as well. "This is Jackson Dobbs. He's with the Kansas City Crime Lab. Dr. Dean Diamant."

Another grunt. "Everett was my father," Jackson explained, finally speaking real words in a gravelly, low-pitched voice.

"Dobbs. Of course." Dr. Diamant's smile became more genuine. "The shape of the head reminds me of your dad. But the hair is shorter, the color of your mother's—and obviously you've lived a rougher life than Everett did. Except for the end, of course." Dr. Diamant winced at the words that came out of his mouth. "I'm sorry. We were all very upset around here when they were killed. Terrified for our own lives."

"Killed?" Reese's heart squeezed in her chest as a light bulb of recognition turned on in her brain. She'd done a show with his father ages ago. Soon after, although she'd been little more than a child at the time, she'd heard the rumors about the kind professor and his wife, who'd been brutally murdered in the parking lot beside the theater. They were stabbed and left to bleed out and die after a performance late one night. Over the years, some of the more fanciful students even claimed that the couple still haunted the place. And she'd brought Jackson back, to what must be a nightmare for him, by handing over that knife. Reese cupped her hands over her mouth, as if she could retract any hurtful words she'd said, or painful memories that she might have triggered in him. "I'm so sorry. I didn't put two and two together this morning that you were related—"

The dean interrupted her apology before extending his hand to introduce himself. "I'm dean of the School of Fine Arts now. I knew your parents. Your father and I taught together. He was a good man. A friend. Your mother worked in the fine arts office. Beautiful woman. Such a tragedy."

Slowly moving his gaze from Reese over to her boss, Jackson reached down over the edge of the stage to shake the dean's extended hand. "I remember you."

Judging by his scowl, it didn't look as if they were very good memories. Maybe Jackson hated everything about the theater and the university. Or maybe that stern stoicism was an unfortunate side effect of his scarred face.

"You were what—ten? twelve?—last time we met? Must have been at the funeral."

Jackson had no comment about Dr. D's tacky trip down memory lane.

"How about a little sensitivity," Reese protested.

But her boss was talking over her again. "You're with the crime lab now? Wait. Are the police here? Has something happened?" Dr. Diamant's gaze swept the auditorium before fully acknowledging Reese. With no flashing lights outside the lobby doors or uniformed officers inside to back up his concerns, he frowned, then reprimanded her. "I should have been informed immediately if there was an issue on campus."

Somehow the crime lab showing up in the theater was her fault? "No one is in any danger. Last night, I found something that I thought might be a piece of evidence. The fact that Mr. Dobbs is here now makes me think I was right."

"What evidence? To what crime? At the theater? Was there an assault? Have we been vandalized again?" He tilted his gaze to Jackson again. "We've had a series of break-ins across campus. Nothing taken. Just some damage. The Deans' Council suspects a fraternity initiation. Campus police have stepped up..." He paused and the color drained from his face again. "Oh, Lord. Does this have something to do with your parents' murders? I know the case was never solved. I'm the one who found them, you know. Your father was already gone. Your mother was badly injured, already unconscious. They were holding hands."

Oh, my God. How heartbreaking.

Jackson came down the stairs, one deliberate step at a time. "I know the details."

Reese had to back up when he stopped between her and the dean. She was torn between inhaling the clean leathery scent that came off Jackson's body, offering him a comforting hug and snickering at the realization that, even standing on the same level, Dr. Diamant still had to angle his head up to hold Jackson's gaze. She was ready for Jackson to ream out the older man for callously rambling on about his parents' tragic deaths.

"I need you to be a lot nicer when you speak to Professor Atkinson."

Professor? Reese was completely caught off guard by Jackson's pronouncement. Had he heard her mini tirade? He was defending *her*?

"What?" The dean's dark eyes darted from Jackson down to her, then back up again. Confusion lined his face. "Are you Reese's boyfriend?" Why would he ask that? Was that the only reason he thought anyone would stand up for her? After a moment, Dr. Diamant glanced at Reese. "Dobbs here isn't what I expected. You're a free spirit. But you're also an academic. He's a public servant."

"He's a scientist," Reese countered, hating the condescending note in the dean's tone. "Even if he was a garbage collector, my personal life wouldn't be any of your business."

Dr. Diamant patted the air, placating her, and lowered his tone as though her argument was unwarranted. "I just thought you'd go for a man with a more bohemian vibe— someone in the arts. I thought you were seeing Professor Brown?" It had been one date. One spark-free disappointment before they agreed they got along better as friends. But Reese never got the chance to correct him. "Of course, you and Dobbs both have a background in the theater, at least by association—"

"Now." Jackson sharpened his articulation without raising the volume of his voice.

"Now? Now what?" For a moment, the dean was puzzled by the single word. Then he offered them both a handsome smile. "My apologies if I offended you. Reese is a valued member of our faculty. And you're a bit of a legacy around here, I suppose, being Everett and Melora's son. It's natural for me to assume you two could be a thing."

Jackson grunted at the dean's rambling excuse for an apology before facing Reese. "I have questions."

She jumped when Jackson's fingers brushed against her upper arm. He immediately drew his hand back and tucked his fingers into the front pocket of his jeans. Reese felt guilty that he might have misinterpreted her startled response.

She was still processing the fact that this big bruiser, who had every right to lash out in pain, had stood up for her against the dean's disrespect. But she wasn't averse to a man of his kindness touching her. Watching Jackson literally put more space between them, Reese reached out and linked her fingers into the crook of his elbow, halting his retreat. Even as she stepped into his side and tightened her grip on his sleeve, she wondered if the vibrations she felt humming between them were tremors of surprise in Jackson's muscles, or her own barely checked emotions spiking through her.

"If you'll excuse us, Dean." Good grief. The man generated heat like a furnace, and Reese fought the urge to lean into him to soak up some of that warmth. "I need to speak to Jackson."

The dean nodded, pointing a finger at her as he retreated up the aisle. "Police business, then. That makes more sense. All right. As long as it doesn't interfere with class, I'll leave you to it. Remember, keep Maisey happy. I'll make sure you have something from her to grade."

She idly wondered if he'd recruit another student to write the paper for her, or even do it himself. Whatever it took to keep their theater angels happy, she supposed.

Dr. Diamant had exited into the lobby before Jackson

dropped his gaze to the spot on his arm where her fingers clung to him. Then, leaving his face downcast, he tilted his gaze to hers. "He's rude."

"Sorry about that."

"He's rude to *you*."

Jackson wasn't a handsome man, and clearly, he wasn't a glib conversationalist. But nice? Polite? So male that women of all ages seemed to notice? And now he was showing how protective he could be? Reese's hormones kicked into hyperdrive, even as that self-preserving instinct that was constantly on guard inside her tensed.

"Yeah. But he's in charge. Of my job and my dissertation." She shrugged. "I don't know whether to be grateful or put out that I've been arguing with him for months without much change. Yet you say one thing to him, and he suddenly listens? He's never apologized before. Of course, that's probably just because you're here. Because you're a *legacy*. He's always super cognizant of the theater's reputation and where our next donation might be coming from."

"Did I overstep?"

"No. I'm grateful for the support. I'm just not used to anyone fighting a battle for me."

His eyes narrowed. "You fight a lot of battles?"

"More than you know." Reese realized she'd been stroking the warm skin along his forearm with her thumb, tracing the path of one of the prominent veins she'd noticed earlier. Suddenly, she was too hot, with him standing so close and his gaze on her so intense. This man saw too much, more than he let on, and it was unsettling. She abruptly pulled away and circled around him to lift her bag off the stage.

"I wasn't offended by those girls."

She looped the strap over her shoulder. "Well, I was. Maisey comes from money, and she's spoiled. I'm supposed to be the one in charge. The professor. The director. The manager. Those are all titles that should command a little respect."

She glanced up to find him nodding. "If your boss spoke with more respect—"

"They'd emulate him?" She'd gotten his point, so there was no reply. "Thank you for standing up for me. I don't know if it will make a difference with Dean Diamant, but it made me feel better to have someone in my corner." She headed up the stairs. "Do you think that knife has something to do with your parents' deaths?"

"Possibly." He followed behind her, taking the stairs two at a time.

Despite the noise coming from the class backstage, they were now alone. Still, she didn't imagine being front and center onstage like this was a place where a quiet, socially awkward man like Jackson Dobbs felt comfortable. Especially if he was here to talk about murder. "So, ask me questions."

Chapter Three

"Someplace private?" Jackson suggested, stepping aside to let Reese stoop beside Zach Oliver's gargoyle.

"Sure. My office is backstage." She heaved the prop into her arms to move it to an out-of-the-way location where no one could, accidentally or intentionally, damage the work of art.

"That heavy?"

She led the way across the stage. "Not bad. The base is solid, but the rest is papier-mâché. Now that it's up on my hip, I...oh."

He pulled the gargoyle from her hands and carried both it and his kit without any trouble.

"Thank you. But I'm not a diva who refuses to haul my own set pieces. Could I at least carry your jacket?"

He ignored her insistence that she could move the heavy prop. "Where?"

"Back here." She hurried ahead to the trio of offices located off the cavernous workroom behind the stage, and unlocked the first door. She pointed to an empty spot on top of the file cabinet while she tossed her bag onto the chair behind the desk. Jackson had the oversize prop situated before she could get back to help him. "Thanks."

She saw her crowded office through his eyes as he swept the room for a place to set his kit before simply lowering it to the thin carpet beside his feet. Reese groaned. There wasn't even an empty chair where she could invite him to sit. Her desk held papers and scripts, research books, a framed picture of her sister's family and an old one of her parents, and a computer. The worktable was covered by a 3D model of her set, along with many props, including a judge's wig she had built out of gray yarn draped over a foam head, and a silver tray that held a broken decanter and several glasses. Another table along the wall was littered with posters and promo items from the previous season's shows and an old-fashioned portable record player, which was also a prop in the current production.

She felt embarrassment warming her cheeks. "Sorry about the mess. Chaos is kind of my thing when I'm directing a play. No time to organize."

"Creative." He nodded, as though that one word explained the mess and maybe even made it acceptable in his eyes. "Dad's was similar."

"Don't stereotype theater people," she defended herself with mock indignity. "It's not always a pigsty."

"Know where things are?"

"Of course."

Her answer seemed to be all he needed to earn an approving nod. "Dad, too."

She smiled with relief that he seemed to understand her messy system of organization. Reese moved to the guest chair on the near side of her desk, and scooped up the stack of costume sketches she'd laid there. "I bet your office is pristine, with everything put away in its own place."

She reached for his jacket to drape over the back of the chair, fighting the urge to pull its heavy weight up to her nose and breathe in deeply. She gestured for him to sit, and turned to find a corner of her desk where she could set the drawings. She shivered when she saw the manila envelope in which she'd stashed the messages that were someone's idea of a clever joke. They'd been left on the windshield of her car or stuffed under the door to her office over the past couple of weeks. Reese slapped the drawings down on top of the envelope. Out of sight, out of mind. They were just words, anyway. Words couldn't hurt her, right? Not on the written page, not in a mysterious phone call. They could undermine her authority or rattle her self-confidence—but they weren't physically dangerous. She just needed to endure long enough for whoever was getting their kicks out of this sneaky game to grow tired of messing with her.

Then she realized that Jackson was standing close enough that she could feel his abundant heat through her blouse and denim jacket. He towered over her, his gaze moving from her to her desk and back again, as if he'd sensed she was hiding something.

Right. She'd been apologizing for the mess and guessing his office wasn't anything like her own. She fixed a smile on her face before tilting her eyes way up to his. "Do you work mostly in your office or in a lab?"

"Lab."

"You don't talk in complete sentences very much, do you?" She could see he wasn't entirely at ease or given to making small talk, but since she wasn't feeling like her usual perky, extroverted self, she started the conversation she assumed he wanted to have with her. "The knife? Did it turn out to be something important?"

"I need to see where you found it."

All business. She could handle that. She suspected Jackson was more comfortable with an investigation-related conversation, although she missed the grumbly, low-pitched protective vibe of him telling Dean Diamant to be more respectful. *I need you to be a lot nicer when you speak to Professor Atkinson.*

Those words had felt like a supportive hand at her back, like Jackson Dobbs saw her as a grown woman. Being sheltered by the big lab geek's abundant heat—like she was important to him—made her feel as if he wanted the rest of the world to know that she wasn't alone in the battles she fought against misconceptions and intimidation tactics.

But this wasn't a date. Jackson wasn't her boyfriend. His visit to the theater had nothing to do with her troubles. And even though she felt an inexplicable connection to him, he was barely more than an acquaintance—although she couldn't deny being fascinated by him, being drawn to him, feeling more secure with him in her world.

Reese combed her fingers through the short curls that fell over her forehead, and shifted her thoughts back into concerned-citizen, theater-caretaker mode as she'd been that morning at the crime lab. "You need to see where I found the box it was in originally? Or where I opened and unpacked the box upstairs?"

"Both."

Reese smiled. He didn't need to say much when he could communicate so succinctly. She checked the chunky watch on her wrist, which had once been her father's. "I have a couple of hours between classes. You want to look now?"

He nodded and reached down to open his CSI kit. By the time she'd hidden her purse in the bottom drawer of her desk and retrieved her keys, he had pulled on a pair of sterile gloves and looped a high-tech camera around his neck. After locking her door, she led him through the noisy construction of the set pieces and flats being built by the stagecraft class. Since the man in charge of the class, Patrick Brown, was wearing noise-canceling earphones, she simply exchanged a wave of acknowledgment with the blond-haired professor and hurried through the sawdust, drills, platforms and plywood to the back wall where floor-to-ceiling shelves stored several boxes, large props and building supplies.

"Sorry about the noise," she apologized, raising her voice a bit. She put a hand on a large dented box on the bottom shelf. "Beatrice Lowry, one of the theater's biggest benefactors, passed away a few months back. About two weeks ago, her husband donated a ton of her stuff to the theater. She must have been collecting it for decades."

"Related to Simon Lowry?"

Of course, he recognized the name of one of Kansas City's wealthiest and most civic-minded families. "Yes. She was his wife. You know him?"

"Of him. My folks went to parties."

"The Lowrys still throw a holiday party for the theater faculty and staff, and host fundraisers for fine arts projects. I heard that their son, Dixon Lowry, will be taking over now that Beatrice has passed. He's Maisey's—one of the rude girls—uncle. They're holding an open house here this week-end for theater faculty and students to help launch the beginning of the main-stage season. I'm guessing that's when the dean will announce renaming the theater in Beatrice's memory." Reese retreated several steps and stretched out her arms. "These are the boxes I haven't gone through yet. They were stacked up out to here. They were a fire hazard since they narrowed the path to the back door, so I moved several of them upstairs to the loft where we store costumes and hand props."

He snapped a few pictures of the area, then pulled out the boxes and opened them. After taking more pictures of the contents and boxes themselves, he moved them back into place. Then he pointed to the commercial shipping label on the outside of each box. "The one with the knife was the same?"

She nodded. "Obviously, Mr. Lowry didn't haul these in himself. I assume they'd all been taped shut by that local shipping company and delivered here. I signed for them."

He traced the Williams University Theater address with his gloved finger. "It's been opened and taped shut more than once."

"So, the knife didn't necessarily come from Simon Lowry's home. Someone could have opened the box, put the knife in, then sealed it shut again?"

Jackson nodded. "Here, or at Lowry's end. No clue."

Reese frowned. "I'm sorry. I didn't really pay attention to that. I just assumed they'd been reopened to stuff in a couple more items before shipping them here. I broke down the boxes as I emptied them. Did I mess up your investigation?"

"I can dust for prints."

Reese paced for a bit, then shared a brief conversation

with Patrick Brown about her choice of paint colors for the set. Finally, she returned to watch Jackson work.

Thorough would be an understatement. He spent almost an hour working in silence, poring over each seam of the boxes with a lighted magnifying tool. A few times he pulled out a jar of black powder and a fat, flared brush to dust a section of the tape or box. Reese knelt beside him to watch him press what looked like a piece of clear tape over the dust marks, and then carefully peel it away and adhere it to a small rectangle of white cardboard. He labeled it with the date, the object and location where he'd lifted the print, along with his initials, before holding it beneath his light to study it.

Reese studied the remarkably clear image, too. "Wow. Even I can see the ridges and swirls of a fingerprint."

"Thumbprint," he corrected.

Reese flipped her hands over and held them next to the card. "Not mine, is it?"

"Too big." He tucked the card into one of the many pockets in his CSI kit. "A man's."

"It could be from one of the movers," she supposed.

Jackson agreed. "Probably bonded, with prints on file. Chelsea will check."

"Who's Chelsea?" It was the first time she'd heard Jackson mention any woman besides the pregnant receptionist at the crime lab.

"Hacker." He packed the rest of his tools and samples into his kit, as well, except for the camera and a flashlight. When he saw Reese frowning up at him, clearly asking him for more of an explanation, he shrugged. "In charge of computers and research at the lab. Tech genius. She can find anything on the web."

"Cool. I wish I could do something useful like that."

Now he was the one frowning, and it hardened his expression enough that she leaned away from him. "You teach."

"I'm not exactly tracking down criminals or saving lives."

"*Shaping* lives." He cleared his throat before continuing in a harsh, gravelly tone. "Whether they know it or not, those students need you. The right teacher can make a difference in how a student's life turns out."

His emphatic response made her think he didn't appreciate her making light of his assertion. "Did a teacher impact your life like that?" When he didn't answer, she searched for a less dramatic explanation. "Your parents both worked in academia. I can understand how you'd value education."

"You..." He struggled to find a word, then surprised her with the one he chose. "...smile."

Reese arched a doubtful eyebrow. "That's useful?"

He quickly refocused on his work, as if he'd admitted something he didn't want her to know. "I don't smile."

"Sure you do," she insisted. "I've seen that little quirk at the corner of your mouth. It may not be a toothy grin, but I totally count that as a smile."

Not only was there no toothy grin, but she didn't even earn that lift at the corner of his firm lips. Instead, he snapped his kit shut. "How many boxes were there?"

Either she'd touched on a sensitive subject or he didn't like her flirting with him. And yeah, she was honest enough to admit that she'd been doing what she could to elicit more conversation, and a few of those smiles. Reese centered herself on a deep breath and tried not to let his swift changes, from polite to friendly to snapping beast to hinting at something deeply emotional and back to impersonally polite again, get to her. "Fourteen. I carried eight of them upstairs and opened them with a box cutter. Then I cleared the shelf space here, and stashed the rest until I could get to them."

"No one helped?"

"You're a little obsessed with me doing things on my own. I assure you, I'm a very capable woman." She braced her hand on his shoulder and pushed herself upright. Good grief. Why did she keep touching the man? His shoulder was broad and muscled and as seemingly unmovable as the rest of him. Reese quickly snatched her hand away. "Sorry. I should have asked before touching you. I keep forgetting my manners. I know I wouldn't like it if someone I'd just met kept putting their hands on me."

"I don't mind," he assured her. He stood. "I know it doesn't mean anything."

Was that why he didn't appreciate her flirting? He didn't believe she was sincere in wanting to get to know him better? Huffing out a sigh of irritation, Reese propped her hands at her hips. "Of course, it means something. If I didn't trust you on some level, I wouldn't be touching you at all." She pointed back to the stage. "And just to be clear, when I pulled away from you out there, it was because you startled me. Not because it was *you* putting your hand on my arm. I *like* touching you. But I'm trying to be polite and cognizant of what *you* might be feeling. It's what good people do."

He grunted at the apology that had morphed into a heated admission of her unexpected attraction to him. "Red-haired temper?"

Her temperature rose as embarrassment flooded her cheeks. But there was something sparking in those pale gray eyes that made her realize he was amused by her inability to let any slight go unchallenged. Reese shook her head as her smile returned. "Wow. You change emotional gears faster than any man I've ever met. If we were old friends, I'd punch you in the arm for teasing me like that."

"We *are* old friends."

Reese frowned. "What do you mean? I thought you seemed familiar to me, but didn't we just meet this morning?"

He shook his head. "Dad directed you in *Annie*."

She'd been ten when the university had put out a casting call throughout Kansas City for youngsters to audition for the orphans and title role of the musical. Reese scrolled through her memories. "That was my first starring role."

"Didn't put it together until I saw you onstage earlier. You've got curves now you didn't have back then. Sang beautifully."

"Thanks."

Jackson shrugged. "A lot of annoying girls in that show."

Reese snapped her fingers as the memory surfaced. "That's right. I remember you now. The big, silent boy. Your dad brought you to rehearsal some nights. You'd sit out in the auditorium and do your homework. Or hang out in the light booth and play with the boards." Jackson was so much older, broader, and bearing the scars of a violent life now. No wonder she hadn't made the connection herself when she'd tracked him down at the crime lab. "I don't think you ever said a word to me. But I was kind of bratty and made myself at home with the whole theater. I sat down beside you one night during a break and went through your schoolbooks. You were reading *Hatchet* by Gary Paulsen." She had no trouble remembering him now. "You let me read it. I hope I thanked you for that."

Jackson nodded, indicating she had, and he pushed his elbow toward her. "You can punch my arm now."

Who knew this big, taciturn man had that wry sense of humor? She wondered how many people actually got to see that humor. Instead of punching the proffered arm, she wound her fingers as far around his warm forearm as they could reach and squeezed. "I am not hitting you. You were a nice boy then, and you're a nice man now, Jackson."

He grunted at the compliment, and Reese had to press her lips together to keep from laughing out loud at his go-to response when he didn't know what to say. She released his arm and headed toward the steel-and-concrete stairs that led to the storage loft. "I'll show you where I unloaded the box."

Once upstairs, Reese stood back while Jackson took pictures and sorted through the costumes and props that had been in the same box with the bloody knife. If she ever had to play a part that called for stoicism or intense focus that never missed a detail, she'd channel Jackson Dobbs. "I can't believe I didn't recognize you." He asked her to point out every item she'd touched, even the items she'd put in the trash. Plus, he scanned her fingerprints with an electronic device to eliminate her trace from the items he bagged and labeled. "You've changed a lot in twenty-three years, too. You're obviously taller, deeper voice, a lot more muscular."

"Uglier," he pointed out. "The Army and time in a boxing ring took a toll on me."

"You have an interesting face. A little beaten up by life, maybe, but interesting." She laughed. "Of course, I didn't notice boys back then the same way I do now. Back then, I only noticed the books they read."

There. His mouth quirked up at the corner and Reese beamed in return. She felt like she'd won a prize for earning that shadow smile.

He ushered her toward the stairs ahead of him.

"You turned me into a Gary Paulsen fan with that book. I've read the entire series since then."

Jackson offered no response, but she could still see the hint of his smile. As they came down, she noticed the stage-craft class had erected the interior walls and framed out the garden doors that would lead out onto the balcony of her set. She felt a little rush of excitement knowing that in the next day or two, they'd move the pieces to the main stage, and they could start setting lights and rehearsing with actual doors and windows. The plan was to have the set in place, if not with the finishing touches, by the Lowrys' open house at the theater this weekend.

But the thought of moving the set reminded her of all the cleaning and straightening up she'd been working on. "If that knife was used in your parents' murders, where has it been? That box hasn't been here for twenty-three years. Did the killer put it there, thinking they were getting rid of it? Did Beatrice Lowry take it from the killer, and has been protecting him all these years? Is someone trying to hurt the Lowrys? Will you investigate their family? The people who were at the university back then?" She crinkled up her nose as an unpleasant thought struck. "Will you investigate me?"

"Man."

Was she really learning to interpret what his terse responses meant? "A man killed your parents?"

He stepped down to the main floor beside her. "Man's strength to subdue my father. Depth of the wounds."

Compassion for him squeezed her heart. "How horrible to know things like that about people you love."

His icy eyes held hers for an endless moment before he gave her the slightest of nods. "Still have the box itself?"

If she knew him better, she'd have given him a hug. But she was learning that Jackson was like an animal that had been abused. He needed time to process his emotions and what he wanted to say, and he was cautious about his interactions with other people. She'd have to be patient about earning his trust and building a relationship with him—provided he wanted to be friends and spend more time with her outside his investigation.

The way she apparently wanted to. Reese turned away from him to hide her reaction to that surprising thought. Why was she even thinking about relationships with everything she had going on in her life? Maybe she was the one who should be more cautious about deepening her friendship with this man. In some ways, she felt as if she had known him twenty-three years. In others, she'd only known him for this one day.

"It's in the recycling dumpster. I didn't see any blood in it, though." She led the way out the back door. "But you might be able to get other information from it."

"Prints. Trace."

He held the door for her, and she pulled the front of her jacket together against the brisk autumn breeze. The sun was high in the sky. But there was a park and walkway that led down to a small bridge over a creek behind the theater. The tall pin oaks that were just starting to turn gold and the rich green pine trees cast long, cool shadows across the back of the building.

"It's like you're gathering all the pieces of a jigsaw puzzle. When you fit them together in the lab, it tells you the story of what happened. I love puzzles." She pulled a crate over to stand on so that she could reach into the bin to pull out the box he wanted. "This is it. I labeled the boxes once I opened them."

He shooed her hand away and retrieved it with his gloved fingers. He spared a few moments to examine it, then he pulled a large, flat paper sack from his kit and unfolded it. Reese held it open while he slid the flat box inside.

"Is that it?" She discovered she was reluctant to see him go. He was probably ready to carry his gear out to his truck or whatever Jackson-size vehicle he drove. "Do you need anything else?"

He pointed to his watch, giving her another look at those forearms. "Nearly two hours. You have class."

Wow. A man who truly listened to what she had to say. She was pleased that he paid attention to what she'd said earlier.

Despite her earlier caution to slow down whatever connections she was building with Jackson, Reese couldn't stop the smile that curved her lips. "I've enjoyed hanging out with you this morning. I'm glad you figured out how we knew each other. I hope you find something useful that can lead you to the answers you need about your parents."

"Not leaving yet."

That little rush of excitement she felt was unexpected and probably misplaced. "You're not?"

"My jacket?"

The hopeful feeling quickly crashed and burned. Jackson didn't want to spend more time with her. This was just good old-fashioned practicality. "Of course."

He opened the door for her, and they walked side by side back to her office.

"I don't suppose there's any way to tell if that knife was in that box for twenty-three years, or if someone hid it in there after it arrived at the theater." He shrugged. There was probably so much science behind the work he did that even a talkative man wouldn't have time to explain it all to her. "Can you figure that out at your lab?"

"Possibly."

"How? You study the other things that were in the box with it? The items you bagged as potential evidence?"

He nodded.

"Do you think..." She was flattered at how he gave her his full attention when she spoke. She was surrounded by college students who were consumed by their social lives and career goals, and fellow staff and supervisors who thought she was beneath them since she wasn't a fully accredited doctor with a PhD yet. She'd been ignored and talked down to throughout her life because of her age or her sex or her height or her youthful looks. Even if she received a terse or growly response, having Jackson Dobbs hanging on to her words, as if they had meaning and she was someone important, was good for her ego. "Is that the knife that killed your parents?"

"Can't say yet. Same type."

So, there was a possibility she'd uncovered an actual murder weapon. "Do you know if it was human blood on the blade and the blouse?"

He nodded. She shivered at the memory of what she'd given him. "That was a lot of blood."

He nodded again.

Reese pushed her key into the doorknob of her office. But instead of the key sliding into the lock, the entire door swung open. She froze in the doorway, a sick feeling curling in the pit of her stomach. Accidents happened, sure, but she swept her gaze across the office, anyway. She knew. Something was off. Changed. Violated. "I swear I locked that. Maybe I didn't get it closed all the way."

But no such luck. There it sat, on the prop table. Another disturbing gift.

A syringe skewered a note into the wig and foam head.

Chapter Four

"Reese?"

She let the anger swell up before the fear could grab hold. "Oh, come on. Not another stupid joke. Coward." She muttered the word under her breath before stepping around Jackson and yelling into the backstage area to no one in particular. "Stay out of my stuff!"

Jackson put his arm out, blocking her path when she reached for the graphic message. "Don't touch."

Then he was pulling out his flashlight and fresh gloves again and studying the object she could barely look at. She yelped when she felt a hand at her back and spun around. "Damn it, Patrick."

The stagecraft professor quickly raised his hands up in apology. "Sorry, I didn't knock. The door was open."

Reese studied him from the receding points of his hairline down to the toes of his work boots before waving aside his apology. "No, I'm sorry. You startled me."

"Doing that a lot," Jackson observed from right behind her. His heat seeped into her body, and she didn't know whether to breathe easier or inch away. Once he seemed assured that she was okay with her visitor, he went back to work.

Patrick Brown flicked his short blond ponytail behind his shoulder, eyeing Jackson. "Everything okay in here? I heard you yell."

"I'm fine." Reese reached out to squeeze his arm to reassure him, and couldn't help but notice that she didn't react to his veins and muscles with that same rush of awareness she had with Jackson. "Someone was in my office. Has your class been backstage with you the whole time?"

"Up until I dismissed them a few minutes ago. Most of them went out the back door, but a few crossed the stage. Exited through the lobby, I suppose."

"Did you loan any of them your master key for the building?"

He nodded. "I asked a couple of boys to put some of the new tools away in my office. Until I can get another storage locker set up. I got it back, though." He pushed his glasses up onto the bridge of his nose and peered around her. "Another note?"

"Yeah." She stepped back so that he could see the syringe in the wig. Since Patrick had been with her that first night she'd found a message tucked underneath her windshield wiper, she couldn't very well hide the fact that her prankster had struck again.

"He's escalating if he's in your personal space." Patrick clasped her arms right above her elbows "You're not hurt, are you?"

"No. More pissed off. And a little rattled." She patted his hand before pulling away from his concerned touch. "I thought I locked my office."

"You did," Jackson said.

Good. She wasn't losing her mind or being careless. Someone else had seen her lock the door.

"I'm not the only one with a master key to this building," Patrick pointed out. "I keep telling Dean we need to change the locks after the vandalism incidents we've had. But he doesn't want the expense on this year's budget. I guess we have to wait until January to beef up security around here." He regarded Jackson warily, as if he thought he posed some kind of threat to her. "You want me to stay?"

"Jackson didn't do this. He's been with me the whole time. He's a friend." She glanced up at him, comparing the boy she remembered watching rehearsals with this mature, rough-featured man. What was wrong with people that they couldn't see him for the gentle giant he was? "I've known him for several years, in fact."

"Really? I haven't seen you around Reese before. Patrick Brown." The two men shook hands. "I'm chief set builder and supervise the tech classes. Reese and I go way back, too."

"Jackson Dobbs. Crime lab."

"You're Everett and Melora's boy. Dean mentioned you were on the premises." Patrick shrugged when Reese asked him when that conversation had happened. "That man gossips more than any old biddy I know. I think he wanted me to keep an eye on you."

"I'm fine with Jackson," Reese insisted. "Perfectly fine. The dean probably wanted you to keep an eye on why Jackson was here. He's paranoid about anything getting in the way of the department's big launch party with the Lowry family."

"Probably," Patrick agreed before turning his attention

back to the larger man in the room. "I was a senior here
when your folks were killed. Your mother tutored me so I
could get through theater history and literature classes." Patrick chuckled at the memory. "I've always been better with
my hands than I ever was with words." Jackson grunted and
Reese bit back a grin. "Well, good luck with your investigation." Patrick backed out the door, thumbing over his shoulder. "I'll be down in my office if you need anything, Reese.
Just holler. I'll come runnin'."

She followed her coworker to the door and waved as he
walked away. "I will. Thanks."

Jackson snapped a half dozen pictures before setting his
camera aside. He carefully removed the syringe, studied
what looked like condensation inside, then dropped it into
a hard plastic container. Reese crossed her arms and leaned
against the doorframe. "What are you doing? This isn't a
crime scene."

He opened his jar of black powder and knelt in front of
the doorknob. "Breaking and entering? Vandalism? Terror-
istic threats?" He continued to process her office. "Tell me
about the other *gifts*." He pointed his brush toward her desk.
"And that envelope."

Reese's shoulders deflated as she resigned herself to getting someone else involved with her troubles. "Some of the
props we're using for the show have been altered, damaged.
The murder weapons, specifically." She pointed to the tray
of broken glass, moving away as he pulled several prints.
That had been the first gift after the notes started arriving.
"One character dies by drinking poison. That tray was sitting on the middle of my desk when I came in after rehearsal
one night. The bottle had been shattered, and the cranberry

juice we use to mimic wine onstage had flooded the tray and soaked into my desk calendar blotter sitting underneath it. At first, I thought one of the stagehands had broken it and was afraid to fess up, so they left it in here anonymously. But there was a note under my windshield wiper in the parking lot that night." Jackson continued to snap pictures of the damage. "Another character is injected with a syringe. I'm afraid to see what shows up when they get to the character who's killed with an axe while chopping wood."

"Can you replace these?"

"Already working on it."

Wearing his sterile gloves, he bagged and labeled the abused props, and set them beside his kit. Then he straightened and nodded toward her desk. "The envelope?"

She pulled the manila envelope from beneath the pile where she'd tried to bury it and handed it to him. "They're distorted versions of the nursery rhyme that's used in the play. All of them are typed on plain white paper. None are signed." She watched a harsh line form between his eyebrows as he read them. "The one on the wig is number four. I'm the only one who touched them, except for whoever left them. If they were dumb enough to leave prints." When he silently asked if he could take them, she nodded. "Each verse is supposed to be about one of ten little soldiers dying, just like in the updated version of the script. But someone has substituted nicknames for redheads in each one. They aren't in order. I don't know if that's significant, or if it just fits the messages they're sending me."

She was a quick study at memorizing lines. She didn't need to see the pages to know what he was reading.

Nine little freckle faces stayed up very late; One overslept herself and then there were eight.

That had been the first message.

Then the culprit had gotten their hands on the props and
added a more unsettling twist to each incident. The shattered
liquor bottle had been the first.

Ten little carrottops went out to dine; One choked her
little self and then there were nine.

The next incident had been her finding a copy of the
script burning in an ashtray on the prop table. If she hadn't
smelled the smoke after rehearsal and gone to investigate,
the fire could have spread and done significant damage to
the theater—or to her or anyone else who was there. Fortunately, she'd been able to put the small blaze out with her
jug of water. But the message had been waiting for her under
her office door.

Two red-hot mamas sitting in the sun; One got frizzled
up and then there was one.

Now she could add getting stabbed with a syringe to the
mix.

Six little fireballs playing with a hive; A bumblebee
stung one and then there were five.

"These are what you mean by a joke?" Jackson asked. She
nodded. "Not funny."

"Not to me." Still feeling a chill, Reese hugged her arms around herself. "I thought they might be fraternity pranks. Or messages from a disgruntled student because I won't let a theater class be an easy A for them. Or I didn't cast someone in the part they wanted. Maybe someone thinks it's funny that I'm directing a perfect murder mystery, and they're leaving me murder gifts that I can't figure out. I don't know. Maybe it's Maisey Sparks, trying to make me look incompetent or paranoid so that the dean will replace me with a director and professor she can manipulate."

Jackson was kneeling again, rearranging things in his kit to fit as many items as possible. "Someone's idea of courtship?"

"Like a student who has a crush on me? You mean someone wants to date me, and thinks this is some sick way to woo me?"

"Woo?"

"People don't use that word anymore, do they?" Reese frowned. She couldn't think of anything more upsetting than being the object of someone's obsession. Again. Reese hadn't quit performing because of her parents' deaths. She'd quit striving for the spotlight because she hadn't been safe. The pedophile who'd targeted the pretty red-haired fourteen-year-old to be his plaything had been arrested, sentenced and subsequently murdered in a New York prison. "I suppose there could be someone out there who thinks if I get scared enough, I'd turn to them for comfort."

Jackson rose like a leviathan in front of her, forcing her to tilt her head. "Who would you turn to?"

Um, you?

But other than that wishful thought, the list was pretty

short. Maybe a friend like Patrick. Although, one boring date
had proved they would never be anything more than friends.
Boyfriends had been few and far between with her work and
school schedule and trust issues. With her father gone, she
couldn't really think of anyone. "Maybe my brother-in-law?
He's a sheriff's deputy in Grangeport."

"That's two hours away. Anyone here in KC?"

Reese forced a grin onto her face, determined to pull herself out of the pain of her past. "Is that your subtle way of
asking if I'm available to go on a date with you?" She felt
bad when a rosy blush tinged his angular cheekbones. *This
guy isn't flirting! Just answer the question.* "Sorry. There's
no one. I... For all I know, you've got a girlfriend. Or a wife."

"Neither."

"Me, neither. I've been too busy getting my PhD and
working to pay for it. I've always felt I have to work extra
hard to get people to take me seriously."

"Why?"

"You really don't see it?" He frowned at the question.
"Well, other than the fact there are still plenty of glass ceil-
ings women have to break through in academia, look at me.
I'm thirty-three years old. If you bound my breasts, I could
still play Little Orphan Annie. Even with the boobs and
hips, all some people see is the curly red hair and freckles.
They see the wannabe child star who never quite made it—
even though that hasn't been my dream for a long time. The
people I want to impress always think I'm younger than I
am. That I'm not serious about my craft or my job. That I
don't have history. That I don't have secrets that wake me
up in the middle of the night. That I haven't seen or been
through things that make me able to empathize with others.

I'm a grown woman. I've already lived more life than I ever thought I would." She shoved her fingers through her curly hair. "I thought about dyeing my hair a dark brown color and straightening it so I'd look older—"

"No." He reached for her hair as if he wanted to touch it, too. But he curled his hand with the crooked fingers into a fist and pulled away. "It's too pretty."

Whether he was remembering their conversation about asking permission to touch, or he was self-conscious about his damaged fingers, she wished he'd been brave enough to run his fingers through her hair. "Dark hair would look horrible with my freckles, anyway. And those I can't change so easily."

He tucked his fingers into the front pockets of his jeans. "I'm judged by my looks, too," he stated quietly. "People have misconceptions."

Two full sentences of real empathy felt like a gift to Reese. "I imagine. At first glance, you're a big, scary dude. Well, at second glance, too," she teased. Did that quirk at the corner of his mouth qualify as a smile? "May I?" When she reached out to touch Jackson's arm beneath the rolled-up cuff of his sleeve, he nodded. Reese rested her hand lightly on his forearm, absorbing his heat, trying to ignore the little frissons of awareness that zinged across the sensitive skin of her palm. "But they're not looking closely enough. During the heat and humidity of a Missouri summer, I'd love to dive into an icy mountain lake the color of your eyes. These arms are quite… Hottie McHotterson. Clearly, you work out. And seriously, Jackson—you may look like a heavyweight prizefighter, but you've been nothing but gentle and kind with me."

"Not good with words." His shoulders lifted with a shrug,

but she noticed that he kept his arm still beneath her touch, as if he was cognizant of possibly scaring her away.

Reese squeezed his forearm, proving that she wasn't afraid of the contact between them. "Not true. You may not use a lot of words, but you communicate just fine. With me. With anyone who pays attention. You have to communicate to work with your friends at the lab, right?" He nodded. "And Dean Diamant sure got your message."

He parted his lips to speak. Instead of producing words, though, he darted his gaze to the open doorway behind her.

"Yo, Ms. A. You coming to class or are we getting a free day? Whoa."

Reese startled for the umpteenth time that day. But Jackson was already moving and planting himself like a wall between her and the door. After bloody knives and veiled threats, she was more unsettled than she'd like to admit. With her hand pressed against her thumping heart, she stepped up beside Jackson to face one of the young men in her class.

"I'll be right there, Chris."

The young man glanced from her up to Jackson and back, then shrugged. "Ok."

He was almost to the stage before she realized that Jackson had extended his undamaged hand toward her. A protective gesture. One that told her student—or anyone else who popped into her office and startled her—that she wasn't alone, that she had a friend who was looking out for her. But by the time she'd noticed the caring overture and reached out to take it, he was already pulling away.

Did he think she had rejected him? Jackson Dobbs was confident and imposing in so many ways. What had happened to make him so gun-shy about putting the moves on her? And why couldn't she make him understand that she wasn't averse to him trying?

With the moment to make that connection and put him at ease having passed, Reese respected the distance he seemed to want and circled around him to her desk. She grabbed her bag from the bottom drawer, slid in her laptop and the flash drive she needed for the class's PowerPoint presentation on stage movement. "I enjoyed spending the morning with you, Jackson. Well, not for the reason you're here. I'm so sorry about your folks. I lost mine, too, but at least I know what happened to them." When he arched an eyebrow with a silent question, she took a cue from him and gave the briefest of synopses. "Car accident. Winter storm. Black ice."

She'd save the details of that heartbreaking night for another time. "It has been nice to get reacquainted and talk to…someone who listens." She turned the lock in the doorknob. "You see me doing this, right?"

He nodded.

"Just close the door behind you when you're finished. I'd better get going before my class runs off. Will you keep me posted if you find out anything about the knife or the pictures you took or…anything?"

Jackson nodded. "I'll look at these *gifts*, too. Whoever this is has to be watching you to know when to deliver them without being seen."

He was right. Whoever was pulling these disturbing pranks had to know her. This wasn't just about the skewed poem and props. "He knows when to call me, too."

"Explain."

"I've been getting mysterious phone calls," she admitted. "You know, when you answer and someone hangs up or no one's there?"

"Here or on your cell?" When she hesitated, he guessed the answer. "Both?"

She nodded. "My contact information is on the university website, so it's not hard to find me. They come within a few hours or so after each of the messages arrives."

"Late at night?"

Of course. Wait until she was alone and it was dark before adding to the torment. "I think he's checking my reaction to his latest gift. I'm assuming it's a guy, at any rate. His breathing sounds...male. He probably gets a thrill out of hearing my voice."

"Part of the game." Whatever game that might be.

"Knowing someone is there, but all you can hear is breathing or background noise? That's always creeped me out." Some of those nightmarish details of the accident were coming out, anyway. Why was it so easy to talk to this man? Was that a trick of not saying much? To get other people to fill up the quiet by pouring out conversation?

"When my parents were in the car wreck, they knew it was bad," she started. "Help wasn't coming in time. My mother called my sister at college. My father called me." Her eyes stung and she blinked back tears that wanted to fall. "I could hear Mom telling Reggie they loved her, loved us both. But it was already too late for Dad. He lost consciousness and succumbed to his injuries without saying a word—just the silence of a connected call. I could hear the wind, groans of pain. I listened to Mom breathing...until I couldn't hear her anymore, either." Man, she could use a hug right about now. But this quiet, cautious man wasn't offering. *Suck it up and get to the point.* "I have a good imagination. When no one's there, it makes me think something's wrong. Very wrong. Not my favorite thing." She swiped at the moisture in her eyes and forced some energy into her posture. "So, on that downer, if you ever call me, be sure to say hello. Don't sit there breathing and wait for me to start talking."

"I won't," he answered as if it was a solemn promise. He shrugged into his jacket and gathered an armful of evidence bags. "When are you done working tonight?"

"After rehearsal? It takes me about twenty to thirty minutes to make sure everything's put away and locked up. And all the students have gone, of course." Mostly likely, he just wanted a simple answer. "Ten o'clock? Ten thirty?"

He moved past her out the door. "See you then."

"Do you think you'll have some answers that quickly? More questions? Jackson?" But he was already striding away with his first armload of evidence bags. He was an enigma. But sweet and shy. Considerate. Protective. And more masculine than any man she'd ever met.

"Ms. A?"

Reese smiled and hurried out to the stage to meet her students. She wasn't sure if Jackson Dobbs had just asked her out on a date, had follow-up questions about the knife or was simply being chivalrous and worried about her safety. But she knew she was looking forward to later tonight.

Chapter Five

Jackson leaned back in the shadows behind the steering wheel of his truck, mentally debating whether he was doing his civic duty, being a creeper or hoping in vain that those sparks of interest he'd felt from Reese that morning were legit, and not a figment of his lonesome imagination.

Yes, he was doing his duty by keeping tabs on an old crime scene and potential witness. Yes, he was keeping an eye on the pranks surrounding Reese that history and his well-honed survival instincts told him might be merely scratching the surface of something much darker and more sinister. And he hated the idea that Reese was caught up in the middle of it.

Yep, he qualified as a creeper, too. The group of girls who filed out the back door of the theater, laughing and talking over each other, paused when they saw the big man lurking in his truck. They fell silent for a split second, then all chimed in again, trading warnings and making a beeline for the one car they all piled into before quickly driving away. Two more groups of college-aged men and women exited the theater and either drove away or headed down the path into the woods that cut through the park separating the education buildings from the dormitories on campus.

And yeah, he was sitting here in the dark of night watching every single one of them.

He was watching and waiting for the curvy little dynamo, whose petite stature belied the size of her personality and the wattage of her smile.

Because spending time with Reese Atkinson was an experience unlike any other he'd ever had with a woman. Twenty-three years ago, when the cute and bubbly star of the show sought him out and included him in her circle of friends. And today, when a bold woman approached him, not once but twice, defending him from the hurtful, mocking words he'd long ago learned to let bounce off his tough hide. And then telling him his eyes were soothing and saying that the bulk and muscle that made him so intimidating made him— what had she called him? *Hottie McHotterson?* Whatever those silly words meant, he'd felt them inside like a breath of sunshine in his dark, distrustful soul.

Yeah, he was cautious, but he wasn't stupid. He liked Reese Atkinson. And he got the feeling she liked him—at least as a friend. So, here he was, sitting alone in a parking lot at 10:15 p.m., ready to do whatever was necessary to protect the first woman who'd made him feel something in a very long time.

A single male student left the theater and headed out along the path into the park. Although Jackson's internal radar alerted with suspicion at the lone figure keeping to the shadows and disappearing among the trees, he stayed put. The guy was walking away, not looking over his shoulder to see if he was being watched. Another pair of students shot out the door and dashed down the path to join the young man. Jackson released the tense breath he'd been holding. Not a threat.

This morning, he'd justified his convoluted offer to meet Reese after rehearsal because she'd given him the first new lead anyone had had on his parents' murders in twenty-three years. Grayson Malone had identified three different blood types on the knife and blouse. Two of the blood smears belonged to his parents. But without fingerprints on the knife, or a sample to match the unknown blood donor to the killer, he wasn't much closer to finding the truth about his mother and father. He squeezed his hand into a fist and rubbed at the ache in his chest. He wanted answers, or a chunk of his life would always feel incomplete. He'd gone into this line of work to find the truth, to honor his parents and bring himself closure. He'd helped the crime lab and the KCPD solve plenty of crimes. But thus far, he'd let his parents down. He hadn't found the peace of mind he needed. He wanted to feel better.

Reese Atkinson's smiles made him feel better.

Her curly red hair and countless freckles that he wanted to explore with his good hand and taste with his lips filled him with a yearning anticipation that had him looking forward instead of staying trapped in his past.

She was caring and forthright in a way that was completely different from how he was raised after his parents' deaths. In Curtis Graham's house, there was no asking permission to touch someone. He'd either gotten yelled at or ignored, and never touched at all. In his uncle's house, affection was earned by achievement—and for a shy, grieving boy who was just trying to get from one day to the next, he had no hope of bonding with the family who'd taken him in. There was no hand-holding or hugs or easy smiles after his parents had passed. In the Army he hadn't expected hugs and softness, so he was never disappointed while he served his country. But in his personal life, he'd always hoped that he'd find unconditional love and support, the tenderness and laughter that he'd known with his mother and father.

Jackson was learning that he had friends among his co-workers at the crime lab—men and women he could depend on and sometimes socialize with. That's why he'd said yes when the lab's computer guru, Chelsea O'Brien, had asked him to be an usher at her wedding in November. Chelsea had given him a hug that day. The quirky, brainy coworker who'd survived an abusive childhood, and nearly died at the hands of a cyberstalker, loved to give hugs, and Jackson admitted he liked having friends who accepted him as he was.

But finding a woman? A family of his own? It was hard to get his uncle's words out of his head sometimes: *Nobody wants you, boy. You've got to make yourself somebody special before anybody's gonna give a damn.*

Not that he thought any of this was a fairy tale, and that Reese was going to magically fall in love with him.

But he really, *really*, wanted to spend more time in the aura of pretty smiles and positive energy that was Reese Atkinson. He wanted a friend from his past, from the good memories in his life. He wanted new memories to savor, good feelings to blot out the darkness of his life.

He intended to see that these pranks didn't snuff out that aura and dim Reese's light. And he was damn well going to make sure that the threats Reese had received weren't a prelude to disaster, like the threats his mother had received in the weeks before her murder.

Jackson silently cursed when the theater door opened

again, and a young couple walked out and wound their arms around each other's waist. He immediately recognized the dark-haired young woman who'd been so rude to Reese. Simon Lowry's granddaughter. Maisey Something—with a different last name than the Lowry fortune. Beautiful in the way of overly made-up fashion models and stylized portraits, but lacking any of the warmth and compassion that oozed out of Reese's pores. The couple leaned against an expensive purple sports car and started making out.

Tired of being stuck with his own thoughts and feeling like a voyeur, Jackson heaved a resolute sigh and opened the door. The couple stopped and looked across the several parking spaces that separated them from Jackson as he climbed down out of his truck. Although the young man had the grace to look a little embarrassed to be caught with his hand under Maisey's shirt, the young woman herself narrowed her eyes and blew a mocking kiss at Jackson.

Whatever. He locked his truck, stuffed the keys in the pocket of his jacket and strode past them toward the theater's back door. He remembered from his parents' time here that the door would lock automatically, and could only be opened from the inside after hours. Still, he would be there, waiting to walk Reese safely to her car as soon as she came outside.

He heard two car doors close and one vehicle drive out of the parking lot. He was already turning at the crunch of gravel on the pavement when a car pulled up to the curb behind him.

Maisey rolled down the passenger-side window of her purple Porsche and yelled at Jackson from behind the wheel. "What are you doing here at my theater, Beast?" When his only reply was to arch an eyebrow at her juvenile attempt to belittle him, she laughed. "You really are Ms. A's boyfriend, hmm? Dean Diamant said you were related to that couple who got killed here. That you were reopening a murder investigation." She revved the engine, probably attempting to show him that she had power and money and could claim the dean as a friend. "Whatever you're up to, don't mess anything up for me. An agent and a producer from New York are coming to the season launch party and to see me in the play. My uncle and granddaddy tell me I'm going to be a star. But not if Ms. A gets in the way. Or you."

Jackson wondered if the young woman was a spoiled diva or extremely insecure, and if she had the means to back up her threats. Asking questions like that wasn't really his thing, but he had no chance to pursue any kind of conversation as she shifted the car into gear and sped away.

Alone once more, Jackson breathed in the cool autumn air and surveyed the parking lot again. The place was down to two vehicles. His truck and Reese's car. He'd asked Chelsea to get her license plate number so he could find it and park close by. He was glad to see her car right beneath a streetlight, but less pleased to see how far away from the theater she had parked if she had to walk that distance on her own. He heard no voices coming from the trees, and saw no one on the path, so those students must have made it back to their dorm rooms.

While the quiet and loneliness was relatively commonplace for him, it didn't sit right that Reese had to face the night or the threats or anything else on her own.

When he heard the click of the bar inside the door being pushed, Jackson swung around and grabbed the door. There she was, her shoulder sagging with the weight of her bag, her eyes looking tired and her short red curls stirring in the breeze.

"Any other incidents?" he asked, realizing a second too late that he hadn't given her room to clear the exit and make sure it was closed. He released the door and backed up a step at her startled gasp and inwardly cursed before tucking his fingers into the front pockets of his jeans to show that he wasn't a threat to her. This woman had a hair trigger when it came to surprises. A man looming over her when she stepped out the door was a big one. She wouldn't be the first woman he'd made uncomfortable by standing so close. And he sure didn't want to add to the stress she'd already had to deal with today. "Sorry."

"Hello to you, too." But she smiled up at him, and that told him he hadn't screwed up too badly. "Did you need to go back inside?" He shook his head and gestured toward their vehicles. "Just here to walk me to my car, kind sir?" Yeah, that smile did make him feel better. She checked to make sure the door was secure before grasping the straps of her quilted carryall and heading out. "Did you find out anything useful at the lab today?"

He wanted to offer to carry something for her. But she'd dinged him for that this morning. Besides, as heavy as the bag looked draped over her shoulder, the straps clutched in both hands, it was all she had. He settled for shortening his stride and falling into step beside her. "No prints on any of the notes."

They'd reached the parking area and stepped off the curb before she spoke again. "What about your parents?"

Grayson's report had been heartbreaking and given him

hope all at the same time. "Mom's and Dad's blood is on the blouse. Knife, too."

Reese halted. "Oh, Jackson. I'm so sorry."

He turned to see the stricken expression on her upturned face. "Grayson couldn't ID a third donor. Samples are too degraded."

"Who's Grayson?"

"Friend at the lab. Blood expert."

"But that confirms the knife was used to kill your parents? You can trace it to the owner or something? The third blood donor must be the killer? Please tell me finding that helps you."

Her eyes were a deep violet blue in the shadow he cast over her. He shifted to the side to let the harsh light from the streetlamp catch in them and make them sparkle again. Oh, hell. Those were tears glistening in her eyes. "I didn't mean to upset you."

"You're the one who should be upset." He watched a tear spill over and magnify the freckles on her cheek. "That's such a violent way to die. I'm sure they fought back. Maybe they even tried to save each other."

He rubbed at the weight pressing on his chest. He'd read the forensic details in the thin evidence file until he had the facts memorized. "Dad was attacked first. Mom may have been collateral damage. May have tried to intervene. But she was the one getting threats."

Jackson heard Reese's pained gasp, felt it deep inside himself, clenching around his heart. She reached up to cover his fist with her hand, and he stilled the habitual movement. "They must have loved each other so much. You were lucky to have them in your life for as long as you did. That's how

I cope with losing my mom and dad—I remember all the wonderful times before they were gone." She slipped her fingers into the center of his fist and stroked his palm, easing his tight grip. "I suppose a man who deals with crime and death has a hard time thinking of the good things. Tell me a good memory about your mom and dad."

Jackson held himself perfectly still beneath her hand. Funny how even though her skin was cool to the touch, he felt something warm and bright seeping into his blood from the contact. With her touch, her patience, a flood of memories from his childhood filled his head. This woman must possess some kind of superpower. He couldn't not feel better when he was with her. He might as well share the most important memory. "They always called me their miracle boy. Mom had several miscarriages. I'm the only child she carried to term."

Another tear ran down her cheek and dripped off her chin, but she was smiling this time. "You were a treasure to them, I'm sure."

Jackson raised his other hand to wipe away the tears she was shedding for *his* loss. But he stopped himself before touching her. He didn't want to scare her away from this intimacy he was feeling.

Her gaze shifted to the hand he dropped back to his side. She sighed and pulled back, tugging the cuff of her blouse from beneath her jacket to dab at her empathetic tears. She headed toward her car again. "Were they robbed? Carjacked?"

Breaking contact was the opposite of what he wanted. He hurried after her. "Nothing taken."

"A crime of passion, then. Is that what it's called when

the attacker loses it in a fit of rage, and goes after someone like that?"

Instead of agreeing or explaining the technical terminology used in their lab reports, Jackson asked. "Do you like pie?"

"What? Is that code...? Um..." She spouted a few partial sentences, looking confused by the question. "It's not my favorite dessert. I'm not a fan of mushy cooked fruit. Why?"

"When I have a bad day, I like to get pie. Pearl's Diner has the best. They're open late." He rambled on, not sure he was making sense. They crossed the last few steps to her car. "You're probably tired. I'll make sure you get inside safely, then you can go home."

"Does Pearl's have ice cream?" He felt her hand at his elbow as she stepped up beside him. "Could they make me a milkshake?" The soft smile on her full pink lips gave him a sliver of hope. "Ask me. If that's what you want."

She knew he was trying to ask her out? Trying and failing. But this beautiful, kind, insightful woman understood. He didn't think she was setting him up for a joke, either. That had happened once in the Army. He'd gone to a bar with some of his platoonmates and thought a woman there was coming on to him. Believing she'd been sincere in wanting to go home with him had been the punch line. While she laughed at his invitation with her friends, he'd gone back to the base and hammered a heavy bag without gloves until his knuckles started to bleed. But this was different. Reese was different. She hadn't done anything to make him think she was playing him. She was worth the risk, right?

Find the words to say what you mean. Spit 'em out. "Want to get a milkshake? With me?"

"I'd love to." The tension in him relaxed at her eager response. She reached up and touched her fingertip to the corner of his mouth. "I like it when you smile. I've had a tough day, too, and could use a little self-indulgence." He held the door to her car while she climbed inside. "I've never been to Pearl's. I've got GPS. But could I follow you and meet you there? Then we won't have to come back to campus."

And she'd have a means of leaving on her own if she discovered she wasn't comfortable with him. That had happened before, too.

Fifteen minutes later, Jackson locked his truck and jogged around the corner to meet Reese when she got out of her car. They'd hit the shift change at the KCPD and dinner break with the fire department. Being so close to the downtown stations, Pearl's Diner was a popular eatery for the city's first responders. The parking spaces in front of the diner were already taken, so they'd had to find spots the next block over. But Jackson wasn't worried about waiting in line. He and his team from the lab sometimes came here after working late on a crime scene, and he knew the servers and cooks at Pearl's kept things moving quickly with their simple, tasty food and reliable service.

Of course, tonight would be different, he thought, as they joined the line waiting to be seated. He probably wasn't scoring many points with the last-minute invitation. And if they had lousy service, he'd be scoring a big fat zero with Reese. Thankfully, she wasn't complaining.

"Two." Jackson held up two fingers when it was their turn to be seated.

The new server who greeted them at the door never looked him in the eye. The dark-haired woman whose name tag read

Mollie glanced at Jackson's chest, maybe raised her gaze up to his chin, then focused her attention squarely on Reese. "This way, please."

Jackson didn't take it personally that she was skittish around him. A lot of people were wary of his size and tough-guy looks. But he suspected there was something more at work here when she walked a wide berth around the tables where only men were sitting. Even the ones where some Kansas City's police officers sat. Was she leery of cops? Or men in general?

"Hey! Mollie, is it?" When an older uniformed customer grabbed her wrist, she literally shied away and bumped into the table across from him. "We need more coffee."

Jackson instinctively touched her elbow to help her gain her balance, and she jerked away again.

"Sorry," she muttered to the front of his jacket. "Sorry," she apologized to the table she'd bumped, causing their drinks to slosh over the sides of their glasses. She immediately pulled a cloth from the belt of her apron and mopped up the mess. "I'll bring refills."

"Good golly, Miss Mollie," the older man who'd grabbed her teased. "How hard can it be to bring a coffeepot around and refill our mugs?"

The waitress cleared her throat and glanced at the impatient customer. "I'll be back as soon as I seat this couple."

"The longer it takes, the smaller your tip."

"Dude. Lighten up." A dark-haired uniformed cop spoke from the table on the other side of the booth divider. "Let her get her feet under her before you become *that* customer the staff gossips about back in the kitchen. She's new and they're obviously slammed tonight."

"Mind your own business, Standage. The little lady and I have reached an understanding. Right, babe?"

More interesting than her reaction to Officer Grabby Hands was that the waitress's eyes locked on to the police officer standing up for her. Those two knew each other.

"Hey," the officer greeted her. Jackson had met Joel Standage when they'd both been part of a murder investigation the previous year. He didn't know Standage well, but he'd gotten a sense that he was good guy.

Still, Mollie looked like she was about to bolt. Even as Jackson moved to position himself between the waitress and her rude customer, Reese stepped up beside the woman and smiled. "Hey. Everything okay? Ignore him. He's not going to do anything stupid with us and your friend across the way around. Where do you want us to sit?"

"He's not my friend. I thought I recognized him. But the man I knew is dead." Mollie tucked a long strand of hair back into her ponytail. "It's fine. I'm fine. Sorry. Come this way." She moved a little faster when she saw how close Jackson was following behind her. But Officer Grabby Hands wasn't going to touch her again. Jackson exchanged a nod with Officer Standage. She seated them at a booth in the corner. She waited for him to slide into the seat across from Reese. She spoke straight to Reese. "Water?"

"Please."

Jackson didn't take offense. Mollie wasn't the first woman to be cautious around him.

"The menus are there on the table. Unless you already know what you want?"

Reese looked across the table at him, then up to the waitress again. "Excuse me."

When Reese grabbed her purse and slipped out of the booth, Jackson assumed she was headed for the ladies' room. Or maybe to say a few choice words to Officer Grabby Hands. Or maybe he was completely wrong about her, and she was rethinking agreeing to this impromptu date and was leaving him.

Chapter Six

The last thing Jackson expected was for Reese to circle to his side of the table and scoot into the seat beside him. She wasn't running away. She was moving closer. Her thigh brushed against his.

Reese reached for his hand between them and laced her fingers together with his before lifting them to rest on top of the table. She was holding on to him in plain view of the waitress and anyone else in the diner to see. Although the top of that curly red hair barely reached his shoulder as she sat beside him, she had taken control of the situation here. Her ease with being close to him put Mollie at ease. Her words even elicited a shy smile from the waitress. "I've heard you make a pretty mean milkshake here at Pearl's."

Mollie nodded. "The menu only lists chocolate, strawberry and vanilla. But since we make ice cream sundaes, too, we can basically create any flavor you want. I like to swirl in an extra shot of syrup. Whipped cream and a cherry, too, if you want."

"You're my kind of woman. Butterscotch?"

"Sure."

"That sounds yummy. I'll take a butterscotch milkshake.

No cherry. But yes to the whipped cream. And my date here—" she glanced at Jackson and squeezed his hand "—would like to know what kind of pie you have."

Date. She'd called him her date.

Yeah, everything felt better when Reese Atkinson was around. Jackson breathed easier and felt the urge to smile. He couldn't even complain that she was holding on to his mangled hand.

"Since it's so late, we don't have everything. But you have a few choices." Mollie listed off the flavors they had left, and Jackson ordered caramel apple.

She was making eye contact with him now. "Warmed up? À la mode?"

"Both," Jackson answered. "And coffee."

Mollie smiled. She'd deemed him safe, thanks to the way Reese acted around him. At least he was less of a threat than the jerk who needed a caffeine fix and a lesson in manners. "Just made a fresh pot. I'll get those right out." She brought them water and coffee, poured a cup for the handsy customer, then headed behind the counter to fix their desserts.

"This *is* a great place." Reese scanned the diner, taking in every detail from the wall-to-wall windows at the front to the black-and-white tiled floor to the soda fountain, complete with red vinyl stools. "I love the kitschy decor. Seems to be a popular place for first responders. No wonder they're open late. They're doing a booming business."

"She was afraid of me. Afraid of every man in here. But she relaxed. Because of you." Jackson looked over his bulky shoulder into Reese's upturned face. "You're good with people."

She shrugged off the compliment. "Nah. That guy was a

jerk. I just offered her a means to escape. It's a woman thing. Like when there's no toilet paper in the stall and you ask a complete stranger in the one next to you to loan you some, they do it. Women help each other out."

Jackson had no idea what that reference to unified female pride meant, but he wasn't going to let her downplay her gift. "You're a star in the theater, on and off the stage. But I think your way with people is your real talent."

She shrugged. "I was just keeping the peace. It stopped you from knocking that jerk's block off. You're scary when you go into protector mode like that. I swear you were suddenly six inches taller when you stepped between Mollie and that guy. You did that at the theater, too, with Dean Diamant. Made *me* take a step back, and you were defending me."

"Reese." He held her gaze and made sure she saw he was serious about the rare gift she had that he could never hope to master. "Take the compliment."

Her freckles disappeared beneath a blush. "Okay. I did a good thing. I helped Mollie feel better herself, and about you. And I defused the tension in the room. Thank you for noticing." He waited for her to release his hand, but she never did, and since he liked the feel of her soft bejeweled fingers laced with his, he made no move to let her go. "It comes from necessity, I suppose. My sister and I have always had to stand up for ourselves. Battling the insurance company, lawyers, creeps in courtrooms, employers, directors, students—"

"Dean Diamant?"

"Him, too. I don't know if I'm an extrovert so much as I'm good at playing one. All my experience in the theater has given me the training to pretend to be whoever I need to be." After a few seconds of silence, she turned their hands over and studied his misshapen fingers. "What happened to your hand? Is it rude to ask?"

He shook his head. "I was a boxer in the Army. Still hit the gym to work out. Repetitive injury. Scar tissue on the bones."

"They don't impact the work you do now?" He shook his head and wiggled his fingers for her. They were stiff, but functioned. She lifted her other hand to trace the crooked arc of his pinkie and ring finger. "Do they hurt?"

Not when she caressed them like that. "The first couple of times I broke them, yeah. They work. They'll never be straight. They'll develop arthritis one day. I can already tell when rain or cold weather is coming."

"Ouch." She sat beside him for several long moments, fiddling with the silver and turquoise rings she wore, adjusting the man's watch that circled her wrist, checking the time. He wondered if she was considering letting go of his hand and moving back to the other side of the booth. She surprised him when she closed both hands around his. "Can I tell you something?"

He waited for her to continue.

She understood that was a yes. "I'm glad you came back tonight. To the theater. That place is creepy at night. Even if you don't believe in ghosts."

"Something happen?" In the one day they'd gotten reacquainted, he knew it wasn't like her to hesitate like this. "Come on, Freckles. You've told me everything else today. Don't stop now."

She suddenly lightened up and chuckled. "Freckles? Really?"

He touched several of the pale pink marks on her hand. "It's like you've been sprinkled with fairy dust."

"They make me look like I'm twelve years old."

His gaze dropped to her full unadorned lips, then boldly skimmed the generous curve of her breasts and the shadow of cleavage between them, curious to know if those freckles went all the way down there, too. Then he lifted his gaze back to the unique violet blue in her eyes. "No man would ever mistake you for a twelve-year-old."

She blushed beautifully and Jackson felt the need to kiss her, to lean down and claim her lips and show her in whatever rough-edged, but honest way he could muster that he had never met another woman who fired up his body, got him out of his brooding thoughts and cracked through the walls of his heart the way she did. Before he could act on the impulse to any degree, Reese pulled her hands away from his. Mollie arrived with their desserts, and Reese tasted a spoonful of her milkshake before raving to the waitress about how deliciously perfect it was with the butterscotch syrup swirled through it.

Jackson took his cue from her and stabbed into his pie, savoring the warm, spicy aroma before tucking a big bite into his mouth. Yes, it was delicious, and certainly gave him pleasure. But he'd rather be holding Reese's hand and sharing more conversation with her.

They ate for a few minutes in silence. Jackson polished off his pie before Reese spoke again. "You're not like any man I've ever met," she said, easing his fears about voicing his attraction to her.

He sipped the hot, strong coffee, keeping his hands busy so he wouldn't reach for her. "That good or bad?"

"It's…intriguing. You don't say much. Sometimes, I feel like you're searching for the right word or worrying too much about how people will react to you. And then, out of the blue, you spout poetry like the fairy dust. I think, maybe, you need to stay in the moment more—not worry about your past or try to foretell the future. I like the things you do say."

Right. His style was about as smooth as that crass cop who'd put his hands on the waitress. He steered the conversation back to a more work-related topic he could handle. "The theater was creepy tonight?"

"I've been spooked by weird stuff all day—dwelling on what all of it means." She set aside the last of her milkshake and finally got to the heart of the problem she'd skimmed over earlier. "You said your mother received threats before she was killed? What about?"

Oh, hell no. He wasn't ready to talk about this with her, was he?

"A grunt is not an answer."

He wasn't even aware that he'd made the noise. But since he'd already acknowledged his concern for Reese's safety, and could see a pattern repeating itself twenty-three years after the fact, he could hardly avoid letting her know the truth. "Love letters, at first. Then not so loving. All anonymous, like yours."

"Do you think whoever sent those letters is the man who killed your mom and dad?"

Jackson set his mug down and looked at her pale expression. Oh, hell. Did she think the messages she'd received meant someone would try to kill her, too?

She looked completely earnest as her hands fisted on the table. "I want to help with your investigation. There are... secrets at that theater. Old ones, new ones. As much as I love it, I'm not comfortable there. I made a mistake of going out with one of the professors—Patrick Brown, the guy with the blond ponytail and glasses?"

Jackson nodded. He remembered Brown, both from today, and from when he'd come to the house for Jackson's mom to tutor him. Twenty-three years ago, Brown's hair had been longer, and he hadn't started balding yet.

"I could tell after one night I just wanted to be friends. But he keeps pushing. My play goes up in two weeks, but props are being destroyed. I have to get everything ready for the Lowrys' reception. I get the feeling that Maisey is trying to get rid of me, and Dean Diamant uses me as his verbal whipping post. It's like…"

"The spotlight's on you?"

She nodded. "I used to love the spotlight. All I wanted to do was act on Broadway."

"You were good enough." He sensed this conversation was taking a turn into difficult territory for her. Without thinking it through, he reached for her hand and held it gently against his thigh. Thankfully, she accepted that small bit of comfort and didn't pull away.

"Turns out, the price of fame wasn't worth the dreams I had."

"What price? This morning you said that secrets wake you up at night. A few minutes ago, you mentioned 'creeps in courtrooms.' Now you tell me you're spooked?" He hunched down to look her straight in the eye. "I need you to always be straightforward with me. Subtext isn't my best thing."

"Okay." Her grip pulsed within his. "I'm scared. Every time I get a note or busted-up prop, I get a sick feeling of déjà vu. I was targeted once before. It started when I was twelve. Just starting my career in New York. There was this man.

He was obsessed with sweet little Reese with the big voice. He wanted to…marry me. He sent notes, flowers, gifts— came to every performance. He'd show up at my dressing room backstage. Restraining orders didn't stop him. He just changed his tactics to get to me." She paused and shivered. "When I was fourteen, he tried to kidnap me. He said he was going to make me his wife, and do things to me that fourteen-year-old me didn't even understand."

"*Tried* to kidnap you? Honey, if he took you for any length of time, you were kidnapped." How was Reese so…good? When crap like that had happened to her? Since she didn't seem to notice the endearment that had slipped out, he didn't draw attention to it by apologizing. But he did make a point of easing the anger from his grip before accidentally crushing her hand. "What happened?"

"My parents were rock stars. They saw me get dragged inside the van. Mom called in the license plate and description of the van while Dad jumped in the car and followed us. NYPD stopped the van with a spike strip, got me out and arrested the guy." She was shivering again. But her skin felt feverish, not cold. "I wasn't his first obsession. He had a record."

Creeps in courtrooms. "You testified against him."

She nodded. "Mom and Dad died coming home from his sentencing hearing."

First thing tomorrow, he'd ask Chelsea to dig up the court transcripts to get a name and location on this guy. "Is he sending the messages now?"

She shook her head. "Child molester? He was killed in prison."

Good. Not that Jackson condoned murder. But he wouldn't
excuse anyone that evil getting close to Reese, either.

Turning toward him in the booth, she pulled back her
shoulders and tilted her chin, like she was about to make
an announcement. Jackson braced, fairly certain he wasn't
going to like where this conversation was leading.

"I'm a grown-up now. I don't need Mommy and Daddy
to save me. I'm not going to let anything like that happen
again. Not to me. Not to one of my students. Not to my theater." Her hand pulled against his with every point she made.
"The messages? Finding a real murder weapon? It's no secret
that I'm the one in charge of the building. I think someone
put that knife there for me to find. The dean ordered me to
take care of those donations. The Lowry family sent them.
How did I get stuck in the middle of all this? If I'm being
targeted again, I intend to fight back. For my parents. For
those girls before me who weren't so lucky dealing with
that creep who took me. If I help you—asking questions,
putting you in touch with some of the people who were involved with the theater when your parents were there—it
would give me some control back. Make me less afraid.
I'd feel less isolated if I knew I was part of a team that was
searching for the truth."

"I'm a scientist, not a cop."

"I'm just asking questions. Keeping my eyes open. Reporting to you so you can do your science thing and come
up with answers we can share with the police."

"Twenty-three years is a long time to get away with murder. He thinks he's smarter than us. Could be dangerous."

She waved her hand in front of him, sweeping from shoulder to shoulder. "You were in the Army. You box. You're

built like a truck. I think you're a lot smarter than most people would ever guess. I have a feeling you're well equipped to keep me safe."

He repeated his objection. "I don't like you in danger."

"Jackson, except for my sister, I have been on my own since I was a teenager. I've dealt with being taken for granted, being laughed at, being underestimated and being alone." She pressed her fist to the tabletop. "I'm tired of *dealing*. I want to fight back. I think someone wants you and KCPD to reopen the investigation into your parents' murders. Maybe the killer has been hiding the truth for twenty-three years, and wants to finally be rid of the guilt. Or an accomplice who knows what happened has finally decided to break their silence."

"Maybe someone wants to kill again. Kill you."

"Maybe it doesn't have a damn thing to do with me, and I'm the unluckiest woman in the world to get stuck between a stalker *and* a killer." She released him to wrap both hands around his forearm, pleading with him. "But I'm not going to just sit here and do nothing. I'm a fighter. Like you. Maybe I don't have the external scars to prove it like you do, but they're there. Please let me help. You can be the brains behind the scenes, and I can be the mouthpiece on the front line."

"No."

She let go and turned away. "Great. I thought you were different. But you're dismissing me just like everybody else. You don't think I can get the job done. All I'm good for is looking cute and smiling."

"No."

"Would you please say something besides no? Tell me what you mean."

"No, you are not putting yourself in danger on the front line of this investigation."

"Oh." Spelling out his concern seemed to give her hope. "So, you don't mind me helping—you just don't want me to get hurt?"

He nodded.

"I can work with that." Her energy renewed, she dug into her bottomless pit of a bag and came up with a pen and small notepad. "Who would you like to talk to? What can I do to help?" She was listing ideas before he made any suggestions. "I can get you in to the Lowrys' party on Saturday. You could be my date. A lot of the people who were part of campus life twenty-three years ago will be there. All the people who have a grudge against me—that I know of—will be there, too."

"No one would believe we're a couple."

"Dean Diamant did. Mollie does. Do you have a tux?"

He didn't. "You'd go without me?"

"I have to be there, no matter what. Use of the theater is my responsibility."

"Then I'll find one."

"Thank you. I'll text you the details." She jotted a note with his name in it before snapping the pad shut and stuffing everything back into her bag. "I like that we've got another date planned. I'm sure I can help."

Although she could certainly ask questions of people who probably wouldn't talk to him, Jackson wasn't so sure her contribution would be worth the risk she'd be taking. "I want to meet you after rehearsals. Sit in on some. I don't want you alone late at night."

"That's good. Anyone who sees us would expect my boyfriend to pick me up."

"No. I want to make sure you're safe."

"Even better."

"I'm not acting."

"Neither am I." She beamed a smile up at him that lit the darkest corners of his soul. "Thank you for hearing me out. And giving me a chance to help fight my own battle."

Jackson paid the bill and left a generous tip before putting on his jacket and walking Reese out the door. He stuck his hands into his pockets so he wouldn't forget this was a first date and didn't do something stupid like act on that kiss he'd fantasized about.

"Look. You said you don't do subtext. I'm guessing you don't have a lot of good experiences with dating. So, let me make this clear." She hooked her hand through the crook of his elbow and stopped him. Then she slipped one hand into his and hugged herself around his arm, tilting her head back to make eye contact. "I'm interested in you."

"Why?"

"A bunch of different reasons. You listen when I talk. You don't dismiss me as inconsequential. You're protective. You don't care about the freckles or the extra pounds—"

"I like the freckles. And the curves."

"You like to read. I do, too. These arms. Some reasons I can't even put into words." Suddenly, her smile vanished, and she pulled away. "Are you interested in me?"

"God, yes."

She laughed with such relief that he smiled. "Good. I want to get to know you better. I want to spend time with you. You okay with that?" He nodded. She linked her fingers with his again and they headed down the sidewalk to her car. "All right, then. I'll be patient. And you keep trying to come out of that shell of yours. It makes me feel special to know that you're making the effort to do that for me."

When they rounded the corner and Jackson saw her squarish little toaster car, he halted.

"What?" Reese followed the direction of his gaze, then cursed and hurried forward before he could stop her. She went out into the street, circling around her car, taking in the damage. "What the hell?"

All four of her tires had been slashed, and two words had been keyed into the driver's side door.

Next time.

"*Next time* what? He'll give me a full-blown heart attack?" Reese demanded. Jackson followed her into the street and put up a hand to warn the approaching traffic to drive around them. She charged ahead of him before he could guide her back to the safety of the sidewalk. "I'm getting one of those cops from the diner." He nearly plowed into her when she suddenly stopped and turned. "Wait. You don't think this was that cop we stood up to for Mollie, do you? Maybe this is something different. Spur-of-the-moment rage. Everything else has happened on campus. And there's no clever message."

Jackson snagged her by the shoulders to stop her from moving away from him again. "There's a damn message. *Next time* he'll hurt you and not your car? *Next time* he'll kill you?"

Yeah. She got the message now. And he felt like a heel for driving the point home.

Reese nodded before twisting away to dig her phone out of her purse. "This has gone too far. I can't dismiss it as a prank anymore. I'm reporting it to the police." She pulled out her phone to punch in 911.

But Jackson already had his out of his pocket, speed-dialing his friend at the KCPD, Aiden Murphy. "Murph? I need a unit at Pearl's Diner right now. Somebody's after a friend of mine." Yes, it was the cute little redhead from this morning. And no, she wasn't hurt. "She's pissed, but fine. Now, Murph."

Once he knew that Aiden and his K-9 partner, Blue, were on their way, along with a priority call to Dispatch to get a black-and-white here even sooner, Jackson scanned up and down the street, peering around the glare of streetlamps and headlights, searching for anyone in the shadows who was watching Reese right now. He noticed she, too, was visually tracking every pedestrian, squinting to see faces inside the cars that drove past.

"This guy is good," Reese bit out between clenched teeth. "I've never seen him. Not once. Why don't you show yourself?" Her shout was drowned out by a car racing past.

Her phone rang in her hand. Her outburst of frustrated anger and fear fizzled out on the second ring. She must have thought it was the guy. She'd said he called her after every incident.

Jackson read the caller ID. Unknown. "On speaker," he ordered, leaning in to listen as she answered.

"Hello?"

Jackson heard someone breathing. Angry huffs of air. A sniffle as if a hard run in the cold air was affecting his sinuses. Then one guttural, ghostly word. "Mine."

When her cheeks went pale and her hand started to drop, he grabbed the phone and put it to his ear. "Who is this?"

The abrupt disconnect echoed in his ear.

"Jackson?" Reese stepped toward him. "Put your arms around me."

Her whole body was shaking against his as he wrapped her up in his embrace and dipped his lips to the crown of her hair. The woman had a death grip on his shirt beneath his jacket, her lush curves pressing against his harder angles as she clung to him. With her face buried against his chest, he couldn't tell if she was sobbing with fear or shaking with anger.

In these moments when Reese had turned to him for comfort, something inside Jackson changed. The threat to Reese woke the warrior inside him. His heart might get shattered at the end of all this when she discovered she no longer needed him. But for now, this woman was his to protect.

She needed him. Needed his strength. Needed his heat. Needed him to hear her words. Needed him to stand tall and do the job he was trained to do. Find answers.

He squeezed her to his chest as tightly as he dared with one arm and raised his phone with the other. "Lexi? Jackson." He'd never been one for pleasantries. He was even less so now that he'd seen firsthand how these threats could hurt the woman he was falling for far too quickly. "I need Chelsea to trace a call for me. And send the team to Pearl's Diner."

Chapter Seven

The man waited until all but the police officer with the dog had left the scene before pulling the top of his hoodie over his head and sliding his hands into his pockets. No one would notice him dressed like this. He moseyed down the sidewalk away from the diner, right along with the curious lookie-loos who'd grown tired of watching the KCPD's response to his handiwork.

The CSIU van was still there, as well as a tow truck and a group of criminalists wearing CSI vests and jackets. They'd taken dozens of pictures and dusted for prints they would never find. One of them had even knelt in front of the message he'd scratched and pressed something like flypaper over it before peeling it off. Probably checking for any kind of trace that would indicate the weapon he'd used.

He ran his thumb over the pocketknife with the etched ivory handle that could only be found in antique stores or on the black market anymore. Typically, he preferred a bigger knife, but he hadn't planned on leaving a message for Red tonight. He was just watching her the way he did many nights. The way he liked to do with his women.

He'd never had a redhead before.

But he'd gotten so damn angry. Reese Atkinson was proving to be a handful of trouble. Sticking her nose into things that were none of her business. Refusing every chance he gave her to comply with his wishes. Being scared, but not scared enough to confide in him. Instead, she'd allied herself with that hulking shadow from her past.

"Big mistake, Red."

He reached his vehicle parked much farther down the street and climbed inside. He picked up his binoculars from the passenger seat and raised them to study the activity around her car. The tow truck driver was loading her ugly little eco car onto the platform at the back of his truck. He let his gaze slide over to the man in the leather jacket who was blocking his view of Red. She liked to collect ugly things.

The man in the car huffed with an angry breath. He needed to cool the fire heating his blood. He watched as Red stepped forward to shake hands with a man walking on a pair of crutches. Just as quickly, she drew back beside Mr. Ugly. Her posture flagged and she looked forlornly over at her car and waved goodbye.

Now he was getting through to her. He was the master of this game. And she'd be the prize when he won.

But the jolly scarred giant could be a problem.

He slipped earlier when he'd spoken on the phone. She could have recognized his voice. Hell, that ape she'd turned to for comfort might have recognized his voice if his memory was any good.

He understood objectively that he had a sickness. That his way of pursuing a relationship wasn't healthy. But the heart wanted what it wanted.

And he wanted Reese Atkinson.

But there she was, hugging her heavy breasts around the

big bruiser's arm as she clung to his hand. She'd gone out with him on a date, practically sat in his lap in the diner.

Red had found the knife he'd used on his beloved Melora. Mel hadn't done what he'd asked of her, either. Melora had been an accident. She'd been his first, but she hadn't been his last. He thought the evidence had been disposed of years ago, but he'd been betrayed. He should be doing all he could to cover his tracks. All he could to find out if someone had accidentally exposed him by sending the knife to the theater—or if the revelation had been done intentionally. But his compulsion ran too deep.

He lowered the binoculars and carefully stowed them in their case and tucked that into the glove box before starting his vehicle.

If Red kept working with the crime lab and the police, he'd probably have to kill her as soon as he took her. Usually, he could scare them into obeying him. For a while, at least. But then they either rebelled or surrendered, and he'd have to dispose of them and start anew. He had a feeling Red would be the kind to fight him every step of the way. But she would be tamed. She would obey him—even if it was only for a few moments before she took her last breath.

But he'd have to get the new boyfriend out of the way. Distract him if he could. Kill him if he couldn't. The behemoth shouldn't be touching what was his.

The figure sitting in the dark shadows of the parked car pounded the steering wheel with his fist.

"She's mine."

JACKSON RAISED HIS head from the microscope where he'd been analyzing the trace Shane Duvall had taken from the door of Reese's car last night. He blinked to clear his vision, then pinched the bridge of his nose between his thumb and forefinger to alleviate the tension gathering there after an afternoon spent studying metal dust, identifying its components via chemical analysis, then evaluating each extracted component. It was time-consuming, painstaking work, and normally, he appreciated extended quiet time alone in the lab.

But this was evidence from the attack on Reese's car, and he was struggling to find his patience. The anonymous coward waging a terror campaign against Reese had escalated last night. Cool and calculating and hiding in the shadows to torment her was dangerous enough. Losing his temper to the point of lashing out at her and actually speaking on the phone was a whole new kind of threat. Unpredictable. Violent. There was no mistaking the rage he'd vented on her car last night.

Next time he might not stop with carving up her car.

If Reese had been anywhere near that guy last night... If he had taken that rage out on her instead of her property...? It was far too easy to imagine Reese's body disfigured by cuts and stab wounds lying in a pool of her own blood. He'd been to enough crime scenes, had taken enough molds of wound tracks, and had dissected and analyzed enough weapons to know what each and every wound would look like.

Jackson curled his hands into the meaty fists he'd once used to take down opponents in the ring and let his own anger course through him. He couldn't lose Reese. Hell, he'd barely found her. He hadn't even kissed her yet, and he had an idea that his life would be incomplete if he never got the opportunity to feel her beautiful mouth beneath his. He liked holding her hand. Loved how she'd gently caressed his broken fingers as if he was something precious instead of a fighting machine or a reclusive monster or a beast.

Put your arms around me. Last night when she'd been shaken up by her stalker's violent attack, he'd needed to hold her. To feel her softness against him. To feel her clinging to him as if she never wanted to let go. He'd almost hauled her up against him before she'd spoken. He needed to hold her to know she was safe and that the threats hadn't broken her beautiful spirit. She'd needed him. She'd needed *him*.

It was a heady discovery that filled him with a new kind of confidence where second-guessing had no place to dwell, where Uncle Curtis's voice and the harsh mantra that said he wasn't good enough to matter to anyone couldn't reach. Hearing Reese say she was interested in him wreaked havoc on all the bad memories that had taught him he was unattractive, worthless, not special enough for any woman to want.

Being with Reese Atkinson made him feel like the victorious boxer again. The valued Army sergeant on patrol with his platoon. The miracle boy his parents had loved.

He was going to hold Reese again.

He was going to kiss her.

He was going to find out who wanted her to be afraid.

Even more important than solving his parents' murders was identifying who was terrorizing Reese. He'd been a child when his parents had been killed. Even if he'd been on campus with them that night, he wouldn't have been able to stop the attack. But he was a grown-ass man now. He was a skilled criminalist, an Army vet and a champion amateur boxer. He'd see Reese safe, and justice served, or he'd die trying.

Jackson opened his hands and exhaled a breath to steady his focus, just as surely as a sniper would calm any movement of their body before taking a kill shot. Then he looked into the microscope again to confirm his findings.

He had a lead.

Nodding, he turned away to type the results into his computer. Then he sent a text to Chelsea in her computer lab with info on a search for her to run.

He heard a knock on the door and looked up as his friends and coworkers Grayson Malone, team leader Lexi Callahan-Murphy, Zoe Stockmann and Shane Duvall strolled in. Clearly, like Jackson, they'd finished running their tests for the day and were in wrap-up mode, unless the team got called to another crime scene.

Grayson pulled out a stool on the opposite side of the stainless steel table where Jackson was working. "Find anything new about the scene we processed outside Pearl's Diner last night? The prints I ran all came back to you or Professor Atkinson."

"You took charge of the scene and put us through our paces." Zoe was the youngest on the team. And, though she was the daughter of the veteran police officer who oversaw the CSIU and liaised with the KCPD, she'd more than earned her position as a solid criminalist. "I don't think I've ever heard you talk so much at one time."

"Exactly." Lexi gently elbowed the younger woman. "I think this sudden explosion of social interaction has something to do with Professor Atkinson. I like her."

Jackson grunted his agreement, then remembered Reese telling him that a grunt was not an answer. He was never going to be verbose, but he had words. "Me, too."

"Obviously." Lexi winked and pulled up a stool beside Grayson.

Great. This impromptu staff meeting was about to turn into an inquisition into his newfound interest in Reese if he didn't steer the conversation back to business. He nodded to Shane Duvall, a single dad whose beard and glasses made him look more like a professor than Reese did. "I processed the trace you took from the carving in the door. Good idea."

Shane grinned at what passed for high praise from Jackson. "Did you find something, big guy?"

"Minute paint chips and steel shavings from the car itself." Jackson moved the sample over to the projector scope and adjusted the image on the screen so he could point out his discovery to everyone. "But I also found evidence of bronze dust in the deepest groove of the *N* in *Next.*"

"There's no bronze in a car chassis, is there?" Zoe asked.

"None at all." The director of the crime lab, Mac Taylor, walked in. "I wondered where my best team had wandered off to. Didn't realize I had called a staff meeting." He went up to the projection and adjusted his glasses to study the image with his one good eye. He'd been blinded in the other eye by an explosion at the old crime lab years before Jackson had come to work for them in this new facility. "You think you can identify the weapon from some dust? I know you're good, but…"

"Not precisely." Jackson did, as Reese had said last night, like to read. As the lab's weapons expert, he'd studied everything from a club made from the branch of a tree to jousting equipment, and from laser scalpels to military assault rifles, along with almost every type of gun or blade in between. "It's nothing modern. Probably from turn of the last century. Bronze is stronger than the iron originally used to forge the earliest of sharp weapons. But it's not as strong as the steel used today. Bronze loses its edge faster and needs to be sharpened more often. I'm guessing the blade itself is misshapen from so many years of honing. Some flecks from the last sharpening stayed in some of the pits or nicks on the blade and were transferred to Reese's car."

"Can we identify the make of knife, at least?" Mac asked.

Jackson nodded. "Based on the depth of the marks and composition of the blade, I'd say we're looking for an antique pocketknife."

Grayson propped his crutches against the edge of the table. "An antique? You said the Bowie knife from the theater that I processed had some age on it. Are we looking for a perp who collects rare knives?"

"That's what I'd like to know." Chelsea O'Brien, soon-to-be Buckner, came into the lab hugging her laptop and a file folder to her chest. She set both on the end of the table and fired up her computer. "I need more search parameters to narrow down your request for antique-knife collectors. I had no idea there were so many knife shows and enthusiasts out there. The Nelson-Atkins Museum has an extensive collection of bronze weaponry. Not much that's as small as a pocketknife, though."

Great. Jackson's lab was turning into a damn party. But, for once, he found he didn't mind being the center of the team's gab sessions, where they hashed out ideas and brainstormed solutions to their scientific queries. Maybe because he knew they were there to help him help Reese. Or maybe because Reese had reminded him that he was as human and valued as anyone else.

She reminded him that he had a voice, and encouraged him to say what he needed to. "This guy isn't stealing them. We'd have reports from museums and vendors. We're looking for a private collector."

"That helps. Kansas City area?" Chelsea asked.

"Yes. This guy is local." He'd have to be to have such regular access to Reese, and to know the area well enough to remain undetected.

Chelsea typed the information into her laptop and started another search before handing him the folder she'd brought in. "Oh, and I've got the scoop on the guy who called your friend last night."

While Jackson skimmed through the data she'd collected, Chelsea explained what she'd found to everyone else. "I'm guessing Edwin Booth isn't his real name. I googled it and found a famous actor from the 1800s—the brother of John Wilkes Booth. I figured it was an alias since your friend works in the theater, and the other threats—"

"Focus, Chels," her friend Lexi reminded her. "We need the facts, not a history lesson."

"Right. Edwin, or whoever he is, paid cash for the phone. He used it the one time last night, and it hasn't been active at all today. Reese—I can call her Reese, can't I? Since she's your friend?" Jackson nodded, and she continued. "At any rate, Reese gave me permission to check her phone records. All the creepy calls that match the time stamps she gave me have come from prepaid disposable phones. Your perp used a different number each time. But the phones came from the same batch that was purchased two years ago." She shoved her sparkly cat-eye glasses up onto the bridge of her nose and frowned an apology to everyone in the room. "Unfortunately, the store doesn't keep security footage from that far back. So, I can't give you a visual on whoever purchased them."

Shane frowned right back. "I thought anything that was digitized on the web stayed there forever?"

"The store has a closed-circuit system on their own network." Chelsea wore an expression that said she was entirely innocent, but still so brilliant no one in the room would understand what she was talking about "I could hack into the store's system. But two years of overwriting the same security footage could lead to a pretty degraded recording, if any readable images still exist. If they were simply deleted, I could try to recover them, but it would take me some time to get a picture of your guy."

"And a court order," Mac reminded her. "Private property."

She turned her earnest hazel eyes to Jackson. "But if you ask, I'll do it."

Ask me. If that's what you want.

Jackson couldn't seem to keep his mind off Reese. The woman was a Jackson Whisperer, reading almost as much from the things he didn't say as the things he did. He was anxious to see her again. Eager to hold her hand—to hold her if she'd let him. And of all the longings he never expected to have, he wanted to talk to her some more.

He checked his watch. It might be close to quitting time here at the crime lab. But Reese would be at the theater until after rehearsal tonight. Ten o'clock seemed like a long time away. Maybe he could invite himself to a rehearsal. Or take her some dinner.

"Jackson?" Chelsea was still waiting for his answer.

He pulled his thoughts squarely back into the room. "Let's hold off on breaking any laws right now."

"Good call," Mac echoed.

"Probably," Chelsea agreed. "Buck will never forgive me if I'm in jail on our wedding." The others laughed. Chelsea picked up her laptop and headed for the door. "I'll get to work on finding your knife collector."

With his investigation into the man who was threatening Reese temporarily stalled until Chelsea got him some suspects with a knife he could compare to the marks on her car, Jackson asked, "Anybody know where I can get a tux in my size by Saturday?"

There was a squeal from the doorway, and Jackson looked up to see Chelsea making a beeline toward him. "You have a date? A fancy date?"

Jackson nodded. "Reception at Williams University."

Chelsea squealed again before coming around the table to hug him. "I really like Reese." Then she was opening her laptop again. "I'm going to find you that tuxedo right now. What size? Color?"

Mac tried to rein in the sudden flurry of questions and gaping mouths around the room. "Um, still work hours, people? Reports are all in? Equipment shut down? Evidence labeled and stored?"

Chelsea waved the boss aside. "My search is already running. This will take me two seconds." She turned her computer around and showed Jackson the map on her screen before clicking on one of the icons and opening an advertisement for him. "Here. There's a big-and-tall store down on the Plaza or at Barrywoods Mall in north KC. They have tuxes in stock. Take your pick. Nothing froufrouey for you. I'm thinking basic black. It's always classy."

Mac threw up his hands, but he was smiling as he stepped away. "On that note, I'm heading back to my office. If it helps, my wife and daughter tell me what color they're wearing before I pick out my tux. For the vest and tie or cummerbund."

"You have to call Reese, have a conversation with her," Lexi advised.

Jackson was flummoxed. "I have to wear a cummerbund? Hell, I didn't even go to senior prom. Look, I'm only going because some of the guests knew my parents and could be potential suspects in their murders. One of them could be targeting Reese now. I don't want her facing any of them on her own."

All the teasing suddenly grew serious. Lexi braced her elbows on the table and leaned toward him. "You think what's happening to Reese is the same thing that happened to your parents?"

Jackson nodded. "I think history may be repeating itself."

Now they were all back in investigative mode.

Chelsea was typing on her computer again. "I'll pull up any unsolved stabbings where the weapon was an antique of some kind."

Shane nodded. "A perp doesn't go twenty-three years between killings unless he's moved out of the area, is in prison or dead. Give me a list of suspect names and I can check where they've been in that time frame."

"Why do you think the two cases are related?" Lexi asked.

"For several weeks...before my parents were murdered..."

Jackson hadn't talked about this until yesterday with Reese. "Mom got threats. Letters. Someone was stalking her, too."

"They're in the case file?" Lexi stood and urged Zoe and Chelsea to the door with her. "Let's pull the cold case file and read through the letters Melora Dobbs received. See if there are any linguistic similarities or production factors we can compare to Reese's."

"Or any unsolved cases Chelsea comes up with?" Zoe suggested.

"Good idea."

"What do you need from us?" Grayson asked. "You know I owe you for helping me when Allie was being stalked."

"You don't owe me anything for helping you save your fiancée," Jackson insisted. "She's good for you."

"Yes, she is." Grayson hooked the cuffs of his crutches onto his forearms and stood. "I'm helping you anyway. You need me to watch Reese's place? Pull bios on her students and coworkers?"

Shane headed toward the door. "I'll get busy running the tests to identify if that was poison or simple condensation in the syringe you retrieved from her office."

Jackson was a little overwhelmed by the support he was receiving. He mattered to these people. He might not have any of the Dobbses or Grahams in his life anymore, but he had *this* family. If he was lucky and didn't screw it up, he might have Reese in his life for a while, too.

"It's not a priority case for the crime lab. It's my case, my time. We have other crimes to solve."

"Does Reese mean something to you?" Grayson asked.

Jackson nodded. "I know it's happening fast. And maybe she doesn't feel the same way—"

"She wouldn't let go of you last night. Even when she

was answering Lexi's and Aiden's questions and introducing herself to the rest of us, she kept her hand in yours or she had you in her line of sight. You mean something to her, too." Grayson adjusted his weight over his prosthetic legs. "It doesn't matter if it happens fast, or it takes years to recognize the connection you have to someone special. What matters is it happened. And if Reese Atkinson is important to you, then she's important to us. We're helping you find out who's after her and if it's related to your parents' murders."

"Thanks." Before his friend reached the door, Jackson stopped him. "Malone. How'd you know Allie was the woman for you?"

His friend turned and smiled. "She didn't put up with any crap from me. She got me out of my head, out of the pity party and anger I'd been living in since I lost my legs. But she still needed me. Not anybody else. Me." Grayson came back and rested a hand on Jackson's shoulder. "Tell me this—how do you feel when she holds your hand or smiles at you?"

"Better." Grayson waited for more of an answer. "Like my past and my scary looks don't matter."

"How do you feel when this guy sends a threat to Reese, damages her things, spies on her, claims her as his?"

"Like I want to rip his head off."

Grayson chuckled and smacked Jackson's shoulder. "It's not scientific. But I think we can safely say she's the one for you."

Chapter Eight

Reese ignored Dixon Lowry wiping his hands on his crisp white handkerchief again while his white-haired father, Simon Lowry, ran his fingers across the gritty oversize stone made by her student property master, Zach Oliver.

"This is papier-mâché and chicken wire, with actual bits of gravel dust incorporated into the finish?" The elder Lowry looked at the young Black man and congratulated him on the realism of his work. "Clever, son."

"Thank you, sir." While his gargoyle sat in Reese's office, waiting to be added to the display case in the lobby, Zach had taken great pains to produce a prop with the look and function they needed for the play. He also knew the importance of impressing their biggest supporter as Reese and Dean Diamant led the father and son duo on a tour to personally check out the venue for the Lowrys' season launch party.

Reese added her own congratulations. "Well done, Zach. This will look like the real thing onstage when we drop it on Inspector Blore. Sound effects, staging and his acting will make the audience believe he's being crushed and killed."

Zach's smile quickly faded when Dixon Lowry added his opinion. "Dad, the glue on that thing is still tacky. You have dust on your jacket already and you have dinner with the Vailes at seven." Dixon was a carbon copy of his septuagenarian father, except for the snow-white hair and the graciousness to others, no matter what their station in his life might be. "You'll have that thing put away before the reception, right? Our guests will be dressed to the nines. They won't want to get gravel goop on their clothes."

"It should be dry by tomorrow morning, sir," Zach apologized before Reese could stop him. "Then I'll move it out of the way to the prop table."

"You're making note of all the things that need to be fixed, Miss Atkinson, yes?" Dixon acknowledged Reese's presence without voicing any approval of the effort Zach had made in meeting both Reese's needs for the show and the scheduling requirements for the reception.

"Don't worry, Dix," the dean assured him. "I'll stay on top of Ms. Atkinson."

Reese clamped her lips down over her huffy sigh. "That's not necessary, Dean. Managing the theater is my job. Besides teaching classes, of course." She held up her notepad. "I have everything planned down to the last detail, and I have been in close contact with your staff and the student help I'll be working with."

Dixon put his hand on his father's elbow and turned him away from the worktable where the fake pediment sat up on two-by-fours to dry. "Come on, Dad. Let's move away from it before you get dirtier or hurt."

"My son thinks I'm old and infirm." The sweet man winked a rheumy blue eye at Reese. "I apologize for his rudeness. I'm enjoying the private tour."

Reese winked right back, thanking him for the apology. "Don't worry. Everything will be good to go Saturday night."

"I know it will." The older gentleman rubbed his hands together. "What's next?"

Reese gestured for Simon to follow her. "This way."

"Dad." It didn't seem right to hear a grown man in his fifties whining to his father. Apparently, the love for the theater that his parents and niece shared hadn't been handed down to Dixon. His custom-tailored suit and manicured nails seemed woefully out of place in this building where hard work and imagination created magic. But he'd promised his father that they'd personally check out the venue for the Lowrys' annual season launch party, so he reluctantly followed Reese and his father into the backstage area. "This is as clean as you can get it?"

Reese turned away to hide the roll of her eyes. This was Patrick Brown's construction area. Of course, there would be dust and sawdust, stacks of wood and cans of paint. She looked across a pair of sawhorses to meet Patrick's gaze and beg him to intervene with their guest.

With a nod to Reese, he stepped forward. "The set onstage is completely built except for the taping and touch-up painting. We'll have that done by the end of the day today so that everything is dry for the party Saturday night. I'll have my classes Friday sweep up and put things away so that our guests can tour the entire theater if they wish."

The dean tossed an arm around his friend's shoulder and guided him back toward the stage and auditorium. "Reese, tell Dix about the schedule for the evening."

Reese couldn't determine if the dean's presence on the tour was to check up on her performance in managing the theater, keep an eye on one of the school's biggest investors or seize the opportunity to catch up with a former fraternity brother from their student days at Williams U. Or maybe he was there for all three reasons. Regardless, she mouthed a thank-you to Patrick and fell into step behind the dean, Simon and Dixon.

Once they were back on the stage, Reese put her director skills to work to describe how the celebration would be staged. "We'll have food and drinks in the lobby, where faculty and students involved with the theater program will mingle with the guests to promote our upcoming season, and answer any questions about the shows, their classes and so on. Then we'll lead tours of the theater, except for the storage loft backstage and the catwalk where we hang the lights—for safety reasons, of course. If anyone wants to go up to the balcony and look in the light and sound booth, I'd be happy to show them that myself. Finally, we'll all gather in the auditorium for remarks from Dean Diamant and the Lowry family."

"And you, as well, dear." Simon Lowry touched her elbow and pointed a gently reprimanding finger at her. "You had a great impact on my late wife. She remembered you from the time you were a child appearing in *Annie*. And your production of *Twelve Angry Men* last season was the best drama she's seen on this stage."

Ignoring the glare Dr. Diamant was shooting her way from behind Simon's back, Reese blushed at the high praise. "Thank you, sir. Those are two of my favorite shows, as well—and very kind words. I appreciated all the support Mrs. Lowry gave to the theater."

"More than you know." Although she found the comment

slightly cryptic, he smiled and patted her arm. "I sense that this place is as important to you as it was to her. Something like that is all you need to say."

"And the rest?" Dixon Lowry tapped his watch. Then he looked at Dean as if expecting him to take up his cause to end this meeting.

Take up the cause he did. The dean moved to divert Simon's attention. "Finally, we'll unveil the temporary sign built by our stagecraft students to commemorate Beatrice's generous donation—The Lowry Theater."

Reese's long hours, late nights and stress chose that moment to catch up with her, and she yawned. Although she quickly raised her hand to mask it, all of her company had seen it. "I'm sorry. I had a really late night. After rehearsal last night…my car was vandalized. It was towed to the crime lab as evidence."

"Evidence?" Dean questioned.

"Yes. It could be related to…a case they're working." Reese wasn't sure how much illegal activity swirling around her these past few weeks she wanted to share with the dean. No doubt he'd find some way to turn around the fact that she was the victim and blame her for bringing the authorities into his theater. "I had to hitch a ride to work with a friend this morning. But he needed to get to work early, so, not much sleep."

"Your friend, Melora Dobbs's son?" Dean asked. "The big guy?"

"Yes. Jackson. He drove me to campus this morning."

"So, you two *are* close," the dean muttered, looking a little disappointed or frustrated or…something…at confirming she and Jackson were more than acquaintances or child-hood friends.

At least, she'd like to be close. Whatever was developing between them seemed to be happening quickly. And though Reese wasn't averse to acting on this bond between them, she had a feeling that Jackson was a slow mover. Clearly, the man had history that tainted the way he presented himself to the world. He'd been hurt or abused or shunned because of his looks and his shyness. She didn't want to risk scaring him away by pushing him too far out of his comfort zone before he was ready. On the other hand, every time she had pushed him yesterday—to talk more, to touch more—he seemed to welcome the encouragement, as if he'd been waiting for her permission to share more with her.

By the end of the night, she'd discovered he could be sur-prisingly bossy—both in his job and in the way he protected her. He'd introduced her to all his friends from the crime lab, then wouldn't let her anywhere near her car, even when one of them had asked her a question. He'd held her hand most of the time, or simply stood between her and the work they were doing. So, the alpha male that most women craved was in there. That just wasn't the part of his personality that he let show much. Until she'd needed his arms and heat to shelter her, and his expertise and take-charge demeanor to make her feel safe.

Jackson was plainspoken when he did have something to say, and he had been adamant that he would provide trans-portation for her while her car was at the crime lab. Her in-surance would pay for a loaner once it was in the shop for repairs, but until then, he insisted on spending as much time watching over her as possible. Despite her argument that he didn't owe her around-the-clock protection, and wasn't responsible for her, he claimed that he had already dropped the ball twice by not preventing yesterday's events in her office and outside the diner. He wasn't going to let her get into a taxi or hired car by herself with a stranger when an obsessed stalker was terrorizing her for reasons they didn't yet know.

The man could be a shy poet. Or sweetly considerate. Or a scary guardian over whatever he chose to protect. She had a feeling he would be completely devoted to the woman he gave his heart to. He was appealing in so many ways. So yes, she wanted to say she was close to Jackson Dobbs.

"What's she talking about, Dean?" Dixon Lowry's barely whispered disbelief was hard to miss. "Her?" He glanced at Reese, then back at Dean. "The son of that man and woman who got murdered here? You know our families have history. *He's* dating her?"

History? What was he talking about? Had his parents known Everett and Melora Dobbs? Probably, since they'd been patrons of the theater even back then. "Do you know something about their deaths?" she asked, feigning innocent curiosity instead of pushing for information to help Jackson's investigation.

Smooth Dixon Lowry glared at her, as if she'd accused him of committing the crime himself. "No. Mom and Dad knew—what was his name? Jackson?—they knew his parents. Isn't that right, Dad?"

Simon nodded. "Yes, son. They were good people. Your mother and I worked with them often. Such a loss to the department and the university."

Dean smiled and turned their guests toward the front of

the stage. "I think the point is that Ms. Atkinson had a rough night, with someone marking up her car."

"And slashing all my tires." Her unwanted fan had done a lot more than leave her a message last night.

Dean glanced back over his shoulder to her. "Are you all right? Were you hurt?"

"I'm fine." Dean Diamant had some acting skills of his own. His concern had sounded legit, even though she suspected it wasn't. He was probably showing himself as the benevolent boss in front of their guests. "Thanks for asking."

Dean shook his head and came over to her. "This isn't related to the other incidents, is it? Do we need to hire security for Saturday night?"

"I've already arranged for campus security to—"

Before she got the chance to explain that she was already being proactive about ensuring the safety of their guests, and that the threats seemed to be focused on her and no one else, Maisey Sparks pulled open the door of the theater and interrupted.

"Uncle Dix! Granddaddy!" Maisey swept down the aisle and up the stairs to the stage, where she hugged her uncle and traded kisses on the cheek. She embraced Simon, as well. Her smile became a sneer when she turned to Reese and dipped into her backpack to hold out a folder. "Here's my paper."

Dr. Diamant took the report and placed it into Reese's hands. "I'm sure you'll find it more than adequate to raise Miss Sparks's grade."

"I'm sure it will." She got his message loud and clear. *He* had done what was necessary to keep the Lowrys happy, whereas she had jeopardized the relationship by holding the young woman to the same standard she expected from all her students. She wasn't sure how much longer she could play the role of the dutiful underling for Dr. Diamant. "Dean, will you show our guests out?"

"Of course. Dix, why don't you come to my office, and we can go over the numbers of your family's donation."

Dixon winked at his old friend. "Got anything hidden in a desk drawer we can sip to warm me up? It's chilly in here."

"You know me too well. This way. Simon? Maisey? Would you like to join us?"

Invite an underage student to share a drink? Reese protested, "Dr. Diamant—"

"There will be plenty of time for you to have a drink to celebrate all your hard work after the reception on Saturday."

"I wasn't fishing for an invitation."

"Maisey, my girl." Simon crooked his elbow and held it out to his granddaughter. "Why don't you help an old man down these steps."

"Of course, Granddad." Maisey linked her arm through Simon's and led him down the stairs and up the aisle in the auditorium. "I'll show you to the dean's office."

Dixon let his father and niece reach the exit before he turned and extended his hand. "Thank you for your time today, Professor. I appreciate you coordinating with our family's caterer and decorator during this difficult time for us."

"I'm happy to help. I'm always proud to show off our theater."

Instead of releasing her hand, he tugged her a little closer, lowering his voice. "And don't worry. I'll keep Dean in line. I won't let him pour Maisey a nip of his whiskey."

Grateful that he understood her concern, Reese forgave him the uncomfortably long contact. "Thank you, sir."

"Dix, please."

"I'll see you Saturday, Dix."

"I'll be back to watch a little bit of rehearsal tonight. I enjoy seeing my niece onstage."

He lifted her hand and kissed it before jogging up the aisle to catch Dean and walk with him out the door. Reese fought the urge to wipe her hand on the side of her jeans. When he was getting his way, Dixon Lowry was all attentive charm like his father. But when he wasn't, the impatient, arrogant, faintly threatening Lowry came out. It explained a lot about Maisey's behavior if Dix was a role model for her. Reese didn't think that was charm so much as he was schmoozing someone he'd be working with this weekend. Or maybe someone he didn't want pondering his weird reaction to learning she was involved with Jackson Dobbs.

The moment the door closed behind her guests, Reese went back to her office. She was relieved to discover it was still locked when she inserted the key. She tossed Maisey's hastily written—possibly not by her—paper on top of her desk and picked up the scarf she'd been knitting for the play to unravel a few of the ends and tie them off with knots so it would look like a project in progress when used in the play. She completed two knots before sighing heavily and setting the prop aside. She circled her desk and sat down to look at Maisey's report. But that didn't hold her interest for long, either.

He's dating her?

Why did she find Dixon Lowry's angry whisper to Dean about her budding relationship with Jackson so condescending?

Our families have history.

What was it about two-thirds of the Lowry family she'd met with today that rubbed her the wrong way?

She shivered in her chair as if shaking off a bad memory. These past few weeks, she'd hated working in the theater almost as much as she had when she'd been the target of a sick man's obsession. She loved so much about the theater and teaching, but men like Dean Diamant and Dixon Lowry and whoever the hell was sending her those messages were ruining the creative life for her.

Maybe she should just move to Grangeport to live with her sister, Reggie, and her family. She could find a small-town businessman with simple goals to settle down with. Or a salt of the earth farmer and be his helpmate in an agrarian life. Of course, that would mean becoming a burden on her big sister again, at least temporarily. More importantly, it would mean giving up her dream of earning her PhD to honor her parents' sacrifice and proving to herself that the traumas of her childhood hadn't scarred her for life. Plus, she really was a city gal. And she wanted to see where this thing with Jackson might go.

Reese groaned aloud and reached for her phone. Typically, when she was upset and needed a place to vent, she called her sister. But her thumbs were already pulling up Jackson's number and sending him a text.

Why are people mean?

She picked up Maisey's paper and started to read.

She'd only reached the end of the introductory paragraph when her phone dinged with a reply.

Another threat?

Reese smiled at that simplest of contact from Mr. Tall, Dark and Silent, and picked up her phone.

No. Just rude people.

Mere seconds passed while she waited for his reply. Instead of a message popping up, her phone rang. She smiled when she saw Jackson's number and answered immediately. "Hey."

"Hey, Reese. This is Jackson."

She giggled at his perfunctory announcement. "I know it's you. We were just texting, and I saw your number."

"You told me to always identify myself when I called."

She had confessed that unnerving little fear, hadn't she? "I know it's a hassle, but it's sweet that you remembered."

"It's not a hassle if it's something you need." Wow. She could fall in love with this guy if she weren't careful. "Who was mean to you?"

"Why? Are you going to beat him up for me?" she teased, needing to lighten up her thoughts and this conversation.

After a pause, Jackson's tone was dead serious. "Is that what you need me to do?"

Reese hastened to reassure him that she wasn't looking for more violence. "No. I don't want you to be an enforcer or my bodyguard. I just wanted to reach out to someone who…" *cares about me.* "Hearing your voice makes me feel better. I feel calmer about being here."

"Something did upset you. Are you safe? Alone?" He'd noticed her use of the word *calmer*.

"For now. There are a few people working backstage. My students will start showing up for rehearsal in a few minutes. I'm locked in my office, so don't worry. I just finished giving a tour to Dixon Lowry and Dean Diamant. Simon Lowry was here, too. He was quite charming. But he seemed tired. Still grieving for his wife, I'm sure."

"Lowry and Diamant know each other?"

"Yeah. Fraternity brothers from back in the day." She toed off her shoes and pulled her stockinged feet up onto the chair, hugging her arm around her knees. "Do you know Dixon Lowry, by any chance? He got weird when I said we were dating."

"Dating?"

"Yes." She pointed out what was obvious to her in case it wasn't obvious to him. "We've had several long conversations, so we're really getting to know each other. You asked me out last night, and I asked you to the reception on Saturday. Those are dates. Hence, we're dating."

"Weird how?" he asked, without replying to her claim that they were a couple at the beginning of their relationship.

Reese shifted topics with him. She wondered if he had accepted her definition of their relationship, or if his idea of being interested in her was different from her idea of being interested in him. "I can't put my finger on it. He was pretty much bored and disinterested while I walked them through the details of Saturday's program. I suspect he was just there for his father's sake. Then Dr. Diamant said we were dating and he kind of panicked. Like he didn't want anyone named Dobbs to have anything to do with the theater, including me. So, you must know Dixon."

"No."

"Would he have known your parents?"

"Don't know."

Okay. So, if there was any connection there, it didn't mean anything to Jackson. Her suspicion radar must be working overtime, seeing clues and bad guys where none existed. "Then to top it all off, Maisey showed up to see her uncle and grandfather and tried to make me feel small."

"You're better than any one of them. Better than all of them put together." The pitch of his deep, gravelly voice dropped when he defended her. "Don't let them make you feel any less special than you are, Freckles."

Reese grinned at the silly endearment he used. "It makes me laugh when you call me that."

She could hear the cautious note in his voice when he said, "Is that all right?"

"Yes. Of course, you can have a pet name for me. It's another example of what people who are dating do." She lifted her gaze to the window of her office door as she heard footsteps and chatter coming from the stage. She was going to have to end this call soon. Then she eyed the new wig of gray wool she was knitting to replace the prop that had been skewered with the syringe, and had a sobering thought. "I just hope this creeper who's sending me messages doesn't use *Freckles* in one of his sick nursery rhymes. I don't want him to taint your nickname for me."

"We'll get this guy. We're developing a profile of the man we're looking for."

"You are? Can you tell me who I should be keeping an eye out for? Is there someone I can draw into a conversation at the reception to get you information? I already asked Dix if he knew anything about your mom and dad, and he just clammed up. He told Dr. Diamant that your parents and his family had history." Reese wrinkled up her nose at the memory. "Then he tried to be all charming and kissed my hand."

Jackson grunted.

"To be honest, it freaked me out after he'd been so put-upon by my tour, and then downright hostile. Like I said, weird."

"Don't confront anyone without me or the police there."

"We were in the middle of a conversation. It came up."

"Still…" Once again, he moved on to the next subject without explaining himself. "The police are looking for someone who's got enough money to be able to afford rare collectible knives—we're talking thousands of dollars or more. Either that, or someone who's really in debt because they're spending all their money on their collection. Or it could be someone older who has been collecting tools and weapons over several years."

Simon Lowry was older and wealthy. But that sweet gentleman had no reason to kill Jackson's parents. Dixon Lowry had the wealthy part down. And she did know someone with an extensive collection of every kind of tool under the sun.

"Patrick has more tools than any man I've ever known. In his office, in locked cabinets backstage, in his truck. Probably at home, too. I know he has a box cutter and a pocketknife. I'm not sure there are other weapons around here, except for props. And there will be several wealthy people here on Saturday. All our patrons are invited. I don't know if any of them are collectors."

Jackson grunted. What did that mean? Confusion? Disgust? Eagerness? She heard a screech of metal and wondered if he had pushed away a stool or chair he was sitting

on. Judging by the even exhales of his breath, she imagined
he was striding out of his lab or office.

"Jackson?"

"Is Brown there right now?"

She heard other voices in the background. Had he flagged
down some of his friends at the lab?

"Yes. He's working in his office, I think."

He took a deep breath. The side conversation he was having with someone else faded away.

"Jackson? You stopped talking again."

"My friend Grayson is going to call campus police. They'll
swing by the theater to keep an eye on things. Just in case."

She was a little frustrated and a lot worried. "Do you suspect Patrick?"

"You said he pressured you to go out with him."

"Yes, but I don't feel threatened by him. He's a friend."

She heard a knock on her door and looked up as Zach
Oliver peeked through the glass and waved.

"I have to go. My students are arriving. You'll be here
after rehearsal again, right? Or should I call a cab?"

"I'm driving you home."

She suspected he'd say that and felt relieved. "Okay." Zach
knocked again. She lowered her feet to the floor and slipped
on her shoes. "I'll be right there."

Zach pushed the door open and picked up several of the
props they'd need for rehearsal. "The set looks cool, Ms. A."

"It does, doesn't it? You go ahead and start setting up the
prop table. I'll be there in a sec."

He left with his props. Wait. How did he open the door
if she'd locked it behind her? Reese hurried over to check
it. Nope. The knob was still secure and wouldn't turn from

the outside. It should have locked automatically behind her. She touched her finger to the latch that retracted and came out to seal the lock into the door jamb. It felt a little sticky, as if someone had taped it open. But there was no tape there now. She shook her head and turned back to her desk. Okay. Now she was creating mysteries where none existed. She probably hadn't pushed it all the way closed.

Reese forced herself to exhale the breath she'd been holding and slow the rapid drumbeat of her pulse. Zach had no reason to hurt her. And he hadn't even been alive when Jackson's parents had been killed. Her imagination was working overtime. "Jackson?"

"Still here."

"Will you say something nice to me before we hang up? Make me feel good about myself? Make me feel safe?"

The silence on the other end of the phone almost made her think he'd hung up. But she'd never heard a click. So, he was still there, listening. Reese was a little disappointed that he was too flustered or just didn't care enough to answer her request. "I'm sorry. I shouldn't have put you on the spot like that."

"I finished reading a new book. A thriller. I figured out the mystery, but it's still good." He shot the words out like a rapid-fire machine gun before taking a breath. "Would you like to borrow it?"

"Really? That's sweet. Bigger than a Gary Paulsen book, maybe, but just like old times. I'd like that." It would be interesting to see if his reading tastes had progressed the way hers had over the years.

"I'll bring it tonight."

She'd forgotten that this guy needed think time before he

spoke. But every word he uttered was worth her patience. "You're making me smile so much right now my face hurts."

"Good. I love your smiles."

Love? No. He didn't mean what she'd heard. *Smiles, Professor. The man is talking about smiles.*

She picked up her director's notebook and headed for the door. "I really do need to go. I'll see you later."

"How many freckles do you have?" he asked from out of the blue, stopping her in her tracks.

"Um, I've never counted them. Why?"

"Are they everywhere?"

She could feel her face heat up. Her freckles were a bit of a lightning rod for her. Some men she dated seemed to work hard to overlook them. Others criticized them. One guy had even asked her to bleach them so she'd look more grown-up. "Why do you want to know?"

"Are they...under your clothes?"

The blush was still there, but confusion and wariness had given way to anticipation. "Are you flirting with me?"

"I'm trying. I haven't had a lot of practice—"

"All over." Uh-uh. She wasn't letting him back down from the most intimate thing he'd said to her yet. "From my forehead down to the tops of my feet. More so where the sun hits my skin, but all over." His groan deepened her smile. "Now you think about all those freckles, Mr. Dobbs, for the next two and a half hours while I'm in rehearsal."

"I will," he said matter-of-factly. "All of them."

"Jackson!"

"Do you feel good about yourself now?"

Delighted with his innuendo, she laughed. A sexy, overtly masculine man wanted to see her freckles, even the ones she hid from the world. How could she not be flattered by his words? "Yes. Much better. Thank you. I'll see you later."

"Count on it."

And that promise made her feel safe.

Chapter Nine

The good feelings of Jackson being silly and sweet and sexy with her didn't last past the second act of the play. Working with the actual set walls and platforms threw off some of the actors. The young man playing the judge had a meltdown because he was struggling to come up with lines he had recited perfectly the previous night.

Which set off Maisey into a whiny tirade about the unprofessionalism of actors making her look bad. Then Dixon Lowry had come to the front of the stage to comfort his niece, despite Reese's suspicion that the young woman was playing up the drama she wasn't really feeling in order to impress her uncle. And the moment she had started to question Maisey's sincerity, Dean had come down to defend Maisey and warn Reese that she needed to regain control of the rehearsal.

Reese had ordered everyone to take a ten-minute break before her redheaded temper spewed out of her mouth. After a private conversation to calm the young actor's nerves, and a reminder to Maisey that putting on a play was a team effort, and they should be supporting each other instead of tearing each other down, they made their way through the third act with the drama limited to the show onstage. The tension during the show's gripping ending was actually pretty darned believable, and she told the cast and crew that they were absolutely going to be ready for an audience the following week. She ignored Dean and Dix altogether, until she took her focus off the stage long enough to realize that both men had left the auditorium.

Reese checked her watch several times once rehearsal had ended, eager to see Jackson again. All things considered, she'd handled her stressors well tonight. But there was something inherently spooky about a cavernous auditorium that reflected every little noise, and a backstage area filled with props and set pieces that created creepy shadows. The actors quickly left. Patrick helped the backstage crew reset the stage for the beginning of the show before they all went home. Somewhere in between all that, the light booth and stage had gone dark, and the only illumination in the building were the security lights in the lobby and by the back door exit, along with the glow through the window of her office.

As theater manager, she made her usual rounds. She checked the timed locks on every external door to make sure they were secure, and then she focused on her own office door. She locked and shut it three separate times, convincing herself that the only way anyone could have gotten in was if they had a master key or they had sabotaged the lock. She'd make a point to ask Jackson about the sticky residue she'd felt on the lock. Then she closed the door and sat at her desk to grade Maisey's paper while she waited for Jackson to knock at the back door.

She finished the paper, quite certain that these weren't Maisey Sparks's words, and that they had been plagiarized

or written by someone else. But without any evidence beyond her gut telling her that this wasn't how the spoiled
student talked, and doubted she would come up with anything as insightful as twentieth-century drama being a met-
aphor for the social issues of the day, she debated whether
it was worth confronting Maisey. With Dean Diamant and
the Lowry name against her, Reese would have a difficult
time proving her case. Although the university had a strict
policy against plagiarism, it might be worth her own sanity
to give Maisey the lowest passing grade possible and let her
move on to be a terror in someone else's class.

And maybe that was a decision she needed to make after
a little more research and a lot more sleep. She put a sticky
note on the paper with the grade she wanted to give, along
with a reminder to do an online search to find similar papers that had been published.

While she was straightening her desk and gathering her
things into her bag, she heard voices, low and indistinct,
coming from the auditorium. Great. Reese heaved a weary
sigh. Had a couple of students hidden inside the building
to make out or do their homework? Or they'd simply fallen
asleep and hadn't realized rehearsal had ended.

It said Theater Manager on her door. It was her job to
go out there and clear the building. She grabbed her keys
and a flashlight, pulled the sweater she was wearing tighter
around her torso and headed out the door. Although the
backstage lights were in the opposite direction, she headed
onto the stage. Her flashlight gave her path plenty of illumination. Besides, she had the ins and outs of this building memorized.

The voices were clearer out here. Not voices. One voice. "Oh, hell," Reese said.

Another prank. One of the sound effects used in the play was being broadcast from the light booth, where the sound controller also worked. It was the recording used onstage by the play's alleged killer that was meant to terrorize the guests in the production, and put them on alert that the murderer intended to kill them all for their crimes.

It was terrifying enough to hear that evenly modulated voice during the show. Hearing it now ticked her off, giving her more work when all she wanted to do was see Jackson and hopefully turn tonight into another date.

Reese marched off the front of the stage and up the aisle, shining her light into the balcony above her. "Hello? Is somebody up there? We're closed for the night. You need to go home." She pushed through the lobby doors and up the stairs to the balcony. "I don't know if you're trying to be funny, but this is an actual crime. Trespassing." She pulled out her phone. "I have campus police on speed dial."

When she unlocked the door to the light booth and saw the blinking lights of the soundboard piping the words into the loudspeaker, she realized it wasn't the recording from the play anymore.

It was her very own personalized poem of terror.

Ten little carrottops went out to dine; One choked her little self and then there were nine.
Nine little freckle faces stayed up very late; One overslept herself and then there were eight.Seven hot little tomatoes chopping up sticks; One chopped herself in halves and then there were six.

Reese shivered and backed out the door. What the hell? She was alone, wasn't she? She'd said good-night to the two young men who ran the lights and sound and watched them walk out the back door together. Maybe it was set on a timer. Computers could do that sort of thing, and all their sound effects were computerized.

But who? Why? What had she ever done to anybody except testify against a monster who was now dead, and refuse to play all of Maisey's and Dean Diamant's games to appease their egos? Was someone trying to scare her away from helping Jackson solve his parents' murders? But these pranks had started before she ever went to the crime lab to meet Jackson.

He'd said his mother had received threats before she was killed.

Was history repeating itself? Had she become the newest obsession of a man who'd gotten away with murder for twenty-three years?

Fear tried to squeeze common sense out of her head, tried to squeeze the bravery out of her heart. But she was stronger than this. This was a game to someone. And she wasn't about to lose any stupid mystery game.

Taking a fortifying breath, she stepped back into the light booth to shut off the vile recording…

And heard footsteps running across the catwalk where the lights were hung overhead. Her pulse hammered in her ears at the sound. There were two ways down off the catwalk—using a super tall extension ladder that was safely stowed backstage, and climbing down the ladder anchored to the wall of the light booth.

Reese slowly turned her gaze to the ladder just a few feet away that led up to the open trapdoor in the ceiling.

Open door. Ladder. Not alone.

"Get out," she whispered, willing her frozen feet to move. The footsteps were coming closer. "Get out. Get out. Get out."

Reese was running now. She slammed the door shut and raced for the stairs. She shoved open a lobby door and ran for the stage, with the cruel words still echoing throughout the theater. The footsteps she heard behind her could be the intruder coming after her. Could be the man running away. It could be her imagination. Could be nothing.

Reese didn't go to her office. She didn't grab her purse. She just ran. The beam of her flashlight found the exit and she pushed her unathletic body into a sprint. She crashed into the back door. Dropped her flashlight. Shoved it open, plowed into a man's chest and screamed.

The broad shoulders blotted out the light from the streetlamps. But then her panting breaths inhaled leather and soap and a scent that was already more familiar to her than her own perfume.

The moment she realized she was pounding on Jackson's chest, she stopped fighting and started grabbing. She crushed fistfuls of his jacket in her hands and pressed her body against his. When he didn't immediately fold his arms around her, she shoved her hands beneath his open jacket and clung to his shirt and the heat of the man underneath.

His hands lightly skimmed her shoulders. "Reese?"

"Just hold me."

Those twin bands of iron wound around her back, lifting her onto her toes as he snugged her tightly against his heat and strength. Reese uttered a noise that was half sob and half groan, like the pain and reviving warmth returning to frostbitten fingers. His fingers crept up to cup the nape of her neck and tunnel into her short curls. His lips grazed the crown of her hair. "Honey, you're shaking. What scared you?"

"Ask questions later. Just hold me a couple of minutes."

While his fierce hold on her never lessened, she was aware of him turning with her to prop his booted foot against the door, blocking it in case whoever was after her tried to come out behind her. "Was someone in there with you? I need to know how to protect you."

She shook her head and snuggled in, willing his strength and protection to chase away the panic and allow reasonable thought to return. Her lips moved against the hard swell of a pectoral muscle, while her pulse aligned itself to the steady drumbeat of his heart beneath her ear. "Another prank. I thought I was in there alone. But the sound effects from the light booth started playing. I went to check it out. Then I heard footsteps and I ran like some stupid damsel in distress." Now she was realizing she wasn't much of a detective or any help to Jackson's investigation. "Damn, I could have snapped a picture with my phone. I could have called campus security or the police. I could have done something useful. Instead, I totally spooked myself."

The fingers in her hair gently massaged her scalp. "Are you skilled in hand-to-hand combat?"

"No."

"Are you armed with a weapon?"

"Of course not."

Jackson leaned back against her arms around his waist

and framed her face between his hands, tilting her face up to his. "Then you didn't do anything stupid. You did what was necessary to keep yourself safe."

The man was eminently practical, and that made her feel better. She reached up to brush her fingertips across the scruff of his square chin. "Thank you."

She was shaking like a leaf on a brisk autumn wind, but she had something solid to cling to now. She could anchor herself to Jackson.

"You're still scared."

"Um, yeah. But I'll be fine. I'm better with you here—"

His lips dropped to hers and he was kissing her, consuming her. Jackson blew past the quick peck on the lips as first contact. He skipped the whole gently exploring, getting acquainted kiss. A fire kindled low in Reese's belly as his mouth blotted out all thoughts except for the sensual assault of his lips on hers. Jackson's kiss was as raw and potent as the man himself. She slipped her hand behind his neck to latch on to him even as his fingers pulsed against her scalp and kept her mouth pinned beneath his. She parted her lips to become a more active participant in the kiss. His tongue slipped in to tangle with hers and Reese groaned. Her breasts grew heavy, and the sensitive tips hardened into tight buds, which rubbed against his chest. She fisted her hands in his shirt and collar, holding on for dear life. The other women he'd dated must not have let him get to the kissing stage in their relationship, because they wouldn't have given up this toe-curling, panty-dampening ability to kiss. She wouldn't.

But all too soon Jackson tore his mouth from hers and straightened. Reese whimpered in disappointment at the loss.

"Are you okay?" he asked, his voice a gravelly rumble, his

beautiful eyes dilated to the point she could barely see their icy gray color. His deep, harsh breaths seemed to match her own. She mutely nodded. "I didn't overstep?"

This time she shook her head from side to side, still in a daze over this man's secret talent. "I haven't been kissed in a while," she whispered. "I've never been kissed like that."

"Is the recording still playing?"

Recording. Reality. Reese squeezed her eyes shut and nodded, forcing her mind back to the danger that had sent her rushing into his arms in the first place. Wow. Jackson's kiss really was a secret weapon when it came to disrupting her thoughts. She hoped that kiss was about more than helping her move past her fears. But they could discuss it later.

She shifted her grip on Jackson to the more neutral location of the front of his jacket. "It's on a loop. I have to shut it off in the light booth. But you'll come with me, right?" He nodded. "The footsteps I heard were on the catwalk right above the light booth. Whoever was there is probably long gone."

He pried her hands from his jacket and tested the door before moving the foot that had been blocking it all this time. "You have keys to get in?"

Reese pulled her keys from her pocket and nodded.

"Let me get my kit from the truck. I'll check it out with you."

She felt chilled by Jackson's abrupt departure toward the parking lot. He had just turned her world upside down and set her heart on the path to falling in love with him. And now he was walking away?

But then she realized he'd only taken a few steps and was

reaching back, his hand outstretched toward her, inviting her to take it. "Freckles?"

With a noisy sigh of relief at knowing he wasn't abandoning her, even for a moment, Reese hurried after him and slipped her hand into his. Jackson's grip tightened around hers and held on the entire time it took to retrieve his CSI kit and go back inside up to the light booth.

There was something extremely unsettling about a mechanical voice, listing off all the ways she could die, over and over. They paused outside the light booth long enough for Jackson to slip on a pair of sterile gloves and kneel down to study the doorknob.

"My prints should be on it," Reese said.

Jackson shook his head. "Wiped clean."

A chill rippled all the way down Reese's spine. "So, someone *was* here with me."

Jackson opened the door and visually swept the room before turning off the computer and silencing the voice. He removed the flash drive and studied it closely before dropping it into an evidence bag. He stretched his hand out to her again, and Reese didn't hesitate to take it. This time he pulled her right into his chest without her giving instructions or permission and held her close. He dropped his chin to the top of her head. "You aren't imagining this. The threat is real."

She nodded her thanks for believing her and settled against him. The embrace was brief as he had work to do, but his support was enough for her to pull away to share her observations and help him while he inspected the sound and light boards. She pointed to the trapdoor in the ceiling above them. "That was open when I was in here before."

"I remember going up to the catwalk a few times with

Dad." He went to the ladder and started climbing. "Turn on the auditorium lights."

"It's okay for me to touch stuff?"

Jackson nodded. "This guy has wiped everything clean. But he might not have been so careful up here."

Reese turned on the lights and watched Jackson disappear through the door above her. A few minutes later, the top half of his body reappeared through the opening. "Get in my kit and hand me the small round brush and the jar of black dusting powder."

She opened his CSI kit and climbed partway up the ladder to hand him the items. "Did you find something?" she asked, before he shut the trapdoor over her head. "I guess that's a yes," she muttered, climbing back down.

She startled when it opened up again. He pointed to his kit. "I need a couple of those clear tape cards."

"Like you used in my office to pull up fingerprints?" He nodded and she quickly pulled the items he needed and climbed the ladder to deliver them. This time, she felt more curious than shut out when he disappeared again. But only a couple of minutes later, the trapdoor opened, and Jackson climbed down. "Did you find something useful?"

He held up two clear fingerprints. "As I suspected, he cleaned up down here, but neglected to wipe down the latch on the catwalk side."

Reese felt another shiver, but this was anticipation, not fear. "You can run those and find a match?"

"If he's in the system. Otherwise, I'll need warrants to obtain prints." He packed the items back in his kit, including the small evidence bag with the flash drive that held the recording inside. "I'll have Chelsea take a look at this.

Maybe she can decrypt the data to find out where it was re-corded. Or see if there are other files on it that will help her pinpoint the owner."

"Can she identify the voice, even though it was mechani-cally altered?"

"You didn't recognize it?"

Reese shook her head. "It's created like the sound effect we use in the play. But it doesn't sound quite like the man who recorded our message for us."

"Who was...?"

Her nightmare was about to become very real if the re-cordings were made by the same actor.

"Dr. Diamant."

Chapter Ten

Reese happily went with Jackson to the crime lab to log the evidence he'd found. Although there was a team on call around the clock to process crime scenes, at night, the building itself felt like a modern, high-tech tomb. The floor-to-ceiling windows in the main hallway reflected the interior lights and blotted out the night outside. Jackson's office and the lab she'd glimpsed gleamed shiny and sterile in the bright lights. Jackson promised to bring her back in the daytime to give her a full tour and reintroduce her to some of the friends he worked with. She nodded at the invitation and gave an appropriate response about wanting to get to know the people who were important to him.

But she was already thinking about what would happen next. The man stalking her had promised *next time* and claimed she was *mine*. Was scaring her at the theater what he meant? Simply that he wasn't done playing these games with her? Or was there something more sinister waiting when he was done tormenting her?

Then they were back in his truck, cruising through the lights and shadows of downtown traffic, heading toward her apartment complex. Jackson must have asked a question she didn't respond to because she felt his hand slide over hers and link them together on the center console.

"Freckles?" He squeezed her hand in his gentle grip. "You okay?"

"What?"

They stopped at a traffic light, and he turned to face her. "I asked if you wanted something to eat. You're a million miles away."

"I'm not hungry."

Rightly understanding that food wasn't at the forefront of her thoughts right now, he said, "Talk to me."

"He hasn't called yet. He always calls after one of these incidents." Reese turned to wrap both her hands around his. The colored lights from the dashboard and the darkness outside the car might have given Jackson's harsh angles and muscular bulk an ominous silhouette. But to Reese, there was something comforting about having all that solid strength to cling to. "Waiting for the other shoe to drop is giving me an ulcer. Maybe that's his grand plan. He wants to stress me out so much that I have a heart attack. Or I pass out, and then he can do whatever he wants to me."

Jackson grunted his displeasure at that possibility.

"And if he thinks all this is funny, that he's getting his jollies by watching me squirm and scream and cuss at him, then I want to punch his lights out. You can teach me how to do that, right?"

"You want me to teach you to box?"

"Maybe? I just want to be able to do something to fight back. It's not right to bully someone like this." She pointed a stern finger at him. "Don't you for one minute think that you are some kind of social misfit because you're not the handsomest guy in the room or the smoothest charmer. This guy is the misfit. He's sick. He's a coward. You're a real man. You stand up for what's right, for someone who needs you. I can talk to you. I like being with you. I trust you. I will take honest and shy over his kind of sick any day of the week."

He glanced behind him in the rearview mirror and pulled into the turn lane. Away from where she lived.

"Where are you going? My apartment is to the right. I'm venting too much. But I don't need pie or a milkshake."

"You shouldn't be alone."

"I'm not alone. I'm with you, thank goodness."

"I need sleep."

"Oh. Of course." Reese pulled her hand from his and hugged her arms around her bag in her lap. "I'm sorry. You don't have to babysit me. Just drop me off and make sure I'm locked up inside."

Jackson shook his head and turned the corner when the light changed. "He'll call when you're alone."

"Probably."

"You'll be afraid."

Duh. She let her frustration creep back into her tone. "Probably."

"I don't like it when you're afraid."

"Well, neither do I. But I'm a grown-up. I'm not Little Orphan Annie anymore. I'm not a child who needs her parents and big sister to take care of her. I can handle this."

"Stay with me."

"Huh?"

He glanced her way across the cab of the truck. "I won't force you to do anything."

"I didn't think you would. But Jackson, I'm already taking up too much of your time. You're not getting to work on your parents' murder case. Staying the night is a big step. We hardly know each other."

"Not true. I know you better than any woman I've ever met."

Even though she agreed that she knew him better than other guys she'd dated for months, she had to stop taking advantage of his good heart and penchant for standing up for her. "I know you're an introvert. Don't you need a break from me and all the chaos I bring into your world?"

"I can handle your chaos," he insisted. "We're dating. I don't want my...girlfriend...to be scared."

Oh, wow. There was so much to love about this man's plainspoken honesty. The urge to argue her point faded. "I'm your girlfriend?"

His eyes captured hers for a split second, but he didn't answer.

Reese repeated herself, but this time as a statement rather than a question. "I'm your girlfriend." She reached over the console to rest her hand on his thigh and felt his muscles quiver beneath his jeans at even that light touch. "I want to stay the night, if you're sure. I don't want to be alone. I feel safe when I'm with you."

Jackson dropped his right hand off the steering wheel to lace his fingers with hers and hold her hand. "I feel better when I know you're safe."

"I don't have any of my things," she pointed out.

"I have a new toothbrush you can use. I'm guessing one of my shirts will be big enough for you to sleep in."

"Pretty sure." There'd be more than enough room. And if his shirt carried his scent, she'd be surrounded by him, guaranteed to sleep in comfort and have sweet dreams—or erotic ones if she thought of his body and those arms and that kiss.

They drove several more blocks in silence until he steered his truck into a residential area. "Jackson?"

"Hmm?"

As much as the rawness in her settled at the security of staying with him, there was a different sort of anticipation humming through her veins. "Since I'm your girlfriend, will you be kissing me again the way you did at the theater?"

He glanced at her with a hungry look, then turned his focus back to the road. "You liked that?"

"No. I loved it. I don't think I've ever shared such a grown-up kiss with a man before. It made all my girlie parts stand up and cheer. And it touched something deep inside me. I've been alone most of my adult life, but I didn't feel alone then. I felt connected, like we were one, like that was how my life was supposed to be."

He frowned at her waxing poetic. "Girlie parts?"

"You do know what those are, right?"

He grunted. But the blush tingeing his cheekbones told her he knew exactly what she was talking about.

She continued to pour out her thoughts and praise him. "You, sir, have been holding out on the women of Kansas City. You've got skills."

"I haven't had that much practice. Just some casual encounters. Kissing wasn't really a necessity."

"Are you saying you're a natural talent?"

"Reese."

"Well, you can practice on me anytime." She squeezed his hand. "But not on anybody else. Because *we're* dating."

"I don't want to kiss anybody else."

"You need to stop saying sweet stuff like that. You're going to make me fall in love with you." The sudden stillness of Jackson's big body seemed to suck all the air out of the truck cab. *Dial it back a notch, Atkinson.* She had to remember that Jackson was a rare man who needed to move at his own pace. Reese smiled and tried to lighten the mood in the truck. "As long as you have a blanket and a pillow, I can sleep on the couch. I'm couch-sized."

He answered with a sound that was more than a grunt and almost a chuckle. "I have a guest room."

Good. She hadn't scared him away. Yet.

"Then I'm guest room–sized."

Their silly, intimate bantering eased the tight grip of fear inside her, and tempered the surprising depth of what she was feeling for this man. By the time they pulled up to a modest but well-maintained brick ranch, Reese was beginning to feel like this might be the ending of any other date with a man she'd stayed up far too late with.

Jackson warned her to stay put and climbed out of the truck first to check the neighboring houses and up and down the street for anything unusual before he opened the door for her, tucked her hand in his and led her inside. While she brushed her teeth and slipped on a gray Kansas City Chiefs T-shirt that hung to her knees, he checked the doors and windows of the house. Once he declared everything was secure, she sank into the double bed in the guest room and bade him good-night. Although she would have loved a good-night kiss, she was learning not to push. Jackson didn't believe how badly she wanted him yet. But he understood how much she needed him, and that was the feeling she'd cling to. He left her door slightly ajar and a night-light on in the bathroom across the hall before he retired to his own bedroom at the end of the hall.

She pulled the covers up to her chin and tucked her nose into the collar of his T-shirt. Yep. It had that clean masculine Jackson smell she was learning to crave. With a deep sigh, she turned onto her side and let the scent and security Jackson provided seep into her senses.

Reese was drifting off when her phone vibrated and lit up on the bedside table. That slight buzz in the night shocked her awake and she knew. It was him.

"No, no, no, no, no."

She pushed back the covers, swung her legs over the edge of the bed and sat up. The blinking light was garish in the slumberous cocoon of Jackson's house. She picked up the phone. Somehow the vibrations in her hand felt like his vile touch on her skin. Reese swiped the answer button and took a deep breath before speaking. "Hello?"

The labored breathing she hated brought tears to her eyes.

"I don't understand what you want. Why are you doing this to me?"

She yelped when her door swung open and Jackson's giant frame filled the doorway. She cowered away from him as he strode to the bed. "Hang up."

Since she was too shocked to immediately comply, he grabbed the phone from her hand and ended the call. Without hesitation, he turned off her phone and tossed it onto the bed, ending any chance of her stalker calling her again.

Reese's head was tipped all the way back to keep Jackson's grim expression in view. But his hand was gentle as he cradled the side of her neck and jaw and wiped away a tear with the pad of his thumb. "He made you cry."

She didn't know whether to nod at the obvious, or make a token stab at arguing she would be okay.

Jackson took the decision from her when he slipped his hands to her shoulders and pulled her to her feet. Then he was bending, curling an arm behind her knees and the other at her back, lifting her off the floor. She tumbled against his chest, coming to her senses enough to realize the man didn't sleep with a shirt on, and he was carrying her from the room.

Reese latched on to his shoulders. "What are you doing?"

"You're sleeping with me."

He seemed like a man who had made up his mind, and she wasn't a woman who wanted to protest his decision.

He laid her gently on his king-size bed and she scooted over as he lay down beside her and pulled the covers, which had been tossed aside at the slight sound she or her phone had made, over them both.

"Come here," he ordered when he saw her putting space between them. He opened up his arms and pulled her to his side. He tugged one of her arms over his bare stomach and held it there while he wrapped his other arm around her shoulders, and urged her to use his chest for a pillow. "You don't have to tell me to hold you. This is where I want you to be."

Reese burrowed into his heat. "This is where I want to be, too."

"I don't know what you see in me. But I'll be damned if I'm going to give you up without a fight."

He dropped a kiss to the crown of her hair, and she turned her lips to kiss the swell of his pectoral muscle. "Whoever made you believe you aren't something special is wrong. I'm falling in love with you, Jackson Dobbs."

He grunted. Of course, he grunted.

Although she hadn't expected a confession in return, she was more worried that he was dismissing the legitimacy of her feelings for him. Stretching up, she cupped the side of his jaw and tilted his face toward hers. Then she closed the short distance between them and pressed a chaste kiss against his lips. When she pulled away, his lips chased hers and he planted a firmer stamp of possession on her mouth.

Then he threaded his fingers into her hair and guided her head back to the pillow of his chest. "Sleep, Freckles," he whispered. "He doesn't get to you tonight."

WHERE WAS SHE?

The man sat in the darkness outside Red's building and wondered why the lights hadn't gone on in her apartment. He rubbed his thumb up and down the etched steel blade of the knife he carried. He loved the feel of cold, hard metal almost as much as he loved the feel of a woman's soft body writhing beneath his. Even if she was as scared as he'd intended, running away from him, she should have been home by now.

He'd been nice to her today. She was almost ready to accept his next overture. She'd turn to him once she realized he was the only one who could protect her, the only one who could make her happy. She'd flashed those smiles and flirted with him for a reason. She wanted him.

He'd been with her tonight. He could have caught her in the light booth if he wanted. He could have chased her down and grabbed her before she ever made it to the back door. But she wasn't ready yet. He was still training her, bending her to his will, breaking her spirit if he had to. She had to learn how to be meek and compliant before she could be his.

All these years, he'd counted on one woman to keep his secret safe. It was fate that the knife had fallen into Red's hands. Now he was putting his fate in her hands. He wouldn't let her disappoint him.

He pulled out his phone and dialed her number. He watched the windows to see if a light came on. He waited with anticipation for her to answer.

He needed to hear her fear. He needed to hear what she would sound like when he made her his.

She had fight in her. She wouldn't surrender easily. But she would surrender.

Just like the others.

He'd tried to forge a relationship with Melora Dobbs. She'd wanted him. He could tell. But her husband stood in the way of them being together. He didn't realize Melora was still at the theater when he'd killed her husband. He had no idea she would try to protect him. No idea that she'd jump between him and his target and get stabbed herself. He'd held her while she bled, apologized, professed his love until he heard others coming and had to leave. The whore had lied to him. Led him on. Let him think they had a future together.

She'd spat in his face. Said she pitied him. Swore retribution in another life.

With her last breaths, she crawled to her dead husband and reached for his hand.

He'd been forced to turn to the one woman who would never betray him for help. He'd lived a good life, a successful life since then. But then the knife showed up in Reese Atkinson's theater.

He thought the woman he'd trusted had gotten rid of it twenty-three years ago. But she'd merely hidden it away.

Had her conscience on her deathbed made her send the knife back to the theater to be found? Did someone else know his secret and plant the knife because they thought it was time for him to pay for his sins? Or was it truly just a freak accident that the expensive knife he'd sacrificed to get away with murder had been found and turned over to the crime lab by that righteous, troublesome redhead?

Finally, she picked up. "Hello?" He heard her breath catch. She tried to sound so brave, but she was crying. "I don't understand what you want. Why are you doing this to me?"

He stroked his knife blade as he listened to her breaking.

Then he heard a man's voice. "Hang up."

Startled, he cut the pad of his thumb on the blade's edge. "No!" he muttered. The damn Dobbs man was interfering again!

The line went dead, and the rage built inside him, and his own blood dripped to the carpet at his feet.

Chapter Eleven

The next morning, Reese sat in the memorial lounge of the Kansas City Crime Lab, sipping her coffee while she watched the organized bustle of criminalists, scientists and police officers come and go to refill their mugs from a seemingly endless pot of coffee, grab a snack or sit down for a fifteen-minute tête-à-tête between meetings and experiments. Jackson had offered to let her sit in his office while he worked in the lab, but she preferred the sun streaming in through the windows and being around people.

She'd already made friends with an amazing dog named Blue, and gotten better acquainted with his KCPD handler, Aiden Murphy. This was the Murph Jackson had called when her car had been vandalized. She'd learned he was married to Jackson's team leader, Lexi Callahan-Murphy, and that he was the police officer assigned to safeguard crime scenes and the criminalists who worked them.

She also shared a conversation with Grayson Malone. The blood expert was a veteran Marine who walked with two prosthetic legs with crutches. He was more serious than Aiden had been, and had even grilled her with a few questions about how she and Jackson had met—she told him about the boy who'd loaned her a book, and the man who'd taken a murder weapon off her hands—and warned her that still waters run deep. But he skimmed over the fact that growing up in his uncle's house after losing his parents hadn't been a good experience for Jackson. When Reese pushed for more information, he told her to ask Jackson. Reese promised to do so and then asked Grayson if he was seeing anyone. He was proud to say that he was engaged to a fellow veteran who'd also dealt with a stalker, and that Allie Tate was the best thing that had ever happened to him. He stressed the importance of keeping Jackson in the loop on any strange feelings of being watched or threatening messages she received. That it was the lines of communication between him and Allie that had ultimately allowed him to rescue her when she'd been taken. Reese promised. And he laughed when she said she was learning to interpret Jackson-speak.

Chelsea O'Brien also stopped in to introduce herself. Reese had heard a lot of good things about the brilliant, talented computer geek. And while Reese knew she was an extrovert who got along well with most people, nothing could have prepared her for the gabfest that was Chelsea. She learned more about the lab; Jackson; Chelsea's fiancé, Buck, and their upcoming marriage; her dogs, who were named after Teenage Mutant Ninja Turtles; and two cats, Peanut Butter and Jelly, in fifteen minutes than she could learn in an entire semester of taking a class. The delightful woman wore glasses with colorful autumn leaves printed on them and an engagement ring that, while simple in design, had a good-sized diamond on it. She pulled up her laptop and showed Reese the tuxedo she'd ordered for Jackson for the party Saturday night and asked her to send a picture of him dressed in something besides jeans and a lab coat. Then Chelsea opened another screen with what looked like two sound wave patterns. Reese leaned in to pay close attention once she realized Chelsea was showing her information about *her* case.

"You were right," Chelsea said. "There were two different voices on the recording Jackson brought me from the theater. I peeled away the mechanical overtones and broke down the speech patterns. Based on pitch, one is male and one is female. Do you recognize either of these voices?"

Closing her eyes to focus on the faint, slightly slowed, voices, and not cringe at the threats she was hearing, Reese nodded. "The first voice is Dean Diamant. I was there when he recorded that for our show. He has such a distinctive voice." When it wasn't lecturing her or undermining her authority with her classes. The second voice made her a little sick to her stomach. "Could you play that one again?"

"Sure."

She heard Jackson's voice from the doorway. "It's Maisey Sparks, isn't it?"

She popped her eyes open and watched him stride toward her, his hand outstretched to take hold of hers. "I believe so. But she can't be behind this terror campaign, can she? I don't think I'm worth that much time and effort in her eyes."

"She could have made the recording for someone else," Chelsea suggested. "For a friend or a professor. If she's the spoiled diva you describe, then maybe she did it for a lark."

Reese nodded. "I can see her doing that. Hell, I can see her doing that in exchange for getting a better grade in someone's class or to get another student to write a paper for her."

Jackson's steady strength seemed to seep right into her bloodstream from where their fingers touched. "Did you identify where the recording was made? Where the flash drive came from?"

"Somewhere on campus." Chelsea pushed her glasses onto the bridge of her nose. "I'm still working on narrowing it down to a specific computer. But I can tell you the rest of the flash drive contains files that have all been deleted."

"What kind of files?" Reese asked.

Chelsea hesitated.

But Jackson didn't. "What was in the files? I know you can retrieve lost data."

"Pictures. Lots and lots of pictures." Chelsea looked from Jackson down to Reese, her face wreathed with an apology. "Of you. Mostly at the theater. But some at your apartment building and running errands, I guess. It's not like you posed for any of them."

The temperature in the room dropped and Reese felt Jackson's arm slide around her shoulders. She reached over to fist her hand in the front of his lab coat. "How long has this been going on?"

"Is that a rhetorical question, or are you asking me?" Chelsea said.

"We're asking," Jackson stated.

Reese nodded.

"The first file was dated this summer. June."

"That's when I took over as theater manager. I'd finished all my PhD classes and the first draft of my dissertation. I've been at the theater almost every day since then."

"If it means anything," Chelsea added, "the pictures were

all deleted yesterday afternoon. About the same time the second recording was added to the flash drive."

Reese loosened her grip on Jackson and reached over to squeeze Chelsea's hand. "Thank you."

The other woman blushed. "I'm just doing my job." She tilted her gaze to Jackson. "And helping out a friend."

Jackson nodded his thanks. "I want to know the minute you figure out which computer that recording came from."

"You will." Chelsea closed her laptop and hugged it to her chest. As she backed out the door, she pointed to Reese. "Make sure Jackson brings you to the wedding. You're officially invited."

"Thanks." Chelsea turned down the hallway and hurried to catch up with a man in a suit and tie. When the older man dipped his head to kiss her, Reese smiled. "I take it that's the fiancé?"

When Jackson didn't answer, she looked up to find him frowning down at her.

"What? What's wrong?" she prodded.

"Do I stay here and hold you? Or should I go back to work?"

Reese smiled at his dilemma. "I'm okay, Jackson. Just because I have the day off doesn't mean you don't have to work. I'm safe here, right?"

Jackson nodded. "You should be."

"Trust me, I can project a really loud scream if I do get in trouble."

"I'll hear you," he promised, either unaware or uncaring that she was teasing.

She leaned away to pull his arm from around her shoulders but kept hold of his hand. "Are you working on an important case?"

"I'm running the prints I took off the top of the light booth last night. And I want to compare the timeline of the threats you've received to the ones my mother did."

"Then you must go back to the lab. I'll be fine here." She glanced around. "I can make a fresh pot of coffee for everyone, and I've got some phone calls to make for the party tomorrow night."

"There are plenty of people around that theater who were there in one form or another twenty-three years ago."

"And there'll be even more tomorrow night." When it looked like he might say something about staying clear of the threat and not going, Reese reached up and touched the side of his face. "You'll be with me. I'll be safe."

He gave her the same curt nod he'd offered Chelsea.

Uh-uh. Their relationship was something more than friendship. She tapped his lips with her index finger, then brought it down to touch her own.

"You want me to kiss you in public?"

"Chelsea and Buck just did it," she reminded him. "I want you to kiss me anytime you want. And I fully intend on kissing you back."

"You're not embarrassed to be seen with me?"

She seethed as she imagined some witch in his past telling him that. No person who really knew Jackson could be embarrassed by his shy, gruff charm. That faceless female hadn't been kissed by him. Hadn't given him the chance to cherish her the way he did Reese. She wondered what it would take to make him see himself the way she did. Possibly just speaking as plainly and succinctly as he did, and showing him by her actions how important he was to her. "To be seen with a stud like you? Hell no. Now, are you going to kiss me, or what?"

The corner of his mouth crooked up in what she supposed passed for a smile. Then he released her grip and put one hand on the high tabletop and one hand on the back of the stool where she was sitting and leaned over her. "Oh, I'm kissing you, all right."

His lips covered hers with the same kind of driving heat he'd shown her last night. Reese brought her hands to his shoulders to hold on at the rush of sensations overtaking her. The kiss was brief. But it was hot. It was thorough. And Reese felt a little unsteady as he pulled away, his eyes hooded and locked on hers.

"Definitely a natural talent." She managed to find words as he licked his lips, as if he could taste her the way she could still taste him. She pushed him out of her space and swatted his backside. "Now get to work. I'll be waiting for you here when you're done."

She watched Jackson stride from the room back to his lab and knew she was in trouble. And not just from a stalker or a killer who might be trying to re-create history.

After forcing herself to get up and make the fresh pot of coffee she'd promised, Reese pulled up a familiar number on her phone and called her sister.

Regina "Reggie" Harrison was a married mother of two at home on maternity leave with her one-month-old baby. Reese got the scoop on the baby and two-year-old her sister was dealing with. Reggie sounded exhausted, but happy as she went on to tell Reese about how supportive her husband was, even though he'd had to go back to work full-time at the sheriff's office a couple of weeks ago.

Reese could tell by the decibels of noise dropping in the background that the baby had just gone down for a nap.

"All right." Reggie heaved a sigh and Reese hoped she had plopped down into a comfy chair. "We've got about twenty minutes before Ryne's video is done, so talk to me. I love you, but I also know you. And I can tell by the tone of your voice that there's something on your mind you want your big sister's opinion on. Please tell me it's a guy." When Reese didn't immediately answer, she imagined her sister sitting straight up. "Shut up. Tell me about him. Is he good to you?"

"Yes." Reese felt herself grow hot as she talked about Jackson. "He listens to me and talks to me like I'm an adult, and not a thirty-three-year-old version of a child star. He's quiet, but when he does say something, it has meaning. And can I tell you about the way this man is built?"

"Please. Lucas and I can't be together for another two weeks. I need something to distract me."

Reese laughed. Reggie and her husband had the kind of marriage Reese aspired to, one full of love and lust, unending support and mutual respect. She knew her sister would never look at another man, and Lucas would never stray to another woman.

"He's a little damaged by life. Some might say he looks like one of the mean, scarred-up henchmen in an action movie. He's tall and muscled. I mean, a lot of muscle—he used to be a heavyweight boxer in the Army. He had a traumatic childhood, and I think that's made him shy, reticent to reveal too much of himself. But he's not that way with me."

"He trusts you."

"I hope so. But it's all happening really fast."

"What's happening really fast? Sex? Pushing you for a commitment?"

"Me falling in love with him."

There was a long pause on the line, and then her sister said, "Tell me everything."

Reese did. She talked about the quiet boy who'd loaned her a book and encouraged her love of reading to their reunion at the crime lab. And though she shared a little bit about finding the knife and continuing to be on the butt end of some mean pranks, Reese focused on the part she needed to share with her sister. "Kissing him is like a meteor hitting the earth, and the world falls out from under your feet. Yet he's there to catch you."

"Good grief, Ree, now I'm feeling hot." Reggie took a long drink from her omnipresent water bottle before speaking again. "I think *I* love this guy."

"You've never even met him."

"I love him because he listens to you. He makes you feel good about yourself. And truly, Ree, this is the first guy since—what, we were teenagers?—who you've called and been this excited to tell me about." Before Reese could explain her concerns about getting closer to Jackson, Reggie issued an invitation. "When do I get to meet him? It doesn't take that long to drive halfway across the state and bring him to dinner here in Grangeport."

"I don't think I can get away right now. With work and the play—"

"Oh, we are totally coming to KC to see your play. He'll be there, right?" Reese hoped. "Have you asked him to come?"

"I'm hoping he will."

"Didn't I raise you better than that? You don't have to wait for a man to make the first move. Especially if he's shy like this one is. Oh, wait. Does he not like theater? That would be a deal breaker for you, wouldn't it?"

"I don't think he dislikes theater. I think he's not too fond of this one."

Reese could imagine the frown on Reggie's face. "He doesn't like the university?"

"You remember that college professor and his wife who were killed here?"

"Professor and Mrs. Dobbs? Yeah. Mom and Dad knew them. You did a show with him."

"They were Jackson's parents."

"Oh, sweetie." Her sister's enthusiasm ebbed, and concern took its place. "I remember going to the funeral. Mom stayed in New York with you, and Dad and I went to represent the family. I think half of Kansas City was there. Certainly, every professor and staff member from the university. He had an uncle there with him. But he still looked stoic. Alone. I don't think his extended family was much of a comfort to him."

"I don't think they were, either." In fact, they may have inflicted more damage on his vulnerable psyche when he'd needed their love and support. Her heart ached for the lonely boy he'd been. Since he hadn't mentioned his uncle, and Grayson Malone had suggested it wasn't a good relationship, she suspected they weren't close. Was it illogical to make the jump that once he'd lost his parents, Jackson hadn't had a good childhood? "I'm helping him reopen the case and find the killer."

"You're helping with a police investigation?"

"Crime lab investigation. They work together. But KCPD makes the arrest. Well, he's hoping with a couple of new leads, he can finally find out who murdered his mother and father."

"What about that other stuff you told me about last week? The weird gifts and messages."

"He's helping with that, too."

"I really like this guy. Listen to me, sweetie. You have to ask him out. Ask him to the show—or to help out with it, even. Fix him dinner and thank him for his efforts. You can't let him get away."

Reese chuckled at Reggie's adamant words. "That's your advice for your little sister? Knock Jackson over the head and drag him into my lair?"

"You said he's unsure of himself because of his looks— wait, he's not a total brute, is he?"

"No! He has beautiful, striking eyes."

"And you already mentioned all the muscles and the sexy voice." Reggie seemed to be evaluating everything Reese had told her. "He's protective of you and respectful?"

"Yes."

"Chase him until he catches you."

"Huh?"

"Just be yourself, sweetie. Let him see that big heart of yours. Give him the reassurance that he needs, then he'll turn the tables on you. He'll scoop you up in his arms and never let you go."

"What if he doesn't like me in that way?"

Reggie made a scoffing noise. "Are you kidding? You're my sister. You are talented and funny and smart, and your heart is bigger than you are. He'd be a fool to let you go. Besides, a man doesn't kiss a woman the way you described unless he likes her in *that way*."

"You don't think this is all happening too fast?"

"A piece of advice from your big sister?"

"Please."

"It doesn't matter how fast or slowly it happens. If he's the right guy, you grab on to him and hold tight."

Reese breathed out a sigh of relief. Her sister's words were reassuring since she was feeling the same way, too. This relationship with Jackson might be happening fast. But it also felt right. "Thanks, Reg. He's about to take his lunch break and drive me home so I can pack up some things for the next few nights. Thanks for the pep talk."

"Wait. You're staying at his place?"

"It's been just one night. I feel safer with him."

Reggie groaned. "You stayed the night with this guy, and you didn't lead with that?"

"All we did was sleep."

"Together?"

"Yes."

"Thanks for the juicy gossip. As much as I love my boys, I needed a break from changing diapers and answering all of Ryne's questions about the bugs he finds in the backyard. I love you, Ree."

"Love you, too, Reg. Hug my nephews and give my brother-in-law a kiss."

"I will. Now go get this guy." Reese was smiling from ear to ear as her sister hung up.

Jackson returned to the lounge, his white lab coat now replaced by his familiar leather jacket. "Ready?"

Reese drank him in for a moment, taking her sister's

words to heart. *It doesn't matter how fast or slowly it happens. If he's the right guy, you grab on to him and hold tight.* She climbed down off her stool and hurried across the room to wind her arms around Jackson's waist and rest her cheek against his chest.

She was pleased to feel his arms settle lightly around her. "What's that for?"

"I just wanted to hug you. Claim you as mine, in case anyone is watching."

Misinterpreting her display of love as a reaction to some kind of threat, he tightened his hold and brushed his lips against the top of her hair. "The lab has security cameras inside and out. And the seventh precinct offices are connected to the other side of the complex. If that guy is anywhere around here, we'll catch him on surveillance. We'll get this guy."

Reese sighed against him, not wanting to correct him after such a fiercely protective tirade. "I know you will." Pulling back, she tilted her face to his. "But that's your serious look. You found out something?"

"I always have a serious look."

"Jackson." She tugged on the front of his jacket, demanding an answer. "What did you find out?"

"The fingerprints have no match in IAFIS."

"In what?"

"The Integrated Automated Fingerprint Identification System. So, we know our guy doesn't have a criminal record."

"You mean he hasn't been caught for anything."

He nodded. "There are other databases Chelsea is searching."

"Like university staff records. We were fingerprinted and had background checks run on us when we were hired there."

He seemed hesitant to add the next bit of information. "My mother started receiving her anonymous love letters and threats about five months before she died."

Even with Jackson holding her, she felt the warmth inside her draining away. "You mean this is going to go on for another four and a half months?"

"Connecting whoever is after you to my parents' murders probably accelerated this guy's timeline."

"So, he could kill me sooner?" She was definitely feeling a chill now. "That's not reassuring."

He rubbed his hands up and down her arms. "Let my team do their thing. Let's go back to your apartment so you can pack a bag. I also need to pick up my tux for tomorrow."

"Jackson?" She didn't finish the question that weighed heavily on her mind until Jackson brushed the curls off her forehead and encouraged her to ask it. "What if we don't figure out who this guy is until it's too late?"

"I will be with you as much as I can. I notified the cold case squad that we were stirring up interest in my parents' murders, and they're sending a couple of detectives to work security at the reception tomorrow night. They'll be checking out suspects while they're there. And if I'm not with you, and he gets to you, you fight. Just like you fought that creep who terrorized you as a child. Be relentless. Fight hard. Fight dirty. And know that if you are not in my sight, and I can't get a hold of you, I will be coming for you."

"What if he tries to hurt you? If he tries to get you out of the way so that he can get to me? The way he took out your father so he could get to your mom. If it's the same guy."

Jackson stood there, a tall, overbuilt pillar of strength

who looked like he'd been bred for one thing. Nodding, Reese reached up and touched the face she loved. "You fight hard, too."

"I promise."

Chapter Twelve

Jackson Dobbs in a tuxedo was the kind of hot that made women pant with desire and men clear a path out of respect. Reese wished there was no party, no alumni or dean she had to cater to. She wanted nothing more than to take Jackson home and rip him out of that tux.

But that would be impractical. And bad for her job-performance review. And it might possibly put an end to her dream of finally earning her PhD.

No, tonight was the theater's big night, and she was in charge of making sure everything ran smoothly. Her student volunteers had all shown up on time, wearing costumes representing the series of plays for the season, or in suits or dresses if they worked backstage. The caterers had all the food she'd ordered to suit every taste and meet every dietary need of their guests. Champagne and sparkling grape juice were flowing, and the guests seemed to enjoy meeting old friends, getting to know the students and touring the theater.

Her own navy-blue gown had a modest neckline that revealed a hint of cleavage, and a simple A-line design that flattered her full figure and was adorned with enough tiny glass beads that the thing felt like it weighed as much as her infant nephew. She carried her flute of sparkling grape juice through the crowd and inched her way toward Jackson, who stood at the wall at the back of the theater, where he could see her both through the open lobby doors to the food tables and displays there, and in the auditorium. The one time she'd led a group up to the light booth, Jackson had joined the tour.

There was something both wildly arousing and super comforting about having such intense focus directed on her throughout the evening. As long as she knew where that attention was coming from.

She sidled up beside him and leaned back against the wall. "Have you talked to anyone this evening? Or are you the tower of doom and gloom off in the corner?"

He dropped his hand down between them and closed it around her fingers. "I've run into some friends of Mom's and Dad's. They expressed their condolences, asked what I've been up to all these years."

Reese squeezed his hand. "I'm sorry. Is that hard for you?"

"I don't mind. The grief gave way to anger and determination a long time ago."

She leaned her head against his shoulder. "I was worried about the crowd being too much for you. I didn't think about the bad memories."

"I'm making good memories now." His gaze continually scanned their surroundings, though he paused to exchange a nod with Max Krolikowski, one of the detectives from the cold case squad here tonight. "Once people discover I'm with you tonight, they rave about what a fantastic job you've done here, and how proud of you I must be." He tilted his head to press a soft kiss to the crown of her hair. "I am."

"Thank you. I wonder if any of the powers that be will notice."

"There are bigger players here than Dean Diamant," he pointed out. "You have the ability to work the room and make everyone from a lowly freshman to your most generous donor feel welcome and important. People notice."

Two of those people she'd worked hard to impress chose that moment to approach her. Reese released Jackson's hand and smiled at the two gentlemen who'd traveled all the way from the theater district in New York to be here tonight. "Mr. McKay. Mr. Haight. I trust you're enjoying your evening?"

"We're having a great time," George Haight, the taller one with the graying hair answered. "The dean may have gotten a little long-winded for my tastes, and Simon was understandably teary-eyed by the unveiling of the theater's new name, but otherwise, it's been a perfectly fine reception."

The shorter, pudgier man with the receding hairline, Linus McKay, echoed the praise. "I've enjoyed talking directly to the students. I'm sure some of them know I'm an agent and are trying to impress me, but for the most part I'm simply reassured to see such a love and knowledge of the theater being instilled in them."

"We do our best." They practically ignored Jackson, but since he didn't seem to mind looked unbothered, she didn't make a big deal out of it. "We're honored that you'll be here this week to sit in on rehearsals and be a guest speaker in some of our classes."

"Yes, yes." Linus snapped his fingers a couple of times,

as if he was trying to recall something. "Do you mind if we ask you a question?"

She felt Jackson's hand slide against the small of her back, shielding her, she supposed, if the question proved upsetting. "If I can answer, sure."

George Haight jumped into the conversation. "I've seen you on Broadway, haven't I?"

"Ages ago."

Linus seemed pleased that she'd confirmed their suspicions. "You starred in the revival of *Annie*, and then did a turn in a drama. What was it?"

"The Innocents."

"Critics loved you. You could have had a long career." A comment once made by her own agent at the time. "Why did you leave?"

She drifted back against the warmth of Jackson's hand. "It was a personal choice. My parents died tragically. I was only fourteen. I needed to be home with my family."

"That's rough. I'm so sorry to hear that." Mr. McKay's sympathy sounded genuine. "Hey, but making it in academia is no small potatoes, either. And now you're inspiring the next generation. That's an awesome calling."

Mr. Haight finally turned the conversation to a less personal topic. "My company sponsors a grant to support theater programs in academic settings. Have you ever considered applying?"

"Really? We're always looking for funding..."

The conversation tapered away, when Reese felt a pair of eyes boring into her like bullets seeking their target. She turned her head to see Maisey Sparks at the end of the aisle.

And she was pissed that Reese was getting the attention of the New York producer and agent.

AFTER MAISEY HAD run off after her uncle Dix to no doubt complain about Reese stealing her opportunity to go to New York, Reese concluded the conversation with the two men. She excused herself from Jackson as well to continue mingling with other guests.

But a peaceful end to her evening was apparently too much to ask for. Once she handed a check over to the lead caterer and told them it was okay to start clearing away their things except for the coffee and desserts that some guests were still enjoying, she made her way back into the theater to the spot where she last saw Jackson chatting with the two detectives.

Instead of finding the three men talking police business, she saw Maisey Sparks wagging her finger at Jackson and spewing lies that would have diminished a lesser man. And bless his heart, Jackson just stood there frowning, as if he wasn't sure what recourse he had against a girl nearly half his age having a temper tantrum. It would be ungentlemanly to simply walk away. And arguing back wasn't really his thing.

A protective rage reenergized her body. She was exhausted, her heels had been pinching her toes for about an hour too long and she was livid to hear the twenty-year-old going after Jackson when she'd been unable to get her satisfaction with her.

"You know Ms. A is only with you because she needs a bodyguard."

Reese did the thing she'd seen Jackson do many times when he was protecting her. She put herself between Jackson and the threat that was getting on her last nerve. She had no trouble tilting her chin and letting Maisey have it. "You are a spoiled, immature brat who doesn't know thing one about what a real man is like. You don't speak to my man with respect? Then you don't speak to him at all."

"Your man? You must be good in bed, Beast," the young woman sneered.

Reese didn't bat an eye. She simply leaned closer and articulated two words. "He is."

Not that she knew that for a fact, but she suspected he would be, given the way he kissed and held her. Besides, she hadn't been lying when she'd told the student to button her lip unless she could speak to Jackson with respect.

Maisey sputtered through the beginning of one sentence, and then another, before she shook her long hair down her back and retreated a step. "My grandfather wants to speak to you."

"Oh?"

"He's up onstage."

"Maybe you should go to New York, Maisey, and forget about college theater." Reese could ignore her role as a mentor and teacher completely. "Just know that it's a lot scarier out there in the big world when you're trying to make a living doing this. No matter how much you love it. No matter how much you want to succeed. No matter how hard you try. There will be a hundred other girls, just as talented, just as pretty, fighting just as hard as you for the same part. And no one in New York will be as supportive of you, or will try to teach you as much as I have."

Maisey literally growled before she gestured up to the stage and stormed away. "Just go."

Reese didn't take a deep breath until the young woman was out of earshot and she felt Jackson's big hands on either side of her waist.

"Her words didn't bother me, Freckles, because her opinion doesn't matter to me. I know she's got issues and is lashing out." She felt Jackson's warm breath tickle her ear and she shivered. "But do you know how hot it is to hear you leap to my defense like that?"

Reese didn't turn to face him. They still had guests, and jumping his bones right now shouldn't be part of the show they'd come to see. "You think I'm hot?"

His teeth closed gently around her earlobe next to the sapphire earring she wore. She gasped and goose bumps erupted up and down her arms. "I don't know if I'm good or not. I've never gotten an official evaluation. But with the right teacher, I'd be willing to try."

With that offer, Reese did turn around. "Are you serious?" Jackson grunted. That was a yes.

Reese beamed him a smile. "I have no doubt you will ace the class."

Jackson leaned over to kiss the top of her head. "Go. Meet with Mr. Lowry. I'll be here when you're ready to go home."

"Did the detectives find out anything new?"

He shooed her away. "Ticktock, Professor. Only another half hour and I can take off this damn bow tie and find out how many freckles are underneath your dress."

Reluctantly, Reese headed down the aisle to the stage one more time. By this time of night, her middle toes were numb and the small of her back ached from being on her feet for so many hours today. Still, with Jackson watching over her and the promise of making love somewhere in her future, she felt energized by the time she stepped up onto the stage and approached the white-haired gentleman who was admiring the Beatrice Lowry Theater sign.

She smiled as Simon Lowry turned to her. "Maisey said you wanted to see me?"

Simon reached for her hands and held both of them in his gnarled fingers. "Yes. I wanted to have a private conversation with you."

Reese glanced around the set where they were standing. "In the middle of the stage?"

Although he chuckled at her incredulity, he quickly dropped his voice to a soft tone she could barely hear and got serious. "I know this seems exposed, but Dix assured me the microphones were all turned off so that no one can hear us. And no one will be suspicious as they would be if we wander off to someplace on our own."

As she leaned closer to hear him, one word popped out. "Suspicious?"

Although he didn't turn his face from hers, his eyes were looking in every direction. The older man *was* afraid of being overheard. "Watch your back, Professor Atkinson. I thought I was doing the right thing. My wife had hidden that knife for all these years. I've always known. But I would never betray my Beatrice. I would never give away what she had done. She was protecting someone she loved."

"What are you talking about, Mr. Lowry?" Reese was confused. What did this wealthy old widower know about the knife she'd found?

"I put it in the box and sent it to the theater for someone to find. When Beatrice died, I thought justice could finally be served. Secrets could be revealed. But I fear all I've done is turn you into a target."

Reese stepped closer. Was this the witness Jackson had been waiting for to step forward? "Mr. Lowry. Who killed Everett and Melora Dobbs? Who was your wife hiding the knife for?" A shadow swung over them and back again. It wasn't unusual for shadows to be created when the stage lights were on. But that unusual shape wasn't similar to any prop or set piece in her play. When the shadow darkened Simon Lowry's head again, she looked up into the fly space and saw the danger swinging over them. "Move!"

She shoved the old man aside as Zach Oliver's beautiful gargoyle came crashing down. The weight of several two-by-fours clipped Reese's right shoulder and she fell on top of Simon. She curled into a ball as everything from her elbow down to her fingers went instantly numb. The frayed rope that had held the gargoyle so precariously in place tumbled down after, and she ducked her head again. Simon howled with agony as the gargoyle lost its head and splintered into a dozen pieces.

"Reese!" She heard Jackson's shout.

Zach ran up onto the stage and knelt beside his master-piece. "My gargoyle."

"Don't touch that!" Jackson warned, racing down to the stage. "It's evidence. Back away, son."

"Yes, sir." Zach hovered over Reese, muttering apology after apology. "Ms. A, I'm so sorry. I didn't do that. I swear. I'm so sorry."

"It's all right, Zach. I believe you." She reached up to squeeze Zach's hand and reassure him, and slowly pulled herself up to a sitting position. "You go down and sit in one of the seats. I'll ask the police if we can salvage it."

The numbness in her shoulder turned into a sharp, shooting pain as feeling returned. The tips of her fingers tingled, and even the small of her back protested the sudden pain radiating outward from where she'd been struck. She looked over to see Simon rolling back and forth on the floor, cradling his arm against his stomach. Although his son, Dix, was kneeling beside him, Reese pushed herself up onto her hands and knees and crawled toward him. "Mr. Lowry? Mr. Lowry, are you hurt?"

Before she could reach him, a rough hand grabbed her around the upper arm and hauled her to her feet. Reese cried out in pain as Dean Diamant shouted angry words at her. "What the hell were you thinking? You broke the man's wrist."

"I saved his life," she argued, trying to twist away from his painful grasp. "I'm fine, too, thanks for asking."

"Don't you get smart with me." He wrenched her arm, aggravating her injury, and she cried out. "He means millions to us."

"Ow! Let go of me!"

"You don't touch her!"

A meaty fist flew past Reese's face and plowed into Dr. Diamant's jaw, freeing her from his harsh grip and knocking him to the floor.

Then Jackson was carefully pulling her around the wreck of Zach's prop. "Are you hurt? Where did it hit you?"

"My shoulder. I'll be fine. Maybe an ice pack and an ibuprofen later. Check on Mr. Lowry."

"Lowry's not my responsibility."

She clutched at the lapel of Jackson's tuxedo jacket and tugged him closer so she could whisper. "He said he's the one who sent the knife to the theater for me to find. That his wife had been hiding it for somebody all this time."

His eyes narrowed with a question.

Reese shook her head. "He didn't say who she was covering for. That's when the gargoyle dropped. Like someone knew what he was saying to me and wanted to shut him up."

"Or maybe Dix was looking to get his inheritance early."

"Will he be okay? We can still ask questions."

"His son is looking after him, and the EMTs are on their way." Jackson glanced over at the remains of the gargoyle Zach was stewing over, then up into the ceiling above them. "I need to get a look at that rope and find out how somebody got that up there."

"There's a tall ladder in the back. But that shouldn't be there. It's not part of the show, and the prop we do drop is a lot lighter and hangs upstage beyond the garden doors." She scoured the crowd, looking for an angry young woman. "Maisey was pretty pissed at me."

"She wouldn't have been able to hang that up there without us seeing her."

"It had to be hung before the reception started."

"You have a list of everyone who was scheduled to speak onstage?"

She nodded. "Simon and Dixon Lowry. Dean Diamant. The president of the university."

"You."

"Patrick."

Scowling, Jackson surveyed the crowd again. "Where

is your wannabe boyfriend? I haven't seen him around for a while."

Reese tugged on his lapel. "He's not my boyfriend. You are."

He covered her hand with his. "I know that. But does Brown?"

Reese took in the chaos around the stage—Zach bemoaning the destruction of his artwork, Dixon Lowry keeping anyone from getting too close to his father, who was lying on the stage, and everyone circling around to get a better look or express their concern. Dr. Diamant sat in one of the chairs that were part of the set, cradling his bruised jaw and rubbing at something in his pocket, probably a stress ball that wasn't doing him a damn bit of good, all the while glaring at her.

"Jackson? I want to go home. Your home. I want to get out of here."

"We can't just yet, hon. You'll need to give a statement to the police."

With her strength quickly ebbing and fear and suspicion seeping in to take its place, Reese leaned heavily against Jackson's arm. Had someone just tried to kill her? Or Simon Lowry? Or was this accident yet another fluke occurrence that happened around her at the theater?

It didn't feel like an accident. And it didn't feel like anyone else had to worry about someone wanting to kill them.

"Now, Jackson. I can't do this anymore."

She felt his eyes studying her. And then he peeled off his jacket, draped it over her shoulders and pulled it together beneath her chin. "Okay. I'll tell the detectives that we're leaving, and call someone else from the lab in to process this mess. Will you be okay to hang out here while I bring my truck around?"

She nodded, but Jackson didn't look convinced.

"Zach, is it?" he asked of the young man sitting a few rows back in the auditorium.

"Yes, sir?"

Jackson helped her down the steps and into the seat next to Zach's. "Will you sit with Professor Atkinson and hold her hand until I can come back in to get her? And don't let anyone bump into her right shoulder. It must be pretty bruised."

"Is she okay?"

"She will be." Jackson dropped his head to claim her lips in a quick, hard kiss before he jogged back onto the stage toward the back door. "If I have anything to say about it, she will be."

SOME TIME LATER, after a hot shower, a cold ice pack and a few hours of blessedly mindless sleep snugged in Jackson's arms, Reese awoke before dawn to the repetitive stroke of Jackson's fingers running up and down her arm.

Sometime during the night, the giant T-shirt she wore had slipped off her shoulder to expose the dark-gray-and-violet-red evidence of where the heavy gargoyle prop had slammed into her. She propped her chin on his chest and raised her gaze to his to show him that she knew he was upset. "Jackson? Are you all right?"

He grunted. "You're not. That bruise on your shoulder is the size of my fist. If that thing had hit you in the head..."

"But it didn't. I'm sorry if it upsets you, but the bruise will fade, and I'll be just fine."

His fingers traveled all the way up her arm, skipped her

injury and settled beneath the fringe of her hair to cup the nape of her neck. "What can I do to make this better?"

"Keep your promise."

"What promise haven't I kept? You know my word is good."

"I know. But you've been worried about me, and I've been snoring on your shoulder, and you may have forgotten. Tonight, at the reception, you indicated that you wanted to make love to me." She might have started this conversation, but she was the one blushing with heat. "Well, actually, I think you said something about counting all the freckles underneath my dress."

His arms shifted around her to hug her more tightly against him. "I want that more than you know."

"Ask me, Jackson. Ask and I'll say yes. I want to forget everything for a while—the messages, the so-called accidents, solving a murder. I want to focus on the best part of these past few days. Finding you."

The long fingers at her nape played with her hair. "I love your hair. It's silky and soft. It curls around my fingers and clings to them. And that fiery color is all you, isn't it." She nodded, loving the words that came out of this taciturn man's mouth when he did choose to speak. "Reese Atkinson, I want to make love to you. Will you let me?"

"Let you? I'm about to beg you."

He shifted in the bed beside her, forcing her to rest her cheek rather than her chin against him. Maybe he didn't want to look her in the eye when he told her this. "My uncle Curtis used to tell me I wasn't special enough for any woman to want me."

"He's the man who raised you?" He nodded. She hugged

her arm around his waist more tightly. "There's something wrong with him for saying that to a child. You believed him, though, didn't you?"

"It was either shine like a star or you didn't exist in Curtis Graham's house." He laughed, but there was no humor in his tone. "I was a homely kid. Too tall and skinny to be able to coordinate everything. I didn't love sports the way he did. Even after I started filling out, his opinion didn't change. I had no chance of earning his love."

"For the record? I hate your uncle Curtis."

"You do get fired up on my behalf, don't you?"

"Red hair," she teased, suspecting he could tell her temper wasn't the reason she felt so protective of him. "What did you do to get away from Uncle Curtis and his wrong way of thinking?"

"I joined the Army and started punching things."

Reese laughed. There was a wry sense of humor hiding inside this man. She propped herself up on her elbows, resting one beside him and one against his chest so she could look into those beautiful gray eyes again. "What did it feel like punching Dean Diamant? I've often wanted to do that. But I didn't think I was strong enough. Or I was worried I'd get fired."

He grinned. "After the way I've heard him talk to you, it felt pretty damn good."

"I imagine."

But the grin quickly faded. His fingers were stroking up and down her back now, tangling in her hair, then traveling down to rest against the curve of her rump. "When he put his hands on you and you cried out in pain, I'd had enough. I'm sorry if that gets you into trouble at the school."

"I wouldn't worry about it. His idea of mentoring a PhD student has strayed a long way from supporting and challenging the doctoral candidate. There is a whole new generation of harassment laws I can cite against him. He might even have defied the school's policies on plagiarism and underage drinking."

"You think you could get him fired?" His hand squeezed her bottom. She liked the weight of his hand there.

"He does have tenure, so it wouldn't be easy. But I don't want to talk about him anymore. I want to talk about us. And freckle exploration."

She rode the rise and fall of his chest as he took in a deep breath. "As willing as I am, I don't have a lot of experience with this," he admitted.

"Because of your uncle not understanding what a treasure you are?" She drew her fingers around the stubble of his jaw and decided he wasn't a beast, at all. He had an interesting face, marked by life and tragedy and what she hoped were a few good memories. It was the face she wanted to look at every morning when she woke up. "But you do have some experience?" He nodded, though his expression remained grim. "It wasn't good?"

"We both got off if that helps."

"You can get off without having an emotional attachment or feeling fulfilled."

"I was a notch in her bedpost. A bet with her friends. She was gone before I woke up in the morning. That's just one of my misadventures with the fairer sex."

Reese hugged him as tightly as she could in this awkward position. "I hate that woman, whoever she was. She's not related to Maisey Sparks or your uncle Curtis, is she? I bet you didn't kiss her the way you've kissed me. No woman in her right mind would leave you if you kissed her like that." Reese started to pull away when she heard the vehemence in her own voice. "But I don't want you practicing on anyone else."

His arms tightened around her, anchoring her in place. "I don't want to practice on anyone else, either."

Good they were on the same page when it came to attraction and fidelity. She smiled at that. "Would you like to see my freckles now?" He nodded and Reese pushed his arm away to sit up on her knees beside him. She tugged her shirt off and tossed it to the foot of the bed. Feeling suddenly self-conscious about baring herself to him, she crossed her arms in front of her to cover her breasts. He might not think himself handsome, but she had too many pounds on too small a figure she wished she could hide. "Sorry. I'm kind of bouncy and soft."

He pulled her hands away and sat up facing her. His eyes were glued to her breasts. "You're perfect." He cupped her breasts the way she just had. Only his touch had everything to do with praise and seduction, not modesty. "I've got big hands, and these fill them." He teased her nipples between his thumbs and the palms of his hands until they tightened into stiff peaks, and she moaned with pleasure that darted straight down to her womb. Then he drew a line into her cleavage and pushed her breasts aside. His observations sounded very scientific, but every caress was fueling the tension inside her. "You do have freckles everywhere." He brushed the underside of one breast, stroked his thumb across the nipple of the other, then buried his nose between her breasts and pressed his lips to one lucky spot. "Here. Here. And here."

"Jackson." She breathed his name as her pulse jumped into hyperdrive and her panties dampened with heat.

"I'm a big man. And you're so petite."

"You'll fit, Jackson. A woman's body is made to stretch and be filled by the person she's making love with. If she's properly prepared."

"With my hand or mouth?"

Just the words made her squirm with desire. She nodded. She wound her arms around his neck and pulled him down to the mattress on top of her. His muscular thigh settled at the juncture of her legs, putting delicious pressure on that most sensitive part of her.

He started to retreat, but she held on tighter. "You're better at this than you know, big guy. How about we start with a kiss."

He dipped his head and proceeded to make her mindless with desire. He trailed kisses down to her breasts. Her hands fisted in his hair and she cried out his name. "What about here?" He pressed a kiss to her stomach, then nudged aside the waistband of her sweats with his nose. "Found more."

He tugged her pants off her hips and one leg. He kissed the seam of her thigh and licked the crease there.

"Jackson!"

"You do have freckles from head to toe." Then he bent her leg at the knee and pushed it up toward her body, exposing her weeping center to his gaze. "Like this?"

"Like what?" Reese squealed a senseless moan as his mouth closed over her sensitive bud. After bringing her to orgasm that way, he shucked off his pants, rolled on a condom and settled himself where she most wanted him to be.

"You sure you're ready for me?"

Still riding the roller coaster that his hands and mouth had taken her on, she made a guttural sound in her throat.

He grinned above her. "A grunt is not an answer."

She grinned, too, wrapping her legs around his hips and digging her heels into his backside. "Now, Jackson. I want *you* right now." He thrust himself inside her and proceeded to take her on another round of the roller coaster she would ride again and again. "I love you, Jackson," she whispered against his skin before she flew off the tracks and into arms she trusted would catch her and never let her go.

Chapter Thirteen

Dress rehearsal Thursday night had been full of miscues—an actress coming onstage in the wrong costume, an actor saying his act 3 monologue during act 2, a supposedly "dead" actor onstage having a sneezing fit and making it pretty near impossible for the other actors onstage—including Maisey—to keep a straight face and move on with the show. In other words, as theater lore would say, a bad dress rehearsal made for a great opening night.

"You guys are ready for this." Reese had taken no director's notes to share with her cast and crew. At this point, there was nothing for her to polish or improve. She needed to let them do their thing. "Thank you for all your hard work. You're going to knock the socks off our audiences this week and next. Hang up your costumes, put away your props, then go home and get a good night's sleep. I'll see you tomorrow for makeup call and sound checks starting at six. Remember, no alcohol, no milk. Drink lots of water. You need to protect your voices for the run of the show."

There was a general chorus of thank-yous and good-nights before the cast and crew left the stage to change in the dressing rooms or reset the equipment for tomorrow night.

Once the last student had disappeared from sight, Reese stretched her arms out to the side and exhaled a weary sigh.

"Your job is done now, right?"

She turned to their lone audience member and smiled as Jackson came down the aisle to hug her tightly enough to lift her onto her toes before he claimed her mouth in a kiss.

There had been a lot of that this week. Hugging. Kissing. Making out when she was tired from the last long rehearsals before opening night when she integrated the tech aspects of the show, such as sound and lighting, into the production. They'd even made love a couple of times when she wasn't so exhausted. Every time she smiled at him, or she took his outstretched hand, she could see the curse of his childhood lifting from his shoulders layer by layer. If she was patient, if he could finally believe that her feelings for him were real, permanent—then Reese might just find her happily-ever-after. Since the launch-party reception, Jackson had come to the theater with her every night except for the one time he and his team had gotten called to work a crime scene outside a bar in a rough part of town. And that night, he'd asked his friend Aiden Murphy, and Aiden's K-9 partner, Blue, to sit in on rehearsal and drive her to Jackson's house when she was done.

"That's the idea," she answered, once her boots touched the floor again. "I've prepared them as best I can. It's their show now."

Jackson followed her onto the stage and picked up a couple of the irreplaceable props and then stowed them in her office after she unlocked the door. The one thing marring her chance at happiness was a big thing—a lot bigger than the gargoyle that had come crashing down on her.

She still hadn't identified the man who was terrorizing her.

And they weren't any closer to finding the man who'd killed Jackson's parents.

The information Simon Lowry had given her had turned out to be a dead end because Dixon Lowry had hired a lawyer, and as long as his father was in the hospital recovering from the surgery on his broken wrist, he wasn't letting him talk to the police or the crime lab or anybody.

Could a relationship between them survive if they never found answers?

Jackson's coworker Chelsea had scoured the records of old newspapers and campus publications to search for any mention of a man tied to Beatrice Lowry besides her husband whom Beatrice would care enough about to help cover up a murder. There was her son, Dixon, of course. And numerous social gatherings and fundraisers that listed most of the people on their suspect list. Dean Diamant, Patrick Brown and Dix had been students or faculty at the university twenty-three years ago. As dear as she'd found Simon to be, he, too, had experience in the theater. What if he was just acting the part of a sweet old man, deflecting suspicion onto someone else after losing track of the murder weapon?

As for pricey knife collections? After the attack during the reception, a judge had issued four search warrants to go through Patrick Brown's tools and comb through Dean Diamant's home and office. Not that that had earned her any brownie points with her coworkers.

If anything, the pressure the KCPD and the crime lab were putting on the investigation was making her stalker more and more unhappy with her. She was getting the creepy phone calls every night now. She wanted to get a new phone number, but Jackson had insisted that the best way to track down this guy was to keep him focused on her. He took her phone the second they knew it was him and carried it into another room so she wouldn't have to listen. While the call was active, the lab could run a trace. They all led back to more disposable cell phones, but Chelsea could pinpoint that the calls were all pinging off the same two cell towers—either the one by her apartment building, or the one closest to the theater. He was definitely following her. Definitely watching for his chance to...what? Make good on any one of the threats he'd made?

"You've got that pensive, hopeless look on your face again." Jackson slipped his arms around her from behind and rested his chin on her shoulder. "We'll get this guy. I promise."

Reese leaned back into his strength for a few seconds before pushing him away. "Will you stay with me once you do?"

"What?"

"Never mind." She stuffed her bag into the bottom drawer of her desk and tucked her keys into her pocket. "I need to make the rounds. Make sure all the students have left and all the doors are locked."

But the doorway was blocked by Jackson's bulky, unyielding body. "Do you doubt my feelings for you?"

Reese drifted back a step and threw her hands out in exasperation. "One of these days you're going to figure out you're not a beast and you can have any beauty you want."

"I don't want anyone else. I wouldn't trust anyone else to accept me the way I am."

"Oh, well, then you're going to get tired of me. Tired of

being with the woman who's always the victim. Tired of being with the woman who has to be watched over 24/7."

"Honey, you're exhausted, frustrated and scared."

"Yeah, I am. And, apparently, that's never going to change."

Jackson's eyes narrowed as he leaned toward her. "You've gone to the dark place where I usually reside. I don't like seeing you there."

"That's just too damn bad, Jackson Dobbs."

"Freckles—"

"Don't call me that stupid nickname!"

"Is there a problem here?" Patrick Brown walked up behind Jackson. He wore his tool belt and clasped a hammer in his fist as if he'd armed himself with a weapon.

Jackson turned, planting himself squarely between Reese and anyone he deemed a threat. If that hammer had been a screwdriver or a pocketknife… Reese almost felt like she was flashing back to a remembered attack. Only, she'd never been stabbed. But she'd seen something, hadn't she? Still, the answers wouldn't come, and whatever she thought was important about that memory blipped out of her head.

"No. There's no problem. Just a disagreement." She walked up to Jackson, linked her arm through his and nudged him aside so that she could leave her office. "Everything's fine, Patrick. You can head on home. I'll check the doors." She glanced up at Jackson. "Why don't you go ahead and get your truck and pull it up to the end of the sidewalk."

Jackson nodded, then grabbed his jacket and followed Patrick. "I'll walk out with you."

Reese felt a flare of annoyance as much as she felt relief that Jackson was making sure she was alone in the building while she made her rounds. Even after she'd picked that stupid fight with him, he was intent on keeping her safe. God, he was a good man. And he had no idea what a catch he was. She'd cleared and locked up both dressing rooms and the greenroom before she heard the back door close behind the two men. She hastened her steps. She needed to apologize to Jackson and explain her own insecurities that had popped up out of sheer frustration and fatigue before her hurtful words drove him back to that grunting, uncommunicative man she'd first met.

Moving with a purpose once again, Reese hurried to secure the lobby doors and run up to the light box she hated so much now, and make sure that door was locked, too.

She was striding across the stage to her office when she heard the sound of clapping coming from the back of the auditorium. One pair of hands. One man. Applauding her.

Feeling dread a hundred times worse than the night she'd heard the skewed nursery rhyme recorded for her, Reese turned.

Dean Diamant must have been hiding in his darkened office. She hadn't seen him, hadn't even known he was in the building tonight. He stopped clapping when she made eye contact with him, and found she couldn't look away.

"Dean," she greeted him, her tone light and surprisingly friendly despite her trepidation. "I didn't see you there." *Good acting job, Reese.* "Were you watching rehearsal? I think we've got a good show."

"You...are a thorn in my side, Ms. A. Reese—I'm never going to call you *Professor*—Atkinson. In my mind you'll always be Red, from the day you first waltzed into my office and batted your eyes at me to the day you die. You're my Red."

"Excuse me?" Reese turned her body slightly away from him and pulled her phone from her pocket. She slid it down her leg where she could call up a number without drawing attention to it. Jackson was the last person she'd texted so his name should be at the top of her call list. She tapped his number. Now what? She couldn't text without looking at her phone, and she couldn't call him without the ringing and his answering giving her away. "I've never batted my eyes at anybody in my life. And I'm not *your* anything." Her gaze dropped to the bandage on his thumb. He'd had that on the night of the reception. Had he cut himself? And what was he clutching so hard between his fingers and palm? He had a knife. That's what he'd been fiddling with the night of the reception, working out his fury on an object that was precious to him. He was carrying a knife.

She ended up texting the buttons she could reach without looking. Probably pure gibberish. She hit Send, typed in more random letters and hit Send again. The messages wouldn't make any sense. But maybe Jackson would be curious enough to come see why she was repeatedly butt-texting him.

Dean just kept walking, moving step by step down the aisle, coming closer. The bruise from Jackson's fist was still visible on his jaw, and the dark look in his eyes stripped away any hints of handsome there. Who was the Beast now?

"Don't bother calling him," he warned.

"Calling who?"

"Your boyfriend. That Neanderthal. The son of my worst enemy and the woman I loved more than my own life."

"Really? If you loved Melora more than your own life, how come she's dead and you're here?" Where was this snarky sarcasm coming from? *Don't poke the beast*, part of her brain warned. The other part urged her to get in his face and tell him she was done letting him ruin her life—letting him ruin Jackson's, as well.

"He can't get to you to you to help now. He can't lay me out flat with one of those brawny fists."

"Don't count on it."

He laughed, but there was far more evil than amusement in the sound. "You've locked him out, my dear. I asked Patrick to make sure he left because I thought he was bothering you. And now he can't get back in, even if he somehow knew you needed him. You've done such a fine job as theater manager that this place is locked up tight every night. Unless, of course, he has a key."

Okay. That was a problem. Jackson didn't have a key. Was Patrick still outside with him with his keys? She had the feeling that Jackson had been intent on making sure Patrick was off the premises while she was here. Could Jackson reach campus police in time to do an emergency breach of the doors to get to her before Dean Ego Pants did?

"You loved Melora Dobbs?"

"With all my heart. I killed Everett to get him out of the way. She wasn't supposed to be here that night. She had a little boy at home to take care of. She wasn't supposed to try to stop me. She wasn't supposed to get in the way."

"How could you let someone you love die like that?"

"Because I knew there'd be others. Instead of saving herself, instead of loving me, she spat in my face and crawled to her husband."

"Others?"

"It has been twenty-three years, Red. Do you honestly think a man like me can't have any woman he wants? Patrons. Other professors. Students. Most cooperated."

Most? What happened to the others, like her, who refused to fall at his feet? Swallowing the bile that threatened to choke her at Dean's selfish explanation for the end of two innocent lives, and possibly more, she asked, "Why did you give the knife to Beatrice Lowry?"

"Because we were lovers back then. She had a soft spot for me."

"I bet she had a bigger soft spot for this theater and keeping scandal away from the place she loved so much."

"You think you're so smart. But you never did see the truth, did you, Red?"

"Reese."

He ignored her and kept advancing. "I wanted to mentor you. I wanted to be your friend. I wanted to be lovers."

She was choking again. By the time she cleared her throat, she heard knocking at the back door. She almost glanced back. But Dean had heard the noise, too.

"Hmm. He's worried. He's suffering. Your big, strong man can't get to you now."

"He's not just strong. He's smart. He's resourceful."

"He's outside."

Right. Chilling thought. Bad guy with knife. She needed to do something here or she was going to wind up bleeding to death like Melora Dobbs. She wouldn't inflict that nightmare twice on any man, especially the man she loved.

"So, Beatrice Lowry was your first lover. Makes sense. You probably met at some theater event. Then she realized how much money she'd lose, or custody of her children, if Simon ever found out. So, she broke it off with you. Then you turned to Melora for comfort over getting dumped for a better man. But she wouldn't give you the time of day. With your ego, you couldn't imagine her not wanting you. There had to be another reason for her turning you away. It must be the husband. How am I doing so far?"

"Pretty accurate. But you'll never be able to prove anything."

"Your blood will match the unidentified blood on that knife."

"I won't give them my blood."

"Well, they're going to know you did a bad thing today," she challenged as he reached into his pocket and pulled out an unusually long ivory-handled pocketknife, and flipped it open.

"But they don't know I'm here. All those pranks you complained to me about, those clever messages—I was here all the time and you never even realized. The only one who knows the hidey-holes and hidden stairwells of this theater better than you is me." Reese tried to quell the panic rising in her veins. That knife looked very, very sharp. "No one knows I'm here tonight except you. When I'm done, no one will find me here. All they'll find is your dead body."

"You're going to kill me because I wouldn't date you?"

"No, Red. I'm going to kill you because you wouldn't cooperate. You wouldn't turn to me for help when those messages started coming. You wouldn't let me comfort you. All you gave me were problem students and you whined about the jobs I asked you to do. I'm going to kill you because you found that damn knife before I could and then you turned it over to the police."

"The crime lab."

Correct terminology didn't matter. "Once I knew that Simon had known about the knife and me all these years, I thought I could get rid of you both before he blabbed the truth to the world."

Reese heard the pounding on the front doors. Jackson had to know something was wrong now. He'd need evidence to prove that Dean Diamant had killed his parents, evidence to prove he was here with her today before he disappeared again.

She needed to get the dean's blood on her.

Reese swallowed hard. Oh, hell, this was not going to be fun.

Yeah, yeah. Bad guy talking. He really wanted her to listen to his whole egotistical speech. That could buy her some time. "I'm going to kill you, Red, because you are more trouble than you're worth."

"Yeah, I've been told I've got a red-haired temperament. I'm a little mouthy. A little independent. A little picky about the man I want to be with."

The moment his foot touched the bottom step, Reese typed in the letters *SOS*, hit Send and ran.

His feet pounded up the stairs behind her as she raced for her office. She shoved her key into the doorknob and cursed. Really? Today was the day the damn lock decided to work? Of course, Dean's keys had made every door as accessible to him as they were to her.

Run!

Leaving her key jammed in the lock, she sprinted backstage. She tipped over the two prop tables behind the set, hoping to create an obstacle course to slow Dean down. But he was gaining on her.

Think!

She couldn't go upstairs. There was only one way in or out of that level. She'd be trapped.

Dean was between her and the back door now.

She wouldn't risk the balcony or catwalk. There were too many places she could trip and fall. Too many ways she could plummet to her death.

She needed a weapon.

"You're just prolonging the inevitable, Red."

She snatched the axe off the prop table on the other side of the stage. It was dull. It was old. Hell, it was fake. But maybe she could at least use it as a club if he got close to her.

She had to make it to the front doors of the auditorium. There was no other way for her to escape.

She charged through the garden doors at the back of the set and ran straight into Dean. He wrapped his arms tightly around her and pointed the tip of his blade at her neck.

Reese screamed. She never even felt the cut, but she could feel the burning aftereffects of the nick in her skin. She whacked at him with the axe, but it merely knocked his hand away and was jarred from her grip. There was no cut, no blood, except for the ooze trickling down her own neck and dotting the sweater she wore. She needed his blood, not hers!

She locked her chin down to her chest, fighting to keep anything vulnerable from the slice of his blade. She stomped on his feet, gouged at his eyes. But his grip was strong, and he wasn't letting go. She reached behind her head and clawed her fingernails through his cheek.

Victory!

Sort of.

Not.

Enraged by the blood she'd drawn from his face, Dean picked her up and slammed her to the floor. Her head struck the stage, leaving her dazed. He straddled her and grabbed a fistful of her hair, yanking her head back to expose her throat, when it sounded like an explosion had gone off in the lobby.

"What the hell...?" Dean muttered.

It was enough of an interruption to blink her eyes clear and pick up the axe that had dropped at her feet.

Glass shattered and fell like thunderous raindrops. An engine roared in her ears. The entire building shook as she swung that axe with every bit of strength she could muster against the side of his head.

An alarm screeched to life with a deafening pulsebeat, and she heard footsteps charging through the auditorium.

"Reese!"

That voice. That blessed voice.

Jackson Dobbs wasn't just the stronger man here today. He was smarter.

Dean swayed above her for a moment, then turned toward the new threat.

"Get off her, you son of a—"

Reese felt the impact of Jackson tackling Dean and taking him to the floor. While the two men traded kicks and punches and grappled for control of the knife, she rolled over and crawled away to a relatively safe distance. Even though he was armed, Dean was at the disadvantage because Jackson was angry, he was protecting her, and he knew how to fight.

Understanding what *her* job was right now, Reese scrambled to her feet and hurried to her office. Now that she wasn't in a panic, she could turn the key in the lock. She shoved the door open and scanned the room for what she needed. There. Next to the fake stone pediment Zach had built for her. A brown paper sack. She turned it over and dumped the contents before shoving her right hand inside. With her other hand she grabbed the duct tape every good theater company kept in stock. She wound it around the neck of the bag, then sealed it around her wrist.

She snagged a rope that looked like the only real weapon she could get her hands on and ran back to the stage in time to see Jackson lift Dean by the collar of his shirt and knock the knife away from his limp hand. Then he hauled back his fist and knocked her attacker out cold before he dropped him to the floor.

"I wanted to do that," she complained. "It might not be as satisfying as you knocking him out. But he made me angry. All 'I'm your mentor, you should worship me.' And 'I tried to scare you into loving me.' He said your mother and I aren't the only women he's manipulated like this, either."

"We'll check it out," Jackson wheezed.

"Good. He needs to go away forever."

"Reese—"

"At least let me tie him up in case he comes to again." She knelt beside Dean's prone body and pulled his hands together behind his back. "He's not getting away with killing your parents and trying to kill me."

"What's that?" Jackson sounded slightly winded as he pointed to the bag on her hand.

"Evidence." She held it up while using that elbow and her left hand to tie as many knots as tightly as she could around Dean's wrists. "It's his blood. I preserved it in an evidence bag like you do. You can compare what's under my fingernails to the unidentified blood on that knife. You can prove that Dean killed your parents."

Jackson sat down hard on the top step at the edge of the stage. "Come here," he ordered in a gruff voice. "Come here now."

"This is taking me a minute. With one hand and all. They're just little half-hitches. But I tied a lot of—"

"You said to ask for what I want."

Reese turned to fully look at his proud, battered face. "Huh?"

"I want you here. In my arms. Now."

She supposed seven knots were enough to subdue an unconscious man. Something was off about Jackson's unusually stern demand. She pushed to her feet and knelt beside him, winding her arms around his neck and squeezing as tightly as she dared. "I'm so sorry about before. I didn't want to fight. I never want to scare you away."

"Fat chance of that." His arm snaked around her waist and he lifted her onto his lap. His fingers caressed her neck. "You're bleeding."

"It's just a nick," she assured him. "I did what you said. I fought hard. I fought dirty. Until you could get to me."

"You fought smart. Texting gibberish like that? I knew something was wrong. By the time I got that *SOS*, I'd already found a way to get inside."

When she braced her hand against his stomach to shift to a more comfortable position, he jerked slightly and groaned. Reese scrambled off his lap and inspected the small pool of crimson staining the front of his shirt. "He stabbed you." She nudged his shoulder to get him to lie down flat on the stage and pushed up his shirt to inspect the wound on the left side of his torso. With the evidence bag preventing her from removing her sweater or blouse, Reese kicked off her ankle boot and peeled off a cotton sock, which she then wadded up and pressed against his wound. "Damn it, you big galoot. You aren't supposed to get hurt. Don't die on me."

He reached up to palm the side of her face and neck. "Honey, I'm not dying. I have plans to be here for opening night of your play. And to dance with you at Buck and Chelsea's wedding. And to celebrate with you when you pass your oral exams and get your PhD. I plan to be here to celebrate all the big moments with you. All the little ones, too."

Reese nodded, sniffing back the tears that stung her eyes. "I want that. I want all of that, too. We're going to toast your parents now that you've caught their killer. I want to visit them in the cemetery and tell them what a smart, brave, caring, strong, sexy man their miracle boy has become—how he served his country, how he protects his city, how he saved my life. I want to tell them how much I love him. How much I need him to be there to share all those big and little moments."

"Freckles." He brushed his thumb along the tears streaming down her cheeks. "Don't cry. Give me bad guys and crime scenes any day of the week. But please don't cry."

"Happy tears, Jackson. Happy tears." She pressed a quick, deep kiss to his lips, then went back to concentrating on his wound. "I have no idea where my phone is now. I probably lost it when he tackled me. We need to call for the police and an ambulance."

"Already done."

"You're sure you're not dying? I'll be pissed off if you are."

"I don't think he nicked anything vital. I'm pretty clear-headed."

"You're still going to the hospital."

"Anything you want, it's yours."

"You. I want you."

"You got me. I love you so much, Reese Atkinson. Even when I wasn't sure I knew how to love, I loved you."

"You're damn good at loving me, Jackson. I'm the luckiest woman in Kansas City. In all the world. I love you, too."

"You'll have to use some of that Lowry money to fix the front doors. And maybe my truck."

She looked back to see the wreck of his truck that he'd crashed through the glass doors at the front of the building. There were cops coming in now, KCPD and campus police both.

"One more kiss before we have company."

Reese cupped Jackson's wonderful, scarred, square face and leaned down to very thoroughly kiss him. "All you have to do is ask."

Epilogue

"I love seeing you in a tuxedo," Reese gushed, letting Jackson help her down from the cab of his new truck. Before he straightened her sparkly wool wrap around her shoulders and shut the door, she was reaching up to adjust the knot in his silvery-blue tie. He'd hastily put it on in the truck at the last stoplight on their way to Chelsea and Buck's wedding at the historic Loose Mansion in downtown Kansas City.

"You like seeing me out of it more," he teased, dutifully standing still while she smoothed his tie over his starched shirt and buttoned his navy-blue jacket. Now that her show was over, she and her brilliant, brave, musclebound criminologist had been spending nearly every night together, either at her apartment or his home.

Reese smiled as she straightened the lapels of his jacket. It thrilled her to no end that Jackson was getting comfortable enough with his social skills to actually flirt and share his dry sense of humor with her. "I really do."

Dean Diamant was in jail awaiting trial for the murder of Jackson's parents as well as stalking and assault charges. The DA's office had taken the death penalty off the table in exchange for information on other victims the dean had stalked and assaulted over the past twenty-three years. But until Dr. Diamant was pronounced guilty and sent to prison for the rest of his life, Jackson had vowed to remain Reese's protector.

While she loved that he wanted to be with her, he'd been a terrible patient, more worried about the fading bruises on her skin instead of allowing her to change the bandages over his own stitches, or wanting to hold her when she had nightmares about her ordeal instead of resting like he should. He'd insisted on attending every performance of the play in the evenings, and working days at the crime lab to pick up the slack from his teammates who were focused on the Diamant case. He'd quizzed her over her dissertation and ridden with her to Grangeport to meet her sister, brother-in-law and nephews instead of staying home to rest. The only time they'd been apart had been those first three nights when the doctors at St. Luke's Medical Center had kept him to pump him full of antibiotics and monitor his recovery from surgery to repair the stab wound that, while it had blessedly missed piercing any vital organs, had torn through skin and muscle and chipped one of his ribs, necessitating that they find and remove the bone fragment before stitching him up.

As if sensing the darker turn of her thoughts and how scared she been at the thought of losing him, Jackson covered her hands with his, stilling them against his chest to halt the last-minute touch-ups to his formal attire that had become random caresses. "I'm okay."

Pulling herself out of her head, she pressed a kiss to his damaged hand. "I know. Sometimes, I just need to feel for myself that my troubles didn't get you killed."

"Not dead," he assured her. "But if you keep petting me like that, we're going to be even later."

Reese's eyes widened at his guttural warning. Was he saying what she thought he was? "The doctor finally cleared you for *normal* activity at yesterday's appointment. You already conducted a thorough freckle exploration when you came to pick me up this afternoon. That's why we're already running behind to get to the wedding." She felt her brief moment of melancholy dissipate. With a resolute sigh, she smiled to know that this good man was still part of her life. "But I don't think the doctor meant you should have sex multiple times throughout the day now."

"I'm a scientist."

Reese blinked. "What does that have to do with anything?"

The corner of his mouth curled up in that shy smile she loved. "Scientific theory requires multiple tests to prove conclusively what the evidence is saying. While I love sleeping with you cuddled up next to me, I wanted to know if being with you was as good as I remember."

His clinical explanation made her giggle. Her man was funny. And sweet. And everything she hadn't known she needed. Bracing her hands against his chest, she stretched up on tiptoe, still falling shy of reaching his mouth. When she whimpered in frustration at her inability to touch her lips to his, Jackson lowered his head. Warming at how attentive he was to her wants and needs, she smiled. "And your scientific conclusion?"

"Better every damn time."

Finally, Jackson covered her mouth with his, reminding her of how their lovemaking had started this morning when he'd arrived at her apartment to pick her up for the wedding. And since she was waiting for his help to zip up her dress before putting it on, she had greeted him in little more than her underwear and a robe. Once the door was locked behind him, it hadn't taken much for him to lift her into his arms, back her against the wall and strip her down to her freckles. He'd mussed her hair and the makeup she'd so carefully applied, but Reese didn't care. His callused hands and needy touches made her body sing long before she'd gotten his shirt undone and his slacks and boxer briefs pushed down over his hips. Despite their frantic need to consume each other, he'd entered her slowly, tenderly, lifting her over the crest before he found his release inside her.

"I didn't know it could be like this," he'd whispered against her ear before lowering her feet to the floor. *"I didn't know it was this good when you loved someone. When you can trust them with your heart."*

"Your words are always a treasure to me, Jackson Dobbs," she'd said, touching her forehead to his. She tilted her eyes up to his handsome gray eyes. *"But you'd better stop talking before you make me cry and ruin the last of my makeup. I love you, too."* Then she pushed against his chest, knowing he only retreated a step because he'd do almost anything she asked. *"You're an usher, remember? Chelsea will never forgive us if we're late."*

Jackson had nodded. He picked up the robe and satiny panties he'd removed and placed them in her hands before he redressed himself. *"Go. You'll need something warm over your dress. It's cold out."* He'd dropped a kiss to the crown of her hair before shooing her toward her bedroom. *"We're leaving in fifteen minutes."*

"Who needs a coat? I'm plenty warm with you around," she teased. Reese wiggled her bare, freckled butt as she hurried down the hall. Jackson's deep-pitched groan made her feel more beautiful and important to him than any words could.

Now they were hurrying hand-in-hand down the sidewalk as fast as her short legs and tea-length gown allowed. But with Jackson to cling to, she never once stumbled on her strappy high-heels or felt the chilly November wind. Chelsea's eclectic tastes and the World War I era mansion gave the wedding a whole Downton Abbey vibe, and Reese had embraced her new friend's theme by raiding the costume department at the theater for a silvery-blue gown with an antique lace overlay and three-quarter lace sleeves.

"Thank goodness you're here. I was about to text you." Lexi Callahan-Murphy, Chelsea's matron-of-honor, greeted them at the door. She wore a vintage peach gown and had an uncharacteristic look of panic on her face. "Sorry, Jackson. I need to borrow your date."

He frowned. "Everything okay?"

Lexi flipped her hand back and forth in the universal response for just so-so. "I'm on Plan C right now." She turned her focus down to Reese and pulled her into her arms. "Beautiful dress, by the way."

"Thanks." Reese returned the taller woman's hug, concerned when she felt that Lexi seemed jittery. "You look lovely, too. What can I help with?"

After Lexi sent Jackson off to hang up her wrap and check in with Grayson Malone, the other usher for this evening's ceremony, she grabbed Reese by the hand, and dragged her up the wide mahogany stairs to the bridal suite on the second floor. "Chels doesn't have any family. Allie—Grayson's Allie—is here, too, but she needs to go down and oversee the guest book and gift table because people are already arriving. I'm supposed to be getting Chelsea dressed right now. But I'm not much help."

"Lexi." Reese stopped and squeezed the other woman's hand. Although she was Jackson's supervisor and team leader at the crime lab, she was also their friend. And right now, she looked a little green around the gills. "Stop and take a breath. Are you okay?"

"It's nothing contagious." Lexi clutched her hand against her stomach and inhaled a deep breath with Reese. Then another.

Not what she'd asked, but okay. "Better?"

Lexi nodded before pushing open the door to the bridal suite.

"Oh good, you're back. Hey, Reese. Glad you could make it." The bride-to-be stood in front of a full-length mirror while Allie Tate, Grayson's girlfriend, fastened the many buttons down the back of Chelsea O'Brien's ivory lace gown. Reese blinked against the sparkle of jewelry on Allie's hand as Chelsea pushed her silver glitter-framed glasses up onto the bridge of her nose and glanced at the clock on the wall. 5:30 p.m. "Buck is a stickler for punctuality. And it may take the next thirty minutes just to get me dressed."

Reese quickly took in the clock, the worried bride, the two miniature poodles lounging on the sofa who were dressed in blue satin vests that matched the wedding party's ties, the short veil draped over a hanger in front of the window and the way Lexi hunched over and pressed the back of her hand to her lips. These women—Jackson's friends and now hers—needed help. Reese rubbed her hands together. "I've been making quick changes in dressing rooms for years. What do you need?"

Chelsea counted off the tasks on her fingers. "Rings tied to dog's vests. Boutonnieres pinned on Buck, his son and the ushers. Allie needs to run downstairs to greet the guests. Veil on my head. Figure out what's wrong with Lexi and get me downstairs to marry Buck."

Lexi picked up the ring boxes on the dresser. "I've got the dogs."

Allie, an athletic, statuesque blonde, handed off button duty to Reese. "If you take over here, I'll bring the boutonnieres to the guys and get them pinned up on my way downstairs to the guest table."

"Of course." Reese had three more buttons fastened before she heard the moaning noise behind her.

She and Chelsea turned to see Lexi grabbing her purse and dashing out the door. "I... Oh... Sorry."

Chelsea squeezed Reese's hand and urged her to follow her matron of honor. "I can at least get the dogs ready. Go. Make sure she's okay."

With a nod, Reese hurried after Lexi and followed her down the hallway. En route, she pulled her phone from the pocket of her dress and texted Jackson.

Is Aiden around? Lexi isn't feeling well. We're in the women's upstairs bathroom.

She pushed open the bathroom door to the sound of Lexi dry heaving in one of the stalls. Reese wet several towels with cool water and handed them to Lexi when she came out. Wow, she looked pale. "Here."

"Thank you." Lexi dabbed at her lips, then pressed the cool towels to the back of her neck before pointing to her bag on the counter beside the sink. "Would you mind? There are some crackers in there."

Reese couldn't help grinning as she opened the bag of crackers and handed one to the other woman. "This isn't the flu or something you ate, is it. My sister went through this with both of her babies. Are congratulations in order?"

Lexi nibbled on the cracker and nodded. "We haven't announced it yet. I wanted to wait until I was three months along. But this morning sickness is no joke."

"Um, it's not morning." Reese led her over to a wooden stool at the end of the row of sinks.

"Exactly. I don't think my body understands the concept of morning sickness. It thinks it's okay to do this all day long."

Lexi's color looked better as she polished off the cracker and rested a moment. "Anything else I can do to help?"

"Just make sure Chels is downstairs at six. She's waited months to marry Buck. I don't think she'll survive if she has to put it off any longer. I'll make sure I'm down there with my bouquet. I just need a few minutes to rest and get my equilibrium back."

"You got it."

There was a sharp knock at the door before it opened slightly and Blue, her husband's K-9 partner, trotted in and went straight to Lexi and laid his head in her lap. Said husband, Aiden, poked his head in. "Lex? You all right? Can I come in?"

Reese smiled at Lexi, petted the dog and opened the door wider. "It's all clear. Go on in." She squeezed Aiden's arm on her way out. "Congratulations." He winked his thanks and went in to take care of his pregnant wife.

Just like preparing for the opening curtain of a show, the last minutes before the ceremony flew by. Reese breathed a sigh of relief as she slipped into the row of chairs near the back of the high-ceilinged garden room beside Jackson right as the music changed to start the wedding. Chelsea was dressed, beautiful, and ready for the crime lab's boss, Mac Taylor, to walk her down the aisle. Buck's grown son, Clark, had leashes for the dogs, and walked them up to the wide mahogany fireplace at the front of the room before removing the rings and standing beside his father as best man. Then, Aiden and Blue walked Lexi into the room. She looked every bit the radiant mother-to-be now after some rest, a snack and some TLC from her husband. Finally, everyone stood as the wedding march played and Chelsea and Mac entered.

Being vertically challenged, once the bride and her stand-in father had walked past, Reese had no view of what was happening at the front of the room. When laughter and a smattering of applause rippled through the rows of guests, Reese tugged on Jackson's arm. "What's going on? I can't see."

"Buck kissed her."

At the minister's request, they all sat down. "He's supposed to wait until the end of the ceremony."

Grayson spoke from his chair on the opposite side of Allie, who sat next to Reese. "I wouldn't tell a man what he can and can't do on his wedding day."

When he squeezed Allie's hand and pressed a kiss to her

temple, the glint of something shiny that she'd seen upstairs registered. Reese pressed her hands together in silent applause and whispered, "That's an engagement ring. Congratulations, you two."

"My Thanksgiving present," Allie explained. "We don't want to steal the spotlight from Chelsea and Buck, so we haven't announced it yet." Reese pantomimed locking her mouth shut and throwing away the key, ensuring she'd keep their secret. Allie looked back at Grayson, who studied her just as intently. "But when my Marine asked, I didn't hesitate to say yes."

"Love you, Lieutenant," Grayson whispered.

"Love you." The couple exchanged a soft kiss.

Jackson stretched his hand in front of Reese to shake Grayson's hand in a silent congratulations. When he saw how Reese was craning her neck to see the ceremony at the front of the room, her big guy simply picked her up out of her chair and sat her on his lap. She settled her hands atop his forearms where they wound around her waist and watched the rest of the wedding surrounded by his warmth and love.

A pregnancy, an engagement and a wedding. Reese was happy for her friends, and even happier that Jackson felt included as an important part of his friends' lives.

But she couldn't help but wonder if he believed he deserved all those things for himself, too. And if he truly understood how much she wanted to be the woman who shared those life-changing events with him.

JACKSON COULDN'T BE happier for his friends. And while he was honored to be a part of their lives, he wondered if he would ever find that kind of lifelong happiness for himself.

He loved Reese, and he believed she loved him. But he was too used to being alone, too used to being the outcast for him to completely believe that she was his for the long haul—that she'd want his babies, that she'd marry him.

Even now, at the reception where Buck and Chelsea and Grayson and Allie had danced nearly every dance together, while Aiden had sat Lexi in a quiet corner to take care of her needs, he sat at a table with Chelsea's pseudo-grandpa, Vinnie Goring, while Reese continued to help Chelsea with her dress and other needs. She chatted with many of the guests, whether she knew them or not, smiled at everyone. Reese was comfortable with crowds and parties, comfortable with people, while he sat off to the side like a growly, oversize version of a wallflower.

He was proud of Reese for stepping up to help his friends this evening. She'd sat by his side through the ceremony and dinner afterward, so everyone here knew she was with him. But he wanted to be in her circle of light, to be part of her world and have her goodness shine in his heart…forever.

But how did he make that happen? Where did he find the words he'd never needed before?

Vinnie Goring wasn't at a loss for words, though. The older gentleman leaned his cane against the table, sipped a drink from his bottle of beer, and continued on, as if Jackson had been focused on him and not the thoughts and frustrations and dreams going back and forth inside his head. "If I could have done, I'd have walked my Ladybug down the aisle. But now that I've got to have the other knee worked on, I'm lucky I'm here at all. Doesn't look like I'll be able to keep the bar going, either. That first father-daughter dance about did me in." Vinnie muttered a curse. "Made me cry in front of everybody. Chels is a good girl. She's gonna let me move into her house since it's all one level, when she moves in with Buck. His son, Clark, is going to help me take care of all the animals while Buck and Chelsea are on their honeymoon." Vinnie exhaled a deep breath. "And I'm boring you to tears, aren't I, young man?" He set his drink down with enough force that Jackson turned and gave the man a quizzical look. Vinnie grinned and nodded his head to the left. "You're a good listener. Though I expect you've got other things on your mind tonight."

Jackson turned to follow the older man's unspoken message. Reese was making her way across the room to him, boldly, with a smile Jackson felt all the way down to his soul. Just like that first day she'd come to the crime lab to give him the bloodied knife that had led to solving his parents' murders, she approached him. *Him. He* was the man she wanted to see.

He was vaguely aware of Vinnie exchanging pleasantries with Reese. He stood when she held out her hand to him. She tilted her head, her gaze never leaving his. "Dance with me?"

Jackson had never danced with a woman before. Even in middle school P.E. where he'd learned the basics, he'd been on his own. At the wide-eyed hesitation that must have been on his face, Reese tugged on his hand. "Hold me in your arms on the dance floor and sway back and forth. You can handle that right?"

When he grunted, she rolled her eyes and laughed. And then her hips were locked against his thighs, and she was in his arms. She tipped her head back and rested her chin against his chest, looking up at him with a smile that made him feel gooey and vulnerable and strong as an ox. "Yeah. This is what I needed."

He lowered his head to steal a kiss and then she tucked her head beneath his chin. He pulled the hand he held into his chest and matched his rhythm to the gentle, mesmerizing sway of her hips. They danced together through two slow tunes, a soft country ballad and an instrumental classic. When the third song started and Reese sang softly against him, Jackson knew he didn't want his time with her to ever end. He'd always wanted what his parents had had together, and Reese Atkinson was the first woman—the only woman—he'd ever believed could be his. The only woman who made him believe he could be hers.

Abruptly, he stopped. He released her to frame her face between his hands. "Do you want to get a dog with me?"

Reese stopped, blinking in confusion. "A dog? Is this like the pie thing?"

If he had a third hand, he would have whacked himself in the back of the head. Not exactly what he'd meant to say. Her gaze narrowed as more words spewed out of his mouth. "There's this place just outside the city called Shadow Protectors Ranch. They rescue and train dogs. I'd like you to have one to be with you during those late nights at the theater when I can't be with you. We'd practically be living together since we'd be sharing ownership of the dog, and the responsibility of caring for..."

Reese pressed her fingers against his lips to silence him. "Are you asking me to move in with you?" He'd meant to say something like that. Her beautiful violet blue eyes studied him for a long moment. "Is that what you really want to ask?"

He was breathing too hard. This moment had suddenly gotten too big for him to contain. "Elope to Vegas with me."

Her eyes widened and color flooded the freckles on her cheeks.

No. He'd done this all wrong. She'd want a big event like Chelsea's wedding. She'd want her sister and family there. All their friends. She'd be so beautiful in a fancy formal gown.

"Yes."

"Yes?" The doubts that had held his heart in check for too many years disappeared in the light of Reese's smile.

"I'll marry you. In Vegas or wherever. If you could wait until the semester is over. I'm thinking maybe Christmas break. Then we'd have time for a honeymoon afterward."

Jackson stopped her planning by lowering his head and kissing her. He crushed her in his arms, lifted her feet off the floor and kissed her again. Reese responded with a matching passion. Her kindness and understanding and need made him feel like the luckiest man in the room. They stood and kissed in the middle of the dance floor until one of his friends good-naturedly shouted at them to get a room.

Jackson reluctantly broke off the kiss and lowered Reese back to the floor. He felt like shouting above the noise and music of the room. He wanted to tell someone, everyone, that Reese Atkinson was his. That he'd asked in his own way, and she'd said yes.

Then she tugged on his lapels and demanded that he look her in the eye. "Until then, I'm moving in, we're sleeping together, and we are totally getting that dog. Are you okay with all that?"

Jackson grunted his happiness and kissed her again.

* * * * *

A DETECTIVE'S DEADLY SECRETS

ANNA J. STEWART

To my own circle of ride-or-die friends: Mary, Cari, Melinda and Judy.

What a boring world this would be without all of you in my life.

Chapter One

FBI special agent Eamon Quinn pulled in behind the Brass Eagle, the downtown Sacramento bar that had become his home away from home over the past few years. Bouncing between the state capital and the Bay Area had begun to take its toll, but working out of both branch offices gave him a wider range of focus. More potential cases. More people to connect with. More predators to stop.

He parked in the back corner, killed the engine and, with a sigh, dropped his head back and closed his eyes.

The adrenaline and energy that had been coursing through him for the better part of a week finally abated. Exhaustion crept into the void and made his eyes droop even as his stomach growled. Beneath the dim glow of the overhead streetlamp, the city, unaware of the nightmarish scene that had played out just a few hours prior, drifted silently into slumber, something Eamon planned to do just as soon as he dragged himself out of the car and up to the third floor.

The back door slammed open. Eamon blinked his eyes open, turned his head and spotted Vince Sutton, owner of the Brass Eagle, as he hefted three giant bags of garbage into the dumpster. He dropped the lid closed, brushed his hands on the back of his jeans and, after a quick glance around the parking lot, headed Eamon's way.

"Been wondering when you'd get here." Vince, all six-plus feet of him, rested a hand on the roof of Eamon's vehicle as Eamon grabbed his duffel out of the back. "Simone called." While Vince had become one of Sacramento's premier private investigators in recent years, it was his marriage to Assistant District Attorney Simone Armstrong that would have clued him in on Eamon's now closed case. Leave it to Simone, who was currently on extended maternity leave, to continue to have both ears perked for information. "Want to talk about it?"

Vince wasn't a coddler. He wasn't a hand-holder. What he was was a realist with a sharp eye for the tough world he and Eamon both inhabited. "Not much to say." Eamon locked his jaw. "Girl's back with her parents." Forever changed, but at least she was alive.

"You got him," Vince said simply, although the takedown had been anything but simple.

The standoff had lasted for almost twelve hours and ended in a hail of bullets.

"He had her for more than two weeks, Eamon. The odds of him surrendering peacefully—"

"You know I don't play the odds." After more than ten years with a dedicated task force in the Crimes Against Children division of the FBI, Eamon had learned a long time ago that expecting a positive outcome was the shortest route to burnout. He always hoped, but even that fire didn't burn as brightly as it once did. Cases like this one rarely ended with the victim being recovered alive. Even knowing that, it didn't stop Eamon from trying to save as many as he could. He really should be considering this one a win.

He hefted his bag over his shoulder and followed Vince into the bar through the back door. "She couldn't have been his only victim," Eamon said. "With this guy dead, we may never know how many there were. Forensics may come up with something, but—"

"But by the time they do, you'll already be on to your next case." Vince finished the frequently spoken thought. "You did good, Eamon. Whatever else happened, that girl is alive partially because of you."

Yeah. But how many had died before they'd discovered the pattern? It was a thought that would keep him awake—in the future. But for now?

"I'm glad to be here for our dinner tomorrow night." Always anxious to lighten the mood rather than darken it, Eamon ignored the way his heart twisted at what the annual get-together with his friends represented. His sister had been gone for more than twenty years now and yet... "Looks like the sleepless nights are treating you okay, Vince," he teased. "Come on. Let's see the latest, Dad."

Vince grimaced, but there was a twinkle in his eye. "I really don't want to be one of *those*—"

"As one of Caleb's honorary uncles, I refuse to let you finish that statement." Eamon held out his hand for Vince's phone, which was now displaying the most recent picture of his and Simone's month-old son. "He definitely got your hairline," Eamon teased.

"But his mother's eyes," Vince said. "Other than him being healthy, that's all I wanted. We're thinking he might have gotten Eden's attitude."

"For both your sakes, I hope that's not true," Eamon laughed. Their friend Eden St. Claire had a bit of a reputation of varying degrees, but despite her prickly flaws, her heart was probably bigger than everyone's combined.

The noise of the familiar Friday night crowd erupted through the swinging doors into the kitchen, which was buzzing with dinner activity. Eamon took a long, deep breath of stomach-tempting grilled onions, roasting meat and that always-there hint of bacon sizzling on the flattop.

"Thanks for the use of the apartment again," Eamon said as Vince stopped to let one of his servers pass. "I wasn't looking forward to the drive back into the city."

"No thanks necessary. Since Jason moved in with Kyla, the place is yours whenever you need it. Besides, you're family." Vince's lips twitched in an uncharacteristic grin. "After the last few years, I'd have thought you'd accepted that. Which reminds me—Jason slipped an invitation to his and Kyla's wedding under your door. And before you argue, attendance is mandatory."

"I thought they were keeping it small."

"They are," Vince said. "But there probably wouldn't be a wedding if you hadn't gone out on a limb with the O'Callahan case. My brother and Kyla aren't ever going to forget you helped save their lives. Neither am I."

"Like you said. Family." Eamon shrugged, not able to voice how much being included in the tight-knit group of ever-growing friends meant to him. He'd spent a lot of years—too many years—alone. Now he had more people in his life than he actually knew what to do with. His contact list had gone from near-empty to blowing up his phone. He readjusted his bag and made his way through the crowd at the bar. "I think I have just enough energy to wait on a burger to take with me upstairs."

"You might want to make time for a drink," Vince suggested and nudged Eamon in the opposite direction of the stairs. "Back corner booth. Pretty brunette with sad eyes. She's been in the past few nights asking after you."

"You're kidding, right?" Eamon wondered if his friend had begun to speak in code. Women didn't come looking for him, but Vince's shrug told him otherwise.

"She stays long enough to finish a club soda and lime. Never orders any food. Normally she's left by now, but as soon as Simone called about your case, I let her know I was almost sure you'd be here tonight." He glanced at his watch. "She's been here a good few hours."

Despite being so tired he had to will his eyes to stay open, Eamon's gaze landed on target. Exhaustion evaporated, replaced by a long-dormant buzzing that accompanied anticipation and, more importantly, long-repressed attraction.

"Lana."

Pretty brunette didn't come close to describing Detective Lana Tate. Every cell in Eamon's body shot to attention. Just the sight of her was enough to supercharge his drained system. She always was—to his mind, at least—the personification of a strong, capable, kick-butt female with enough smooth edges to make the smooth bourbon she preferred seem sharp.

Eamon blew out a small, steadying breath. He hadn't often met women who ticked all his appeal boxes: independent, athletic, smart, wicked sense of humor, dedicated.

They'd laughed together, worked together, coasted case highs and lows together. Lana was one of the best cops he'd ever worked with, and the case they'd closed had earned both of them commendations and, in Lana's case, a promotion.

There had only been one thing wrong with her.

Lana Tate had been very, *very* married.

"I'm going to take that look on your face to mean *Lana* is a welcome surprise." Vince grabbed Eamon's bag and slung it over his shoulder. "I'll have the kitchen send out that burger and a double order of fries. In case you want to share. With Lana," he added with a grin that had Eamon suspecting Vince was going to be making a follow-up call to his wife to fill in the blanks.

"Thanks, Vince." Eamon scrubbed his suddenly damp palms down the front of his jeans. No one had ever made him feel quite as nervous as Lana Tate. Clearly the time since he'd last seen her hadn't done much to temper that sensation. One glimpse of her and he felt as if he'd been shot out of a cannon, straight back to his insecure teenage years crushing on the head cheerleader. Not that Lana...

She turned her head, dark eyes catching his in the blink of a heartbeat, and in that moment, he forgot to breathe. Her smile, when it curved those amazing, plump, unpainted lips of hers, carried an unfamiliar hint of uncertainty.

"I'm feeling the urge to quote Bogart," Eamon said by way of a greeting as he took the final few steps to her table and slid in across from her.

"I trust you to resist the urge." One hand clenched into a fist while the other tightened around the half-filled glass in front of her, and she let out a sigh of relief as her eyes softened. "Hope you don't mind me dropping in on you this way. I know it's been a while."

Eighteen months, twenty-two days, but who's counting?

"Thanks, Travis," Eamon said to the bartender who set a beer in front of him. "You want another?" he asked Lana, who shook her head.

"I'm good."

"Burger will be out in a few, Eamon," Travis said before moving off.

Seeing her close-up now, Eamon couldn't help but think Lana appeared almost as an apparition of the woman he remembered. She'd lost weight, and not in a way that appeared healthy. She looked gaunt. Fragile, even. At the funeral he'd understood it. But now?

She sipped her drink, her hand trembling a bit when she set it down. Eamon focused on keeping his expression passive even as concern cycloned inside him. There was a familiar tension tightening her body, from her fingertips all the way down to her toes. She was pulled taut and appeared to be waiting for someone to snap her free. He'd seen this before, a number of times, in his fellow agents. In other cops. In dozens of people with high-stress, demanding jobs.

The wedding ring she used to wear on her finger now hung suspended on a thin gold chain, along with the familiar key pendant he'd never known her to be without.

He pulled the bowl of spicy pretzels and peanuts closer, tamping down on his growing worry. "So." He munched in an effort to keep his nerves at bay. "How long have you been?"

"Been what?" Lana blinked as if coming out of a fog.

"Sober." He inclined his chin toward her glass. "How long have you been sober?"

"Oh." She closed her eyes and let out a breath that, when she looked at him again, allowed the Lana he remembered to shine through ever so slightly. She opened her fisted palm to reveal the round plastic chip noting ninety days' sobriety. "I should have realized you'd... You never miss anything." She shoved the chip into her front pocket before flipping over her cell phone that had been facedown on the table. "Four months, seventeen days." Her smile was quick and cursory. "Six hours."

"Not counting the minutes, then?" He nodded with approval. "If me drinking will bother you, I can—" He signaled Travis, pushed his beer to the edge of the table, but Lana's hand whipped out and caught his. Her hold on him was so tight so instantly, every alarm bell in his head went off.

"It doesn't. You're fine." She hesitated. "I know it's strange. Me just showing up like this, tracking you down. I'm sorry we fell out of touch. I was a mess after the funeral." There was an intensity in her voice that didn't quite seem like Lana. "I should have... I know I said it at the time, but I appreciated you being there. Marcus would have appreciated it as well."

His gaze dropped back to the wedding band she still wore. "He was a good man, Lana. And it was a big loss for you. You don't owe me an apology. The phone works both ways. I could have called and checked in." Looking at her now, he realized he should have.

How many times had he stared at his cell phone, looking at her contact information, finger hovered above the "call" button, knowing her voice was only a few seconds away? But that might have given up his deepest secret. That he'd been in love with her almost from the moment they'd first met.

That he'd have given anything, *anything*, if she hadn't been married. And then she hadn't been and the idea of being near her while she was still grieving… No. The best course of action—for the both of them—had been to put as much distance between them as possible. She'd needed to grieve and move on with her life—without him hovering, waiting, hoping that perhaps someday she'd see him as more than a shoulder to cry on and someone to turn to.

But as much as he wanted to be a part of her life, he did not want to be the rebound guy. The man who helped her move past her sorrow and on to someone else. Eamon was capable of a lot, but that he was not equipped to deal with.

When he'd first seen her in the bar tonight, fresh hope had sprung to life, but whatever that hope might have been was now tempered by the cloud of sadness that enveloped her.

"I've spent a couple of nights in here hoping to catch you," she said quietly, then looked down at their hands as Eamon resisted the overwhelming temptation to slip his fingers between hers. "I meant it. You drinking isn't going to derail or tempt me. Please, Eamon. Don't change anything for me."

"All right." Because he knew those in recovery needed to get used to being in a world of temptation, he nodded and pulled his drink back in front of him. He did take a long drink, but it was more to get rid of it than to prove any type of point.

"When I stopped by the FBI field office in San Francisco, they said you were working a case up here. Special Agent Sarah Nelson told me about the Brass Eagle." Lana glanced around the bar, lips curving at the sight of meticulously polished and maintained wood, shiny vinyl-padded seats and the large brass-cast emblem of the Marines hanging over the bar. "She said you crash here when you're in town. The owner sounds like he's a good friend."

"He is. Both Vince and his wife. They're two of many, as it turns out." Eamon tried to ignore the fact he was still holding Lana's hand. More to the point, that she was still holding his. Clinging to his, her fingers tensing as if he were some kind of life preserver. He could feel the slight chill from the glass on her skin, but also a tremor he was unaccustomed to.

"That's nice," she murmured. "I don't remember you having many friends."

"I've put many ghosts to rest. A lot's happened since we last spoke."

"Yes," she practically whispered to herself as she glanced out the window. "It certainly has." Before he could press for elaboration, she turned her attention back to him. "I take it since you're back here your case is over? Good result?"

"Mixed." He knew when someone was making small talk, even if that talk revolved around work. "Repeat sex offender broke probation and lured a teenager across state lines a few weeks back. We managed to track him down through his activity on the dark web. Girl's been returned to her parents, but he's—"

"Dead," Lana finished for him, as the "mixed" was understood. "One of the lessons you taught me," she said in a tone far too light for the topic. "Offenders like that should be taken alive if at all possible. It's the only way you find out about their previous victims. If there were any."

In this case there was no "if" about it. But Eamon's opportunity to bear witness and get confessions on the record was flat-out gone. "True as that might be, I'm not going to cry in my beer over him. On the bright side, the girl won't have to testify and her parents won't have to sit through a trial." And hear firsthand what had been done to their child.

Therapy, on the other hand, was a different story. The family was going to need a lot of it.

"Answers have always been important to you," Lana murmured.

"They have." Eamon inclined his head. Was it his imagination or had this conversation suddenly turned into some kind of test?

"Because of Chloe." She was watching him now, with that pinpoint assessing stare she'd honed as a cop. It was the first time since he'd sat down that he saw a hint of the woman he'd worked with. "Because of your sister. You knew what it was like to have questions. To not have closure."

"Closure's a myth." He didn't particularly like the harsh Eden-like tone in the statement, but the declaration was one of his friend's familiar mantras. He lifted his beer again, almost in a mock toast to Eden St. Claire and her life lessons. "Took me until we finally solved Chloe's case and found her killer that I finally accepted that."

"But the answers, they had to have helped you a little at least. Didn't they?" Was that hope in Lana's voice?

"I stopped spiraling, if that's what you mean. I didn't feel caught up in the vortex of what-ifs and if-onlys." He took another drink. "I don't dream about my sister as often," he admitted. "At least now when I do, she's not pleading with me to find her killer." Or accusing him of not doing enough. "She's at peace now. That's something." Instead, he heard the ghostly sounds of her laughter on the air or in the wind chime hanging on the balcony of his San Francisco apartment. No, Chloe had been able to move on.

Now, instead of being driven by anger, he found himself amused by having earned himself a mischievous guardian angel who continuously attempted to remind him there was more to life than work. He could remember her with fondness and affection now, rather than guilt and grief. "Answers are great, but Chloe's still dead, Lana. Nothing is ever going to bring her back." His sister was eternally nine years old, with crooked pigtails and mismatched sneakers. A brief life but one that had impacted so many of those she'd loved. Was that a legacy? Eamon blinked slowly. He liked to think it was.

"So, what's going on with you, Lana? You're a ways from Seattle. Once upon a time you told me it would take something close to a truckload of C-4 to blast you out of the station house for anything remotely resembling a vacation."

"Seattle PD finally made me take all that time off I had stored up." Her smile flickered as if her own nerves were attacking. She pulled her hand free from his and tucked a loose tendril of hair behind her ear before she sat back. "You look good, Eamon. Whatever else you say, I can see putting those ghosts of yours to rest has helped. I'm hoping maybe you can help me do the same. If you have the time."

"I've got a few days while the internal affairs board clears me for active duty." Eamon's response was tempered by the knowledge Vince had been right about her sad eyes. He remembered her spark, Lana's zest for life that seemed superhuman and brought out the best in everyone around her. "What's going on, Lana?"

"I've been working on a special case. A closed case. For a while now. Months." She ducked her head but not before he saw her flinch. "Almost a year, actually."

"A year?" Eamon's eyes widened. What special case could she be talking about? "You're sniffing around someone else's work?" Didn't matter which law enforcement agency one worked for; cases were sacrosanct even after they were put to bed.

Agents, cops, they knew to stay on their side of the fence or risk ruffling more than feathers. He'd meant to tease her, to coax something close to that amazing smile of hers that he used to dream about. But no hint of a smile emerged; only a stoic hanging on to hope by a spider's-web-thin thread shone in her eyes. "Lana?"

"They didn't leave me any choice." Both her hands fisted and she knocked them against the table. The defiance in her whisper sent a chill down his spine. "I didn't remember at first. Everything was so…loud in my head after Marcus died. But I know what I heard, Eamon. I've had so much time to think now. Before, I was too caught up in having lost him, but…they've tried to convince me otherwise, the investigating officers, my superiors. My partner. Make that former partner," she added with another wince, filling Eamon's head with even more questions.

"But I know, I *know* I'm right," she said, her voice low. "If I tell you…" She broke off, her brow furrowing as if in a silent argument with herself. "I don't think I have anyone left I can talk to about this. If you say no—"

"Hey." He grabbed her hand again so he could surrender to temptation and slip his fingers through hers. "I made you a promise after we first worked together, what was it, three, four years ago? I said then that if you needed me for anything, *anything*, all you had to do was ask." It had been an easy promise to make to a woman he had no business caring for.

"I know. I kept telling myself that on the flight down." Her lips twitched as if he'd triggered a spark of humor. "The truth is I can't keep doing this on my own. I'm out of ideas. Out of leads. Out of anyone who will talk to me. If I don't get to the bottom of this, I'm really scared I'm going to lose my mind."

"That isn't going to happen." Especially if he could do anything to stop it. "Whatever it is, you've got my help." He refrained from mentioning that if she'd burned as many bridges as she was alluding to, chances were he wouldn't be able to rebuild them.

"You say that now," she hedged with a disbelieving shake of her head.

"There's nothing you can say that'll change my mind." He squeezed her hand to help her focus. "When I make a promise, I keep it. Let's have it, Lana."

She let out a long, controlled breath. "I need you to help me find out who murdered my husband."

Chapter Two

It took Lana all of five seconds to kick herself for not coming to Eamon months ago. Doing so might have stopped her continued spiral that, honestly, had yet to slow. The second she saw him head toward her in the bar, the part of her that had been existing purely on adrenaline and speculation had finally calmed.

Every single facet of her life had shifted on its foundation since Marcus's death eighteen months ago, but nothing was on shakier ground than her faith: faith in her surroundings, faith in her abilities as a cop, faith in the few friends she had left.

But seeing Eamon felt like a first step in rebuilding it.

She should have believed he'd be the stand-up man she'd always known.

He could have easily done what so many others had: shake his head in disbelief or, worse, humor her. Attempt to convince her she was reading too much into memories that probably weren't reliable. Persuade her she hadn't heard what she'd heard. Insist she was making something more out of the "accident" that had left Marcus Tate, her husband of three years, dead.

Out of habit, she reached up for the necklace on which Marcus's and her wedding bands now resided, along with the key pendant Marcus had given her as an engagement present. Feeling the cool gold against her fingertips centered her most of the time. It reminded her not of what she once had, nor even of what she'd lost, but of what she had to do.

She held her breath, still expecting Eamon to look at her with abject confusion and disbelief, shake his head and walk away.

But FBI special agent Eamon Quinn didn't do any of those things. And this was where her faith, tenuous as it was, began to reknit. Not only did he not do any of those things, but she would bet every penny she had that the idea never even occurred to him.

He was a man of honor who kept his friends—however estranged—close and protected.

A very handsome man of honor, she found herself noticing. Not that she hadn't made note of it before. Of course she had. Eamon Quinn was the kind of man no one could ignore or miss in a crowd. Tall, broad-shouldered, steady, and built to masculine perfection, thanks to the workout routine she remembered he'd stuck to since he'd been a recruit at the FBI academy. The red hair and sharp hazel eyes spoke to the Celtic roots of his ancestors. A man from another century, possibly more suited to wandering the Highlands in a kilt with a sword strapped to his back than wearing a suit with a gun at his side.

Her cheeks warmed at the thoughts slipping through her mind. Marcus had often teased her that Eamon looked at her as definitely more than a friend, but she'd never particularly seen it. She wondered if she was seeing it now, however, with the way Eamon held on to her even as his eyes searched her face for what she suspected were questions he now had himself.

There was something unsettling yet empowering about having his entire focus trained on her. Her fingertips tingled with the impulse to reach across the wooden table and stroke the lines of concern marring his brow.

The calm, unreadable expression on his face left her mentally scrambling, but only for a few minutes. He didn't speak. He didn't nod or give any indication he'd heard—or misheard—her. He merely pushed himself out of the booth, headed over to the bar to surrender his drink. She quickly tucked the rings and chain back under her shirt. A few minutes later Eamon accepted an oversize paper sack and returned to the table.

"Let's go."

"Where?" Not that she wasn't going to follow. The fact he hadn't told her she was out of luck with him was cause enough for her to go wherever he led. And, of course, she had nowhere else to go. She'd meant it earlier when she'd said she was out of options.

He stepped back as she climbed out of the booth, large satchel tight against her side. Eamon kept a gentle hand on her back as he guided her around the tables and customers toward the staircase at the end of the hallway where the restrooms were.

"Third floor," Eamon murmured as she grabbed hold of the railing. "Although I have serious doubts you have enough stamina in you to make it past two."

The same grit and determination that had put her at the top of her police academy class kicked in and, despite her churning, empty stomach and slightly shaky legs, she made it to the landing without fully collapsing. "Shows what you know," she told him as he walked around her, digging his keys out of his pocket.

"Yeah. Silly me, challenging your capabilities so I didn't have to throw you over my shoulder like a sack of potatoes."

Lana's lips twitched before they twisted into a scowl as he unlocked the door and pushed it open.

Once again, he stood back and waved her ahead of him. "After you, Detective."

How the man could make her professional title sound like the beginning of a seduction was beyond her. A full duffel bag sat inside the door of the tidy, practically furnished space. She bent down almost immediately and picked up an embossed white envelope that had made its way halfway into the room. "Special delivery. Fancy."

"Thanks." He plucked it out of her fingers with a quick smile, set it on the edge of a computer desk over in the corner. "Wedding invitation for the end of June. This is their subtle way of reminding me to write it down on my calendar. Don't suppose you're free to be my plus-one."

She blinked, a bit shocked at the question but even more astonished at the color that flooded his cheeks. "Um…"

"Kidding." He held up his hand, shook his head, but the frown she caught on his face before he turned his back on her had a load of new questions landing on her. "You know me. Just getting all the awkwardness out of the way before we get to work."

"I'm not in a position to plan anything for tomorrow, let alone three weeks from now."

"No problem. It's more about me fending off my friends'

continued attempts to fix me up. Showing up alone at a wedding may be the final straw they've been waiting for."

She heard the affection in his voice when he spoke about his friends. More importantly, she heard the ease with which he embraced them. The last time she and Eamon had gone out to dinner more than a few years ago, Eamon had lamented the fact he'd only stayed in touch with a few people from his childhood. The fact he now, at least by comparison, had what appeared to be a wide circle of friends eased some of the concern she'd always felt for him. Especially now that she'd become well acquainted with living a very solitary life.

She was all out of friends at this point. She'd gone about things in the wrong way, caused too many problems, and hadn't considered the risks others might be taking. She'd ignored all the warnings and advice, so much so she literally had no one left she could call on. Except Eamon.

All that said, she didn't think he'd appreciate hearing he was her final option.

"It's nice up here." The view from the windows overlooked downtown Sacramento with an illuminated view of the golden Tower Bridge. It was a skyline she wasn't familiar with and it certainly didn't come close to rivaling that of her beloved home city of Seattle. With the cloudless, late-spring-plunging-into-summer night sky kissing the tip-tops of a mishmash of architectural feats, she could understand what continued to draw Eamon back to the River City.

The apartment didn't seem completely his. She didn't see any personal mementos out in the open. Not that she knew whether he was a collector or displayed such things. Their interactions really hadn't delved that deep. It wasn't that the apartment wasn't cozy and lovely. But it didn't scream Eamon Quinn either.

"Left upper cabinet by the sink," he told her as he carried the paper bag over to the table between two windows. "Vince added a second burger to my order, so grab some plates and napkins, will you?"

She didn't have the heart to tell him the thought of food had been making her queasy for the better part of the past year. But as she sniffed the air and caught the telltale promise of bacon, onions and oil-hot fries, she could feel her salivating glands activate. Maybe she could eat.

The magic of Eamon, she told herself. He'd always had a way of setting everything right.

She pulled out a chair and sat. He grabbed a couple of bottles of water out of the fridge nestled at the far end of the galley-style kitchen, then detoured to the desk and popped open the invitation. "Looks like Kyla won the first battle," he said as he skimmed the information. "She got the venue she wanted for her wedding. I bet Simone had something to do with that," he added with a chuckle, a sound that took her a bit by surprise. "That woman has contacts. Jason said that vineyard was booked up months ago." He set the pair of insert cards aside and joined her at the table to unload the cardboard containers. "I'm assuming your tastes haven't changed so much you'll refuse what I ordered for you."

"Food is food." She shrugged and, given the expression on his face, surprised both of them by snagging a steaming hot fry and popping it in her mouth. Her stomach immediately growled, as if being reminded of food for the first time in forever. "Are we going to wait for dessert before you begin interrogating me?"

"What makes you think I have dessert?"

"Because you're you." It felt good, oddly so, reminiscing on tidbits of information she probably should have forgotten years ago. "Your one constant whenever we worked together. Carbs and sugar."

"With some occasional protein thrown in," he added as he folded up the bag and set it on the counter. "For the record, I don't plan on interrogating you, Lana."

"Why not?" She focused on the food, because it gave her something to do other than feel nervous whenever she looked at him. "You wouldn't be the first."

Eamon was supposed to be her safety net. Her one reliable option left in a life gone roller-coaster wild. She wasn't supposed to be feeling, well, anything other than at ease around him. Instead, her insides buzzed as if she'd dragged an entire nest of bald-faced hornets with her from Washington.

"All right, then." He sounded almost resigned. "What changed your mind about Marcus's death? When we spoke at the funeral, it seemed pretty cut-and-dried that it was an accident."

"A hit-and-run." She dropped a knife into the burger and cut it in half. "At the time I didn't see how it could be anything else. Not with how it happened. I was in a fog back then, Eamon. His death knocked me sideways. I wasn't thinking straight for months." The drinking hadn't helped. It had been a fast and easy way to dull the pain, and then it had been the only way she could get through the day.

And then through the nights.

"I shouldn't have gone back to work so fast. I see that now. But what else was I going to do?" She knew she didn't have to explain herself to Eamon. "Without Marcus, the only thing I had left was my work."

"What happened?" Eamon's tone remained light. Calm. As if they weren't discussing one of the most intimate and devastating events of her life.

"I had this…" She blew out a breath. "I guess you could call it a flashback. I'd only been back on the job for a couple of weeks. My partner and I were called to the scene of an accident." She hesitated, took a bite of her food, mainly because she knew that once she got into the details of what she'd been chasing, she'd probably lose whatever appetite she had. "It was a hit-and-run and I reacted…badly."

"No one could blame you for that," Eamon said.

"Actually, yeah, they could." She swallowed hard. "But it was my own fault. Because I'd never said anything. Didn't tell anyone…" She looked over his shoulder, at the stunning seascape painting mounted on the wall behind him. The interplay of colors and imagery of jagged cliffs overlooking a stormy ocean niggled something in the back of her mind. "Is that a Renault?"

Eamon glanced around, lifted one shoulder. "Sure is. Is this a stalling tactic or do you follow Greta's work?"

Both. "Greta. You call her Greta?"

"I tend to use people's names when I speak with them." His lips twitched as he refocused on his meal. "Greta Renault is a friend. She's also married to a local detective I've worked with on and off. If you stick in town awhile, I can get you in for a sneak peek at the gallery she's going to be opening by the end of summer."

"That might be worth enduring a notorious Sacramento summer for," she murmured, enjoying the normal conversation. She'd missed normal. "She had a show up in Seattle a couple of years ago." Lana neglected to mention it had been one of the last events she and Marcus had attended together. "I only spoke with her briefly. The place was packed, but I must have walked around looking at her work for hours. It felt like visiting another world. I can't believe you have one just hanging there like it's—"

"Art?" Eamon grinned. "Funny how that happens when you put a frame around something. I haven't had the heart to take it to my apartment in San Francisco yet. It seems at home here."

"Marcus refused to buy one. He said he wasn't open to the competition." The comment slipped out so effortlessly and without so much as a stab of pain that she wondered if she'd imagined she'd said it. "He was teasing, of course. He actually did make a bid on one, but it was already sold. Sorry." She sat back, pressed her fingers to her temples. "I'm all over the place. I've been on my own with all this for so long I think maybe I've forgotten how to have an actual conversation."

"You're doing fine." He reached over and nudged her plate closer. "You'd probably do better if your brain had something to work off. What is it you didn't tell anyone before?"

She was standing on the precipice of a moment. This was usually when things went in one of two directions. Either the person listening interpreted her statement as being trapped in the circle of never-ending grief and guilt or that she'd been imagining things and her mind was only trying to help her heal. At this point, Eamon was her last shot at making sense of the entire situation.

"I was on the phone with Marcus when it happened. When

he was hit by that car." She said it rip-the-bandage-off quick. "I heard the entire thing. It wasn't an accident."

Eamon swallowed, set his burger down and picked up his napkin, wiped his mouth. She watched him, her own pulse hammering in her throat to the point she could hear it pounding in her ears. She could only imagine what he was thinking. The same thing her former partner thought. Her bosses thought. The investigating officers she'd browbeaten a few short weeks ago into finally showing her the accident report thought. Each of those responses had been expected and, in a way, motivating. But she wasn't sure she could bear it if Eamon jumped on that thought train along with them.

"I'm not lying."

He frowned. "I don't think you are."

"I'm not imagining things either. Marcus was walking back to his car after a late dinner meeting with his boss when he called me. He'd had to reschedule his return flight and was due to fly back first thing in the morning. He was worried I'd be angry."

"Why would you be angry?"

Now was not the time to be stingy with the details. "We'd had a huge fight before he left. I didn't like how often he was away, all these last-minute out-of-town meetings he got called to. All of a sudden he'd be gone days or even weeks at a time. Of course, he countered by reminding me he wasn't thrilled about the hours I spent at the station and with murder victims." She hesitated. "I think we were both terrified at the idea of starting a family and that was just our way of trying to hash things out."

"Ah." He nodded. "I understand."

She gave him credit for not sounding completely shocked.

It had been a decision she'd struggled with for months, but when she'd finally made it, it had just made sense. "I thought I was pregnant, a couple of months earlier. For those few minutes, before the test results come in, you see all the directions your life can go. When I found out I wasn't, we were both, I don't know, sad. I told him when he called that night that I was willing to make some changes, transfer departments if we really wanted to give it a shot."

"You were going to leave Homicide?"

"I know. Impossible for me, right? I mean, I know a lot of women can make it work, Homicide and having a family, but you know my history, Eamon. I grew up a latchkey kid. My parents were always working, hardly ever around, and when they were—"

"You wished you were anywhere else," Eamon finished. "Yeah, I remember you telling me."

"He grew up in foster care. He didn't really have any stability or direction until he was a teenager. Still, I believed in Marcus, in us. So I was ready to make a go of the kid thing, which is what I told Marcus when he called. I'd initiated the necessary changes so we could start our own family." Her heart twisted at the ghostly memory of her husband's laughter ringing over the phone. "Turns out his last-minute meeting with his boss was his idea so he could let her know he was going to take some time off, reevaluate his priorities." For a future that would never come to pass.

"We were laughing about our similar plan when I heard this horrible thump." She heard that sound every time she closed her eyes. "Then the tires screeched and there was an odd crackling sound before another thud." That sound bodies made when they hit the ground without any resistance.

After almost a decade in Homicide, she'd finally experienced something that had horrified her to the point of emotional paralysis. "I don't think I realized I was screaming his name until…" Until her head had stopped spinning and she'd all but yelled herself hoarse.

Eamon stretched his hand across the table, caught hers and, for the second time that night, steadied her to the point her lungs relaxed and the memory slipped back into the dark places where she stored it up tight. "Why didn't you tell me?" he whispered. "That you'd heard it all happen?"

"Honestly? At the time, I thought maybe I did imagine it. That I was just looking for some way, any way, to cope."

"And later?"

She shook her head. "I didn't think you'd believe me." Now that she'd started, she couldn't stop. Especially when she had someone willing to listen. To hear her. "There was someone who picked up his phone after he was hit. A woman. She told me he'd been hurt and she'd seen it happen, and that she'd called 911. They were waiting with him until they got there. She…" Lana took a shaky breath. "She held the phone up to Marcus's ear so I could talk to him and I tried to. I tried so hard to tell him everything was going to be all right, but I think I knew. From the second I heard that thump, I knew he wasn't going to come home. The next thing I remember is his phone went dead. When my phone rang again, it was the Boston police telling me what had happened." She took a long, deep breath to relax even as her hold on Eamon's hand tightened. "I've had eighteen months to come to terms with all this, Eamon. I've spent a good chunk of that time focused on what I heard that night. I was not imagining things. It wasn't an accident. I know it wasn't. You need to believe me."

"I do."

She couldn't have heard him correctly. She'd hoped. Even prayed. But she'd also spent the past few days preparing herself for the fact that any conversation with Eamon might very well end just like the others had. However, her tenuous faith in him had been proved right... Her breath shuddered in her chest and her lungs expanded for the first time in months. "You do?"

"Based on what you've told me. You said the tires screeching came after the thump. Makes me think no one hit the brakes ahead of time to avoid him."

"Exactly." Her throat constricted around the word. Her heart beat so fast it was as if it were trying to catch up with her breath. "That's exactly what I told my boss, Captain Davis, but she said the local police back there had numerous eyewitness accounts that contradicted that."

"Cops will always accept eyewitness testimony over ear testimony every time. You know that."

"Especially when said witnesses are unbiased observers." She sighed. "My commanding officer suggested I was looking for new ways to cope. To find answers where there weren't any questions. If I had a nickel for every time she said 'accidents happen'..."

"Accidents do happen," Eamon said. "But I'm not going to say that's definitely the case here. Not without doing a bit of investigating myself."

It hadn't occurred to her how freeing it might feel to have someone listen to her and actually hear what she'd said. Suddenly her growling stomach's insistence wasn't nearly the nuisance it had been. She almost didn't have time to process the actual taste of the food before she'd eaten the first half of her burger, then reached for the second. If Eamon's expression told her anything, it was that he was tongue-tied due to amusement and self-satisfaction at having been proved right.

"You just made the last few days of waiting around worth it." She made herself slow down, give her stomach time to adjust to functioning fully again. "Where do you think we should start?"

"We can start with what you've done so far to prove your theory about the hit-and-run."

"What I've done?"

He closed his take-out container and stood up to stash it in the fridge. "You admitted you've been working on this for the past…what? Year? Eighteen months? Who have you talked to?"

"About that." One of the things that made him a stellar agent was the fact he remembered every little thing he ever heard or learned.

"You also hinted at the fact I'm one of your last options moving forward. So." He washed his hands, set the paper bag in a bin by the door for recycling. "How many people involved with Marcus's case have you ticked off?"

All of them. From the Boston police commissioner, to the on-site detectives, right down to the patrol officers who had been first on scene. "I'm sure there are some who would be willing to talk to us. To you," she added. "If you don't mention my name."

"Seattle PD didn't tell you to take your vacation days, did they, Lana?"

"There are all kinds of ways to tell someone something." She couldn't quite meet his gaze. "I've been honest about his case, Eamon."

"Now you need to be honest about your actions. I can't go into this blind, Lana, or worse, misinformed. If you want me to dig in, I need to know what roadblocks are waiting for me. Preparation is going to be half the battle."

Whether she was full or his warning killed her appetite, she couldn't be certain. Either way, she was done eating. "I've got a list of everyone I spoke with. I've got notes about those conversations." So many notes that didn't make any sense. "As far as my vacation is concerned, I might have been a bit too loose with the word. I'm on indefinite leave."

"You mean you've been suspended."

She shrugged.

"And when did that leave start?" he asked.

She found it amazing how high she could feel one minute before plummeting to the bottom of the barrel. She stood, shoved her hands into the front pockets of her jeans and rocked back on her heels. "A little over four months ago." She could feel the sobriety chip slip between her fingers where it provided both comfort and pressure. Eamon wasn't dumb. He could put two and two together.

"So, was it your investigating Marcus's death or your drinking that triggered your suspension?" He didn't sound angry. In fact, he didn't even sound disappointed. More like he was gathering pertinent information to move forward with. It should have come as a relief, but instead it annoyed her.

"One has an awful lot to do with the other," she said. With disturbing ease, she pushed aside the doubt that statement brought up. "Heading home to an empty house every night was tough, and the only way I could stop obsessing about how he died was to have a few drinks at the end of the day."

And then the days had gotten longer. The drinks more plentiful. "I took some shortcuts I shouldn't have. Didn't pay attention as closely as I maybe once did. I'm better now." She could only hope he didn't pick up the doubt in her voice.

"But your obsession with these questions of yours has kicked in."

"I need answers," she said flatly. "I came to you because I know you know what that's like. I don't mean to make it sound like what happened to Marcus is in any way as horrific as what happened to Chloe."

He shook his head. "For you, it is. You don't owe me an apology for that. I'll do what I can to help, Lana. But there are only two outcomes here, right?"

It took all her energy not to cringe.

"We either discover you're right, or we find out you're wrong. At the moment we're at fifty-fifty. You get that?"

"I know what I heard." She wasn't about to entertain the notion she was wrong. "My reputation as a detective might be ruined, but I can't stop trusting what few instincts I've got left. Marcus was murdered. If I give in to doubt, I may as well walk away right now."

He looked at her for a long moment. And she looked back. She saw a friend, a man she knew she could rely on. And she saw doubt shining in those tranquil, albeit determined, eyes that held fewer shadows than they once did.

"All right." Eamon picked up his plate and carried it over to the sink.

"Yeah?" She felt a jolt of excitement charge through her system when he glanced over his shoulder and nodded. "You'll help me?"

"Of course I'll help you."

"Okay." She breathed out air she had been holding for months. "All right. So, what's the plan?"

"The plan is to make a plan. Tomorrow," he said quietly as he washed and set the dishes into the rack to dry. "As much as I'd like to dive in right away, I haven't slept more than three hours a night for the past week. I've got to get some shut-eye."

"Right. Of course." She winced. She should have paid closer attention. He did look wiped out. But just the sight of him had been so welcome she hadn't let herself notice just how exhausted he must be. "I'll head back to my motel, see if I can get some sleep myself." Fat chance. She was as wired as she'd been on her first undercover assignment.

"Or." He indicated the sliding doors into the bedroom. "You could crash in there and I'll take the sofa."

"What? Absolutely not." She shook her head.

"Then you take the sofa," he insisted. "We both know you're going to work off this energy you have on that laptop I'm sure you've got set up wherever you've bunked into."

"For the record, my laptop is in the trunk of my rental in the parking lot, and the motel I found near Old Town is perfectly satisfactory." Overstatement of the decade, but given her threadbare finances these days—four months without an income was proving more difficult than expected—the cheap, fifty-buck-a-night motel had been what she could afford. It had also been the first one she'd come across when she'd hit downtown Sacramento. "But I'll take you up on your offer of the sofa." She needed the added incentive of his presence to keep her on the straight and narrow. She recognized the energy zinging through her system. It was a boost that made her feel invincible, and that feeling was rarely a good thing for those in recovery. But there were other ways to burn off that energy. "Truly, the sofa looks great."

"Hang on." He disappeared into the bedroom, returned with a stack of sheets, a lightweight blanket and a selection of T-shirts and boxers.

She grinned and plucked up a plaid pair of said shorts and dangled them in the air. "Guess that answers the question as to whether you're a boxers or a briefs kinda man."

"I'm too tired to laugh." He set the rest of the stack on the edge of the plush sofa with a pull-out strap that would instantly transform the sofa into a bed. When he turned, she was standing right behind him.

"Thank you, Eamon." She was close enough she could feel the warmth of his body, smell the remnants of aftershave drifting off his heated skin. "You'll never know how much it means that you listened. That you're willing to help."

The sudden tension in his body had her inclining her head, her mind filled with new puzzles tempting her to solve them. She lifted a hand to his face, and her fingers tingled at the sensation of red stubble on his cheek. Lana rose up on her toes, just enough to put their mouths at equal level, but before she leaned in, his hands caught her shoulders.

"Don't, Lana."

"Oh." She blinked, embarrassment flooding through her like a dam had broken. "Jeez. Of course. That was… Wow." She tried to step back, but he tightened his hands and kept her in place even as she squeezed her eyes shut so as not to look at him. "I guess I let gratitude cloud my judgment. Overstepped those friendship boundaries. Won't happen again."

"Please don't say that."

His murmured plea had her questioning her hearing once more. It almost sounded as if... "Don't say sorry?"

"Don't say it won't happen again." He took what she interpreted as a reluctant step forward. "We're both exhausted. It's been a long few days for each of us. Now isn't the time to be making decisions we can't change after the fact."

"So..." She frowned, confused. "You're not saying no. You're just saying not right now."

He lifted his hand, cupped her face in his palm and very gently brushed his mouth against hers. "I'm saying sleep on this and let me know if you feel the same in the morning."

She pressed her lips together, trapping the spicy taste of him. The butterflies in her belly, the zinging in her fingertips as she touched his bare arm, left her speaking before thinking. "What time in the morning?"

He chuckled, ducked his head and pressed his forehead against hers. "I want you clearheaded and thinking straight when you come to my bed." He stood up straight, just enough to put a hair's-breadth distance between them. "Lest you think this is me being chivalrous and levelheaded, I'll tell you that this might be the most difficult decision I've made in my life. My bed, any bed, is where I've wanted you for a very long time. I just want to make sure you're there for the right reasons."

"I can think of a couple of reasons off the top of my head," she teased, unwilling to dwell on the fact that his statement had just thrown her into an entirely new level of confusion. Eamon wanted her? *Wanted her* wanted her? As impulsive as her attempt to kiss him had been, she honestly hadn't considered...

"How about we keep the changes in our relationship to

a minimum until we get you on the other side of Marcus's death, yeah?" Eamon suggested.

Curse the man for making sense. He knew grief had brought her to his door. He wasn't going to take advantage of that. Or of her. Surprising? Not at all. Irritating? Only so far as she now realized the sofa was not going to be particularly comfortable for her for very long.

"As I've reached my politeness quota for the day," Eamon said, "I'm going to grab a quick shower. I'll leave you plenty of hot water." He pressed his mouth to her forehead, but only increased her frown lines by doing so. How had she managed to spin the one remaining stable part of her life off its axis? "Good night, Lana."

"Yeah," she whispered as he disappeared behind the bathroom door and left her churning with new regret and longing. "Good night."

Chapter Three

The mattress dipped behind Eamon and he shifted, rolling onto his back as Lana's silhouette moved. The curvy outline of her frame was all too familiar even in the darkness. He'd imagined this moment so many times, longed for reality to call and place her in his arms, a place he'd tried desperately for years to tell himself she didn't belong.

"Eamon." His name on her lips had him reaching out his hand, brushing his fingers against the warm softness of her cheek, down the side of her neck, over her rounded shoulders. Her scent, an intoxicating combination of subtle floral and the barest hint of citrus, wafted around him, drawing him up even as he pulled her close.

He shouldn't be doing this. He shouldn't even be thinking this. She'd come to him for help, not only to solve the supposed mystery of her husband's death, but to push her through the grief that was as prominent as the staccato beating of his heart.

Her name sat poised behind his lips, lips that could only search out hers to quell the building desire inside him. A desire that, for the first time in his memory, felt as if it might actually be abated by her touch.

The moment his mouth brushed hers, she evaporated. Her entire being vanished in a shimmering burst of mist that left his hands filled with nothing but unfulfilled promise and his ears ringing with a constant beat he couldn't tune out.

A ringing that grew louder by the moment.

Eamon's entire body jerked as he pulled himself out of the dream. His fingers tingled, as if the sensation of being with her was still pulsing through his system. He groaned, dropped an arm over his eyes as he rolled onto his back and tried to ignore the frustration and disappointment crashing through him.

He sighed, dropped his arm and stared up at the ceiling, frowning as that incessant ringing continued, only now it had an added buzzing he soon realized possessed the power to drive him over the edge.

Eamon sat up, reached for his cell he'd plugged in on the nightstand, only to find it completely dormant and, if he had to guess, a bit cranky at having been disturbed during its charging sequence.

He shoved himself up, adjusting his drawstring black pajama bottoms as he pried open the sliding door into the living room. The buzzing and ringing intensified as he identified the culprit.

Lana's cell phone vibrated against the glass coffee table scant inches away from where she slept, burrowed so deep in the cushions of the sofa he suspected he'd need an excavation crew to get her out. No wonder she hadn't heard her cell. But even as he lifted the phone, he felt reassured she felt safe enough with him to sleep so deeply. Only a small part of him hoped she was having as good a time in dreamland as he had been. He could only imagine how often he'd regret declining her offer.

There were fewer things he wanted in life more than Lana Tate in his bed. But he'd meant what he'd told her earlier: he wanted her there clearheaded, doubt-free and for the right reasons.

At least now there was hope of it happening. That thought lifted his mood considerably as he checked the screen of her phone.

It had gone quiet, but only for a few seconds before it started up again. He walked back into his room and lifted the blinds to look out over the alley between the Brass Eagle and the independent bookstore that had opened a few months ago. It always amazed him how eerily quiet those midnight hours could get, even in a major city the size of Sacramento. So quiet he could hear the buzzing of the streetlamps, one of which streamed far too brightly through the now unobstructed pane.

"Detective Tate's phone." Whoever was calling clearly was determined to reach her, and seeing as he couldn't reach through the phone and strangle the caller, answering seemed the lesser of two evils.

"Lana Tate?" The squeaky, uncertain voice on the other end left Eamon wondering if this was a pip-squeak of an informant.

"She's unavailable at the moment." He scrubbed his free hand over his eyes, longing for the sleep that had proved anything but restful. "Can I help you with something?"

"Uh." The hesitation sounded couched in uncertainty. "Sorry. This is the number she left at the front desk."

The background noise pushed its way through Eamon's

foggy mind. He could hear sirens and car engines and more than a number of voices bellowing and shouting.

"Front desk where?" Eamon snapped on the bedside table lamp and was instantly alert.

"Shine A Light Motel. I'm the night clerk. She checked in three days ago but I didn't see her come back tonight. The officers on scene—"

"Back up. Slow down," Eamon ordered in his practiced, calm tone. "What's your name?"

"Myron. But my friends call me Skates."

It sounded as if Myron, aka Skates, was younger than the cell phone Eamon was currently holding. "Skates, I'm FBI special agent Eamon Quinn. I'm a friend of Detective Tate's."

"FBI? She's a cop? Whoa, man, I didn't get that from her at all when she—"

"What's going on?"

"Right. Sorry. I've never had anything happen like this. I mean, take a name, a credit card and phone number. That's all I'm supposed to do, but I'm not cut out for—"

"Skates?" Eamon's voice sharpened.

"Sorry. You should see what's going on around this place. It's like I'm in a movie or something. There's a fire. They think it started in room 113. That's Ms. Tate's room."

"Anyone hurt?"

"Nah, man. I don't think so. We evacuated the entire place."

"Who's the officer in charge?" Eamon demanded as he walked over to his duffel and pulled out the last set of clean clothes he had.

"Officer Bowman and his partner. I didn't get her name. Should I have? I can go ask—"

"No. But I need you to go to Officer Bowman and tell him you spoke with me and that I'll be there with Detective Tate shortly. Can you do that, Skates?"

"Yeah, man. I can. He's standing right there by his patrol—"

"I'll speak to you when I get there. Thanks, Skates." He hung up, tossed Lana's cell onto his bed and got dressed. He was still pulling a black T-shirt over his jeans when he brought her phone out to her. Even as he stood over her, he hated to wake her. But he didn't have a choice. "Lana." He set her phone down, reached out a hand and touched her shoulder. "Lana. Wake up."

It shouldn't have surprised him, the force with which she shot out of a dead sleep. In the dim glow from his bedroom, the gold rings dangling from the chain around her neck glinted in the light. He stepped back and held his arms up and stared down at the sidearm she'd whipped out from beneath her pillow. The panic and fear in her eyes told him a number of things first and foremost. Most importantly that she clearly hadn't told him everything that had been going on.

Cops, law enforcement people in general, could wake at an instant and be on alert; power naps were second nature and vital to maintaining control over long cases especially. But there was a ghostly shadow in her gaze that had Eamon going against his training as he very carefully, very gently reached out and grasped the barrel of her weapon.

"You're okay, Lana." He pushed the gun down, pressed his fingers against hers to loosen her grip as he pulled the firearm free. It had to be her backup piece. They'd have taken away her sidearm along with her badge, thanks to the suspension. "I'm sorry I had to wake you." It was a lie. Now at least, since he'd seen just how skittish she was. "The manager at your motel called. There's been a fire. They think it started near your room." He walked around, turned on the table lamp. "You didn't leave a curling iron plugged in or something, did you?"

"What?" She shoved her long hair out of her face, frowning up at him as her eyes cleared. "Sorry. Fire? At the motel? I don't own a curling iron."

It was then he saw the bottle of Scotch he'd bought a few weeks ago next to the lamp. And the empty tumbler next to it. Something inside him twisted. He picked up the glass, held it in his hand. And looked at her.

"Don't look at me that way, Eamon. The glass is clean," she muttered, shaking her head. "I'll admit I got thirsty, but I didn't take a drink. I went to sleep instead. Happens all the time."

He shook his head, attempted to quell the disappointment churning inside him. Not necessarily in her, but in himself for not having realized how far off-kilter their earlier discussion must have pushed her. "You need to get dressed."

"Right. Fire at the motel. I heard that." She nodded, shoved up, then dropped back down. "My room?"

"Seems so. I know the officers on scene. We need to get there. Now."

"Ever wonder if the universe has it in for you, Special Agent Quinn?" She snatched up the jeans and T-shirt she'd tossed over the back of one of the chairs and, after turning her back on him, stripped out of the sleepwear he'd given her. "I don't know how I got the gigantic Kick Me sign on my back, but I want it off."

Speaking of her back, the sight of Lana's bare skin glistening against the soft light from the living room lamp had his hand tightening around the gun he still held. She made stripping down and getting dressed look like a choreographed ballet straight off the Met stage. The fluidity with which she moved, the efficiency as she whipped her hair out from under the collar before she jammed her long legs into her jeans, had him memorizing the sight for what he knew would be the stuff of dreams for years to come.

"You want to know what I'm thinking at the moment?" Lana demanded as she held out her hand for her gun, shoved it into the back waistband of her jeans. "I'm thinking what I wouldn't give for you not to have believed me last night when I told you about Marcus. Someone setting my motel on fire would give me one major reason to say how right I was."

Nothing to argue about there. "Who knew you were coming to see me?"

"No one." She spun around, zipped up her jeans and, after digging into her back pocket, pulled out an elastic for her hair. "I left on impulse, for the most part. My social calendar hasn't exactly been filled, so there was only one dinner I needed to cancel. I asked my neighbor to water Marcus's plants. She's done a better job at keeping those things alive than I have. Even if I had mentioned you, as far as I knew you were in San Francisco. And I told you, I didn't even decide where I was going to stay until I got off the freeway."

"You didn't notice anyone following you?"

"No." She frowned. "But I wouldn't have really thought to look, would I?" She scrubbed both hands down her face. "I probably should have."

Eamon wasn't about to pile on to her self-realization. "You

said you've been looking into Marcus's accident for months. You talk to anyone recently?"

"I called his former assistant at the law firm a few days before I left." Her sigh betrayed her exhaustion, but now that he'd started asking questions, he couldn't stop. "I might have asked if she had a list of Marcus's clients I could see, but she's a kid, Eamon. Twenty-three, just out of college. She was trying not to cry while we spoke. She only wants to help."

"Doesn't mean she didn't tell anyone she spoke with you. What about the list you asked for? Did she send it?"

"Yeah." She nodded. "I haven't gotten around to looking at it in detail yet. I've got it on my laptop, though."

In her car, thankfully. "And I need you to make a list of—"

"Everyone I've spoken to since I started digging around?" The strained patience in her voice actually made him feel better. "I haven't lost all my policing abilities, Eamon. I know not to leave a laptop in a motel room. Not only does it stay with me, I've got cloud access to it on my phone." She motioned to her cell on the coffee table, then frowned. "How did you answer it?"

"Answer what?"

"My cell. It's facial recognition or a code. FYI, you look nothing like me. How did you answer it?"

"Thirty-three-oh-eight."

Her eyes narrowed.

"You're a 49er fan living in Seahawk country." Eamon was grateful to be able to tease her about something. "Roger Craig and Steve Young's jersey numbers. You have signed ones hanging in your house."

"Remind me to change that code to my backup when this is over," she muttered.

"Sixteen-eight-seven." His grin widened at her glare. "Montana and Dwight Clark. You told me once your dad used to watch 'The Catch' on a loop to gear up for football season."

"Your memory terrifies me," she said as she headed to the door. "Your car or mine?"

THEY TOOK HIS SUV, but not until after Lana made a pit stop and grabbed her computer bag out of the trunk of the rental and stashed it in the back of Eamon's SUV. It might have taken her a while to get fully conscious, but now that she was, she felt like she'd been zapped by yet another energy beam. Sitting still for any length of time was going to be an issue. She could just tell.

Which meant she regretted the decision to ride shotgun within seconds of him exiting the parking lot at the back of the Brass Eagle. Staring out at the night sky punctuated by glaring streetlamps only gave her time to think. And all those thoughts spinning untethered only made her begin to spiral and feel as if she might suffocate.

She'd been a cop for eleven years. It was all she'd ever wanted to do after spending most of her childhood watching old cop show reruns. She was a good cop. A really good one. She rubbed hard fingers across her forehead. At least, she had been. Unlike a lot of officers, she'd loved her time on patrol. She'd built up a good communications network working the streets. People knew her and she made it a point to know them. Situation, status, even criminal tendencies didn't define a person—but knowing someone's name, on the other hand, went a long way to building trust. Whether they gave it or she remembered it, there was something powerful about that exchange that kept her reputation solid among the people she'd sworn to protect.

As good a patrol officer as she'd been, she was an even better detective. She prided herself on looking outside the box, examining angles that might otherwise go unnoticed or ignored. Every investigation was different, just as every person was. It was her responsibility to be open to absolutely everything.

But that was before she'd been on the other end of an investigation. Before she'd come up against the stone wall of instant "it was an accident" mindset that had never, from the second she'd heard the words, rung completely true. Of course, that was hindsight telling her this.

Instinct was as vital to a detective as evidence. She couldn't follow one without the other, and every instinct, even as it had lain dormant beneath the grief of losing her husband, had screamed at her that something was very, very wrong.

By the time she'd been able to hear those screams, she was so far beyond a reasonable time frame that there was no one left to believe her. Or advocate for her. Instead of being listened to, she'd been humored and tolerated and, later, if the attitude of her fellow detectives back in Seattle was any indication, pitied.

"I can hear you thinking all the way over here." Eamon's voice broke into her thoughts before they turned to the dangerous coping mechanism that had gotten her suspended from the force. "Want to talk it out?"

"Not really. Pity parties are best attended solo."

He frowned, made a left turn and headed for the plumes of gray-tinged smoke in the distance, blocking out what few stars twinkled above. "There's nothing self-pitying about you, Lana. We cope how we cope at the time. Right or wrong. Hasn't your sponsor taught you that?"

"I don't have a sponsor." She'd gone to meetings, off and on, for the past few months. She'd listened to others, empathized and sympathized, but she hadn't been able to take that final step and open herself up with her own experiences. Heck, she hadn't even been able to bring herself to utter that sober-life confirming line *Hi, I'm Lana and I'm an...*

She shook her head to clear it. It had taken her three tries to make it past thirty days. Stop and start. Strengthen, then fall off the wagon. Where was the power in sharing failure like that?

Every time she'd made the decision to get sober, she got stronger. At least, that was what she told herself. She'd gone back occasionally, most recently to claim her ninety-day chip. But she didn't share. She didn't...confess and purge. All she'd needed was the physical reminder of what was possible. "Sometimes it's difficult to remember I need to take things a day at a time."

"Sometimes it's an hour or even a minute at a time." He glanced at her. "Friend of mine reminded me of that on more than one occasion. He still goes to meetings when he feels the need."

"How long does he have?"

"Not really sure," Eamon said. "Years at least. He only looks at the day he's living in, not the past. But he'll be the first to admit some days are harder than others. It helps he has a lot to live for now. Second chance with his wife. New baby. And by *new* I mean the little guy's just over a month old."

Envy slipped through her like midnight fog on the bay. What she wouldn't give to have that life. That mindset. Instead, she seemed to get a perverse kind of pleasure challenging herself to see how long she could stare into a bottle before she decided whether to drink or not.

"It's strange, to hear you talk about your friends and their families," she said, more to herself than to him. "I don't think we ever really talked about that kind of stuff when we worked together." Doing so now seemed a better solution to regaining control.

"You liked to keep your personal life separate from the job," Eamon said. "I understood that. For the record, I'm honorary uncle to not one, but three little'uns, thanks to Eden, Allie and Simone."

"Those were your sister's friends." Lana recalled him mentioning them when he'd told her about his sister. They'd been with her the night Chloe had disappeared, when the girls had been camping in one of their backyards. Her body had been found a few days later in a field of flowers. "You mentioned them a few times. Three kiddos, huh?"

"Make that soon to be five, actually," Eamon boasted. "Eden's expecting her second girl in a few months. Chloe Ann is looking forward to being a big sister. Or so she thinks," he added with a quick smile. "And then Greta's due... What is it?" He scrunched his brow. "Around Halloween? Getting hard to keep track."

"Chloe Ann?" Lana's throat tightened around the familiar name. "Eden named her daughter after your sister?"

"Yeah." There was no mistaking the tinge of sadness in his voice. "The three of them—Eden, Simone and Allie— had an agreement. First girl born among them got the name."

"You love it, don't you? The big family bit."

"I really do. Surprising, right? Turns out I always had it, even when I didn't realize it." He stopped at a red light and farther along she could see spinning lights. "After Chloe was murdered, my parents couldn't take staying here. Then my father couldn't take staying, period. It was just me and Mom for a lot of years in the Bay Area. She tried to start over, but she was stuck. Couldn't move on. A good part of her died with Chloe, I think. It just took another twenty years for her body to follow." His hands tightened on the steering wheel. "She passed three weeks after we found the person responsible. Mom's with her now. At least, that's what I like to believe. I miss my mom a lot, but she wasn't meant to be here without Chloe. And now I have another family, here in Sacramento."

"Family is what you make, not always what you're born to," Lana said more to herself than to him. Something else to be envious of. "You haven't married, though, have you?"

"Me? No."

An odd wave of relief washed over her. "Why not? Never found the right woman?"

"Right woman wasn't available."

Her eyes went wide before she ducked her chin and berated herself for slipping into the role he'd assigned. He'd said something about having wanted her in his bed, but that was entirely different from wanting to be in someone's life 100 percent. Not that being involved with Eamon would be a bad thing. Quite the contrary. Now that she thought about it, it almost felt...

"Well, this is interesting."

"What?" She glanced up as Eamon pulled into the parking lot of the two-story motel that, at this moment, looked as if it had been reset in a war zone.

"Familiar faces. Detective faces. They must have found something." He parked near the office beside an almost identical dark SUV. "Coming?"

"Yeah." She unbuckled her belt, pulled out her sidearm and stashed it in Eamon's glove compartment, then double-checked that she had her phone before kicking her purse under the front seat.

When she caught up to him, she nearly missed a step. The front of the motel was singed and smoking, black soot covering most of the facade. Smoke continued to billow into the sky, but whatever live flames had licked the building clean had been extinguished by the two fire trucks parked haphazardly in the lot.

A couple of the cars had taken hits as well. Hoods had black splotches and piles of ash floating away in the breeze. Windshields were blown out and scorch marks littered the asphalt. And there, in the center of it all, room 113.

She coughed, choked on the smoke and ash in the air. "Was anyone hurt?"

"Not that I'm aware of," Eamon said.

"There's the good news, at least. That place is a total loss," she said to Eamon, who nodded in agreement. "Guess I'm going to have to go shopping for some clothes. And shoes. My favorite pair of work boots were in there." She planted her hands on her hips, stared at the destruction, even as she felt slightly ill at the thought of being the potential cause. She blinked quickly and tried to get her eyes to stop burning. "Tell me there was a gas leak or something."

"Afraid we can't do that." She turned at the voice and

found a pair of plainclothes detectives nearby. One was taller than the other, a bit ganglier than the other, but both were fit. The one who spoke had dark hair while the other was blond, with a charming grin she suspected stayed permanently in place. "Eamon," the dark-haired cop said. "The night manager told Bowie you'd be stopping by. This her?"

"If by *her* you mean Detective Lana Tate, then yes." Lana offered her hand. "I am her. Detective?"

"Cole Delaney," he said easily. "This is my partner, Detective Jack McTavish."

"Pleased to meet you, Lana," Jack said. "We've heard absolutely nothing about you." He aimed that widening smile at Eamon, who rolled his eyes in a way that actually had Lana chuckling. "And it's Jack, please. Sorry about your room and your belongings."

"Hi, Jack. Thanks." Lana felt instantly at ease with both men, no doubt because she knew Eamon considered them friends. "Eamon said only uniforms were on scene. What changed and brought in two detectives?"

"Night manager mentioned someone had set a fire in Lana's room when I spoke with him earlier," Eamon supplied.

"Night manager got it partially right," Cole said. "Arson investigators can't get in until the morning, but the crew found beer bottle remnants right near the bed."

"Well, I know that wasn't from you," Eamon said. "She hates beer," he added at Cole's blank stare.

A chill raced down Lana's spine despite the warm night. "Molotov cocktail?"

"That'd be my guess," Cole said with a nod. "We'll get a full report in a day or so. In the meantime, the entire motel's been evacuated. Bowie and Clarke are working with the local Red Cross to find alternate housing for the displaced customers and residents. Not much else we can do here except get in the way."

"Residents." Her stomach dropped straight to her toes. "I should have... Where will they go?"

"Local motels have been working with the city to get the homeless off the streets," Eamon said. "A lot of them get subsidies to offer temporary housing to assist in helping them use addresses for employment and benefits. They'll find a place. Don't worry."

"It was literally the first place I saw when I hit town." Guilt had her swallowing hard. "Now they're back on the street because of me."

"No," Jack said. "They're displaced because someone threw a bomb through your window. This isn't your fault, Lana. But you can bet we're going to find whoever is responsible. Both for you and for them."

"An optimist detective," Lana said with a tight smile. "Didn't realize those still existed."

"Why don't you come by the station later today, give a statement?"

"And fill us in on the case you've been working," Cole said, rather than suggested.

Eamon's light touch on the base of her spine stopped her from tensing at the request. "We'll do that. Give you time to get a little shopping in first, right, Lana?"

Lana glared at him. Her idea of shopping was one-clicking to fill her closet. But that wasn't here nor there. She had come to Sacramento to ask Eamon for help, not get anyone else involved. She glanced toward the burned-out motel, nausea churning in her stomach.

"Works for me," Jack agreed. "I need to pick up a case of soy sauce on my way home. Greta's putting it on everything. Have to say, though, soy sauce on vanilla ice cream? Not half bad."

"If you say so," Cole muttered. "Beats Eden's cravings for milk and Doritos."

"The trials of soon-to-be fathers." That earned Eamon a slug on the shoulder before the detectives moved off to their cars. "What are the odds the firefighters let us anywhere near your room?" he asked her once their taillights disappeared down the street.

"I'd say somewhere between nil and nada," Lana said.

"Better to ask forgiveness than permission."

She stayed close, stepping over fire hoses and around equipment set out for easy access. The water was still spewing from overhead as the firefighters continued to keep the flames from reigniting. Rivulets of water soaked her shoes and made her toes squish against the dampness. They made it as close as a car that was parked a few doors down from Lana's room before they were stopped.

Eamon had his badge out so quick it was as if he'd blinked it into existence. "Agent Quinn, FBI," he said to the female firefighter who had stepped in front of him. She was on the short side, definitely the stout side, and had *Harvelle* spelled out along the front of her helmet. "Detective Tate," he added with an incline of his head toward Lana. "We were hoping to get a look at the point of origin."

"No can do, Agent," the woman said. "I let anyone pass, I'll be on KP duty for a month. Trust me, no one wants that." She kept her tone light, but the determination in her gaze told Lana this wasn't her first go-around in this kind of situation.

"I'm happy to talk to my captain, see if he'd be up for giving you a briefing, but this is as far as either of you goes."

"Got an ETA on that possible briefing?" Eamon asked.

"Ten, maybe fifteen minutes? He's on his way down from the roof now." She pointed behind them. "I'll send him your way when there's a break."

"Sounds good. Thanks."

"Were you expecting them to tell us more than Cole and Jack did?" she asked as he steered her toward the manager's office.

"Not even a little bit," Eamon said. "Just thought it was worth a shot." He scrunched his nose. "Hate fires. That stink stays in your nose for days."

"We could try to replace it with the stink of the coffee they have at the reception desk," she suggested.

"Caffeine would not be a bad idea."

"Is it ever?" She hugged her arms around her torso as they made their way across the parking lot to the office with the bumped-out window paralleling the street. "You ever wonder why they haven't started a caffeine anonymous group? CAG. Cag. Has a good ring to it."

Eamon's lips twitched. "Talk about a group the majority of the human race would have a need to join. Nice to hear your sense of humor is still intact, Tate."

"I aim to entertain, Special Agent." A sense of humor in this job was vital. "Since we've got time, I'm going to grab my laptop out of your car. Start getting those lists together you want to look at. Keys?"

He dug into his pocket and tossed her the fob. "I'll be inside talking to Skates."

"Who?"

"You'll find out," he warned before he headed inside.

From a distance, Lana beeped the alarm off and hit the release on the back hatch. She leaned in, grabbed for the strap of her bag, but it was caught in the seam between the back seats. She leaned farther in just as the side window exploded.

She yelped, pulled her legs in behind her and tucked into a ball as she was showered in glass. She heard the distinctive sound of a bullet hitting the side of the car, then another, and a third.

Automatically, she reached behind her for her weapon. She cursed. She'd stashed it in the glove box. Lana lifted her head slightly, guesstimating her odds of making it not only over the back seat, but all the way to the front. Another shot hit, this time coming through the open door, angling toward the gas tank. Her heart pounded in her ears as she considered her options. Outside, she'd only be a bigger target. Inside, she had to move. She needed to do something before one of those bullets hit the tank.

She only had to make it over the back seat to wedge between the driver and passenger...

Lana reached up, grabbed the top of the back seats and began to haul herself up, but another shot took out not only the second side window, but the one across from it. Air whooshed in through the car as she ducked back down.

She heard shouts and cries from all around her and the squeal of brakes before she felt firm hands wrap around her ankles and pull.

"No! Don't!" she cried as jagged fragments of glass cut into her arms and through her shirt. She could feel a deep scrape form up her right side. She was instantly released and she sat up. "Sorry," she said to a shocked-looking Eamon.

"There's glass everywhere." She plucked her shirt away from her body. Her blood dotted and bled through the rips and tears. "I don't have any other clothes at the moment."

She hadn't meant it to be funny, but the darkness in his gaze lifted. He held out a hand and she shoved herself forward and out of the car. Once her feet hit the ground, she breathed a bit easier. At least until she felt Eamon's hands on her again, skimming over every bit of her for injuries. She was trying to remind herself to breathe when he caught her face between his hands, peered down at her with such abject concern she barely saw a trace of the agent she knew.

"You're okay?" he demanded as three firefighters made their way over. "You're sure?"

"I'm okay. Nothing a few tubes of Neosporin won't fix." She laid her hands on his arms and squeezed a couple of times to get his attention. "Eamon, I'm fine. They missed." She glanced behind her, to the pile of glass on the floor of his car. There wasn't a window left other than the cracked windshield. "Well, they missed me, but oh, man. I am so sorry. Your car is totaled."

"Company car," he said stiffly. "I'll get another."

"Everyone okay?" It was the man Harvelle had identified as her captain who reached them first.

"Yes," Lana insisted. "I ducked in time," she said in a loud voice, noticing Eamon's skeptical expression.

"Best check the manager's office," Eamon suggested. "Bullets took out a couple of windows before Skates hit the floor."

"Right." The captain nodded. "We've got EMTs on-site. I'll send them over."

"Where are you going?" Eamon demanded when she pulled out of his hold and hurried to the passenger-side door.

She had her sidearm in her hand in seconds, double-checking the load and the chambered round before she shoved it into the back of her jeans. "Last time I leave it behind," she said as he stepped up beside her. She returned to the back, grabbed her laptop case and slung the strap over her shoulder. "You get a look at the car?"

"Late-model sedan. Dark blue or black. Partial plate."

"Anyone hurt?" she demanded.

"Other than you?" He grabbed her arms, held them out. "You're covered in cuts." He plucked out a shard of glass from her hair.

She dismissed his concern even as his touch warmed her. "What about the motel guests and residents? No one was hit, were they?"

"Not as far as I know," Eamon said. "The shooter seemed to know where they were aiming. And who they were shooting at."

"Yeah." She bent over, pulled her hair out of the elastic. Glass fragments rained onto the pavement as her hands began to shake. "Looks like that target on my back's getting bigger. Think maybe I asked someone the wrong questions about Marcus's death?"

"No," Eamon said slowly as he drew her close and slipped an arm around her shoulders. "I think you asked the right ones."

Chapter Four

"Here." Eamon's offer of a filled mug of coffee earned him an irritated, albeit reassuring, glare from Lana. She'd settled herself at the square table closest to the door in the break room at the Major Crimes division of the Sacramento Police Department with unsurprising ease. "Trust me, it's better than what was back at the motel. What I drank of it before the bullets started flying," he added at her smirk as he re-supplied the coffee condiments out of the bottom cabinet.

Lana sipped her coffee, looked surprised, then sipped again. "Not bad for cop coffee."

"Eden gave the department that fancy coffee machine for Christmas a couple of years ago," Eamon told her. "She said her husband's safety was reliant on his caffeine intake being sustainable and continuous. But truthfully? I think it's because she spends a lot of time here herself," he added at Lana's arched brow. He was on the edge of babbling. Something he rarely did except when he got scared.

Hearing those bullets hit the car where he knew Lana was inside might just qualify as the most terrified he'd been in a very long time. Given his profession and his own close calls, that was saying something. Normally, compartmentalizing things like this came easy, but then he'd learned early on that nothing was easy when Lana Tate was involved.

There were parts of him still quaking even as reawakened parts were already working on figuring out the fastest way out of the mess they found themselves in. He wanted to be on the other side of whatever this was, to get those answers she was so desperate for. He was keeping an open mind, or at least trying to. Lana needed someone to believe her. Believe in her.

Normally he'd be anxious to close a case to do just that: close it. But this time, it was what potentially waited for him on the other side of that case that drove him. Would there still be sparks between him and Lana outside of a professional environment?

There had been plenty of sparks last night. The second she'd touched him in the bar—let alone what had almost happened in his apartment—he'd been engulfed by a desire he'd long denied himself. A desire that was back in full force and in a way that put the motel flames to shame.

The sooner they put any questions about Marcus Tate to rest, the better. For Lana's own safety, most of all. That said, before the call from the motel, he wasn't entirely convinced her stalwart belief in her husband's death being anything other than an accident wasn't manifested grief. But since then her motel room had been torched and she'd been shot at like a plastic duck in an amusement park gallery.

That gave her story more than enough credibility.

On the other side of the door, the dulled voices of the ending night shift echoed in the distance. The changing of the guard, so to speak, was upon them with uniformed officers and detectives finishing up their rotations and readying themselves to head home. Eamon exchanged pleasantries with a number of them as they came in and out and earned a knowing expression from Lana that told him she was more than a little impressed at his friendliness with the local department.

If TV and movies were to be believed, the competition and animosity among and between law enforcement agencies made working together virtually impossible. The truth was that anger and resentment were rare. On more than one occasion, his arrival on scene to take over an investigation from local law enforcement had been welcomed and heartily accepted. But reality like that didn't make for good script writing, he supposed.

Everyone who swore an oath to serve and protect, be it local, state or federal, had one priority: to make things right and get the job done. If that meant working together, that was what they did. Egos rarely entered into it. That wasn't to say there weren't problem agents. Eamon had run into too many of those, but more often than not, the working relationship was smooth and mutually respectful.

Which was why Eamon often found himself at the Major Crimes division here in Sacramento. ADA Simone Armstrong-Sutton laughingly stated this was his office away from his office. Fair enough. He'd worked on more than a couple of cases with this department, with cops he respected and admired. While the local FBI office suited him fine and he got along well with his fellow agents, he couldn't help but be pulled toward the camaraderie he felt with these detectives and cops.

"Eamon." A short, compact Latino man rapped his knuckles on the door frame and stuck his head in as Eamon poured himself a second cup of coffee.

"Lieutenant Santos." Eamon glanced over the older man's shoulder. "I didn't realize you were in already, sir."

"Yes, well, an overnight motel fire and an out-of-state detective getting shot at in the parking lot of the same motel meant my phone was ringing earlier than normal. You two okay? Detective Tate, is it? Lieutenant Santos." He stepped inside, stretched out his hand in greeting, then handed the mug he was holding over to Eamon for a refill. "Delaney and McTavish are on their way in. I told them you were waiting for them."

"It made more sense for us to hang out here than to go driving around after the fact, Lieutenant." Eamon didn't have to spell out his concerns. Whoever had targeted Lana could very well still be keeping tabs on her to try again.

"Agreed." Santos nodded. "Incidentally, just got the report Patrol found an abandoned car fitting the description you gave as the one used in the shooting. It's being taken in for processing."

"I'll be stunned if it produces anything," Lana said, rubbing her temple as if staving off a headache.

"Looks like you two really got caught up in something. Care to explain?"

Lana's suddenly guarded expression had Eamon choosing his words carefully. "Uh, with all due respect, Lieutenant—"

"Let me rephrase." Lieutenant Santos's dark eyes sharpened. "As a professional courtesy, I'd like a report, please. Or should I put in another call to your superior?" He looked at Eamon for a long moment before turning his attention on Lana. "Captain Davis is who you report to, isn't it, Detective?"

"Yes, sir." Lana took a deep drink of coffee and uncurled from her chair. "At the best of times, at least. I'm currently on suspension for...various reasons."

"Yes. I know."

"You do?" Eamon asked as Lana cringed.

"Early morning phone calls often result in me making some of my own. They do provide one with a wealth of information."

"Ah." Lana turned concerned eyes to Eamon. "I see."

"Normally we're advised when an out-of-town law enforcement officer is here to work," Lieutenant Santos said.

"Yes, well, I'm not exactly here in an official capacity," Lana admitted. "But then I suppose you know that as well."

"Captain Davis suggested as much. She had some interesting things to say about you, Detective," the lieutenant said. "She didn't sound particularly surprised to hear you'd gotten into a spot of trouble down here."

"I would imagine she wasn't." Lana's smile was fleeting. "Am I to assume she filled you in on my...situation?"

Eamon's heart hurt for her. It was always difficult to own up to professional shortcomings and personal foibles. In law enforcement, especially for a woman, it could be even more complicated and rife with potential consequences.

"I got the gist of it." Lieutenant Santos's expression shifted to unreadable. "I'm sorry about your husband."

Eamon saw Lana visibly swallow. "Thank you, sir."

"I've seen what happens when detectives take on cases that are so incredibly personal. Complications often arise." The lieutenant came inside the break room, rested his back against the wall, arms crossed over his chest. "I understand you and Agent Quinn have worked together previously."

"On a few cases up in Seattle. A missing person. One kidnapping. He's a friend," Lana said in a way that put a big ding in those growing hopes of Eamon's. "I came to him for help. I thought his perspective might be useful."

"Then clearly, despite your captain's claims to the contrary, your judgment remains intact," Lieutenant Santos said. "Given the morning's events, I'm going to assume you've agreed to assist, Eamon?"

"Yes, sir." It didn't matter that Santos wasn't his superior. The man's rank and experience, as well as his past support of Eamon, demanded Eamon's professionalism and respect. He'd worked with the commanding officer enough to know Santos looked beyond rules and regulations to see the people behind the badge and the curveballs life often gave them. "I plan to stick with this, with her, until it's resolved."

"I'd expect nothing less." Santos turned an assessing gaze on Lana. "Captain Davis said you're convinced there's something more to your husband's death. That it wasn't an accident."

"That would be accurate, sir."

"Given the events of the past few hours, I think it's safe to say you might be on to something," he observed.

"I do seem to be the common denominator," Lana stated. "And given I haven't been working any other cases for the past few months—"

"Clearly you flipped someone's switch," Santos said. "Will this be an official federal investigation, then?"

"To be determined," Eamon said and ignored the frown of surprise from Lana. "I've already spoken with my superior back in San Francisco." Not a great idea to wake said superior up before dawn, but the hail of bullets had dampened his usual caution. "I'll be extending my post-case leave with some of the vacation and sick days I've accrued in the past—"

"Lifetime?" Santos said. "Rumor has it you can barely spell *vacation*, let alone apply for it, Special Agent."

"Yes, sir." Eamon's smile eased.

"I have no doubt you can find outside assistance with your investigation," Santos said. "Still, I'll make arrangements for Detectives McTavish and Delaney to have some flexibility with their caseload. If you need their help, just ask. Provided—" he raised a finger "—you keep me in the loop and updated as to your progress. Both of you," he said with a pointed look at Lana before the ding of the elevator had him pivoting toward the windows looking out into the bullpen. "Speaking of my two best detectives."

Eamon snorted behind his mug of coffee and Santos shot him a look that warned Eamon that comment was not to be shared.

"Here they are, loaded down with a healthy amount of sugar." Santos's amusement was fleeting as Cole and Jack approached. "Detective Tate, suspension or no suspension, you're still a sworn law enforcement officer. I ask that you remember that," Santos warned as Jack, big pink bakery box in hand, entered the break room. "But I also ask that you come to me if you need anything while you're here."

"Thank you, sir. I appreciate that," Lana said with a nod as the lieutenant moved toward the counter to doctor up the coffee Eamon had fixed for him.

"This is my version of a shield," Jack said to his commanding officer before setting the box on the table and facing Eamon. "We were gone from the motel, what? Three minutes? Before the bullets started flying. That has got to be a record."

"It was eight minutes, actually," Lana said. "Personal best for me. Usually it's at least a half hour before someone starts using me for target practice."

Eamon wasn't surprised Jack didn't laugh. The man might be more easygoing than his partner, but he took his job and responsibilities seriously. Eamon had no doubt Jack was second-guessing his and Cole's decision to leave the scene.

"And here I was wondering what could have possibly gotten you suspended, Detective Tate." Santos approached, napkin in hand, and flipped open the box to grab one of the half dozen apple fritters tucked inside. "I would like a briefing on your unofficial case within the hour, please," he ordered before leaving them alone.

"That was...unexpected," Lana said to Eamon as she watched the lieutenant return to his office across the bullpen.

"He trusts us," Jack said with a glance at Eamon. "All of us. That earns us some leeway."

"Not too much, however." Cole, having changed into a clean shirt and tie, hefted an oversize, reusable shopping bag toward Lana. "Eden, my wife, sends her regards in the form of clothes," he told Lana. "She doesn't anticipate fitting into any of these in the near future, so keep what you like."

"She sent these for me?" Lana rose and accepted the bag with overly wide eyes. "She doesn't even know me."

The surprise in Lana's voice triggered a wave of sympathy inside Eamon. How lucky he was to have the friends he did.

"Yeah, well, blame this guy." Cole jerked a thumb in Eamon's direction. "Guy goes and earns himself big-brother status back when we were young, so you're accepted by default."

"I'm not that much older than the rest of you," Eamon grumbled and eyed a maple bar.

"You're pushing forty faster than we are." Cole's dry tone felt surprisingly warm. "In any case, Eden's ready to rock and roll as soon as you give her something to work with."

"Rock and roll with what?" Lana asked.

"Right." Eamon ran a hand across the back of his neck. "That unofficial assistance Lieutenant Santos mentioned earlier? Eden's part of it. She has a talent for digging up information people don't want found. Or accessed."

"I've got a call in to Jason, too," Jack said. "He's carrying a full load of classes now that he's going for his psychology degree, but he said he can jump in when and if we need him. He thinks in different ways than the rest of us," he added at Lana's continued blank stare.

"That's Jack-speak for saying that once upon a time Jason worked on the other side of the law," Eamon explained. "He's better now."

"I don't…" Lana's voice hitched. "I don't know what to say."

"Eamon asked for our help," Jack said matter-of-factly.

"I had some favors to call in," Eamon said with a shrug at Lana's disbelieving look. "Why don't you go get cleaned up and changed? I'll get these two filled in on the recent developments."

She plucked at her holey and torn shirt and winced. "Good idea." Her low voice suggested she was having difficulty processing this. But then her head snapped up and suddenly she was on the move. "Please tell Eden thanks from me. I'll be back in just a sec, yeah?" She grabbed a chocolate-sprinkled doughnut on her way out to change.

Eamon stood where he was, coffee in hand, trying not to notice the two detectives looking at him as if they expected him to self-combust in the next ten seconds.

"That's her, isn't it? The woman you couldn't forget," Jack said as he took Lana's vacated seat. "And before you answer, please consider I have fifty bucks riding on this answer with Greta. Rumor is you've never been serious about anyone because you were already hooked."

"Please." Cole shook his head. "You even have to ask? Look at him. He's not just hooked. He's sunk."

"It's not what you think," Eamon said, not quite certain why he felt the need to deflect. Immediately, the temptation she'd offered last night leaped to mind.

He cringed, drank more coffee. Okay, maybe he did know.

"Oh, I think it's definitely what we think," Jack teased. "The after-fire target practice just ups the ante. You want to give us the short version of what L.T. already knows?"

"Lana's been asking questions about her husband's death that was almost two years ago." It seemed best to just be honest about things. That it had the added benefit of shutting his friends up? Bonus. "There's a lot going on. A lot I'm not even in on yet, but she came here looking for help. I've said I'll give it to her." He eyed the two detectives. "And I think we'll need your help."

Chapter Five

If Lana ever met Eden St. Claire, she'd shower the woman with enthusiastic thanks. After gobbling down the doughnut like a starving woman, Lana found two pairs of practically brand-new jeans in the bag, along with a rainbow of tanks and T-shirts that, while a bit brighter on the color spectrum than Lana was accustomed to, fit almost to a tee. The sleepwear was practical and the simple black knee-length dress reminded Lana of one she had in her closet back home. The fact there wasn't anything frilly, sparkly or overly feminine made Lana suspect she'd found a kindred spirit in the clothing sense.

The waist-length, black lightweight zip-up sweatshirt seemed perfect for the indecisive weather, which had yet to take that final plunge into summer.

There was also a pair of flip-flops with tags attached, and a pair of hiking boots that came pretty close to replacing the ones she'd lost in the motel room fire, and slightly scuffed black flats Lana suspected were meant to go with the dress.

All in all, she'd hit the jackpot when it came to resetting her clothing supply. The dreaded shopping excursion she had on her mind for later had been reduced to a quick stop for underwear and socks. Score.

The fact Eden had also included a zip-top cosmetic bag filled with various toiletries and personal products told her Eden was a sensible woman who planned for various contingencies, proved by the fact she'd also included a box of condoms in the bottom of the bag. Cheeks blazing, Lana folded and stuffed everything into the zipper duffel Eden had tossed in. Obviously Eamon's friends, Eden at least, believed they were more than work buddies. The idea didn't unsettle her exactly, but it did add to her rising confusion. She'd come out to ask for Eamon's help, not start something...personal.

She took a slow, shuddering breath. Last night had been revelatory. Eamon had feelings for her. Dread and uncertainty spiraled around each other and lodged in her lungs. He hadn't been pushy about it. To the contrary, when she'd made her intentions regarding their physical attraction obvious, he'd firmly put some distance between them just in case she wasn't thinking clearly.

Except, she had been. Maybe more clearly than she had in months. Maybe that was part of the problem. And, okay, perhaps he was partially correct in that she'd been looking for a quick, no-ties tumble to serve as a distraction for everything that had thrown her off course. There was nothing wrong with that. But there was something wrong with her thinking Eamon Quinn was the quick-tumble kind of man.

This was a dangerous path to go down. Trying to shake herself free of the increasingly unsettling thoughts, she went over to the sink to splash water on her face. She hadn't felt anything remotely sexual since Marcus had died. It was as if losing him had made that side of her disappear, but moments after being in Eamon's presence, feeling his touch, his simple, hand-to-hand touch, she'd felt that long-dormant fire ignite almost to a full burn.

She stood up, stared at herself in the mirror and wondered, not for the first time, what Eamon saw in her. She stripped off her shirt, wadded it up and tossed it in the trash, then dabbed at the scrapes and cuts the EMTs had done their best to treat. Her stubbornness, her tenacity, it was all etched into a rather angular face that carried little softness even when she smiled. She wasn't a conventionally pretty woman, she thought, but she was a woman who knew what she was and what she was good at. It was what Marcus had always said he saw in her.

Maybe Eamon saw that, too.

She pulled her necklace free from between her breasts, looked down at the pair of rings that, at times, called out to her as if from a different life. The rings and key pendant acted as both anchor and memory personified. The good and the bad. Happy and...

Part of her waited for the guilt to descend, but that wasn't going to happen to a realist like her. Marcus was gone. There was nothing to cling to that would ever bring him back and he, more than anyone, would have wanted her to get on with her life. Heck, they'd had this discussion about what if the worst happened. The only difference was the conversation had been triggered by Lana's dangerous profession.

She wasn't clinging to the rings as a reminder of their marriage. She didn't need that. She was wearing them as a reminder that Marcus's life had meant something. Even now she could practically hear her husband teasing her for attempting to usurp sentimentality, something she wasn't particularly known for.

"Who are you kidding?" she muttered to herself as she tucked the rings back into the center of her bra and quickly put on a raspberry-colored T-shirt and a clean pair of jeans. "He'd be seriously outraged at how you've handled this whole thing." Except, neither of them could have predicted Marcus's death would leave her with so many unanswered questions and suspicions.

If it wasn't guilt getting in the way of seeing the potential with Eamon, what was it? She pressed a hand against the bare skin over her heart. No. She frowned, shook her head. She wasn't a romantic. She had never let herself become so lost in the fantasy of what she and Marcus had shared that she couldn't consider what else might be out there for her.

Her heart skipped a beat. Up until recently, this was when she'd be taking a shot—or more—of whiskey to calm her nerves. But while the nerves might settle, the booze would also dull her reactions, not to mention taint the emotional wherewithal she needed to make full use of Eamon's expertise and investigative connections. She closed her eyes, took a long, deep breath.

Eamon.

Before she'd seen him again, she'd considered him a bit of a life raft in very choppy waters. One that she was fairly convinced she could grab hold of and feel safe.

Now? She lifted shaky fingers to her lips that still felt warm from his kiss. Now she had unexpected images of things that hadn't happened, had never been in her realm of possibilities. And not just the potential sex. Emotional promise. And risk.

Doubt of an entirely different kind crept over her with the stealth of a midnight shadow. She didn't have it in her to love again. She'd given it a chance to work with Marcus and she'd been left broken. She never wanted to give that big a piece of herself away again.

But Eamon...

Even as the thought passed through her mind, she found herself rationalizing.

There wasn't a better man she could think of to take another risk on than Eamon Quinn. It could be the distance, the years that had passed, making her think such things. They'd had little to no contact after the last case they'd worked on together, other than his brief appearance at Marcus's funeral, and even that existed only in foggy memory. And yet...

And yet it was as if no time had passed at all.

"Gah." She ducked her head and splashed more water onto her face. Stupid close calls and near-death experiences. She should be used to them by now, but somehow they always messed with her head and left her dwelling on things she had no business addressing.

Eamon Quinn wasn't asking anything of her. He sure wasn't demanding anything close to love. But he should. Eamon needed love in his life. He *deserved* love, love she wasn't in any position to offer. She was way too messed up for a relationship. She probably always would be.

She gripped the edges of the slightly stained porcelain sink and dropped her chin to her chest. How arrogant of her to believe he was thinking about anything near happily-ever-after or happily-for-now. He was a man who returned the desire she'd finally acknowledged she felt for him. That was all.

The rap of knuckles on the door had her swiping the tears

from her cheeks. "Lana?" Eamon's voice didn't bring quite the amount of comfort it usually did. "You find something that fits?"

"Yeah," she croaked. She cleared her throat and grabbed a handful of paper towels to dry her hands and face. "Yeah, I'm good. Out in a minute."

"We've moved to the conference room."

Conference room. Perfect. The more people around, the better. It was being alone with Eamon that was likely to get her into trouble. She needed to get her head on straight. She hadn't come down here to pursue a relationship or give in to a surprising and distracting physical attraction. She'd come for help to find out the truth about Marcus's death. That was what she had to focus on.

Which was what she did as she gathered up her new duffel and headed out of the bathroom. The second she was out in the hall and heard the familiar clamor of cop talk and muted conversation, the doubts instantly vanished.

There was a universal truth among law enforcement personnel that said any serving officer could step inside any dedicated building and instantly find their way around. It was as if some kind of invisible homing beacon had been implanted in their brains the second they graduated the academy.

She did consider that this particular division of the Sacramento Police Department had a bit more polish than most she'd been in, her own Seattle offices included.

Not wanting to interrupt, she quietly closed the conference room door behind her.

"Six, six thirty." A woman's voice came over the tablet screen set up in the center of the conference table. "We've got the food taken care of. All you have to do is show up. Oh, hey, there. You must be Detective Tate."

"Sorry to keep you all waiting." Lana set her bag down. She wasn't entirely sure what to think about the fifth face reflecting back at her from a tablet screen. The woman on the other side of the screen had her strawberry blond hair messily knotted on top of her head. The expression on the woman's round face appeared to be part skepticism, part excitement. Behind her sat a pile of file folders, one very old printer and a one-eyed, ragged stuffed bear perched precariously on the edge of a stack of storybooks. The wall that served as a backdrop to her video screen was covered in newspaper clippings and printed-out articles circling around various disappearances, unsolved murders and suspicious deaths. The pieces of the puzzle came together in one simple answer.

"I'm betting you're Eden." Lana approached the tablet as if walking up to a friend. "Thanks for the survival package," she said and earned a smile of approval from the other woman. "I'm not sure I'll need everything you included, but—"

"Better safe than sorry." Eden dismissed her embarrassment. "Nice to meet you, Detective."

"Lana, please." Lana couldn't have missed the ever-so-there hint of disapproval at the title and neither, it seemed, had Eden's husband. Cole was sitting back in his chair, a few fingers covering his now curving lips as something akin to admiration and amusement flickered in his eyes.

"Eden's going to take notes, do research you might need. That kind of stuff," Lieutenant Santos said. "What she will not be doing is any gathering of information via asking questions in person. Correct?"

"You've turned me into an admin." Eden's animated grumble had Lana's lips twitching. "Not that there's anything wrong with that."

"Strangely enough," Lieutenant Santos replied, "Molotov cocktails and flying bullets tend to make me leery about putting a pregnant civilian front and center of a case."

"Yeah, yeah." Eden grumbled more. "For the record, I would have agreed had I been consulted. If I can't find my feet, I can't very well be useful on them."

Detective Cole Delaney, Eden's husband, didn't look entirely convinced. "She works better ticked off—don't worry," Cole told Lana. "You want to get us up to speed on your late husband's case?"

Lana took a deep breath and sat in the chair beside Eamon. "What do you already know?" Santos got comfortable in a chair at the far end of the long table.

"Eamon's given us the outline," Jack said from his seat across from her. "Marcus Tate was killed in a hit-and-run eighteen months ago in Boston." He ran through the metadata of the accident: time, location, basic report details. "Officers called to the scene closed it pretty quickly. Detectives followed. Witness statements, of which there were five, all pretty much said the same thing. Mr. Tate was cutting across the street from a local restaurant. It was dark. At least one of the streetlamps was out and a silver SUV clipped him just as he reached his car." Jack glanced up. "He died at the scene shortly after the ambulance arrived."

Lana wished, more than anything, for the level of detachment Jack possessed while reciting the details. But as she'd learned the last few months, some wishes were never meant to be granted.

"What the report apparently doesn't say," Eamon said in a tone that had Lana's attention snapping his way, "is that Marcus was on the phone with Lana when the accident occurred."

Eden swore. "You heard it happen?"

Lana swallowed hard. "I did, yes."

"There was a woman who picked up Marcus's cell shortly after the accident," Eamon said. "She told Lana what happened."

Jack flipped through the printed-out pages. "I'm not seeing any mention of any witness who said they spoke with you, Lana."

"That was one of the first things that struck me when I finally got hold of the reports." She hadn't liked hounding the detectives and officers, nor did she enjoy going over their heads to their superiors. But she'd needed to see for herself what the official record stated. If only to prove she wasn't losing her mind.

"Can you fill in some of the blanks, Lana?" Eden asked. "You and your husband lived in Seattle, correct? Obviously you work for the Seattle PD, but what did Marcus do?"

"He was an attorney. Business contracts and acquisitions mainly, for a company called A&O Solutions." Lana tapped restless fingers on the table. "They're part think tank, part consultancy. They recruited him when he was still in college, thanks to his mentor. They covered his tuition and housing cost, and once he graduated, he went to work for them. A couple of years later he passed the Massachusetts State Bar. He had to travel a lot and most of the times his trips were last-minute. He always said he loved his work. He said it made him feel important. Like he was making a difference." And it had paid well, which, after growing up in the system, had been a plus for Marcus.

"I'm betting his job probably covered a wide range of responsibilities," Eamon said. "The few times I met him, he never went into particular detail about his job. Any idea of the particulars? Any problems he was having with clients or accounts?"

"None. As far as I knew, everything was fine." Lana shrugged. "He didn't complain about anything work-related."

"The *A* and *O* stand for Alpha and Omega," Eden read off her computer. "Subtle. Their client list is a who's who of the rich and powerful. Businesses, private individuals, other multimillion-dollar companies."

"Takeovers in play? Political agendas?" Cole slipped in. "If Marcus was working on something like that, it might explain why someone would have wanted him—"

"Dead," Lana finished for him even as she steeled herself. "Don't worry. I'm past breaking down at this point." One thing about not having any answers was that there were no wrong suppositions. "Marcus and I didn't talk a lot about work." She hesitated. That wasn't entirely true. "We didn't talk a lot about *his* work. Most of his clients required NDAs, and he was never entirely sure what he could talk about, so we agreed early on we wouldn't discuss any of it."

She glanced at the screen where Eden was glaring and typing furiously.

"That's her transcribing face," Cole told her. "She's making note of everything we say."

"The devil's always in the details," Eden murmured, then kinked her head to the side. "Better speed this up. I hear signs of life from Chloe Ann's room. Our girl's Little Miss Cranky Pants until her first glass of juice."

"Like mother, like daughter," Cole muttered.

"So Marcus didn't tell you what he was working on for this particular trip to Boston?" Eden asked.

"Not at first, no. Turned out to be more personal than business-related," she added and only hesitated a moment before saying, "He was going to take a leave of absence so we could start a family."

"What a shame," Jack said without the expected look of pity masking itself as sympathy. "Did he go to Boston a lot?"

"Often enough he kept an apartment there. It's where the company is based." She glanced at Eamon, uncertain how much detail she should share. "He'd flown there the day before to meet with his boss, Felice Covington. She head-hunted him back in his college days, but he first met her when she visited one of the youth centers he attended as a foster kid. They were close. Not that kind of close," she clarified at Jack's raised brow. "Marcus was in foster care from a very young age. Felice belongs to a number of charities that focus on children's issues. It's her pet project with A&O. If she saw promise in someone, she took them on. Sponsored them, both financially and in their education. She considered it a good investment for the future. I think, in a lot of ways, she served as a mother figure for him. For a lot of young people, actually."

"That must make for a very loyal workforce," Cole observed.

"I met her at Marcus's funeral," Eamon said. "Very posh. Very polished, with an underlying hint of steel. Wicked sense of humor, too, if I recall."

"I would consider that an apt description," Lana agreed. "She also has infinite patience until she doesn't. The woman can burn through ice with a quick look alone."

"She has an impressive résumé and portfolio." Jack scanned the screen of his own laptop. "I'm seeing dozens of offices and properties all over the world. She's this successful and yet I've never heard of her. Or A&O Solutions, for that matter. Interesting."

"She likes to fly under the radar. But she's very generous." Lana nodded. "She arranged for us to stay in one of her homes for our honeymoon."

"Where was that?" Eden said as her fingers continued clicking.

"British Virgin Islands." Lana was grateful for the good memories. "Marcus said it would give me a taste of what he was hoping to achieve for us. He had expensive dreams." It was one way they were completely opposite to one another. Lana's dreams were more practical and down-to-earth. She'd have been happy with a white picket fence. Marcus wasn't going to be satisfied until he had an iron gate. Ordinary, Marcus had teased, referring to her choice. It had become a kind of joke between them. One she hadn't found particularly amusing.

"How often did he travel overseas?" Eamon asked.

"Pretty regularly." She shrugged. "He was high up the food chain at A&O. Honestly, I was too focused on my work to pay that close attention. I knew when something big happened, if there was a problem that cropped up or something was bothering him, not that he offered any details. Otherwise…"

"What kind of problems?" Santos asked.

"There were a few issues with employees. People not pulling their weight. Oftentimes Marcus was called in to fire them. It was a talent of his, apparently." Lana frowned. "I remember him having to take a trip to Tokyo because one of A&O's board members died while on vacation with his family. Marcus is who they sent to make sure all the arrangements were made and the family assisted with getting back home."

"When was this?" Cole asked, glancing at his wife, who was nodding in approval.

"Um, a couple of months before Marcus was killed. When I asked Felice if there was a possibility Marcus might have been killed because of his work, she assured me she didn't see how. Nothing he—or the business—was involved in was dangerous."

"So you've been to Felice with your suspicions?" Eamon finished his coffee and rose to get another.

"She was the first one I spoke with, actually." Lana had hoped to be convinced she was wrong, that there was nothing worth pursuing, but Felice had not put her mind at ease. "Like I said, she and Marcus were close. Honestly, I think I'd have been lost without her right after Marcus died. She took care of everything for me. The funeral arrangements, the life insurance coverage that paid off the house. She probably would have sold his apartment in Boston, except for some tax reason he put my name, not his, on the title." She barely remembered him telling her about it when he bought the place.

She'd planned to stay there when she'd gone back to Boston the one time to ask questions, but all she'd gotten was the runaround from the Boston PD. She'd also attempted to go straight to the police commissioner and made it as far as the lobby door before she'd lost the nerve to go inside. In the end, she'd ended up going back and booking a room at the airport hotel. "It was a relief, letting her deal with it all," Lana admitted.

"When was the last time you spoke with her?" Eamon asked.

"Right before I left Seattle." She pulled out her cell and checked her call records. "She's the dinner I had to cancel that I told you about," she added to Eamon. "I said I'd let her know about rescheduling."

"She's based in Seattle?" Eamon asked.

"No. Boston. She was coming out for business," Lana explained. "That's usually when we get together."

"What about Marcus's work stuff?" Cole asked. "Did he have a home office?"

"Yes." Again, she'd seen it more as a status symbol than a practicality. "Not that he used it very often. He kept work out of the house as much as he could."

"Did you find anything in his office when you went through the room?" Jack asked.

"No." She frowned. "No, Felice and one of her assistants went through his office shortly after the accident. Those NDAs aren't anything to play around with." Now that she was being questioned, Lana could see all the mistakes she'd made handling things. Mistakes she never would have made had this been one of her homicide cases. "Hindsight," she murmured. "I'm feeling like an idiot talking to you all right now. There's so much I'm seeing. I should have gone through his office before she got to it. Maybe there was something there."

"More likely you'd have ended up violating an NDA and gotten yourself into trouble," Eamon suggested.

"I managed to get in trouble anyway," she attempted to joke. "That's my talent. The least I could have done is actually produce something because of it."

"You've never been one for breaking the rules, Lana," Eamon said. "Don't try to convince yourself otherwise or feel guilty for being who you are."

It was on the tip of Lana's tongue to tell him that breaking the rules was one of the reasons behind her suspension, but that wasn't an admission she wanted to make in front of the group. Right now they seemed willing to help her. They didn't need to know about…the rest.

"No one thinks clearly in the middle of a storm." Eden continued tapping on her keyboard. "And that's what grief is. A storm. Sometimes it's a fast-moving one. Other times it's molasses-slow. You have to wait until the worst of it passes. Beating yourself up about something that could have opened a whole other can of worms is only going to weigh you down. Letting stuff like that go might even help clear up other things that feel muddled."

"She knows what she's talking about," Eamon murmured.

Lana smiled, grateful for the sentiment. And the support.

"Trauma is tricky. Just when you think you've gotten over the worst of it, it'll start eating away at you again," Eden added.

It hadn't helped, having the people she thought she could trust accuse her of making things up in order to cope with her loss. But rather than make her back off and rethink things, their disbelief had driven Lana even harder, which had definitely put her in a precarious position, professionally at least.

"I don't care what all those witnesses said," she told the people surrounding her now. "There was no sound of brakes before the car hit him. I know that as certainly as I'm sitting in this chair right now."

"No one here is going to argue with you, Lana." Eamon reached across the table and covered her hand with his, curled his fingers around hers until she felt the warm comfort of his touch seeping into her skin. "I promise, you don't have to fight us about this."

Considering she'd been fighting with just about everyone involved so far, she found that difficult to believe. "Boston PD closed the case. Everyone in this room knows what that means. We also all know how we'd each react if someone came at us with questions about a case we'd closed."

"Maybe," Cole said.

"Probably," Eamon agreed.

"Could depend on the case," Jack tossed in and earned some raised brows. "Each of us have had cases that left questions open. Loose threads, for want of a better term. Cases we didn't have the luxury of spending more time on, but enough answers were found that we moved on. Could be these officers had questions that didn't go anywhere at the time or they didn't feel they were in the right position to ask."

"That's an opening to use to stick your nose back in," Lana observed.

"Yes, it is." Lieutenant Santos sat back, stretched out his arms and tapped his fingers on the table. "I'm friends with Eleanor McKenna. I can reach out, see if she'd be willing to take another look, give me her thoughts."

"Maybe find out if the officers on scene didn't put in

something they wish they had?" Eamon suggested. "Hindsight being what it is."

"You know Commissioner McKenna?" Lana asked as her stomach dropped to her tingling toes. The McKenna family was legendary in law enforcement circles. Their lineage traced back to the early days of Boston and the first organized police department in the nation. The commissioner hadn't only solidified her reputation as a premier figure of law and order, but her children had kept the legacy going by joining various branches of federal agencies, including the Secret Service and the ATF.

"Ellie and I go back a ways," Santos said. "A number of years ago she gave a series of lectures on law enforcement career options beyond the norm. It was geared toward young women, seeing as at the time she was one of the first female police commissioners in the country, but we struck up a friendship. Let me see what I can find out."

"Ah." Lana swallowed hard as regret clogged her throat. "Just so you know, my name might set off a few warning bells with her. Suffice it to say, I don't think I made the best impression."

Out of the corner of her eye, Lana saw Eamon glance at her. It took all her effort not to meet his gaze.

"Noted," Santos said with a quick nod before he left the conference room. "Keep me apprised of your progress."

"Wow." Some of the knots Lana hadn't realized were there loosened inside her. "I guess maybe I finally made the right decision about something. Coming here." She finally looked at Eamon. For the first time in what felt like forever, hope sprang to life. She should be wondering why these people, who didn't know her from a stranger on the street, were willing to stick their necks out for her. But she knew the answer.

They were doing it because of Eamon. Because Eamon trusted her. Believed in her. Lana pressed a hand against her fluttering stomach. She could only hope that trust wasn't misplaced. "I don't even know what to say."

"I do," Eden said. "Lana, can you put together a time line of everything you've laid out for us? Seeing as you're focusing on things you might not have paid attention to before, maybe start before the hit-and-run? By the way, did they ever find the car?"

"Not that I know of," Lana said. Hit-and-run. Not accident. That turn of phrase alone would have made the trip down here worth it. Appreciation and gratitude washed over her like a warm tide from the Pacific. It wasn't only Eamon who believed her.

"We've also got a list of Marcus's clients, thanks to his assistant," Eamon said.

"Fab. I'll mark that off the to-do list, then," Eden said. "What's his assistant's name, Lana?"

"Cynthia Randolph."

"She didn't argue about confidentiality?" Eamon asked.

"No," Lana said. "Now that I think about it, I remember being surprised at how quickly she sent the list."

"Does strike me as odd." Cole nodded his thanks as Jack took his mug for a refill from the machine on the back counter. "Considering the NDAs."

Lana's stomach twisted into a new knot. Maybe if she'd been paying closer attention, she might have connected these threads earlier. Even as she thought it, her hands trembled. She snatched them back into her lap.

"Cynthia," Eden murmured as she narrowed her eyes at the screen. "I'm not finding her listed on the A&O Solutions website. I'll check her on LinkedIn. Go around that way."

Lana frowned. "I have her phone number—"

"Eden'll ask for it if she needs it," Eamon assured her. "Woman can find a needle in a needle stack with those programs of hers. Plus she loves a challenge."

"She also has exceptional hearing," Eden said without looking at them.

"All reasons I married her," Cole confirmed. "She also has the uncanny ability to attract the wrong kind of attention."

"What kind of attention is that?" Lana asked.

"The serial-killer kind," Jack announced and earned a glare from Eden. "Oh, come on, E. It's been years. You can't still be upset about it."

"They chained me up in a meat locker and left me to freeze to death," Eden mumbled. "Not to mention I never could wear my favorite boots again. What's not to feel bitter about?"

"Hang on. The Iceman." Lana balked. "That was you? You're Eden on Ice. Oh, man. I should have put that together sooner. The entire Seattle PD reads your blog. You really need to turn that into a podcast."

"Please don't give her ideas," Cole ordered.

"Way ahead of you," Eden announced. "Seeing as I'm going to be tied closer to the house now that number two is on the way, I need to find a way to… Hey, Sunshine. Good morning!" Eden bent out of view for a moment, and when she popped back up, her arms and lap were filled with a snuggly, still-sleepy-eyed toddler. "There's Daddy and your uncles."

"Hey, Chloe Ann." Jack shoved Cole out of the way so

he could take up most of the bandwidth. "How do you like that keyboard Uncle Jack got you?"

"Musical instruments as gifts for toddlers are *e-v-i-l*," Eden spelled out with a sharp look at her husband's partner. "Unfortunately for us, she loves it."

"Of course she does," Jack teased.

"Ack!" Chloe Ann covered her eyes with her hands, then threw them out to the side. "Peek ah you!"

"Kid's going to be thirty and still calling you Ack," Cole teased.

"It's better than Amu," Eamon said and earned a squeal of delight from the little girl as she grabbed for and dislodged the camera, her sleep-tousled curls bouncing around her face.

"Okay, when she goes for the hardware, it's time to say goodbye." Eden struggled to get the camera back on straight while keeping Chloe Ann settled on her lap. "I've got a lot to run with. Dinner, our place, remember, Eamon. Six thirty-ish. I hope you'll join us, Lana. It would be nice to meet you in person." Eden aimed a pointed look at her husband. "Cole, please be careful. Maybe let Eamon take the lead on this one? No offense, Lana, but I'd prefer he not get caught in the line of whoever is firing at you."

She'd prefer no one got caught in that line of fire, but Lana nodded. "Noted and agreed. Thanks for your help, Eden."

"Haven't done anything yet, but I love a good mystery. Say bye to Lana, Chloe Ann."

"Bye, Lala!"

"Oh." Lana blinked as the screen went dark. Unexpected

tears blurred her eyes, but she blinked them back. "Well, that's just delightful."

"More than delightful," Eamon said as he got to his feet. "It means you're officially part of the family."

Chapter Six

This was getting to be a habit, Eamon thought, when he found Lana asleep on his sofa much later that afternoon. This time, instead of being burrowed into the cushions and blankets like a hibernating hedgehog, she had one hand thrown over her eyes and a humming laptop resting on her gently rising stomach. The scrapes on her arms weren't quite so angrily red, but they were still there. A reminder of how close some of those bullets had come.

And yet…he frowned. And yet they'd missed.

He was trying to not get ahead of himself, to not embrace the comfort and excitement he felt at having Lana in such close proximity. While he'd thought of her often over the years, he'd purposely buried himself in work so as not to have to think about the fact he should have called. Reached out and checked in. It was difficult, being in competition with a dead man. There was no winning against Marcus and the life he and Lana had had together. As much as Eamon had been tempted to pursue something romantic with her, the idea of being turned away, turned down or slipped firmly into the friend zone was a chance he hadn't been willing to take. Better to stay safe than sorry.

Now?

Now she'd been the one to take that first step that had terrified him to his core. Somehow she'd tapped into his dreams of them walking the same road together and set them on it herself. The road wasn't cemented with certainty by any means. There were plenty of obstacles to overcome if this was going to be something long-term and serious. But her sleeping on his sofa was definitely progress in what he'd all but given up hope on.

Funny how things worked out.

Eamon glanced at his watch, buttoned his cuff. They had more than an hour before needing to be at Eden and Cole's, but he wanted to give Lana plenty of time to try to worm her way out of having dinner with his friends. He wouldn't let her, of course, but still.

The last thing he wanted was to leave her alone in the rather spartan apartment. She did not need alone time with everything that was going on. Especially after she'd spent the day typing nonstop on her laptop, putting that time line together for Eden. He'd been relieved when she'd crashed a little while ago. The woman needed a serious recharge.

He had a secret weapon in his back pocket, should she put up too much of a fight about going out. And enough verbal bombs to lob back at her should she throw excuses his way. He was as prepared as he was ever going to be.

"You look like you're going to a movie premiere in Hollywood."

Eamon blinked, not having noticed her watching him as he stood in the middle of the living room staring at her. "Thanks. You think?" His smile was quick. "It's always nice when your work attire doubles as formal wear for a party."

She snorted. "Like you've worn that suit to work. And a party? I thought it was dinner?"

"It's a bit of both. And it's not just me. It's we, remember?" He walked over, clicked her laptop closed and set it on the table beside her.

"Eden was just being polite inviting me."

"Shows how much you know. Eden doesn't do polite." Eamon heard the expected sigh of resignation escape her lips. "And it's not a party by its usual definition. More of a get-together for a common celebration."

"I'm not really in a party get-together mood." She scowled and pushed herself up on her arms, looked up at him. "What's the occasion?"

He hesitated. "If I tell you, you'll think I'm guilting you into coming."

"Try me," she challenged.

Suddenly his collar button felt too tight. "It's Chloe's birthday."

"Oh!" Lana swung her legs around. "Well, that's different, then, isn't it? What is she, two? Did you get her a... Oh." She went a little pale even as her cheeks tinted. "Oh, not Eden's Chloe Ann. You meant your sister Chloe. Today is your sister's birthday?"

"It was a few weeks ago, actually." His smile felt forced, but the pain didn't last nearly as long as it once did. "We were supposed to have the celebration earlier this month, but I got called in on that case. As soon as we closed it, Eden threw it together. Simone is usually our organizer, but with Caleb just being born, Eden took the lead this time. Just as well. Security in Eden's building is top-notch. Nothing to worry about, you being out in public." He was preemptively negating any argument she could come up with.

"Eamon, this is family stuff. You don't want me there."

"On the contrary." So far she was not disappointing him with her protests. "I would very much like for you to come."

"What, like as your date?" She snort-laughed before catching his expression. "Oh. You do actually mean..."

"Only if you're okay with it." He walked over to the fridge, his loafers smacking smartly against the hardwood floor. Withdrawing a chilled bottle of water, he twisted off the cap and drank, more to calm his own nerves than to give her time to consider his request. "We can look at this as a test run of sorts, for when we're on the other side of—"

"The off-book investigation into my late husband's murder?" She suddenly seemed quite interested in the blanket she'd tossed over the back of the sofa. "I just made things awkward, didn't I? Always bringing Marcus into things."

"No, you didn't." He clasped the bottle in one hand and returned to sit in the low leather chair near the sofa. "I don't mind you talking about Marcus, Lana. It doesn't bother me. And I don't want it to bother you." He was a man used to putting all his cards on the table. He wasn't about to change now on the one topic that could drive a wedge between them. "He's always going to be a part of you. But if it's too soon—"

"It's not." He took the fact she cut him off as a very good sign. "I'm just...a lot to take right now. I'm a mess, Eamon. Between my job being in jeopardy, not to mention my reputation, I don't understand how I can be remotely appealing."

"And yet you are." He could have joked and told her he liked a challenge, but now wasn't the time for humor or teasing. "Circumstances and life's obstacles aside, I see you as

I've always seen you, Lana. As a woman I like very much. I'd like to see where things go between us, and not just in there." He gestured to the bedroom. "We've both been witness to some pretty dark events. I think maybe we can agree that life's too short to waste an opportunity simply because the timing might be inconvenient."

She closed her eyes. "You really are a dying breed, Eamon Quinn. I had no idea you were such a romantic."

"I endeavor to continue to surprise." Never in his life had he felt so strong an urge to wish away the tension and worry he saw on her face. The semipermanent wincing. The way she carried herself, as if she was going to take a step in the wrong direction and set off a chain reaction of pain. Those aspects faded from time to time, but he wanted them to disappear. Forever. "You came looking for me to help pull you out of what you've been buried in alone for so long. Coming with me tonight will most definitely help you do that."

"Well, I did like Eden. And Cole and Jack."

"See? You already know four of us. The rest'll be easy. It's not an inquisition, you know. It's just good people, good food and good memories," he pressed. "And did I mention Greta Renault will be there?"

"Seriously?" She sank back in the cushions and went wide-eyed. "You're not just saying that to get me to leave this apartment?"

"I am not." His secret weapon deployed, he felt a zing of delight that it had worked. "She owns the building where Eden and Cole live. And it's where her private gallery is being built. You know—" he took a long drink of water "—in case you wanted that sneak peek I promised you."

"You do not play fair." He could see the doubt battling against desire. "All right. I'll come."

Eamon feigned offense even as his plan fell into place. "I should have known the art would be more of a selling point than yours truly. So if that's a yes, maybe try to relax and enjoy yourself."

"And what happens tomorrow?" Now she opened her eyes and looked at him.

"What do you mean?"

"You know what I mean," she warned. "Between us."

"What would have happened today if last night had gone as you'd planned?"

She only stared at him, her expression unreadable, for once, despite him being able to almost see the thoughts spinning in her head.

He knew what he'd like to have happen, but he wasn't going to press the issue. He'd meant what he'd said about not wanting to dismiss or ignore the fact Marcus had existed. But he also wanted to make sure there weren't any ghosts following her into his bedroom.

"How about we make a deal? We won't try to predict tomorrow, nor will we dwell on the past. And you can focus on trying to have a good time." He set his water down. "Why don't you go get changed? If I know Eden, she stashed something appropriate in that bag she sent you."

"She did, actually. It's not fancy or anything."

"Neither is the dinner. Go on. Bathroom's all yours. Just one thing." He pushed himself up as she rose, caught her hand and tugged her against him. Before she could speak, before he could breathe, he lowered his mouth to hers.

It was one thing to have thought about, dreamed about,

kissing Lana Tate. It was another to actually do it. The instant his lips caught hers, it was as if he'd been on life support and suddenly zapped back to life. Every cell in his body sang as he tasted and teased and dived in. Capturing the moan that escaped her mouth in his own had him releasing her hand so he could slide his arms around her back and bring her in closer.

He knew the instant her shock wore off as her mouth opened and she took a tentative taste of him before her arms encircled his neck. His entire body tightened; parts of his body hardened, and he relished the sensation of her breasts crushed against his chest, even as he struggled to draw in breath and stay on his feet.

When he tilted his head back, her fingers tangled in the hair at the base of his neck, clearly wanting to begin again. Her breath came in short, surprising gasps as she raised her chin, dark eyes filled with dazed confusion and surprise as they met his gaze.

"Guess that answers that question." She drew her hand forward, down his chest, then back up to brush her fingers against his swollen lips. "Probably a good thing we never tried that before, yeah?"

Definitely a good thing. "I'm thinking, all things considered, our timing is pretty great." He couldn't resist. He kissed her again but resisted the tug of her arms to take it further. "And if this were any other night, I'd say forget dinner and take you to bed."

"But it isn't any other night," she whispered. She stroked a finger down the side of his face. "I'll go get dressed, yeah?"

He almost changed his mind. "Yeah." Eamon stepped back and watched her pull out something from her bag by the sofa, pick up her cell phone, then walk across the room to the bathroom. She turned in the doorway after clicking on the light, faced him with the glow behind her. For the first time since he'd seen her in the bar last night, she looked almost...happy.

"I won't be long." Her cell buzzed. Lana rolled her eyes, glanced at the screen and sighed as she answered. "Hi, Felice. You know, I was just talking about you today..." She closed the bathroom door.

Eamon remained where he was, staring at the door. She could take as long as she wanted. Because he'd be waiting for her. No matter what.

"WHAT DID FELICE have to say?" Eamon asked as he pulled into a parking spot across the street from a four-story building with enough architectural interest to tell Lana it had been constructed almost a century before.

She'd debated answering the call from her late husband's boss, but the truth was, now was not the time to cut ties.

"She came across some photos of Marcus she thought I'd want to see. From when he was a boy." Lana waited for the wince, or the cringe, or the grief to pool in her stomach, but it didn't. Another one of those steps forward, she supposed. "I got the feeling she wanted an excuse to call, so she made one up." She glanced at Eamon, saw him frown. "I'd seen the pictures before. We have one of them framed at the house. She misses him, I think almost as much as I do."

"Ah." He nodded. "Good talk, then?"

"I guess." It wasn't that she didn't like talking to Felice. She did. And she appreciated everything Marcus's boss had done for her, but she couldn't help feeling the call was...intrusive. As if maybe there wasn't the room for Felice in her life as there had once been. Did that mean she was moving on?

Oh, she hoped so. She was tired of feeling as if she was stuck neck-deep in quicksand, slowly sinking into darkness.

Eamon climbed out of the car and came around to open her door.

"I think I've forgotten how to do this." Lana turned and dropped her feet out of the replacement SUV Eamon had picked up earlier that afternoon at the FBI depot. She stared at his outstretched hand, slightly confused as to what to do. Taking his hand felt as if she was taking that final step into a different world. A world where she and Eamon were more than just friends.

"Forgotten how to do what?" Eamon asked far too innocently.

"You know what." She accepted his hand and stepped out of the car. While he locked up, she quickly adjusted the simple black wraparound dress that, honestly, was something she could have pulled out of her own closet. The shoes were a little snug, but she could manage for a few hours. She scrunched her toes. Hopefully.

As he lifted her hand, the butterfly charms on the bracelet she wore caught the last bit of sunshine. Other than her wedding set, it had been one of the few pieces of jewelry she frequently wore: a memento of a trip she and Marcus had taken to Butterfly Harbor on their first anniversary. The small coastal town situated near Monterey had become one of their favorite vacation spots. She'd fallen in love with the shops and the Victorian Inn, situated at the top of the cliffs, and looked forward to the morning greeting of monarch butterflies that flitted past when they opened the balcony shutters.

"Do you really think we can do this?" she whispered.

"What? Have dinner?"

She arched a brow at him.

"Oh." His grin returned. That amazing, surprisingly boyish, teasing grin that made her stomach flip over. "You mean do we want to push the boundaries of friendship?"

"Not that either." She chuckled. He really was determined to put her at ease. "Do you think we can forget what happened last night at the motel?" It certainly hadn't escaped her thoughts that not so long ago she'd been shot at and her motel room had been burned to a crisp. "Even for a little while?"

"I'm darned sure going to try. On the off chance I didn't mention it before, because I have been thinking it…" Eamon pocketed the car key, took a familiar assessing look around them, before slipping his arm behind her and guiding her across the street toward a four-story building that took up a good half of the downtown city block. "You look beautiful."

"No wonder you get so many confessions. You could charm the spots off a giraffe." She smoothed a nervous hand over her hair, which she'd left down for a change. It felt odd, going to a dinner party when the rest of her life felt as if it was spinning off its axis, but with Eamon beside her she felt steadier. Stronger.

Irritation slid through her. Her confidence and inner strength shouldn't be so dependent on anyone else, but… it was Eamon's confidence in her, his affection for her, that made her feel as if everything was going to be all right. For the first time in a very long time, she was believing in herself again. What a remarkable gift for him to give her.

As they approached the rather elegant front door of the building, Lana spotted a couple striding their way. The man was tall, with dark hair and perfectly trimmed beard, and his attention—all his attention, it seemed—was directed to the beautiful Black woman tucked securely under one arm.

"Eamon! You made it." The woman broke away from her partner and hurried forward, her flowing dress matching the long scarf woven through her curly black hair. The second she reached him, she stepped into a welcoming hug and kissed his cheek. "Seems like every time we see you someone's in trouble. You don't come around often enough just because, you know."

"I know. I'm working on it. Jason." Eamon nodded to the man who joined them. "Thanks for coming."

"Glad to be here. You must be Detective Tate. Jason Sutton. This is my fiancée, Kyla."

"Oh." Lana exchanged handshakes with them both as her stomach fluttered with nerves. Give her a murder scene or a hostage standoff and she managed great. Strangers and socializing? She was way out of practice. "Of course. Kyla and Jason of the wedding invitation under the door," she joked. "It's a pleasure to meet you both. Congratulations."

"Thanks." Kyla reached for Jason's hand. "Eamon, I've finally figured out what your job should be for the wedding. Other than groomsman."

"Yeah?" Eamon grinned as he climbed the three steps to the double-glass, brass-handled doors. "Something other than picking up the kegs for the bachelor party? What's that?"

"Help him pick out a suit. He's dragging his feet."

"My best man—" Jason rolled his eyes.

"Is at a loss suit-wise," Kyla said, cutting him off. "Vince has it easy. Marine uniform, bam, he's done," she said to Lana. "I'd appreciate it if you'd lend your expertise, Agent Fashion Plate Eamon. You wear a suit every day of your life and yet this one tonight puts you in an entirely different league. That's what he needs. If only for as long as it takes for photographs."

"Comments like that make me wish we were eloping," Jason teased.

Lana had to side with Kyla on this one. At least as far as Eamon was concerned. There was no way Eamon had ever worn this particular dark suit to the office. The neatly pressed black slacks and jacket were perfectly tailored, nipped in at the waist, and, with the crisp white button-down shirt he'd left unbuttoned at the collar, made him look as if he'd just stepped out of one of those TV commercials for men's cologne. One of the good ones.

"Consider him taken care of," Eamon said as the door was pushed open from the inside by a fortysomething man wearing a simple black suit of his own. His jet-black hair displayed slight hints of blue in the overhead light. "I've got some connections. Good evening, Estavo."

"Agent Quinn, hello. Ms. Bertrand. Mr. Sutton." He stepped back to let them all enter, and once they were all in the foyer and the door was closed and locked behind them, he glanced at Lana. He made his way to the small curving desk in the center of the lobby. "May I get your name, please, ma'am?"

"Detective Lana Tate." She opened the purse she carried. It was larger than she'd have liked for an event like this evening, but she wanted enough room for her gun. "Do you need my—"

"No ID necessary, but thank you," Estavo assured her. He lifted the receiver to the antique-style phone on the desk. "I'll call ahead and let Eden and Cole know you're on your way up."

Lana couldn't stop her mouth from falling open as she looked around the lobby that could have been transported out of a 1940s hotel from New York. The floor was white marble flecked with gold and gray, the walls painted in alternating stripes of the same colors. Elegance personified, from the multiple groupings of comfortable, cushioned gold chairs to the large round table situated between the security desk and another pair of glass doors that mirrored the ones leading into the building. Atop the table sat a tall and wide vase filled with a huge spray of beautiful spring flowers.

"Is that the gallery?" She wasn't sure why she whispered and felt a bit embarrassed that she had.

"It will be," Eamon said. "You want that peek now?"

Even before she answered, he gave Estavo a quick look. "Why don't you two go ahead?" Eamon told their companions. "We'll be up in a bit."

"Okay." Kyla looked a bit confused as she and Jason headed toward the wrought iron elevator that reminded Lana of something out of an old movie. It wasn't the way the steel clanged as Jason closed the elevator door, but the jarring grinding of metal as the car disappeared up and out of sight.

"You remembered," Lana murmured.

"That you hate elevators? Hard to forget," Eamon said as they followed Estavo toward the locked doors of the gallery. "I had to climb fifteen flights of stairs because of you not so long ago. I still think I left half of my right lung in that building."

"It was only ten flights," she argued. "And it was just as well. Those kidnappers didn't expect a flood of agents to hit from both the elevator and the stairwell."

"I believe Ms. Renault left a surprise for you on the western wall, Agent Quinn," Estavo said as they stepped inside. Then he quickly returned to his desk.

"So, a doorman. In Sacramento." Lana was tempted to toe out of her shoes for fear she might mar the marble floor. "That's different."

"Private security masquerading as private security, actually," Eamon said. "A friend of ours recently contracted out as the West Coast representative of a private security firm. With Greta opening her gallery in the building and some previous events that have taken place, it's bringing her some peace of mind. Someone's at that desk twenty-four seven. There's also security cameras covering just about every angle of this place. At least if she starts sleepwalking again we can track her."

Lana barely heard a word he said. The stark white walls might seem cold and sterile, but as a future display area for Greta Renault's paintings, they were the perfect backdrop. A maze of walls, some higher than others, most of which had fabric swatches of different measurements hanging as if testing frame sizes, created a walkway and experience that made the gallery seem far larger than the actual space.

"Originally Greta was only going to showcase her own work," Eamon said as they made their way to the west wall. "But since she's been pregnant, she hasn't been painting as much. Plus she's sold off a lot of her collection. She's sponsoring a number of artists' shows in between her own showings. And she's not limiting the mediums. Photography, sculpture, and she's particularly fond of mosaics at the moment. She's also working on arrangements with some of the local high school art departments to display their students' work as well. Ah. Here it is." They took one last turn to the left. "Looks like she finally finished it."

Lana stared, frozen in place, at the enormous painted canvas. The trees of the forest had been painted in such a perspective as to make onlookers feel as if they'd stepped into the trees. The light shimmering from above cast a glow about the solitary figure in white, a woman with long silver hair in a robe that, while painted, appeared to be as soft as silk. She had one hand cradling her stomach, which was full with her child, while her other hand brushed against the ray caressing a nearby branch. Beyond her, a waterfall tumbled from far above and plumed up in mist that sprayed her feet.

"I can see her face." Lana moved closer, mesmerized. "Every other painting I've ever seen of hers, the woman's back has been turned toward us. But this one? She's smiling." Something akin to joy burst through Lana, as if something had broken open and hope had spilled out. "I always thought her paintings carried this hint of sadness. Of longing and grief."

"They did." Eamon rested a hand on the small of her back. "Greta spent a lot of years trapped in her past. I don't know how much of her history you know—"

"Nothing beyond what she's talked about publicly." She knew Greta's parents had been a powerful couple in Hollywood back in the day. A troubled noir actress and her filmmaker husband. They'd died tragically when Greta was just a little girl. But it was an event that defined a good portion of her life since. In recent interviews, Greta had been open about her struggle with various issues, including agoraphobia and, for a while, paranoia. The latter, fortunately, had been proved to be an outside manipulation in an attempt to steal her money. The agoraphobia? Jack McTavish had helped with that. A lot. Perhaps even more than her art. "She's happy now." Tears burned the back of Lana's throat. "That's what this painting shows. That she's happy. With Jack. And the baby they're going to have. *Transformation*." She read the description card on the wall beside the work.

"She said we'd be the first to see it. Besides Jack," Eamon said. "Life can change when you want it to. At least, that's the message I'm getting from it."

"One of the messages," Lana said. "Thank you, Eamon." She turned, lifted her hands to his face and drew his mouth to hers. She kissed him. Not in the way she longed to, but in a way that she hoped conveyed both gratitude and the promise of making the changes she wanted to. "I think I'm ready to go upstairs and meet the rest of your friends."

Chapter Seven

"I take it as a good sign we haven't overwhelmed your girl-friend."

Eamon glanced as Eden St. Claire nudged his arm and grinned at him. Her face was a bit rounder than normal, her hair a bit messier. But the color in her cheeks and the smile on her face erased the final fragments of the tragedy that had bonded them as children. He'd lost Chloe, his sister, but along the way he'd gained a few others, if not by blood, certainly by affection.

"You're going to get every bit of mileage you can out of that, aren't you?" Because he knew it would annoy her, he lifted that same arm and slung it around her shoulders. From where they stood, just outside Eden's kitchen, he could see the breadth of the vast loft apartment that was filled with everyone Eden considered family. Glancing over his shoulder to the line of windows behind him, he saw a more modern building that had, in the last year or so, become a major employment hub for Sacramento.

He'd had absolutely no doubt about Lana fitting in with his friends. She might not have been overly anxious to dive into the pool of his social circle. It gave him some satisfaction to know she'd agreed to come because of him. Not that she would have been walking into a lion's den. There wasn't a more gracious, welcoming group of people, as far as he was concerned. She'd stayed close at his side through the initial welcome and the first round of appetizers. She'd happily acquired a bottle of sparkly, flavored seltzer water that Eamon himself couldn't stand. Within moments of their arrival, however, Lana had been swept away by Simone Armstrong-Sutton, who somehow managed to make a soft gray lounge suit look as if she were having tea with the Queen.

Dr. Allie Kellan, sporting her usual dark-haired pixie cut and a sweater set that reminded him of a summer sunset, pulled both women onto one of the well-broken-in leather sofas situated in front of the fireplace. The three of them had had their heads together ever since, with the sound of Lana's genuine laughter lightening his heart.

She fit. With them. With him. As precisely and perfectly as he'd allowed himself to imagine.

Eamon sipped his beer, tried to smother a chuckle at the sight of Detective Cole Delaney, PI Vince Sutton and former firefighter turned private investigator Max Kellan huddled in the corner of the room, arms filled with offspring of varying ages. Cole caught Chloe Ann's hand in his before she could bop baby Caleb on the nose, while Max jostled back and forth to calm a four-month-old Sabrina, who was clearly demanding something her father could not provide.

"Lala!" Chloe Ann yelled loud enough to drop the room into instant silence. Cole, clearly used to doing his daughter's bidding, especially when she was kicking him in the stomach, bent down and released her into the wild. She hit the ground running. Kyla and Jason stepped back while water rescue specialist turned DART instructor Darcy and her husband of five months, Riordan Malloy, lifted their glasses to avoid spilling as Darcy spun around like she was caught in a tailwind.

Eamon watched, a bit surprised, as Chloe Ann propelled herself straight into Lana's arms. He held his breath, but not for long. Lana immediately set her soda down and reached to pick Chloe Ann up to settle her in her lap. The conversation started up again, this time with more smiles than had been in place before and with Chloe Ann reaching up and patting Lana's cheek.

"Well." Eden put a hand over Eamon's heart and cleared her throat. "If I'd had any doubts about her, they'd certainly be gone now." She looked up at him. "I like her."

"Yeah," Eamon whispered. Pride filled whatever space love hadn't taken up in his heart. "So do I."

"And now I understand why I could never convince you to let me set you up on a date."

"I admit nothing." He wasn't about to give her more than necessary. Eden St. Claire collected information the way most people collected dust bunnies. "She came with me tonight even though she didn't want to."

"Why didn't she want to come?" Eden frowned as the doorbell chimed and Cole, standing nearby, opened the door to let Dr. Ashley McTavish-Palmer and her husband, Slade, in. Seeing the two of them together always triggered a niggle of unease when Eamon thought how close they'd come to losing them last year when Ashley had found herself caught in a planned prison break. Slade had been undercover in the prison at the time, fortunately, and had managed to get both of them out alive. But only barely.

"Sorry we're late!" Ashley called out in greeting and waved at Eden. "Couldn't get out of the ER."

"We've got a house full of workaholics," Eden grumbled.

"Takes one to know one," Eamon teased.

"I'm coming around on that front," Eden admitted. "And you just changed the subject. Why didn't Lana want to come? We're a fun group."

"What you are is family," Eamon said. "That's a big thing to step into when you weren't expecting it." Or when you didn't know how to deal with it. Lana's upbringing hadn't been exactly picturesque, which had made the peace she'd found with Marcus all the more precious. "She argued with me before she agreed."

"But she did agree." Eden rocked back on her heels. "Interesting."

"She knew tonight was about Chloe," he said simply. "That's all it took."

Eden scrunched her face. "Well, doesn't that just move her up the ladder of acceptability. I did a background search on her."

"Figured you would." Eamon took another sip. "What is it you think I don't know? She was open about everything, including her suspension."

"So you know that came as a result of her drinking on the job and that she assaulted a fellow officer?"

He swallowed hard, did his best not to cringe. "I've not been made privy to the exact details of that event, actually."

"Hmm." Eden's approval seemed to have slipped a notch.

"I'm going to go out on a limb and say he deserved it," he said easily even as his stomach knotted.

"But you knew about the drinking."

"I know she's got a sobriety chip in her pocket and that she clings to it when she's stressed." He didn't think Lana would appreciate him having picked up on that behavioral pattern. "She's got four months sober, Eden. She's trying."

"Not saying she isn't. Just wanted to be sure you knew what you were getting into."

"None of us is perfect, E."

"I am well aware," Eden said and rested her head on his shoulder. "You know we love you, right? We don't want to see you getting into something that's going to get you hurt. That's all we were doing. Protecting you."

We? Eamon glanced over to Cole and Jack. Yeah, no way Eden would have gone poking around in Lana's record without sharing it with the dynamic duo. "Getting hurt is part of the risk. Otherwise what's the point? I appreciate having a lookout." He glanced down and swore he saw tears in her eyes. "Eden? Are you crying? Did I make you cry?"

"Please." She swiped at the tear that escaped. "These days the laundry makes me cry. Leave me alone," she laughed when he kissed the top of her head. "This big-brother thing makes me weepy."

"Good to know how to get to you. Hey, Ashley, Slade." Eamon greeted the newcomers as Eden made her way back into the kitchen to see to dinner. "Hard day in the ER?" he asked Jack's sister, who worked at Folsom General supervising the emergency room.

"I've had worse." Ashley pulled the bottle they'd brought out of her husband's hand. "And I need some wine. Slade?"

"Nothing right now, thanks." Slade held on to his wife's hand until she walked away. "So." The former undercover FBI agent shifted position to scan the room. After years of being undercover, he never ever kept his back to a room. Even one filled with people he knew. "Heard you were on scene of that fire downtown last night. And that there was an after event to close out the morning?"

"Private security has definitely aided your sense of humor," Eamon said. "All that was missing were the marshmallows and graham crackers. Could have had ourselves a real s'mores fest."

"Even with the flying bullets," Slade added.

"Who blabbed?"

"I wouldn't call it blabbing, exactly," Slade added at Eamon's doubtful expression. "Eden ran into a few walls where A&O Solutions and that client list is concerned. She thought maybe I might have some insights. The details as to your early morning activities came shortly after." He glanced over his shoulder as Ashley emerged with a large wineglass filled halfway with red in one hand and an open bottle of beer in the other.

"In case you change your mind." She brushed past him, handed off the beer to Slade and gave the latter a look that suggested to Eamon their tardiness had nothing to do with the emergency room being overcrowded.

"Your new job provide you with insights?" Eamon asked.

"Let's just say I don't miss all the rules and regulations that come with a badge." It wasn't just Slade's humor that had lightened, but his tone and the way he carried himself. He would never be rid of the intensity he naturally exuded, but the tension Eamon had seen from the first moment they'd met had abated. Eamon glanced toward Ashley, who was admiring Kyla's engagement ring before she beelined right for Vince and a baby fix thanks to Caleb and Sabrina.

"Okay. Do you have any insights you care to share with me or do I need to wait for Eden's status report?"

"I do hate to steal Eden's thunder." Slade ducked his chin, his lips curving. "Suffice it to say, I did a little poking around. And the firewalls protecting A&O Solutions' servers and systems? They're no joke. Could probably hack into the Pentagon more easily. Apparently A&O Solutions has been on the feds' radar for quite some time."

"Seriously?" Eamon frowned. "Why haven't I heard anything?"

"Above your pay grade. Above most everyone's. Just asking questions was enough to set off alarm bells."

"I get the hinky part where A&O Solutions is concerned," Eamon mused. "Most businesses that cloak themselves in subterfuge and mystery have something untoward going on, and it's obvious they're making a ton of cash, but—"

"Uh-huh. I don't think there's a way to finish that thought that won't disturb you," Slade said. "I ended up on a phone call with my boss. The second I mentioned A&O Solutions, he told me to hold my questions until he got out here." Slade eyed Eamon. "He didn't want any discussion over the phone."

This conversation definitely wasn't making him feel better. "Wouldn't it have been easier for you to go out to DC?"

"I don't like venturing too far from home," Slade said. "Part of the deal I made when I signed on with Minotaur Security. But if my boss is getting on a plane tonight? He's spooked. And you and your Detective Tate have stepped in something big. He wants to meet with you. The sooner, the better."

Chills raced down Eamon's spine. "So much for hoping you would put my mind at ease." His gaze wandered back to Lana, sitting with his friends, bouncing little Chloe Ann on her knee as the tyke shoved a miniature cupcake into her mouth, frosting and all. "When is he getting in?"

"First thing in the morning. I'm meeting him around ten at the Hyatt Regency on L Street." Slade met his gaze. "You two want in?"

Lana glanced up just then, met Eamon's eyes, her brow furrowing slightly as if asking him what was wrong. He instantly relaxed his face, offered a smile and toasted her with his bottle.

"Yeah," he told Slade. "We'll be there."

Chapter Eight

Lana blinked her eyes open and, for a moment, had to puzzle out where she was. Even after a short time, she'd gotten used to sleeping on Eamon's sofa. The idea of waking up somewhere else, like in his bed, was going to take some adjustment.

She tucked her chin into her chest, rolled over just enough to peer through the slight opening of the sliding barn door. She could hear the tap-tap-tap of a keyboard in the living room and Eamon's low voice holding a conversation with someone on the phone, she assumed. She inhaled the familiar aroma of continuously brewing coffee emanating from the kitchen. The sunshine streaming through the windows was somewhat of a surprise, or maybe she was just allowing herself to notice some of these things for a change.

She frowned, laying gentle fingers over the gray comforter. Funny. She didn't remember falling asleep in here. In fact...

She sat up, shoved her hair out of her face and glared at the door. She distinctly recalled crashing on the sofa after coming home from Eden's. It had been late. Far later than she'd expected to be. By the time 1:00 a.m. rolled around—

with the under-three sect having long since crashed, either in their beds or in their carriers—she and Eamon had made their way back to the Brass Eagle and his apartment.

She'd been tired. A good kind of tired for a change. Not the she'd-run-herself-into-the-ground-so-she-didn't-have-to-think exhausted.

She hadn't been so tired, however, that she hadn't wondered if perhaps this was the perfect evening to finally breach the barriers of their friendship and venture into more carnal territory.

But Eamon had seemed... She wasn't sure if *off* was the correct phrase, but it seemed to fit, even now. Something was on his mind. Something he either needed to or didn't want to discuss with her.

Which was no doubt how she found herself alone in his bed.

She threw back the covers, scooted to the end of the mattress and, as she swung her legs over the edge, found those personal mementos and pictures she'd thought lacking in the rest of the living space. A trifold brass frame sat on the nightstand beside her cell phone. Three photographs that made her heart break.

One image was of a teenage Eamon—apparently he hadn't gone through the same awkward, geeky stage every other teenager on the planet had. She could see the man's face in that of the boy. His smile was brighter, his eyes lively, his posture relaxed. He had his arm slung around the shoulders of an overall-clad young girl with crooked pigtails and an overly wide smile as they goofed in front of the camera.

"Chloe." The name came out almost like a prayer even as Lana let her gaze slide to the center photograph of the same

little girl, at around the same age, only this time she was sur-
rounded by three friends—friends Lana had met last night.
Rough-and-tumble, cautious-eyed Eden. Elegant, protective
Simone. And wide-eyed, analytical Allie.

The four of them stood arm in arm beneath a fantastic
tree house that, to Lana's roughened heart, seemed impossible to envision, let alone experience.

Lastly, the third picture had her reaching out and lifting
it off the nightstand.

A larger group this time, as large as the gathering last
night. Taken in a setting similar to that of Eden's apartment,
with the Sacramento skyline as their backdrop. Greta Renault, barefoot and in an ethereal white dress reminiscent
of the frequent figure in her paintings, was embraced by
her groom, Jack McTavish, and surrounded by their friends.
Correction, Lana noted. Their family. The fact the group
included Eamon lightened her heart. He stood a good two
inches taller than the rest of them, and those hazel eyes of
his displayed at least a fraction of the joy reflected in the
first photo.

She traced a finger over his face, smiled. He looked happy.
The shadows she remembered in his eyes were gone even
then. After he'd left the ghost of his sister's death in the past.
How she envied that. Even as she thought it, she realized that
last night—the time she was in the presence of these people—she'd felt the same. As if the group provided a kind of
magic that healed hearts. And souls.

Lana set the frame back where it was, unplugged her cell
and made her way to the door to slide it open.

Eamon glanced over, a cell phone up to his ear. He held up
a finger, offered a quick smile, then lowered his voice as she

set her phone on the table beside his open laptop and made a beeline for the coffee machine and her morning jolt. While the coffee finished brewing, she dug around in the cabinets and fridge for something to eat, finally settling on a banana that was more than ready to be turned into bread or muffins.

"That's right, no, I appreciate you letting me know," Eamon said. "I agree. It's not information we were hoping for... Yes, sir. I'll get to work on it as soon as I'm back in the office." He glanced up when Lana, having finished her banana, brought the pot over to refill his mug. "Yes, sir. You, too." He clicked off but the smile curving his lips didn't come close to reaching his eyes. "Morning."

"Morning." She faced him, leaned back against the cabinets. "Was that Lieutenant Santos?"

"No. My supervisor at the Bureau," he said, clearly working through his distraction. "A case I've been on for the past year is about to blow up. Judge we went to for a warrant won't sign off. Says we don't have enough evidence yet. Guess there's a reason they call him Ironclad Cahill." He scrubbed both hands down his face. "Guy doesn't sign a warrant until he knows it'll lead to a conviction. And we can't get that without the warrant."

"What about a different judge?"

"Burned through them already. The sad thing is, Cahill's right. He's a good check for what we do have and it's just not enough."

"I'm sorry." She cringed. She knew only too well the difficulties red tape could often cause. Sometimes it felt as if their hands were tied when it came to helping people. "What more do you need?"

"Don't know, actually." The defeated expression on his

face hurt her heart. No more than his own was hurt working in the Crimes Against Children division. "Guess when I'm back in the office, we'll have to start over. The hope was this guy could be the loose thread we pull to unravel the organization, find out where the photos are being distributed from, hopefully trace the source of who's taking them."

He shook his head as if trying to clear it. "Sorry to lay all this on you. Not what you came out here for."

"Don't be sorry." She'd never been so grateful to be a listener for someone else. She turned, doctored up her coffee and sipped. "After everything I've thrown at you the past couple of days, I'm more than happy to lend whatever meager expertise I can." She'd dealt with her share of child sex abuse cases and she'd hated every single one. There was a certain vile toxicity that came with that kind of work. Some people, like Eamon, seemed to have an immunity to it. Others? Well, most cops couldn't deal with it, certainly not for any length of time. Eamon had been working cases like these his entire FBI career. She forced herself to turn back around and look at him. "How do you do it?"

"Do what?"

She could tell by his response he knew precisely what she was referring to. "These cases. Deal with these children, what's been done to them? The people responsible. Day after day. Eamon, it has to get to you."

"Of course it does." A shadow passed over his face before he ducked his head, grasped the handle of his coffee mug but didn't drink. "But how do you walk away from something you're good at?"

It was a fair question. One she'd asked herself frequently over the past few months. She'd been a cop all her life. She didn't know how to do or be anything else. "I guess maybe you don't until you become so self-destructive or dangerous that you aren't given a choice."

"You know, it's strange," Eamon said. "I joined the FBI because of what happened to Chloe. I wanted to stop what happened to her from happening to any other child. To any other family. I figured I couldn't find or stop him, so I'd focus on doing the next best thing—stopping others. Making those responsible face justice for their crimes and the damage they do."

"I hear the *but*."

"But." His eyes looked almost pleading when they met hers. "Sometimes I can't help but feel as if I'm trying to empty an ocean of ugliness with a teaspoon."

"Maybe it's time you think about handing off the teaspoon to someone else."

"And do what?" His smile was quick, but not quick enough to cover the grief in his eyes. "I've considered that a lot since we closed Chloe's case. And then I remember how many other Chloes are out there. How do I walk away from that, Lana? How do I walk away from them? How do I ask someone who has a family, who probably shouldn't be bringing all this home with them, to take over for me because I'm, what, tired?"

She wouldn't say he was tired. There were only so many times a heart could be broken before it refused to heal.

She opened her mouth, wanted to tell him it was okay to put himself first, to find a new path and walk away. But no response formed. It wasn't any of her business how he continued his career, the decisions he made for his future. That said, Lana could only imagine how his job ate away at him.

She worried that someday there wouldn't be anything left of the Eamon she…

"Okay, enough psychoanalyzing the agent," Eamon announced and clicked his laptop closed. "You sleep okay?"

Recognizing deflection, she let him have his distraction since she wanted him to avoid spiraling down that dark tunnel she was all too familiar with. "Better than I have in a long time." Lana once again rested her back against the cabinets and held her mug in both hands as she sipped. "Having trouble recalling how I ended up in there, however."

"Oh, that was me."

"No." She gasped playfully and earned the delightful reward of seeing Eamon blush. "And here I thought the nighttime fairies carried me into your room."

He sat back in his chair looking, Lana thought without a second of remorse, something like a hero out of a medieval romance novel with that red hair and fit biceps that had her insides warming. All that was missing was a kilt and a sword strapped across his chest and that unbeatable dragon he continued to attempt to slay. She had a general idea what those arms felt like when they embraced her, but she wanted a more complete picture. A more complete experience. An experience that would only create new complications she couldn't afford. Complications and worry she wasn't in a position to responsibly deal with.

That said, what this man did for a simple white T-shirt really should be deemed illegal.

"I had some work to catch up on and I didn't want to take the chance of waking you up," he explained.

"So I gathered with that call," she murmured, waiting

for additional information that didn't come. "So. You were up all night?"

"Pretty much." He sighed, raised his arms over his head and stretched. "Got out of the chair around three this morning and did some push-ups to wake myself up."

Catching a glimpse of his bare torso as his shirt lifted away from the hem of his jeans made her feel as if there was a blast furnace coming to life inside her. "Sorry I missed that," she said. "So, you weren't very chatty last night on the way back here after the party at Eden's." Time to try to push open that door he seemed determined to keep closed.

"No. It looked as if you and Greta hit it off," he said. "Was she everything you expected?"

"Everything and more." Lana couldn't help but smile fondly at the idea of having become friends with one of her favorite artists. "She gave me a tour of her art studio and put my name on the guest list of the official opening of the gallery."

"That was nice of her."

"She also showed me the nursery and the mural she's painting." The fairy-tale-inspired forest scene reminded Lana very much of the painting she'd seen in the gallery last night.

"At least she isn't painting the ceiling." Eamon chuckled. "Jack was convinced he was going to have to talk her out of building a scaffold à la Michelangelo. I know it's indelicate to say, but I think her due date must be off. She's showing a lot more than Eden, Simone or Allie did at five months."

"Her due date is accurate." Lana hid her smile behind her mug.

"Everything's okay, isn't it?" Eamon's instant shift from amused to concerned had her wishing she'd kept her comment to herself. "There's nothing wrong with Greta or the baby, is there? Not that she'd have said anything—"

"She's fine. She was just super excited to share something she hadn't told Jack yet. Although, to be fair, I'm shocked he hasn't figured it out for himself." She hesitated, waited to see if he'd catch on. "She's having twins."

"Twins," Eamon repeated. "Jack's getting two babies at once?" He threw back his head and laughed. A sight and sound that lightened her heart considerably. "This is the best news I've heard in ages. He's going to freak out. In a good way," he added quickly. "So you're in on the secret, huh?"

She shrugged. "Greta's been dying to tell someone, but she's afraid everyone else is going to spill the beans before she can surprise Jack. She probably figured I'm safe since I don't know everyone as well as everyone else does." One benefit of being an outsider, she supposed. It made her privy to some fun information. "You can't tell him. Or let on you know."

"Don't worry. Her secret's safe with me. Aw, man. Twins." He shook his head. "I don't know if there's a better way to start the day than with that kind of news."

"I completely agree." And now that he was in a better mood… "What were you and Slade talking about so intently?"

"When?"

She eyed him as he shifted into familiar protective mode. It was a mode she recognized mainly because she had the tendency to do the same thing herself. Whenever she didn't want to share something disturbing with Marcus about a case or an investigation or a victim, she'd danced around his inquiries as if she were a lifelong ballerina who had earned her prima status.

"Last night when Chloe Ann shoved that whole cupcake into her mouth and got frosting up her nose," she said in an attempt to keep the mood light. "What's going on, Eamon? You're evading. What don't you want to talk to me about?" She narrowed her eyes. "That wasn't Lieutenant Santos you were just talking with but did he call earlier?"

"He did, actually."

"And are you going to share whatever information he told you or do I get to play twenty questions this morning?"

"I don't think your questions are going to come close to the right answers."

"Fair warning—there isn't enough coffee in this apartment for either of us to survive my irritation, Eamon. Spill."

"He was able to speak with Commissioner McKenna yesterday afternoon. Suffice it to say, your suspicion was correct and she did remember you."

She stared into the depths of her coffee. "I'd be surprised if she didn't."

"Mmm-hmm."

Lana pressed her lips together. She knew that tone. It was Eamon's version of sliding into DEFCON 1. Her stomach churned around the banana she now knew she shouldn't have eaten.

"You said you'd reached out to the commissioner for help with Marcus's case," Eamon said. "You didn't tell us you flew back to Boston and camped out in her office waiting room for more than half a day. And then came back the next day. And the next. Apparently Security had to escort you out every time."

"Security should have stopped me before I hit the elevator after the first day." Her attempt at humor fell as flat as the floor beneath her feet. Humiliation wound up from her toes all the way to the top of her head. That sick, ashamed feeling she'd worked so hard to suppress these past months twisted into an even bigger knot of regret. "Those few weeks are a bit fuzzy," Lana admitted. "I remember more about the seedy hotel and airport bars than I do visiting her office. I'm sorry," she said on a sigh. "I should have told you."

"You should have told me a lot of things."

She could feel his eyes on her, but resisted the temptation to glance over. She didn't think she could bear seeing disappointment on his face. Disappointment she would completely understand.

"Was this trip to Boston before or after you punched your partner and broke his nose?" Eamon asked.

"Before." Her entire body went hot. Her hands tightened around the mug and she set it down before it shattered in her hold. It was difficult enough, admitting to herself that she'd hit bottom. How did she admit it to a man she cared for?

"What did he say? Your partner," Eamon clarified at her look of confusion. "What did he say that made you punch him?"

It helped that he asked. It helped that he understood she had to have been pushed awfully far before she struck back. "He told me to get over it. Marcus's death." Her voice caught and she cleared her throat. "He told me to just get over it and move on."

"Ah."

"He didn't know I'd heard Marcus die. No one did." She could sense the nod he gave. She wasn't one to scare easily, but the idea of turning around and seeing disapproval on his face terrified her more than she cared to admit. But she did it anyway, because there was no moving forward with him, with this investigation, as long as the past stood between them. "Not that it would have changed anything if he did know. The guy's always been a jerk."

"Sounds like. I was right, then," he said as he met her shaky gaze. "I told Eden he'd probably said something to deserve it. I'm surprised you only broke his nose."

"So was my captain," Lana admitted. "The fact he said what he said in front of a room full of detectives worked a little in my favor." A very little. That her partner already had reports filed against him for disrespectful behavior also helped.

It still burned, though, that it was those reports and not her own, up until then, exemplary record that had left her suspended rather than fired. Still, it did take three of her fellow detectives to pry her off him and that, to this day, felt like a badge of honor of sorts. "I don't have any excuses for what happened," she told him. "It just confirmed what I already knew. I'd gone back to work too soon. Hadn't processed any of my feelings the way I should have. And I wasn't particularly eager to seek counseling." Counseling for cops was a double-edged sword at times, especially for women in law enforcement. Any signs of weakness could be easily exploited.

The main miscalculation she'd made was how much worse the drinking made things. "I accepted my suspension without question," she continued and turned her back. "And I'll accept whatever consequences remain to be handed down, but in the meantime, I did what I needed to do to get myself straight. I needed to in order to think and work this through. So I could..." She trailed off before she admitted something she hadn't even admitted to herself.

"So you could what?"

His hands gently rested on her shoulders, squeezing as she let out a shuddering breath. She hadn't even heard him get out of the chair. The man moved like a shadow, quiet, stealthy and just a little bit intimidating. She wanted to reach up, to take hold of his hand and not let go, but instead she splayed her palms on the counter.

"Lana, there is nothing you can't tell me. If you don't understand that by now, then what are we doing?"

What were they doing? She hated the tightness in her throat, the way the tears burned. Tears she knew to be useless and ridiculous. "I needed to get straight and sober so I could come to you. I didn't want to give you any excuse to turn me away. To make you doubt what I knew to be true." She stopped short of admitting the rest: that she never ever wanted to be the object of his pity or sympathy.

"You were my plan," she told him. "I knew if I was going to find out what really happened to Marcus I would need your help, and I couldn't do that until I stopped drinking. It took me some time, after my suspension, to make it happen, but I did it. I made mistakes on my way, but I got to where I needed to be, Eamon." She lifted her chin and took a deep breath. "I got to you."

"WE DIDN'T FINISH our conversation, you know," Lana said as she emerged from the bathroom after her shower.

"What conversation was that?" Eamon asked from his place at the small square kitchen window. He wasn't stand-

ing directly in front of it, but off to one side, where the occupants of the dark-colored SUV across the street couldn't
see him. He'd jumped in the shower first, got dressed in
four minutes flat so he could retake sentry duty while Lana
took her time.

Eamon glanced over his shoulder, saw she'd chosen a
bright pink beacon of a T-shirt that no doubt could be seen
from space. Her hair was still damp and hung around her
shoulders. Her face, makeup-free as usual, carried some actual color in it this morning. He didn't like to take the credit,
but wondered if she was feeling more stable around him. Or
maybe he was just imagining or seeing what he wanted to.

"Our conversation about Lieutenant Santos calling." She
picked up the gun she'd left on the sofa side table and slipped
it into the back waistband of her snug jeans. "Have you been
standing there the entire time I was in the shower?"

"Yep." He sipped his coffee, waited for the return call
from Jason Sutton with the results on the plate trace. "Good
shower?"

"Lonely," she said in a way he knew was an attempt to
get a reaction.

"All you have to do is ask," he said easily when she popped
up on her toes to look over his shoulder. She grabbed hold of
him, one hand on his back, the other on his shoulder. Both
warmed him all the way to his marrow. "See them?"

"Dark SUV, rental car, across the street? They're hard
to miss."

"Especially when we got back at one in the morning with
no one else around." He'd kept an eye on them every hour
on the hour since then. "They followed us from Eden and
Cole's. Been parked there ever since we got back."

She swore with such magnificence he had to grin. "You think those are the ones who firebombed my motel room? The ones who shot at me?"

"I'm going to assume so." If they weren't, they were part of a bigger team, and that wasn't something Eamon was happy to consider. Still, he wasn't ruling anything out.

"What's with all the cloak-and-dagger stuff?" she demanded and, to his chagrin, fixed yet another pot of coffee they didn't need. "If I have something they want, why not come right at me?"

"They did come right at you, actually. Email's up on my computer. Initial report from the fire department on the motel fire."

"And?"

"You don't want to read it yourself?" He debated about pulling an Axel Foley and sticking a banana up the SUV's tailpipe, but he had yet to see that work in real life. Now wasn't the time to experiment. But it might be an opportunity to turn the tables and get some information. He'd already worked out a plan on that front. All it was going to take was a couple of people for backup and one perfectly timed phone call.

"I think we're past the point of either of us keeping secrets from one another," Lana said. "Let me have it. What's in the report?"

"The lock on your motel room door was busted in. Handle and door frame, too." He couldn't help but replay that first night she'd arrived and feel grateful she'd accepted his invitation to use his couch.

"They came in looking for me first, then torched the place

when I wasn't there." She sat at the table with her coffee. "Why? To scare me?"

"Didn't work, did it?" Whoever was trying to intimidate her didn't have the first clue who they were dealing with. Or they were underestimating her frame of mind. Maybe because they'd been told what to expect by someone familiar with her recent erratic behavior. Someone who didn't realize she'd gotten herself together. "Hired help," he said as his cell phone vibrated. "That's Jason." He answered the call. "You find anything?"

"At six thirty in the morning you're lucky I can find my phone. Car's rented under the name of Steve Stark. Someone's been watching too many superhero movies."

"Criminal masterminds they are not," Eamon muttered.

"The card he used at the airport agency is a business account registered to Klein Technologies, but their website? It's a facade. Nothing deep or informative, just a showpiece should anyone go looking."

Which they did. "It's a shell company."

"More like a matryoshka company. You know, those Russian nesting dolls with a doll in a doll—"

"I am familiar."

"Right. Well, halfway down the rabbit hole, I found what you suspected. A&O Solutions pulls the strings. You want me to dig deeper?"

"No, thanks." Jason was good, but the last thing Eamon wanted was to alert anyone at A&O that they were on to them. "I've got the rest handled. Appreciate the quick assist, Jason. Next Thursday, ten a.m. I'll pick you up."

"For what?" Jason asked.

"Your suit fitting. I know you didn't want to go tux—"

"I'm not a tux kind of guy."

But Kyla was definitely a tux kinda woman, and by now Eamon had been to enough weddings to understand keeping the bride happy was the most important thing. "Ten a.m. Thursday. Be ready." He hung up just as a white panel van pulled up beside the SUV. Windows opened, a package was handed over and the SUV's driver glanced up and nodded.

"Breakfast delivery?" Eamon inclined his head for Lana to join him. This time she stepped in front of him. He could smell the bath gel from the shower drifting off her skin in tempting, sea-inspired waves. It was all he could do to keep his hands to himself and not slip his palm down the soft curve of her hip.

"Doubtful. No plates. What did Jason say?"

Exactly what Eamon had anticipated, but wanted confirmed. "If they followed us from Eden's, that means they've been on our tail for a while." And he hadn't noticed. Not something that was sitting well with him. "Who all have you spoken to since you got to Sacramento?"

"Just you. And your friends." Lana glanced over her shoulder at him. She was close. So close the heat of her body warmed his. He was almost distracted enough to miss it, but he didn't. The realization of what he'd accepted hours before. "Felice." The woman's name came out more like a curse than an answer. "She called me before we left last night."

It wasn't disbelief or dismay he heard in her voice, but irritation, disappointment. And more than a touch of anger. "That car out there was rented by a shell company Jason traced back to a nonexistent entity." He chose his words carefully. "It's A&O Solutions."

"Seriously? You think someone there is behind this?"

Eamon bit the inside of his cheek. Well, she'd almost gotten it right. He couldn't exactly blame her for wanting to cling to the notion that her husband's boss, his mentor, was someone she could count on and trust.

"But that doesn't make sense." The anger remained as she looked back out the window. "If I had something of Marcus's, something they wanted, all they had to do was ask. Why didn't Felice just ask?"

"Maybe she did? Or maybe she couldn't." Eamon had yet to land on an answer. "Or perhaps she might have, had you been anyone or anything else."

He could almost hear her frown before she turned and faced him.

"You're a cop, Lana. Even worse, you're an honest cop. She probably can't take the chance of you coming across whatever it is she thinks you have."

"You make it sound as if she's some kind of criminal mastermind or something."

"For the record, I'm leaning more toward the former, not the latter."

"Stop leaning at all. This is my life we're talking about, Eamon. I don't have anything they want."

"That you know of." He was already ten steps in front of her, but for now he could wait for her to catch up. And accept the truth of what was developing in front of them.

"I hate this. I detest not knowing what's going on in my own life."

At least she was thinking straight. He could use that, use her anger and her determination to prove his suspicions wrong to both their advantages.

"I know. And this news probably won't help clear anything

up. Lieutenant Santos's conversation with Commissioner McKenna went beyond her passing interactions with you and her familiarity with the hit-and-run file. She checked in with the officers who reported on Marcus's accident. One took his vacation time almost immediately after, then resigned before coming back. She can't find him."

"And the other?"

"The other told the commissioner he had nothing to add to the official report and that if she had additional questions she could speak with his union rep. The detectives? Same exact response."

She grimaced. "Not a normal reaction if you don't have anything to hide."

"No," Eamon agreed. "It's not." It was, in fact, a big red flag. One he suspected the Boston police commissioner was not going to accept lightly.

He could imagine seeing the wheels turning in Lana's mind. Eyes that flashed between confusion, dismay and back to confusion. "What is going on? What was Marcus involved in, Eamon?"

"Apparently those were Commissioner McKenna's questions as well. Lieutenant Santos said she's not opening a formal inquiry, but that she has one of her best people already handling it."

"Well, I guess that's something. Is that all Lieutenant Santos said?"

"Not quite." Eamon looked over her shoulder as the second car pulled away. "Commissioner McKenna did some checking of her own, ran all the names associated with Marcus that were on record just to see if anything popped. One thing did."

"Yeah?"

"Cynthia Randolph."

"Marcus's assistant at the law firm?" Lana's eyes went wide. "What about her?"

"There was a car accident the day after she spoke with you, after she sent you Marcus's client list." There wasn't any other way to put it... "I'm sorry, Lana, but she's dead."

Chapter Nine

The back door of the Brass Eagle closed behind Lana as she stepped out into the parking lot. Without casting a glance to the surveillance van she knew was waiting to follow her, she took a moment to inhale a lungful of early morning air before she made her way around to the front of the building. No sooner had she reached the locked front door than her phone rang.

Heart skipping a few beats, she stopped to answer the call. "Don't tell me—you decided you wanted coffee after all."

"Been practicing that line, haven't you?" Eamon's voice carried the strained smile she had no doubt was on his face. She glanced up, pretending he wasn't in the surveillance van but still upstairs waiting for her to return.

She stopped, tucked the cell under her chin and bent down and retied her shoe. "Just staying in character."

"Remember," he continued, "all you have to do is take a walk to the coffee shop. We just want to confirm you're the target and then draw them away from here. Cole and Jack are on standby if we need backup."

There was no determining where her nerves started and her anxiety ended, and it was taking a lot of her energy to conceal both. She chose to believe Eamon's repeated "reminder" was him being extra cautious; the alternative was admitting he was concerned about her. Eamon Quinn didn't do worried, as far as she knew. She didn't want to be the reason he started now.

"Max is monitoring communications from the Eagle," he continued.

"Copy that," Max confirmed over her earpiece.

"You won't be alone for a second," Eamon stated. "We'll be right there with you. In your ear the whole time."

It was on the tip of her tongue to remind him she could take care of herself, but she supposed, after the past year, she needed to prove it. So she slipped right back into the role she'd written for herself as caffeine-supplying girlfriend.

"You know espresso makes you jumpy." It wasn't difficult, making sure her voice carried toward the SUV that was still parked across the street. The same two men still occupied the front seats. Honestly, if she didn't know better, she'd have thought someone stuck two mannequins inside as a practical joke. "Okay, here we go." She stood up, brushed her hands on the back of her jeans and headed off down the street.

Her and Eamon's thrown-together plan to draw the car away from the bar and the surrounding businesses and homes made sense. He hadn't been thrilled with the idea of using her as bait, but what other choice did they have? Collateral damage had to be considered, especially now that the body count was rising.

The last thing she wanted was any more innocent people to get caught in whatever cross fire she caused. Their best chance at drawing them out and giving them an opportunity to approach was to put her out in plain view. Alone.

That was assuming, of course, that an approach was their priority. The other night at the motel it seemed they'd had other ideas about what to do with her.

Lana purposely didn't look in the SUV's direction as she walked. The truth was, she was grateful to be out on her own for a while, away from Eamon and his increasingly confusing, distracting presence. She'd gotten used to not caring about anyone, not wanting to care, but after even a few hours in his company, she was so deep into caring she could feel herself slipping into emotions she'd sworn she'd never embrace again.

She pinched her lips tight, remembering that talking to herself wasn't an option unless she wanted to have a full-on confession session. How stupid to have thought she was beyond being able to be shocked. Wrong yet again. Learning her late husband's assistant had been killed, possibly as a result of Lana's reckless questions, added a weight to her soul.

Guilt made her thirsty, and not for water. She should have been grateful he'd stuck that bottle of Scotch of his back in the cabinet. If it had still been out...

She shook herself free of that thought. Quenching that thirst was only going to mess things up even more, but she'd appreciated the excuse to get out of the building that was filled with her greatest temptation. She should feel lucky Eamon and Vince were trusting her enough to make this play and draw out the men surveilling the apartment. Besides, throwing herself into work she hadn't been able to do for months was a good way to push herself through the cravings.

Part of her wanted to believe it was just a car accident,

a coincidence, but who was she kidding? She'd been a cop long enough to know coincidences like that weren't likely. Cynthia Randolph's death was tied to Marcus's, which tied it directly back to Lana. It was up to her to get answers—and justice—for both of them.

Her stomach knotted hard enough to make her wince. People like Eamon, people who trusted her, were poised to get hurt. And what about his friends and their families? If she didn't get to the bottom of this soon, she'd just be acting as an anchor dragging them all down. That was not something she planned to be responsible for. No matter what she had to do.

As far as those men in the SUV were concerned, however, she had one simple plan in mind. There was little she liked more than proving someone wrong.

Unless it was making them regret underestimating her.

"You've got this, Lana." Eamon's voice brought her back to the present. "And we've got you."

Her chin inched up. His confidence in her was the shot of adrenaline she needed. Now wasn't the time to play it safe. Now was the time to go full bore and confront whatever monster she'd awakened. As anxious as she was, she kept her pace slow and casual, as if taking a Sunday morning walk with two potential killers on her tail was an everyday occurrence.

She flexed her hands that were shaking as if she was a rookie out on her first assignment, even as she could feel the muscle memory begin to return.

It was all coming back to her. Not in drips, but in subtle waves that built upon one another. The energy surge, the way the plan ran through her mind, over and over as a kind of mantra, even as she reminded herself to stay fluid and be ready for anything.

The focus on keeping her actions completely normal and predictable was helping tame that guilt that continued to threaten her. "I'll be back before you know it," she said to Eamon. "Keep the sheets warm for me."

"She does know you aren't the only person on the line, right?" Vince Sutton's deep voice had Lana's lips twitching.

"All part of the fun," Lana said before Eamon could respond.

Eamon had found himself a really great group of people to surround himself with. People who were there for him the instant he called. Neither Max nor Vince had cast any looks of doubt or concern her way after Eamon filled them in on their plan. Vince had set her up with the special two-way ear pods while Max cut a small hole in the seam of her right sneaker to place an infinitesimal tracking device into her shoe. Any temptation she might have felt to protest would have been silenced by Eamon's warning expression.

Instead she'd rolled her eyes and offered a ghost of a shrug of acceptance. It had been the only indication he was concerned she was up to the job.

She *was* up to this, she told herself. She *was* okay.

Had it been anyone else in the van other than Eamon, however, she might not have been so easily convinced.

Lana straightened her ear pods as she kept her sights focused on the hole-in-the-wall coffee shop that, according to Eamon at least, gave a certain chain a definite run for its money. She was barely a block into her walk when she heard an engine start up and rumble to life.

"Okay, we're on," Eamon said quietly. "They're pulling out now, Lana. Be ready for anything."

"Copy that." Hands tucked into the pockets of her borrowed zip-up hoodie, she kept her gaze straight ahead even as the anger percolated in her blood, hotter and stronger than any coffee machine was capable of brewing. She was either bait or a target. Or, worst case, she was both. It wasn't easy, accepting Eamon's supposition that Felice Covington was behind all of this. It was a bitter pill to swallow, that a woman Lana considered a friend had ulterior motives where maintaining their relationship was concerned. Lana thought of Felice as someone to lean on while Felice thought of her as…as what? A pawn? A tool? A source of information?

The idea that their get-togethers were nothing more than surveillance check-ins made her slightly sick and eroded the already fragile trust Lana still possessed.

"Crossing over to 8th Street." She caught sight of the SUV as she glanced down the street before crossing against the light. They wouldn't be able to follow, as it was a one-way street. Instead they'd be forced to circle around and approach from a different direction—one that should be easy to see coming.

In the distance she could hear the church bells ringing at the Cathedral of the Blessed Sacrament, calling worshippers to Sunday service. A homeless woman pushed her overfilled grocery cart along the sidewalk on the other side of the street. A pair of joggers came to a quick pause at the corner, glancing both ways before continuing on their way. The white noise of the jumble of freeways reminded her of the sound of the ocean roaring.

Lana kept her pace steady and casual. Three blocks down, another four blocks over. Now was not the time to get anxious or get ahead of herself or obsess about what came next. One step at a time. One day at a time.

Jumping to conclusions and fixating over possibilities rather than responsibly looking for answers and following a plan had been partially responsible for getting her suspended.

She had to be careful. If for no other reason than Eamon was a part of this now and the last thing she wanted to do was put his career—or his life—in jeopardy. If someone was going to have to take chances, it was darned well going to be her. She wouldn't survive anything happening to him.

Her stomach swirled at the very idea. She wouldn't want to.

"Okay, Lana. Looks like they're going to circle around to catch sight of you again. Stay alert."

"What else would I be?" Probably not a question she wanted an answer to. "Max? You got me on your screen?"

"Sure do." Max Kellan, Vince's partner in his private investigation business and Dr. Allie Hollister-Kellan's husband, sounded like the epitome of calm. "One nice big green blip."

"Not too big, I hope." The back of her neck prickled. She stopped, looked behind her, but found only an empty street. "You still have that SUV in your sight?"

"That's affirmative," Vince said. "Why? You see something?"

"No." But she felt something. Or did she? Her instincts weren't exactly firing on all cylinders these days. "No, I'm good. Just felt like someone..." She didn't finish that thought for fear Eamon would pull the plug. "Where are you exactly?"

"Close. They're coming up two blocks in front of you, Lana."

"We've got a couple of delivery vans between us and them right now," Vince said. "But we've got them."

"Right. Okay." The sign to the Jumped Up Café hung overhead in the distance and reminded her to get her bearings.

She counted nearly every step of the remaining blocks and forced herself to glance into the small shop windows as she passed. A dry cleaner. A yoga studio. A number of papered windows that promised new businesses opening soon. The remnants of an old pet store took up a corner space while next door, Sir Barks-a-Lot, a dog grooming business, was clearly a recent addition to the area, with its brightly painted windows featuring a Jack Russell terrier wearing a suit of armor.

She splashed through a puddle caused by an overwatered patch of grass as an older man walking his dog passed and offered her a bright good morning.

"Okay, we're circling back in your direction." The relief in Eamon's voice didn't make her feel better. She shivered, still unable to shake the sensation that she was being followed. "Lana? You okay? What's wrong?"

"I don't know." The traffic light changed as she pulled open the door to the coffee shop. The van that drove past had her glancing over her shoulder, frowning.

"Eamon, that van we saw with the SUV this morning, the one that passed off a package to the SUV? I just saw it again." Was she imagining things, or had the driver looked at her?

The hesitation was brief but enough to get her blood pumping. "You're sure?"

"Yes." She caught a flash of a shadow out of the corner of her eye and turned, scanning the empty street behind her. "No plates, same as the one this morning." Driving around without plates was a sure way to tempt a run-in with local police. At least it had been when she'd been a patrol officer.

"Max, check if there are any security cameras in the area," Vince said. "If you need help accessing, buzz Jason and get him on it."

"Working on it now," Max said.

She couldn't just keep standing around outside the café. Not without looking suspicious. "I'm headed inside," Lana murmured and stepped into Jumped Up.

"Remember, get in, get your coffee, get out and go to the park. You would have seen it. It's the one across the street," Eamon said. "Stay in the open. Our target just rounded the block again."

"He's turned into the alley behind the café," Vince said.

"We're parking at the end of the alley, Lana."

"Mmm-hmm." It was the only response she could give without sounding as if she were talking to herself. She took a deep breath and allowed the warm, toasty aromas of hot butter mingling with pungent ground beans to pull away at least some of her stress.

Any other time she'd have loved to revel in the dark-wooded, Pacific Northwest feel of the café. With the dim lights and small guest tables, it reminded her of one of her favorite spots up in Seattle.

Most of the tables were occupied. A young mother broke off a chunk of banana to hand to her stroller-trapped toddler. A pair of college students seated at the window counter on bar stools tapped away on laptops while sipping out of frothy eco-friendly cups. Two older men were halfway through a game of chess that, to Lana's eye, looked like it would soon end in a checkmate, while a group of senior citizens compared prescriptions and tried to outbrag one another in the chronic conditions department. She might have smiled if her heart wasn't pounding in her ears. Just your ordinary neighborhood coffee stop.

The handwritten chalk menu overhead boasted everything from a blackberry dark roast to a word salad offering that had just as many syllables as the coffee beans it probably took to brew.

Lana got in line, bided her time and resisted the impulse to look behind her anytime the door opened.

Instead she focused on the glass pastry cabinet containing dozens of in-house baked goods while one of the employees was busy filling the sandwich trays for what Lana was sure was the upcoming lunch rush. Her stomach growled in anticipation of something she didn't dare ingest.

She'd have to come back another time. When her heart wasn't lodged solidly in her throat.

Lana took a step to the side, her eyes refocusing on the glass of the display cabinet in time to clash with the gaze of a man standing two people behind her. She slid her eyes away, then back again, only to see him shift behind the person in front of him.

Was she being paranoid? The back of her neck continued to prickle.

She could hear Vince and Eamon talking, though, discussing the plethora of delivery vans and trucks making their way in and out of the alley. Sunday morning deliveries setting up the eateries in the area for the upcoming week.

Lana wasn't in a position to talk to them or respond. What she could do was memorize everything about the man who continued to shift in and out of her sight. Tall, slender to the point of being almost skeletal, with close-set dark eyes and a locked jaw that she suspected might be made of steel. The dark suit he wore cost more than her first car, and his long jacket looked too heavy for the early summer weather currently assaulting the Valley.

Her pulse jumped, but she remained calm, pretended to continue to peruse the pastry offerings before she ordered her coffee.

"Thanks," she said a while later when she accepted the large cup. "Do you have a public bathroom?"

"Right back there." The server pointed to the narrow hallway on the other side of the counter.

"Thanks." Lana flashed a smile and circled around, noticing her tail had stepped out of line and taken a seat by the door.

She made her way to the one bathroom, hesitated with her hand on the door, glanced back to confirm her tail was still there. He was. And he'd shifted his chair out in order to keep her in his line of sight. Her gaze shifted down to the gun secured at his side.

"Lana?" Eamon asked as she ducked inside and locked the door. Her hands were shaking again. Her pulse raced, as if her system didn't know what to do with the adrenaline anymore. "You went awfully quiet. What's going on?"

"Not sure." Self-doubt battled against reason. It would make sense for them to have someone else on foot; someone she and Eamon hadn't anticipated, but this was why she'd reminded herself to stay fluid. Expect everything and have contingencies in place for whatever might come to pass.

It was, she recalled, one of her early lessons from her two years as an undercover narcotics detective. One thing she did know. She didn't want Eamon blowing his cover by having to come in and pull her out. Or worse, rescue her. The very thought was bitter on her tongue.

"You sound stressed. Talk to me, Lana." Eamon's urging didn't do anything to calm her down.

She looked down, fisted her hands to make them stop shaking. "Someone followed me inside. And yes, before you ask, I'm sure. He's waiting by the front door and he's armed. Eamon, if I've put these people in danger—"

"No one's going to try anything in publi—"

"They shot up a motel in the middle of the night," she reminded him and heard the panic in her voice. "I don't think a coffee shop is going to offer a deterrent."

Now wasn't the time to lose it. She braced her hands on the edges of the sink, ducked her head and tried to shove the images of Cynthia Randolph out of her mind. The thoughts of the family the woman had left behind—her parents and a brother, if Lana recalled correctly. The ripple effects were devastating and she was done causing them.

"Okay, it's okay." Eamon's voice in her ear again. "Just stick with the plan and make your way to the park. We'll be there in a couple of minutes. Max? We could probably use some backup—"

"No!" Lana cut him off. "No, Max, you stay at the bar.

I mean it, Eamon. I don't want anyone else in the line of fire because of me. Just... I just need a minute." Her mind quickly sifted through her options. She couldn't erase the image of that mother and her baby, or the chess-playing pair. Going out the front door could very well get them hurt. That only left one option.

"Lana. You want out, you say the word," Eamon said. "We'll find another way."

"We both know there is no other way," she said. "They've already killed two people that we know of." She didn't want any more blood on her hands.

"Lana—"

"I'm going out the back." She picked up her coffee and carefully opened the door.

"Lana, no. I repeat, no on the back exit. The SUV—"

The occupants of that SUV were going to find a way to get what they wanted one way or the other. At least with her tracker, Eamon, Vince and Max would be able to see where the bad guys took her and maybe even lead her to Felice and the answers they sought. "I've got at least one guy with a gun on one side and the possibility of escape on the other," she told Eamon. "I'm going with option number two."

She didn't stop to look toward the front but focused on the neon Exit sign over the back door. She hadn't bothered with a purse, had her cell in the back pocket of her jeans, her ID, a credit card and some cash in the other. All she had in her hand was her coffee, which she could throw in someone's face as a last resort.

"Lana—" Eamon's anger came through loud and clear, but it was hopefully something she'd deal with later. "They're right outside. Don't you dare... Vince—"

She heard swearing and the blaring of horns as she pushed on the bar and opened the door into the alley.

Lana couldn't decide who was more surprised. The driver of the SUV or his copilot in the passenger seat. She turned slightly, saw the man from the café running down the hall toward her, his hand already on the butt of his gun.

"You guys looking for me?"

The passenger looked out, confusion marring his thick brow. The man had a neck thicker than her thigh, and it wasn't helped by the black turtleneck he wore, or the black knit cap obscuring most of his forehead.

"You going to open the door or what?" she demanded as she popped the plastic lid off her large, steaming coffee.

He looked back at his partner. The other man's shrug confirmed her earlier suspicion that they were not dealing with rocket scientists. She felt some of the tension and fear melt away. Abducting her hadn't been their objective. Otherwise they wouldn't be balking now. She'd taken them by surprise, which gave her the advantage.

"Lana, I swear, if you get into that car…" Eamon's voice trailed off, probably, she thought, because he didn't want to voice what she knew he was thinking.

The back door of the coffeehouse burst open. Lana pivoted and tossed the contents of her cup right in the man's face. He jumped back. The door slammed closed just as the passenger in the SUV jumped out and yanked open the back door for her.

"Lana, don't you do it," Eamon shouted. It took her a second to realize she hadn't heard him through her earpiece, but from down the alley, where he was racing straight for her.

She couldn't afford to keep watching him. They needed

answers. She needed to get this case closed once and for all. And right now the only path she had to do that was in that SUV.

She climbed into the car. The door barely closed before the passenger was back inside shouting, "Go!"

Lana was thrown back in her seat as the car took off down the alley and made a sharp, tire-screeching turn onto the street. She turned around, eyes pinned on the alley as Vince's van made an equally sharp turn to pursue.

"What are we supposed to do now?" the driver demanded of his partner.

"Don't know." His hands were shaking as he pulled out his cell phone.

Lana frowned. She'd never encountered such uncertain criminals before. "Who do you work for?" she shouted over the roar of the engine.

"Shut up!" the driver yelled. "Do we go to the rendez-vous?"

"The rail yards? Yeah." Cell phone guy nodded and dialed. "They said if we got into trouble to head there."

Curious, Lana carefully slipped her finger into the door handle and pulled, but they'd engaged the child locks. Her window didn't work either. "Eamon." She kept her voice low as they continued to argue. "We're headed to the rail yards." The area was in the early stages of redevelopment. She couldn't imagine anyone was there on a Sunday. At least, she hoped not. "Eamon?" She pressed a finger against her ear, looked behind her as they sped away and put distance between them and Vince's van.

"Eamon?" She tried one more time, only to realize that the voices in her ear had gone silent.

Chapter Ten

"I can't hear her," Eamon yelled into the dash screen as he rebuckled his belt, now that he was back in the van. "Max? Why can't I hear her?"

"Signal's jammed," Vince answered in his marine-calm voice that scraped along the edge of Eamon's nerves. "Probably why we couldn't get a signal off them back at the bar. She's okay, Eamon. She's alive."

"She was alive when she got in the SUV," Eamon corrected, wondering if his heart was ever going to beat again. He pinned his gaze on the roof of the SUV that was gradually gaining distance on them. "We don't know what she is now. What was she thinking, getting into that car?"

"She was probably thinking she doesn't want anyone else getting hurt on account of her." Vince's matter-of-fact statement made sense, but it didn't sit well with Eamon. "I'd be more concerned about who the guy in the café was. Max? You get anywhere on surveillance in the area?"

"Yeah, hang on." Max's voice and activities were muffled before a second voice echoed on the other end. "Jason just got here. He's setting up and will hack into the feeds I was able to pick up on."

"If Jason gets busted for this, I'm going to expect a federal bailout," Vince warned Eamon. "Lana went with her gut." He switched lanes, stayed a good three car lengths behind the SUV. "We weren't there and we weren't in her head. Give her the benefit of the doubt."

"I should have been with her," Eamon said. "And her gut is what got her suspended from the force in the first place."

"Beating yourself up about this isn't going to do any good. Max? You've got us on your map, right? Where are we headed?"

"Three choices. Old Sac, I-5 or…"

"The rail yards." Vince and Eamon spoke at the same time.

"Max, you stay on her tracker and let us know the second it comes back on line."

"Way ahead of you. Jace, let's…"

Eamon blocked out the chatter. "She was jumpy. I should have seen it. Telling her about Cynthia Randolph probably pushed her over the edge." He should have gone with her. They should have revamped their plan so she wouldn't have been alone.

"Stop woulda coulda shoulda-ing," Vince ordered. "And stop thinking with your…heart," he said with a wince. "You're a good FBI agent, Eamon. Start acting like it. You can begin by remembering she's a cop with a decade's worth of experience behind her. You know her. Better than the rest of us do. What was she thinking when she got into that car?"

It took some doing, filtering through the last few minutes to dig out what Vince was asking for. "Collateral damage. She'd do whatever she could to stop the fallout from affecting too many people."

"All right. Good. Max? You got anything on those cameras yet?"

"Not yet. Jason's having some issues getting into the... What?"

"Someone's in the system already." Jason's voice snapped through over Max's. "I'm trying to get in around them, but it's going to take some time so they don't know we're piggybacking in on their hack."

"Do whatever you can," Vince ordered. "Whoever that guy was in the coffee shop scared her more than the two guys in the SUV. And keep in mind, they drove off with her. They didn't shoot her then and there."

"Ah, the bright side," Eamon muttered. His hands fisted against his thighs. How had he not seen what was going on behind those eyes of hers? "When we do find her, I'm never going to speak to her again."

Vince surprised him by grinning. "Must be love." He glanced over at Eamon, his smile widening. "You never did hear the whole story about me and Simone getting back together, did you?"

"I heard enough," Eamon said. "Enough to know you've been where I am now."

"We'll get Lana back," Vince promised. "None of us are going to let her get away from you. I promise."

"Don't go making promises you can't keep," Eamon warned. "There! We were right. They're taking the turnoff for the rail yards."

"Okay. Okay, I'm going to back off. Give them some space and time to think." Vince eased his foot off the gas. "We don't want them feeling cornered. She didn't get into that SUV without an idea, Eamon. I know it's hard right now, but you need to ease up, okay? I'm going to call Jack and Cole in. Chances are we'll need local law enforcement's support."

"Okay, we're in!" Jason shouted over the line. "Max and I are going through the security footage from the parking lot across the street from the café. Give us a second…"

"There! Screenshot him, right there," Max said.

Eamon's pulse kicked up.

"Putting it through my facial rec program now…" Jason murmured.

"What facial rec program?" Eamon asked. "Did you hack into the FBI again?"

"Of course not," Jason said with a fair amount of offense.

"He's been developing one himself," Vince explained. "When he's not working at the teen center or studying for his degree."

"Gotta do something to put food on the table," Jason said. "And I've already got interest from a private security company, thanks to a mutual friend."

"Slade," Eamon said, then shook his head. "I forgot, we're supposed to meet him—" He pulled out his cell and dialed. "Hey, Slade. Sorry, but I think Lana and I are going to be a little late for our meeting."

"Let me guess," Slade said in an overly calm tone so similar to Vince's that Eamon had to glance over to make sure Vince was still in the car with him. "Does this have anything to do with a visit to Jumped Up and an in-progress pursuit through downtown Sac?"

Eamon frowned. "I don't really know how to respond to that." He clicked onto speaker and held out his phone. "You've got me and Vince. And yes, we're currently tailing an SUV with Lana inside."

"Ah, guys?" Jason's suddenly uncertain voice filled the car. "I've got an ID on the guy following Lana into the café. His name's Boris Klineman. He's a former spook."

"CIA," Vince muttered. "Awesome. Just what we needed."

"What on earth does the CIA want with Lana?" Eamon asked.

"Nothing," Slade said. "Boris doesn't work for the CIA any longer." He paused. "He works with me."

"OKAY, GUYS, THIS has been fun, but I've changed my mind. You really need to drop me off." Lana's sudden bravado had little to do with the panic coursing through her system and more to do with the fact that the men in the front seat looked more freaked out than she did. The rumbling and bumping their way through the rail yards was giving her a headache and sending the box on the seat beside her into some kind of frenetic fit. "Whoever you're working for, I'm betting they didn't see adding kidnapping to your résumés."

"You just…" The passenger swung around and pointed his cell phone at her. "Just shut up. We need to think."

"No." Now wasn't the time to be quiet. Causing more confusion was going to get her out of this car faster than anything else. Except maybe them shooting her and throwing her out the door. "What you need to do is to stop this car and let me go. Whoever that was back at the café—"

"You mean your boyfriend?" the driver spit.

"Actually, I was talking about the tall guy with the gun. But yes, the agent, too." She wasn't entirely sure how to feel about referring to Eamon as her boyfriend. It seemed so… juvenile. "Who I can guarantee by now knows exactly where you're headed. You aren't getting away. Not while I'm in the car with you. Give it a few minutes." She pointed behind her. "You'll see him again."

"FBI?" The passenger lost most of the color in his face. "Um...they didn't say anything about the feds being involved."

"Shocker. Someone lied to you." And she had a pretty good idea who.

Lana scooted forward in her seat as they pulled off the road and onto the endless gravel expanse. They bumped and jostled their way over the mishmash of old train tracks, avoiding various piles of rebar, steel beams and piping for upcoming projects. "Stop the car and let me out. I'll make sure everyone knows I got in willingly. No kidnapping charges." She crossed a finger over her heart before holding up three fingers when the passenger looked back at her. "Promise. Girl Scout's honor." Total bluff. She'd never been anything close to a scout.

"Gonz, maybe we should do what she says." The driver's hands tensed on the wheel as they slowed. "They've already paid us. We can just..."

Gonz? What, had she been abducted by a pair of Muppet wannabes?

"We finish the job," Gonz said, his thick brows vee-ing over equally dark eyes. All of a sudden the two men didn't look much like men, but rather overgrown kids who were in way over their heads. "As soon as we ditch the fed, we take our cash and make a run for the border to Mexico."

"You aren't going to ditch the fed." They were giving her a migraine.

"Yes, we are. We already have..." Gonz twisted around in his seat again, looked out the back window. "I don't believe it. She's right. He's still back there. Hack, I thought you said we lost them."

"He's giving you space," Lana said quietly. "To give me time to show you the error of your ways. From what I can see, the job was simply to watch and report. Right? Look—" Lana began as they hit another rail and she bounced high enough to hit her head on the roof. "Ow." She pressed a hand against the top of her head and grabbed the box before it slid to the floor. "Okay, that hurt. You two aren't in anything you can't get out of right now. Trust me. I know. I'm a cop."

"Disgraced cop, from what we heard," the driver said.

"Nice." Lana smirked. "What's your name, Hatch?"

"Hack." He glanced over his shoulder. "Short for Hacksaw."

"You wish," Gonz snort-laughed as they hit another bump that sent both Lana and the box beside her into the air once more.

"Leave that alone," Gonz snapped as Lana pushed the box back against the passenger seat. "That's ours."

"Let me guess," Lana said. "Your payment? How much is my life and privacy worth?" Hand-delivered this morning right out in the open where anyone could have seen. Her heart skipped a beat. Where anyone could and did see. She ran her finger over the cellophane tape holding the lid closed. "Were you supposed to be paid in cash?"

"Didn't think so," Hack said, glancing back before he had to take a hard right to avoid another stacked set of rails. "Thought it was going to all be online. We set up a new account and everything."

"Would you shut up!" Gonz ordered.

"Sure." She pried up a corner of the tape and pulled it

back. "I bet you did." Resting the box on her legs, she removed the rest of the tape. The two sides popped open. Without taking the lid off fully, she could see the red light of a digital timer counting down. She closed her eyes, forced herself to take a deep breath. "Stop the car."

"We've been through this already—" Gonz began, only to stop midprotest when she opened her eyes and looked into his. "What? What is it?"

"Stop the car. Right now. Hack, stop!" Her palms went clammy as she swallowed hard.

"Stop, Hack. Stop!" Gonz yelled.

Hack slammed on the brakes. It took all Lana's effort not to scream, but she kept the box steady.

As the timer continued to tick down.

One minute fifteen seconds. Fourteen seconds...thirteen...

She looked behind them, saw Eamon and Vince barreling across the rails toward them. "We need to get out of the car." She slid the box onto the seat and sucked in a breath when the contents shifted. "Unlock the doors, Hack. For all of us."

The two men were staring blankly at the bomb packed neatly into their payment box.

"Just in case you needed more information," she said in such a tight voice she feared her throat would close, "there's enough C-4 in this box to blast you and a good portion of this rail yard into the afterlife. So by all means, please. Take your time and think about it."

Fifty-nine seconds. Fifty-eight. Fifty-seven...

"Right." Hack nodded and clicked open the locks. "Prison's better than dead." He hopped out of the car at the same time Gonz did.

She grasped the handle and opened her door. With her eyes glued to the bomb, she gently released her hold as she lifted one foot out of the car.

She heard the sound of tires over gravel ramping up behind her. "Eamon!" she yelled, hoping, praying he could hear her. "Eamon, for the love of... Stay back." She twisted and her foot caught. She landed face-first in the dirt and gravel.

In her head, she could see the clock ticking down. Forty seconds, thirty-nine...

She wrenched her foot free of the car, shoved herself up, stumbled again as she tried to catch her balance.

"Stay back!" she yelled at Eamon as he leaped out of the car and raced toward her, Vince right on his heels. "There's a bomb!"

Twenty...nineteen...eighteen.

Her feet couldn't get any traction and she slipped and shoved herself forward, fearing, knowing she wasn't going to make it clear.

She nearly tripped again, only to find herself caught by two pairs of hands that kept her upright. "Eamon."

But it wasn't Eamon. Eamon was being dragged back by Vince, who was pulling them behind the van for protection.

"Run!" Gonz yelled as he and Hack all but lifted her off the ground and put as much distance between them and the SUV as they could.

"Five...four...three..." She couldn't help but continue the countdown.

"Get down!" Eamon's voice erupted over her the instant before the car blew up.

The shock wave took the three of them down, face-first, right in a pile of jagged debris. Heat blasted over them. She couldn't hear anything but the sound of her own heart hammering so hard in her chest she felt her ribs might crack.

She had no idea how long she lay there, how long she breathed in dust and dirt, smelled the acrid stench of burning fuel, metal and plastic. Lana cried out when rough hands grabbed her shoulders and rolled her over.

"Lana!" Eamon's voice broke through her foggy thoughts faster than his face appeared in front of her. "Lana, you okay? Can you hear me?"

She shook her head, coughed as he sat her up, moved behind her and wrapped an arm securely around her.

She blinked, tears streaming from her eyes as she watched the black plumes of smoke erupting from the bank of flames.

She could hear shouting then. And sirens. And…everything. Everything in the world seemed to be lodged firmly in her ears. She plucked an ear pod free and the odd noise vanished instantly.

"I've got it." Eamon popped the other one out, pulled her back so she was sitting up straighter. "You okay?" he demanded and carefully ran his hands up and down her arms and legs as if checking for any injuries. "What about you two?" She felt him shift and reach back first for Hack, then Gonz.

"I'm okay," she choked out as an odd energy zinged through her. "That was…seriously close."

"Too close," Eamon muttered. "Here come the reinforcements," he said as a fleet of emergency vehicles and other cars headed their way. She saw Vince turn and wave his arms, motioning for them to detour to his right, before he headed toward her.

"Hey." Lana attempted to grin up at him, but had to blink a few times to put him into focus. "You found me."

"Never lost you." Vince crouched, reached out and touched a finger to her cheek, and it was then she noticed the combination of relief and concern on his usually unreadable face. "Told you we had your back." He turned his head toward Gonz and Hack as they stumbled to their feet. "Fastest turnaround from criminal to hero I've ever seen." He stood, helped haul them up as two groups of paramedics jogged over, medical kits in hand. Behind them, two squad cars, lights spinning, emptied out, followed by Cole and Jack emerging from their SUVs.

"We need to get them to the hospital," Eamon ordered.

Lana heard something in his voice, something she couldn't quite identify. Or maybe she didn't want to.

"That bomb was meant for them," she whispered, in part due to her raw throat. "It was the package we saw delivered from the van." She pulled her legs in under her, but didn't get the chance to even try to stand. Eamon scooped her up into his arms. "Ah, jeez, Eamon. Don't do this. I can walk."

"I'm not talking to you right now."

"Yes, you are." Her attempt at humor was greeted by a steely-eyed glare. Because he seemed to need it, because she needed it, she lifted her arms around his neck and buried her face against him. "Don't be angry with me, Eamon. It's not even ten a.m."

"The way I'm feeling right now, I'll probably be angry until the end of time." He began to walk, bypassed the EMTs and took her straight to the back of one of the ambulances. "You got into that car. After I specifically told you not to."

"Funny how I have my own mind." She clung to him

even after he set her on the edge of the back of the open ambulance. "I couldn't take the chance the guy with the gun wouldn't hurt anyone."

"But you had no problem risking yourself."

"It's the job," she shot back and was rewarded by a hacking, lung-searing coughing fit. One of the EMTs, a young blonde woman with a pixie cut, placed an oxygen mask over her mouth. Lana took a few deep breaths before she shoved it aside. "I'd never have forgiven myself if something happened to any of those people, Eamon."

He stood beside her, rested a hand on the back of her head and drew her against his chest. "I know. You were more than willing to die for all of them."

She nodded, reveled in the feel of the fabric of his shirt against her cheek.

"I do have one question for you. Before they take you off to the ER."

She shook her head, pushed back. "I don't want—"

"I don't care what you want at this moment." He bent over, his face so close to hers she could feel his breath, as hot as the fire that continued to burn in the distance. "You're so willing to die for strangers. I want to know, I need to know, if you are just as willing to live." He cupped her face in the palm of his hand. "For me."

She had no doubt, not in that moment at least, that he could see into her very soul. "I—"

"Don't answer now." He pressed his mouth to hers. She tasted her own tears when he pulled away. "Think about it first. Because if the answer is yes, I plan to hold you to it."

Chapter Eleven

"Yes, sir, I'm certain Agent Barbosa will lead the team just as well, if not better, than I could at the moment." Eamon paced his way around the perimeter of the ambulance bay of the emergency room of Mercy General. Besides the chaos around him, the cell reception inside was horrific. Although chaos suited his state of mind at the moment. "I'm happy to assist where I can from a distance."

"Assist with what?"

He glanced over his shoulder, keeping a rein on the irritation that surged through his system. Eamon cupped his phone against his chest and glared at Lana. "Aren't you supposed to be on a gurney?"

Her eyes narrowed, but before she responded, the muffled sound of his boss's voice had Eamon lifting the phone again. "Yes, sir. I appreciate the update. I'll check in soon." He pocketed his cell. "It's not enough you semi-assaulted a former CIA operative a few hours ago in a coffee shop. Now you've broken out of the hospital."

"I didn't break—I walked. And why does it take longer to discharge you from the emergency room than it does to be examined?" She straightened the sweatshirt that one of the patrol officers had passed along to her at the scene. "I'm fine. And I know the doctor already told you."

Oh, the doctor had told him all right. Apparently countless scrapes, bruises, heat burns and a minor sprained ankle weren't cause for hospital admission, despite Eamon's plea to the contrary. What he wouldn't give to have her put under lock and key, preferably with a guard on her door.

"Vince is on his way to pick us up."

Lana had refused to let him ride in the ambulance with her. After he and Vince gave their statements and handed Gonz and Hack off to the sheriff's department, he'd had a quick conversation with Lieutenant Santos, who was not thrilled to be called to yet another fire-related incident connected to Lana. Vince dropped him off at the hospital before he headed home to check in and switch vehicles. Since then, he'd spent his time pacing, catching up on emails and getting thoroughly acquainted with Mercy General's spotty reception.

"Do we need to make a break for it before an orderly comes after you?"

"I'm fine." Her limp was barely noticeable as she moved toward him. "They've got their hands full with actual sick people. What's going on? They call you back on a case?"

"They wanted to." He spotted a small park bench across the lot by the exit. "Let's get you off that ankle."

"If I have to say I'm fine one more time I'm going to slug you in your badge." She touched a hand to his arm. "New case? Ongoing?"

"Doesn't matter. It's being taken care of."

"You're still angry."

"Now, why would I be angry?" Even now the terror he

hadn't felt in more than twenty years pressed in on him. Until today, he hadn't thought anything could rival the uncertainty and fear Chloe's murder had triggered. But that was before Lana had nearly gotten herself blown to smithereens. "You did what you thought needed doing."

"Yes, I did." The steadiness in her voice only irritated him further. "The same thing you would have done in my position."

"Don't be so sure."

"But I am sure. I know what you're going to say, Eamon." Her breathy voice, the rush of words—he could tell she'd been rehearsing what to tell him. "I could feel you radiating tension all the way back in my partition. And thanks, but I'm not going to sit down, because once I do, I won't want to get up anytime soon."

"Lana—"

"Don't." She turned on him, rested her hands on his chest. "Don't keep dwelling on the what-ifs. Believe me, it's only going to make things worse."

He looked at her, unable to see anything other than the red splotches from the heat burns and the scrapes on her face and neck. The barely-there evidence of something worse that could have happened.

"There's no need for an I-told-you-so, or a lecture on not following orders. For the record, I... Oh."

He dipped his head and kissed her. A kiss devoid of the anger and fear that had been building up over the past few hours. A kiss he'd never anticipated giving, especially not so publicly and impulsively. It was a kiss that, he hoped, would silence and comfort him and, maybe, if he was lucky, begin to restore his equilibrium.

"Okay." She curled her fingers into the fabric of his shirt when he lifted his head. "Have to admit, I didn't see that coming."

"Me either." He rested his forehead against hers, closed his eyes and, for a moment, reveled in the knowledge that she was alive, that she was safe and that she was in the one place he wanted her: his arms.

"I thought for sure I was going to have to wear you down in order to get you to do that."

He smiled in spite of his still-unsteady emotions. "I'm about to say something that will probably tick you off, but I need to get it out."

"Okay." Her voice was slightly muffled by his shirt, as she'd pressed her face against him.

"Don't ever do anything like that again."

"Eamon." He felt her entire body tense, from the top of her spine all the way down to her toes. But when she leaned her head back and gazed at him, there was nothing but understanding in those amazing depths. Along with the barest hint of humor. "I can't promise that."

"You could try."

"It's not just that I can't." She shook her head. "I don't want to. I haven't felt this alive, this useful, this *capable*, since before Marcus died. It's like I spent the past two years in this unbreakable fog, but when I was in that hallway near the bathroom, when I had to make that split-second decision, it all came back. That adrenaline rush, that going on instinct. An instinct that, for the first time in a long time, I felt as if I could actually trust." She reached up, flattened her palms on either side of his face and tugged his mouth down to hers for another kiss. "You gave me that. A chance at redemption. All the rest of it—the mistakes you think I may have made—"

"The mistakes you *did* make."

"No. There were no mistakes." The certainty, the confidence he'd been looking for ever since he'd first seen her sitting in the Brass Eagle waiting for him at that table, it was all back and seemingly, amazingly, firmly in place. He didn't know whether to be relieved...or worried. He was on the precipice of getting everything he'd ever wanted: her. Was he about to lose her because she'd found her true self again?

"I really am trying not to dwell on what-ifs myself," she said. "But what if I hadn't gotten into that SUV when I did, Eamon? What if I'd gone out the front door instead and that car remained parked there? Because that was the plan. They were told to follow me and stay put. In that alley behind the café."

"Lana—"

"There were dozens of people inside. Families. Babies." Her brow creased, as if she could envision the horror of a different result. "They could have all been killed when that bomb went off. I'm not going to regret preventing that from happening."

"I know you're right." It hurt to admit, but he owed it to her. He didn't want her to think, for one second, that he wasn't proud of her, even if she had scared a good ten years off his life. "As an FBI agent, I don't have an argument to make. But as the man who..." He stopped himself from saying the words, but not fast enough he didn't see the shock in her eyes. "I guess I'm just going to have to get used to you being a badass again."

"I guess you are." She kissed him for a second time,

smiled against his mouth when a horn honked. "I think that's Vince."

"Yeah." He tightened his arms around her before he released her. "Slade texted a little while ago. Since we missed our appointment with them at the hotel, he and his boss are waiting for us at the Brass Eagle. I think we're about to get read in on the story behind A&O Solutions."

"It's about time." She slid her hand down his arm, slipped her fingers through his and held on. "We okay?"

He nodded and squeezed her hand. "We're okay."

HE MIGHT NOT have said the words, but she'd heard them. At least, Lana wanted to think she had, but the truth was, she was afraid she was reading too much into the moment between them. Between the adrenaline rush and subsequent crash, she suspected she could sleep for a week. It wasn't every day a woman saw her entire life—past, present and potential future—flash before her eyes.

Her stomach growled so loud once they entered the kitchen of the Brass Eagle that she made Vince laugh and take pity on her. He detoured to have his kitchen staff get them some food while she and Eamon made their way to where Slade was sliding out of a booth by the window.

She'd only met Slade Palmer once at dinner the previous night. If she hadn't, she might not have recognized him. Gone were the casual jeans and T-shirt that put most of his tattoos on display. Instead, this man was in full professional mode, right down to the sharply pressed dark slacks and crisp button-down shirt. The laptop he had open on the table was housed in a briefcase and reminded her of the kind of thing she saw in spy movies.

"You two sure know how to start the day with a bang," Slade said.

"How long did it take you to come up with that one?" Eamon said as they shook hands.

"Longer than I'd like to admit. Heard you had a close call." Slade brushed a hand over her shoulder. "Glad you're okay."

"Thanks."

"This is my boss, Aiden McKenna. He owns Minotaur Security."

The man seated across from him got to his feet, turned and offered his hand. He rivaled Eamon in height and build, but where Eamon was red-haired and fair, this man's hair was so dark it had shimmers of blue, and those green eyes of his were as sharp as broken bottle glass. There was a punch of attractiveness about him that Lana suspected had left many swooning in his wake. "Pleasure to meet the woman who knocked one of my best men down a few pegs. I'm going to have to add coffee defense training to my employees' schedule."

"My apologies to… Boris, was it?" Lana said.

"I will pass them along." Aiden straightened. "I'll also add my sentiments to Slade's. Happy to see you're both all right."

"McKenna." Lana frowned, trying to place the name. She glanced back at Eamon. "Any relation to the Boston police commissioner?"

"Only slightly." Aiden's lips curved. "She's my mother."

Lana's mind raced. The man was still looking at her with nothing less than approval and acceptance. Maybe Commissioner McKenna hadn't shared anything about their previous experience.

"Well, that explains that," Eamon said as he accepted the

greeting. "We heard through the grapevine Commissioner McKenna was sending her best man to talk with us."

"Is that what she said?" Aiden straightened his shoulders. "I'll have to be sure to mention that when I see her for dinner next month. And time it for when my siblings are in earshot."

"Great. Now you probably started a family feud," Lana teased Eamon and did her best to bury her nerves. "Are you guys hungry?" She gestured back to the kitchen, where she and Eamon had ordered what was becoming their standard burger fare.

"We grabbed something on the way over, actually," Slade said and, after a nod from Aiden, held out his hand. "Lana, would you mind giving me your cell phone?"

"My phone? Why?" Even as she asked, she pulled her cell out of the back pocket of her jeans.

As soon as he had it, Slade plugged it into his laptop, typed something in, scanned the screen. "Yes, it's like you thought."

"What thought?" Lana asked. "What's going on? What did you find on my phone?"

"We'll get to that," Aiden told her before he produced what looked like a cell phone charger. He set it on the window ledge, flipped a small switch on the side.

"What is that? A signal jammer?" Eamon asked. "I haven't seen one that small before."

"Perks of the trade," Aiden said.

"You're saying my cell is bugged?" Lana asked. "It hasn't been out of my sight in months."

"There are multiple ways to track someone these days," Slade reminded her. "Or to hack into their devices."

"You being tracked would explain an awful lot, Lana," Eamon suggested.

"Awesome. For the record, this conversation is already ranking at the bottom of my desired activities list for the day. And I almost got myself blown up this morning." Lana tugged off her sweatshirt and hung it on the hook on the back of the booth while Eamon dipped behind the bar and came back with a water for her and a filled mug of coffee for himself. She glared at him as she waved him into the booth and slid in next to him.

"You really want liquid caffeine right now?" he asked.

She didn't answer but took a large gulp of her water. Before she sat down, she'd felt as if she hadn't had anything to eat in months. She'd been famished. Now? Eamon's thigh pressed against hers, sending her thoughts into a completely different arena. There was nothing like almost dying to remind you to live.

"Vince filled us in," Slade said as Vince appeared with a plate of onion rings and a trio of dipping sauces. Rather than returning to the kitchen, the private investigator grabbed a chair and planted himself at the end of the table.

"On what he could, at least," Aiden added.

"Sac police took the two men into custody," Eamon told them after giving them a quick rundown. "From what I hear, they're not holding anything back on the details."

"Let me guess," Aiden said. "Local guys. More brawn than brains. Questionable history with the law. Contacted online, supposed payout, also online, from a company that dead-ends about two shell companies in?"

Aiden made it sound as if what had happened this morning was an everyday occurrence. "They were smart enough to stop the car when they saw the bomb." Lana reached for a still-hot ring and submerged half of it into the house-made ranch before biting in. "But yeah, from what I gathered, they were in it for a quick buck. I wouldn't call them harmless exactly, but—"

"They came through in the end." Eamon reached his hand under the table and took a hold of hers. "I don't think it would require much to convince them to testify against A&O Solutions."

Slade and Aiden exchanged looks.

"What?" Lana asked.

"There are about a half dozen shell companies in between these two and A&O. It's something, but it's not anything we can build a solid case on. A&O has their business locked down so tight not even oxygen gets out. I bet right now they're already severing any ties with the shell that hired these two. Or at least that's the way it used to be." Aiden reached into a soft-sided briefcase Lana had missed before. He pulled out a stack of file folders, set them in front of him, along with a tablet computer that was already on. "There's a reason I came out here instead of passing this information to Slade over the phone." Aiden rested a hand on the top file. "What I'm about to share with you needs to be kept strictly confidential. For the foreseeable future, at least."

Vince glanced up at one of his servers who was refilling coffees. The young woman's eyes went wide at Aiden's comment.

"Hold off on the food for a little while, Maya, please?" Vince said even as Lana's stomach growled. "I'll give you a heads-up when we're ready."

"Sure thing, boss." She hurried back into the kitchen, no doubt to share what she'd overheard.

"You want to take this upstairs, where it's more private?" Eamon offered.

"No," Aiden said. "This'll be fine." His eyes flickered to the cell phone he'd set near Eamon's shoulder at the window. The screen displayed the area behind him, giving him a wide field of vision outside.

Lana kept her expression passive as her mind raced. Until this moment, she hadn't considered there might be a replacement crew keeping an eye on her. Unless...unless she wasn't the only one Aiden was worried about.

"For the record, I was a little freaked out before," she admitted. "Now you're starting to scare me."

"Told you she was paying attention," Slade said to Aiden, who nodded in what Lana interpreted as approval. "You're on, Aiden."

Lana dropped her gaze to her cell lying dormant on the table, hooked up to what she assumed at this point was some kind of technological life support. Under the table, she squeezed Eamon's hand. Why did she feel as if she was about to take a massive dip down one huge drop of a roller coaster?

"I'm a rip-the-bandage-off-the-skin kinda guy, so I'm just going to jump in," Aiden said. "A little over three years ago, based on a reliable tip, the Department of Justice opened an investigation into A&O Solutions for a variety of crimes including, but not necessarily limited to, money laundering, corporate espionage, blackmail, conspiracy..." Aiden hesitated. "Murder."

"You can't be serious." Lana had guessed right—that

coaster drop robbed her of breath. "You're suggesting A&O Solutions is what? Some kind of front for organized crime?"

"It's not a suggestion, Lana," Aiden said. "It's a fact. They've been operating in this vein almost since the company was established back in the eighties. They have their hands in everything. And not just in this country. All over the world."

"That human trafficking ring I was investigating last year? The one my cousin got caught up in?" Slade said to Eamon. "Aiden's seen evidence that suggests A&O had a hand in the initial financing of their operation."

"I can't believe this." Lana could only stare as a buzzing roared in her ears. "There has to be some mistake." Even as the protest escaped, she knew it wouldn't go anywhere. Information like this wouldn't be shared, however limited, if there wasn't irrefutable evidence of its validity. "Forget the fact Marcus never would have been involved in anything illegal. I've been to Christmas parties with these people," she said. "Office events, baby showers! Heck, a whole group of us went to Bermuda… What you're accusing them of makes it sound as if they're operating like something out of a bad spy movie."

"Lana, let him present his case," Eamon urged before he turned his attention back to Aiden. "I'm sor—"

"Don't apologize for me," Lana snapped and attempted to tug her hand free, but he hung on. "It's not the last four years of your life they're calling into question."

"That's not what they're doing." Eamon's jaw tensed. "Is it?"

Lana's stomach sank when neither Aiden nor Slade answered. "You'll let me know if I need a lawyer, yeah?" Between this revelation and her cell phone, she was beginning to wonder.

"I think we need to hear what they have to say," Vince said in a clear attempt to play peacemaker. "I've started picking up some government contract work, and while I'm sure my contacts and connections aren't nearly as good as yours," he said to Aiden, "I haven't come across anything about an investigation like this. Or about A&O itself."

"Good." Aiden nodded. "That means the wall of silence is holding. This entire thing is as high up as it can go. But that doesn't mean A&O isn't aware of it. They've got their own connections, their own operatives, everywhere. It's one of the reasons they've survived as long as they have. Secrecy isn't just a job requirement at A&O Solutions. It's a creed."

"Sounds like some weird secret society to me," Lana muttered. "One with a major profit margin."

"Clearly A&O isn't the only one with connections," Eamon said. "You found out about it, Aiden."

"It took calling in just about every favor I was owed." Aiden didn't blink. "I've got ten years with the Secret Service behind me and I left on relatively good terms." A hint of regret flashed in his eyes. A quick flash, but it was there. "That's always afforded me some significant goodwill. In the three years it's taken me to build Minotaur into what it is, I've been lucky and rarely missed a step. But when I started asking questions about A&O Solutions? I got major pushback. Pushback I've never experienced in all of my professional life. I'm not downplaying it when I say my reputation meant absolutely nothing where A&O was concerned. After seeing what little evidence my contacts were willing to share, I understand now why they literally suspect everyone of possibly being connected to them in one way or another. Even me."

"Just to expound on that," Slade said. "He's not joking about his standing in the business. His reputation was good enough to lure me into the private sector after how I parted ways with the FBI. Don't think I would have done that for anyone else. No offense," he added to Vince, who shrugged it off.

Lana glanced at Eamon, silently asking him what Slade's story was. "I'll tell you later," he answered.

"All this is to say that the information Aiden has is credible, Lana," Slade said. "He wouldn't be here if he didn't believe in it. And he wouldn't be taking a chance telling you if he didn't think the two of you could be trusted. Listen, please. It's important you let him tell you what he knows."

"Fine. Yeah, okay." Now it was Lana who shrugged, and as she did, she had the sickening feeling her life had just taken a significant turn.

"Eamon requested Cynthia Randolph's accident report and autopsy results."

"You did?" Lana asked.

"I did." Eamon accepted the file Aiden handed over. Lana leaned closer and scanned the information along with him.

"Her car is still being processed by Boston authorities," Aiden said. "But the DOJ has assigned a special forensics team to the lab. Last I heard, they hadn't found any evidence of tampering, but they're taking their time. If something's there, they'll find it."

"'Cause of death—blunt force trauma,'" Eamon read.

"Poor girl." Lana's stomach twisted around the onion rings she suddenly regretted eating. "She was really sweet. Innocent, you know? Smart, talented, dedicated. Marcus adored her. Whatever the report ends up saying, it can't be a coincidence she died after I spoke with her." She hesitated. "After she gave me Marcus's client list." Her heart skipped a beat. A list that, if what Aiden and Slade said was true, could very well be an investigative Holy Grail. But one that might set off cataclysmic alarms and fallout. "Eden." She grabbed Eamon's arm. "Eamon, Eden has that list. We have to get it back, make sure no one knows—"

"Way ahead of you, Lana," Aiden said.

"Eden reached out to me the other day," Slade said. "Looking for help with some information she'd found on the list. That's why I called Aiden. Something didn't seem right, and as soon as I mentioned Marcus and A&O Solutions—"

"Suffice it to say, Eden is fine," Aiden said, cutting him off. "I've already assigned one of my protection teams to Detective Delaney's family, and another two teams are watching the building and its other occupants."

Lana, thinking of the very pregnant Greta Renault, breathed a little easier. "Okay. That's good to know."

"No one's going to get anywhere near anyone in that building," Aiden assured her. "We aren't taking any chances with the lot of you. Especially after this morning. My guess? A&O has had someone watching you for months."

"Longer." Suddenly all those unexpected visits and inquisitive calls from Felice made sense. "I should have been more careful. Certainly more cautious. If I had been, maybe Cynthia—"

"I told you not to blame yourself," Eamon said.

"Don't—"

"Eamon's right. Don't blame yourself." Aiden's tone had

a bit of a military clip to it. "Cynthia worked for A&O Solutions, Lana. She was on borrowed time and her expiration clock started ticking as soon as Marcus was killed. Speaking of Marcus, I need to ask you questions about him and his work."

"Ask whatever you want," Lana said with a shrug. "But like I told Eamon, we didn't talk about his work very much." If all they were telling her was true, she finally began to understand why. Even as she started to question everything she knew about the man she'd married.

"What do you know?" Slade asked.

"He was recruited out of college, thanks to Felice Covington. She'd sponsored him through school, helped him get financing, housing, stuff like that. Then he went to law school and straight to work for A&O. He was already head of their legal department when we met four, almost five years ago."

"You met in Seattle?"

"Yeah. He was there scouting spaces for a possible satellite office that never opened. I stopped for a drink with my partner at the time and Marcus chatted me up at the bar. We went out to dinner the next night, and it took off from there." The sentimentality of those memories was quickly becoming tarnished under the weight of reality. "He was the first guy I'd met who wasn't intimidated that I was a cop." He'd told her countless times it was one of the things he loved most about her—her independence and down-to-earth mentality. Doubt circled like a bloodthirsty shark and she braced herself, holding her breath in anticipation of Aiden telling her that her meeting—and marrying—Marcus had been some kind of setup.

"But you didn't talk about his business that much?"

"Hardly ever. When something was bothering him, I guess, but he never let things get to him very much." She was beginning to second-guess everything. Everything about Marcus. Everything about their life together.

"How about a man named Felix Sorento?" Slade asked. "Did Marcus ever mention him?"

"Sure." She breathed a bit easier and glanced at Eamon. "He was the A&O board member who died while on vacation with his family in Japan. It was a heart attack, I think?" That pool of dread was expanding inside her. "Why? What does Felix Sorento have to do—"

"Felix Sorento was the man who tipped off the DOJ about A&O Solutions. He was going to be their main witness in the case," Aiden said.

"Sorento was a whistleblower?" She balked. "You're kidding. No, of course you aren't kidding," she said quickly. "Sorry. Stupid question. I don't know why I keep doing that." She winced as she wished she'd just let whatever truth they were on the verge of uncovering be buried with Marcus. "What made him turn on A&O?"

"There was a young woman, Julia Conti…" Aiden paused when Lana nodded. "You knew her?"

"Yes, actually. Marcus hired her. She worked at A&O for a few years. There was a gas leak in her apartment building and she…died." Lana swallowed hard. "It wasn't an accident, was it?"

"DOJ reinvestigated. No," Slade said. "It wasn't an accident."

"Sorento and Conti had been having an affair for months. A few weeks after her death, Sorento made the approach to

DOJ, said he was convinced Conti had been killed because of something she'd seen or heard at the company headquarters."

"Marcus was devastated by her death," Lana whispered. "I'd never seen him so shaken before. It was the one time he refused an assignment. He let someone else make the arrangements for her funeral."

"Sorento agreed to give testimony about the company's business practices and their suspected criminal dealings in exchange for immunity and relocating him and his family. It took years to work out the details, and during that time he continued collecting information on A&O and passing it off to his contact at DOJ. He was due to testify the week after his trip to Japan."

"The rabbit hole just gets deeper. This whole thing..." Lana broke off, took a deep breath. "Okay, I'm just going to ask. What does any of this have to do with Marcus specifically?"

Slade exchanged a look with Aiden, a look she herself had used multiple times when questioning witnesses. Or suspects.

Was that where this was going? But hadn't they already said they didn't suspect her of being involved with A&O? She pulled her hand free of Eamon's and wiped her suddenly damp palms hard against her thighs. "If you want to hook me up to a lie detector, do it," she said. "I have nothing to lose and nothing to hide. Ask whatever it is you want to ask." At this point she was ready for anything.

"All right," Aiden said slowly. "When did you first hear about Felix Sorento?"

"Not until Marcus got the call that he'd died." She cast desperate eyes to Slade, then to Eamon. "It was at two, maybe three in the morning? We joked about me usually being the one who got the midnight calls. He got on a flight later that day."

"I don't suppose you remember the exact date he left?" Slade asked.

"I do, actually." An odd sensation began swirling inside her. Something cold. Chilling. Ominous. She lifted her hand to grip the key and wedding bands hanging around her neck. "It was right before our anniversary, which is on March eighteenth. I'd just caught this armed robbery–homicide case that was going to take serious overtime. I didn't think I could take even a night off to celebrate, so I was actually relieved when Marcus had to leave town a few days before then. Yeah. He flew out on the fifteenth. And before you ask, I remember because he made a joke about the Ides of March."

"And what did he say he was going for?" Aiden asked.

"To help the family. Sorento's wife and two sons were with him. Marcus was supposed to take care of all the travel arrangements, deal with the local officials. Make certain the family didn't have to worry or think about anything other than each other. Marcus even planned the funeral himself. It's what he did. He took care of people."

"Lana," Eamon said in that overly patient tone of his.

"Don't Lana me," she snapped. "It's obvious they're leading up to something that I'm either not going to like or they think I had something to do with." Whatever was coming was going to hurt.

"We do not think you're involved," Slade said. "If we did, Aiden would have suggested we hold this conversation in a more official federal setting."

"Oh, well, then happy happy joy joy." She swallowed a

rush of angry tears. "That leaves option number one on the table. Just spit it out already, Aiden. What is it you think—"

"Felix Sorento didn't die on the fifteenth of March, Lana." Aiden pulled a solitary sheet of paper out of one of his folders and set it in front of her. "This is an official copy of the death certificate. As you can see, he died on the eighteenth."

She tasted bile in the back of her throat and stared at the document. It blurred for a moment before her vision cleared. "No." She touched tentative fingers to the paper. "No, that can't be right. Marcus only left Seattle on the fifteenth. I know he did."

"I don't think they're disputing Marcus's travel dates, Lana." Eamon's tone could only be interpreted as cautious. "Are you, Aiden?"

Lana ignored his hand that reached for hers. Instead, she shoved both of hers under her thighs and dug her nails into the vinyl. She couldn't explain the overwhelming urge to run that sped through her, but suddenly she felt trapped by information she couldn't seem to process. But the longer she looked at the death certificate, the deeper she felt she was falling.

"There's a logical explanation," she whispered. "There has to be. I mean, how could he have known Felix Sorento was dead before he…died?" And yet he'd told her it was a heart attack that had killed Felix Sorento. Three days before he actually did.

She looked at Eamon, but for the first time since she'd met with him in this same booth a few nights ago, she saw doubt on his face. "Eamon?" She glanced at Vince, then Slade, and finally she focused on Aiden McKenna. "What is it you're saying?"

Aiden hesitated.

"Show her," Slade said. "She has a right to know, Aiden."

Another file folder, this one in blue, was placed in front of her. Aiden flipped it open. "These photos are stills from the security feed at Tokyo's central garden. Notice the date."

She followed his finger to the bottom corner. "March eighteenth." She leaned closer. "That's Marcus." She pointed to Marcus wearing the beige trench coat she'd bought him for Christmas. He was standing off to the side with another man whose back was to the camera. Tall, lanky, with shiny dark hair. Marcus was clearly handing him something.

Slade flipped to the next picture. Same date. Same Marcus in the same coat in the same place, only the man he'd been speaking with had moved off, heading toward a small group on a guided tour of the garden. A man, woman and two young boys.

"Is that Felix Sorento?" She spoke as if from outside her body. Her ears were roaring so loudly she almost couldn't hear Aiden's response.

"Yes." He flipped to the next picture showing Marcus's companion walking past, directly behind Sorento, his right hand raised.

The next photo showed Sorento pitched over, clutching his left arm. The final image was of Sorento on the ground, his family and garden employees hovering. She shifted through the rest, the images coming together like a kind of macabre flip-book. Marcus's companion circled back, before the two walked off in the opposite direction and out of sight.

"The cause of death was correct. Sorento did die of a heart attack," Aiden said. "He'd had a heart condition for years that he took digitalis for, but it was under control and had been for a while."

"At the request of the DOJ, a subsequent tox panel was performed," Slade said. "It confirmed what the DOJ suspected. Felix Sorento was poisoned. An overdose of oleander caused the heart attack."

"Oleander." Lana felt the blood drain from her face. "You're certain it was oleander?"

Aiden nodded. "One hundred percent."

"What?" Eamon asked.

"I don't know. It could be nothing." But that wasn't the way her luck was running, was it? She cleared her throat, attempted to put her thoughts in order even as panic threatened to cut off her air. "Neither Marcus nor I had a lot of time for hobbies," she choked out. "But Marcus, one of the reasons he loved the house we bought was because of the greenhouse in the backyard. He liked to garden." She raised terrified eyes to Aiden and Slade. "He had an affinity for medicinal plants, even dangerous ones. Foxglove. Pennyroyal. Dogbane. He had a bunch of books on their historical uses, how they were cultivated. I've been trying to…keep them all alive since he died. They were the only things he really paid much attention to other than me. I'm terrible with them, but I couldn't just let them… There must be seven or eight oleander plants."

She shoved the photos away, rested her head in her hands.

"I know this is difficult to hear," Aiden started.

"That the man I was married to for three years was actually moonlighting as a floral hit man for a crime syndicate?" She dropped her arms on the table and looked at him. "What makes you think that would be hard to hear?"

"He might have planned it…" Eamon rested a hand on her back and she hated that her initial reaction was to shake him off. "But he didn't do the killing himself."

"Really?" She could feel the tears burning behind her eyes, but she was determined not to let a solitary one fall. "Semantics? You really think that was candy he was handing off to that guy? Looked like a hypodermic needle to me."

"That was the official assessment, actually," Aiden said. "But Eamon makes a fair point, and it was one Slade and I considered before we came here to speak with you. We don't think Marcus was a hit man necessarily."

"Oh, good." She patted a hand against her chest. "What a relief."

"You know what a fixer is, right?"

"They specialize in taking care of certain types of problems for the people who can afford them," Eamon said. "They're like corporate caretakers who are sent out to solve potential issues, prevent scandals. Cover up wrongdoings."

"Stop witnesses from talking to the Department of Justice," Vince added. "Fixers make sure the rich and powerful aren't held responsible for their actions."

"The best ones tend to know their way around the justice system. Being a lawyer would definitely be a bonus," Aiden said.

"So Marcus wasn't a killer—he was just someone who provided the weapons and opportunity." She didn't have any energy left with which to fight. "The distinction, while negligible, is noted." Lana turned her head, lowered her voice before it broke. "Can I have the key to your apartment, please, Eamon?"

"Sure." He pulled it out of his pocket. "I can come with—"

"No." She shoved out of the booth, knocking her knees against Vince's chair. "No, I'd rather be sick in private, thanks. I'll..." She'd what? She honestly didn't know what she was going to do other than put one foot in front of the other, which she managed to do.

The nausea intensified in that all-too familiar post-drunk way, only instead of cloudy, vague regrets, she had the abject terror of realization swirling through her system. She was a cop. A decorated one who had been admired. It was all she'd ever wanted to be.

Justice. Law and order. Right and wrong. It had all been crystal clear to her since before she'd first stepped foot into the academy, and yet...

And yet she'd married a man who had apparently been an integral cog in the organized crime wheel that turned not only within the confines of the United States, but all over the world.

What was worse than that?

She had no trouble believing it was true. And that was the truly sickening part.

He wasn't the man she thought he was. How could he be and be responsible for what she'd seen in those photos? And she had seen it. In his eyes. Even from a distance, she'd seen the detached determination, the flash of, what—approval?—when the deed was done.

Lana dived up the stairs, taking them two at a time to the third floor; her hands shook as she shoved the key into the lock. She stumbled into the apartment and hit the bathroom floor on all fours, just in time to empty her stomach of its meager contents into the toilet.

She heaved and choked and cried until her ribs and throat

ached. When she sat back and swiped her cheeks she did so with an anger and ferocity that left her skin raw.

The rage coursing through her, the anger at the fact that every single thing Aiden McKenna had told and shown her fit the puzzle she'd been trying so hard to put together. She couldn't argue with any of it. Not one little bit. Everything Marcus had ever been about had been a lie.

A lie she'd bought into, hook, line and sinker.

Fury shoved her to her feet. Determination had her cleaning up and throwing cold water on her face, brushing her teeth and pushing herself out of the bathroom and into the open space of Eamon's apartment.

She stood there, chest heaving as she tried to grab hold of some thread of decency about the man she'd been married to. The man she should have seen through.

"What a fool I was. How could I have been so naive?" She'd never once questioned. Never once believed he was anything other than who he portrayed himself to be. And none of it, not one word he'd spoken to her, had been true. "Why me?" She stared at the window. "Why did he have to pick me?" Was it the challenge of her being a cop? Or was it some kind of assignment from his employer, a way to keep an ear on the rumblings within law enforcement so they could be ready when and if the government came calling?

The very idea had her doubling over, crouching into a ball, until she braced her hands on the floor, head bent over her knees. When she opened her eyes, the necklace hung free, and the key pendant and wedding bands she'd kept safe these last months dangled and shimmered in the afternoon sun streaming through the blinds.

She gripped the chain in one hand, ripped it over her head

and, as she stood back up, tossed it onto the kitchen table before striding over to the cabinets. This time she knew where to find it and she did. The bottle of Scotch felt cool and comforting in her hand.

The empty glass she dragged down clattered onto the counter that she rested her hands on before she bent over, her forehead brushing the polished marble edge.

The temptation and promise of absolute oblivion, of erasing the pain slicing through her, throbbed so painfully she nearly sobbed. Without looking, she grabbed hold of the bottle, focused on the feel of it against her palm as she found herself silently begging for the strength to stop.

"Lana."

She squeezed her eyes so tight stars exploded behind them.

"He lied to me." The loathing in her voice shocked her. "Every single day, simply by existing, he lied to me. He was a killer. A manipulator. A user. And I didn't see it." She turned her head, looked at Eamon standing there, so tall and handsome and strong, in the doorway of his makeshift home. Looking at her with so much understanding, the shame ripped through her like a tidal wave. "I didn't see anything except what he wanted me to see. No wonder I broke as a cop. He broke me."

"Not possible." Eamon barely made a noise as he walked across the room to stand beside her. He didn't touch her. Didn't move the glass. Or the bottle. Nor did he pull her hand free of the death grip that numbed her fingers.

He simply rested a hand on her forearm, his gentle fingers offering a moment of comfort she couldn't help but think she didn't deserve.

"I can't tell you not to take that drink."

"Sure you can," she whispered and choked on a laugh.

"All right, then. I won't." He moved closer, until the warmth of his body began to ease the chill of hers. "You're the only one who can make that decision, Lana. But you and I both know that nothing you're holding on to right now is going to make any of this better."

The tears she'd fought against so hard emerged once more. She struggled to keep them from falling, but instead she saw the tears splash onto the floor. "I don't want to drink." But the desire, the bone-deep yearning that felt like another entity surging inside her, slapped back, a challenge she either had to surrender to or triumph over.

She stood up, knowing she could step back and Eamon would put the bottle in the cabinet, along with the glass. But it wasn't up to him to do this. It was up to her.

Eamon released his hold as she picked up the bottle and took a step around him to the sink, where she emptied the Scotch straight into the drain. "I'll reimburse you," she said in a futile attempt at humor. When the final glug of alcohol spilled out, she let the bottle clatter in the sink as he turned her into his arms. She rose up on her toes, locked her arms around his neck as he held on, his arms the only thing that felt real. Lana buried her face in his neck, inhaled the male scent of his aftershave, lost herself in the feel of his skin against hers.

"You were right. Holding that bottle wasn't going to make it better," she whispered. "But holding on to you does."

"I think that's the nicest thing you've ever said to me." He turned his head, pressed his mouth against the side of her neck. "I know this is the last thing you want to hear right now, and it's probably the absolute worst time to tell you, but I'm going to say it." He pulled back, just enough to look into her eyes, to lift a hand to her face and stroke her cheek. "I love you. Trust might be in short supply for you right now, but I think I'm pretty good in that department where you're concerned. If you can't believe anything else right now, believe me. I love you."

She felt the doubt circling once more, attempting to grab hold, to convince her she had no right believing anything anyone ever said to her again, and yet...

She couldn't imagine going through these last days without him. These last hours. The last few minutes. There wasn't anything else in this world that could keep her on her feet, that could keep her moving forward, like Eamon Quinn.

"Yeah," she said and smiled back at him as her eyes filled yet again. "Yeah, you're quite reliable with the truth." It should have come as a surprise that she had won this man's heart, and she wished, with all of hers, that she trusted herself enough to tell him she felt the same. But she couldn't. She could barely trust what she could see with her own eyes at the moment, let alone what her heart might be screaming at her.

Not yet, anyway. Not until she was finally free of the past that only now did she realize had no basis in reality. Reality...

She frowned, her mind finally skipping over the stones of betrayal as she hit on something Aiden and Slade hadn't addressed. "There's more. There has to be more." She pulled free of Eamon, stepped back, cast a cursory look to the necklace she'd thrown on the table. "Eamon, there's a question we haven't even asked, not them, not ourselves."

"What's that?"

"Marcus." She steeled herself to step into the arena for the final battle for answers. "If he was such a vital employee, if what he did was so important for A&O Solutions, then why is he dead? Eamon, why did they kill him?"

Eamon blinked, his expression shifting from affectionate back to serious again. "That's a really good question."

"Yes, it is. And I think I know where we can find the explanation. The one place Felice couldn't get to." She stalked over to her bag, dug inside and pulled out her set of keys that included, among other things, the key to Marcus's apartment. "We need to get to Boston."

Chapter Twelve

Since the age of fourteen, Eamon had made it one of his primary goals to get to the end of his life without regrets. It was that mindset, and almost thirty years of focusing on that goal, that had him admitting out loud the one thing that, if said at the wrong time, could blow a hole in any hope he might have for a future with Lana Tate.

He'd known her, loved her, for more than three years, but until that moment when he walked into the apartment and found her hunched over that bottle of Scotch, he hadn't realized how desperately he'd needed to confess his feelings. Not to stop her from taking a drink. He'd been right about that—there was nothing he could do to prevent her from drinking if that was what she decided to do.

Eamon had needed to tell her because in those seconds, he truly feared he was going to lose her. Maybe for good this time.

Perhaps his timing could have been better. Admitting to being in love with her so quickly after she'd discovered the truth about her late husband's double life probably wasn't the best idea he'd ever had. She was on shaky ground where everything was concerned, let alone an awful thing so potentially wrought with complications. And no, she hadn't responded with professions of her undying affection for him. But she hadn't rejected his admission either. She hadn't run and hid or thrown it back in his face. She'd held on to him, clung to him. Accepted him.

And that, he told himself as the fog of possible regret faded away, was more than enough. For now.

The cockpit door of the private Bombardier Challenger popped open and Lana stepped out, looking surprisingly calm despite her longtime aversion to small aircrafts. She stopped at the built-in drink station, grabbed a bottle of water out of the mini-fridge, offered him one.

"Thanks." He watched, amused, as she made her way past the sofa-like seat and plopped down in front of where he was seated in one of the four leather-upholstered swivel seats. Behind them, both Slade and Vince had slept their way across the country, each stretched out in one of the other chairs, while Aiden McKenna had been plugged into his laptop and on a call with various members of his staff, checking in on current jobs and potential assignments.

"Well?" Eamon asked Lana. "Feel better about this thing now that you've spent some time in the copilot seat?"

"Let's just say I've felt worse." She slammed a death grip on the arm of the sofa when the plane did another slight shimmy. "I can't stop thinking about a friend telling me the smaller the plane, the rougher the ride."

"Trust me, this baby is as smooth as ice compared to others I've flown in." Aiden popped his earphones out and closed his computer. "I had to hand out Dramamine to my people whenever we boarded my first jet."

"Yay, progress," Lana said with a hint of a smile before

her gaze drifted to the window and she looked out into the night sky. "I'll be very glad to get on the ground. The captain said we should be landing in Boston in about twenty minutes or so."

Eamon glanced at his watch. "Puts us into Boston International at around midnight local time."

"Hear that, Slade? Vince?" Aiden reached back and gave Slade's black work boots a nudge. "Little over an hour and you'll get an actual bed."

"Hallelujah." Slade stayed exactly as he had been for the past six and a half hours, legs stretched out, arms crossed over his chest.

Vince sat up, instantly wide-awake, thanks to his military training with the Marines. "Coffee." He scrubbed both hands down his face. "Need coffee."

"Help yourself." Aiden motioned to the fully decked-out espresso and coffee machine above the refrigerator.

"Make that two, please." Slade sighed and folded himself back into a seated position.

"I thought you didn't like to travel too far from home," Lana said.

"Ashley and I make exceptions for family." Slade's smile was quick but genuine enough. Gratitude surged inside Eamon. "To be honest, I think we could have filled up the plane with all the people who want to help. Apparently Eden and Cole had quite the discussion about her ability to be backup from a stationary position."

"She probably just wanted to ride in the plane," Eamon said.

"Good to know that's a temptation," Aiden said as the plane began its ear-popping descent. "She's really good on the research side of things. The work she's done on that client list you turned over is going to save DOJ a ton of time. I know she typically focuses on cold cases, but do you know if she's ever considered contract work?"

Lana's gaze jumped to Eamon's. She was thinking what he was. That Eden was looking for other employment options now that she was expecting her second baby. "I would feel safe in saying it's worth an approach," Eamon said. "Especially if there's schedule flexibility in the offering."

"Agreed." Lana stared down at her cell phone, which had been lying on the table beside Eamon's for most of the flight.

"Having second thoughts about us keeping that malware active that Felice sent to your cell with those pictures of Marcus?" Aiden asked.

"Only because I feel like the darned thing is possessed." She sighed. "I want it gone, but if we remove the program, A&O or at the very least Felice is going to know we're on to them. All the more reason to leave it turned off. Speaking of Felice, she texted me at least three times before we left California. I mentioned the apartment. Let her know it was on my mind."

"Planting the seed." Aiden nodded. "That's good."

"One thing I don't get," Eamon said. "If your assumption is right, Lana, and Marcus has something in his apartment that A&O wants, why not just go in and get it? They know the address."

"Biometrics," Lana said. "Growing up, Marcus's favorite TV show was *The Jetsons*. He was always reading up on the newest gadgets, systems. Programs. This particular apartment building is one of the first to use the Xenon Two Thousand."

"Quadruple-layered security," Aiden said at Eamon's blank look. "Key, fingerprint, personal access code, full biometric scan. And as close to a hack-proof server as I've ever encountered. Try to bump a lock in that building or use a passkey without other verification? Instant lockdown and the cops are called. It's all four or no joy. And don't get me started on the steel-plated elevators."

"Please no one tell my brother about this," Vince said. "Jason would sell his soul for a chance to hack the thing."

"I thought you said you'd never been there," Eamon said to Lana. "How will you—"

"Xenon sent out a special programming team for my print and scan. Kind of like what they do to make 3D models. I am literally the only person who can walk into that apartment."

"Makes it a darned good hiding place," Aiden agreed. "Smart."

"Also explains why you're still alive, Lana," Slade said. "They need you to get in."

Aiden smirked. "All their resources and A&O couldn't get into a simple two-bedroom apartment. Gotta love the irony."

"They lured me here," Lana said. "They wanted me to come to this place. Seems only fair I should return the favor and lure them in, too."

Eamon gnashed his back teeth together. He understood the advantage of being able to use Lana as bait for this case, but that didn't mean he had to like it. Besides, there was no faster way to tick off Lana Tate than to go all protective bodyguard on her.

"Stick close to the truth," Eamon said instead. "Just say you decided to follow her advice and came out to check the apartment before you sell. She'll take the bait."

"But wait until we've got our surveillance lined up before you respond to her text," Aiden said. "We want to make sure we've got all the angles covered."

"We've run a background check on the dozen or so other tenants in the building," Slade said. "We didn't find anyone else with any employment history with or connections to A&O Solutions. And we dug pretty deep."

"I'll take that as good news. I won't feel like I'm walking into some kind of den of thieves." Lana's repeated attempt at humor did not work on Eamon.

"We also sent a team to the building earlier this afternoon as a maintenance crew," Slade added. "We found a way to hook into the internal and external security feeds. We'll have you in sight until you get into the apartment at least."

"But not after?" Eamon asked.

"Oddly enough, there aren't any security cameras in the apartments," Aiden said. "She'll be fine, Eamon. We'll be right outside the entire time."

"So when are we going to do this?" Lana asked. "Tonight?"

"Negative," Aiden said. "Even if you hadn't had a close call this morning, it's been a long day for the rest of us. I want us coming at this with a clear and well-rested mindset. We'll assume, since your phone's been off, she won't know you're here. In the meantime, we'll get everyone checked into a hotel for the night. Don't worry," Aiden said to Eamon when he frowned. "My mother recommended it. It's a place that's been used for stashing witnesses and those in protective custody. It's also a favorite of politicians and celebrities, so the security's better than most. Trust me. It's safe. Even from A&O."

"All right," Eamon said as the lights of the airport appeared in the distance. Out of the corner of his eye, when Vince asked anyone else if they wanted coffee, Eamon noticed Lana pulling out her sobriety chip that she clasped between her hands, almost as if it were a talisman.

Uncertainty wove through him, and he opened his mouth to say something. Vince cleared his throat and, when Eamon glanced up at him, shook his head. Instead, when Vince made his way to the back of the plane, he inclined his head in a way that had Eamon getting up to follow.

"Now isn't the time," Vince murmured as Eamon joined him near one of the compartments that housed a selection of nonperishable snacks. "If she wants your help, she'll ask for it."

"You know?"

"That she's an alcoholic? She came into the bar three nights in a row, didn't drink anything other than club soda and had that chip in her hand most of the time. Plus I haven't seen her drink anything stronger than a soda. Yeah," Vince said. "I know. How long does she have?"

"Four months and change." He didn't particularly like the idea of talking about her behind her back this way, but if anyone was going to understand... "That's all I know."

"You know she's struggling," Vince said. "That's enough."

"Maybe." Eamon wasn't so sure. "It's not easy."

"Being in love with an alcoholic, even a recovering one, never is." Vince plucked out a couple of packages of trail mix and handed him one. "Just ask my wife."

"Still? But you've been sober for years." Eamon shook his head, not wanting to believe. "I've never seen you—"

"And hopefully you won't, but I'll never say never. There

are periods I have to take it a day at a time. And others when it's an hour at a time. I can go months without a meeting and then something crops up that sends me right back for a refresher and reset."

"It's such a difficult road to walk," Eamon said. "And yours is even harder, owning and running a bar."

"I'm a glutton for punishment." Vince's lips twitched. "Strangely enough, it's not as hard as you'd think. It's easier when you've got some stability and people to lean on." He hesitated, as if debating to continue.

"What?" Eamon urged. If Vince's impulse was to say something, it was worth hearing. Whether Eamon wanted to or not.

"Simone started going to Al-Anon meetings when we got back together. She said she needed to understand more, and to be aware of pitfalls and triggers. I'm sure she'd be willing to sponsor you or give you information about where you can go."

Eamon looked over at Lana, who had settled back in her seat and looked a bit less stressed. "I don't want to get ahead of myself. Lana and I aren't exactly official or anything."

"Then you're the only one who doesn't see it." Vince ducked his chin. "Together or not, your feelings for her aren't going anywhere. Tackle the challenges head-on, Eamon, but don't make it the focal point of your relationship. She's far more than her disease and dependency."

Eamon let out a long breath. "Is it me, or does this feel like a really bad time to be sending her into the lion's den of A&O Solutions?"

"Maybe. Or it could be the perfect time. She's had a lot thrown at her in the last couple of years, the last few days, but she's still standing. Still fighting. She hasn't had a genuine safety net in a really long time, but you've given her that. She's been alone and that can feed an addiction more powerfully than any treatment can combat. If she can stay sober during the rough patches, it'll make the good times ahead even better. All you can do is love and support her, so long as you understand the difference between support and enabling."

"And how do I do that?"

"By leaning on your friends." He rested a hand on Eamon's shoulder. "I'll text Simone once we land, let her know you'll be in touch when you get home. Take it a step at a time, Eamon. Just one step at a time."

LANA FLIPPED THE switch on the bathroom fan and swiped a towel across the steamed-up mirror. After a long day and an even longer flight, she'd hoped the state-of-the-art shower would ease the ache in her muscles and siphon the stress of the day straight down the drain.

Instead, she found herself keyed up as the promise of what awaited her in just a few hours loomed large. The only thing worse than the anticipation was how antsy she'd gotten without being able to use her cell phone. She pulled the towel off her head and tossed it over the shower door.

"Lana?" Eamon knocked on the bathroom door. "Aiden had room service send up something to eat. It's ready when you are."

It was on the tip of her tongue to tell him she wasn't hungry, but she was. She'd been too nervous to eat on the plane. Too nervous about a lot of things. She stood in the middle of the spacious white-and-gold bathroom and wished everything could stop. Just for a little while. Long enough to catch her breath, to get her bearings and her thoughts in order.

"I'll be out in a sec." She gave herself credit for sounding utterly fine. She'd never felt this way before, as if some kind of pressure-sealed door had opened and she'd taken a step into the inevitable. The last two years, maybe the last six, had been leading her right to where she was now. Standing between what was and what could be.

What could be. She turned, pressed her fingertips against the steam-slick door. It had been a long time, too long a time, since she'd had a clear plan of action in her mind about anything.

The desire to find out the truth about Marcus's death had been planted long before it fully bloomed. But it had been there, lurking beneath her grief and loss and her self-destructive way of coping with losing him. It wasn't until she'd followed the impulse to find Eamon that she'd made progress.

It wasn't until she was with Eamon that she'd finally been able to see the reality of her life with Marcus. Lies.

It had all been lies. Who he was. What he was. Nothing Marcus had ever said to her had been the truth. How could it have been, when the biggest part of him had been something utterly abhorrent to her?

There was anger now. More anger than she knew what to do with. Some at herself for being duped for so long, but mostly anger at Marcus for not being the man she'd believed him to be.

There was no way to fix this. No way to get out from under the truth. She'd been married to a criminal who was responsible for...for offenses and horrors possibly too numerous to count.

She rubbed a hand just over the towel knotted between her breasts. How could she be standing here, thinking what she was thinking, feeling what she was feeling, given everything that had happened? How could she possibly trust herself again when it came to a man?

"Because he's Eamon." Honorable, devoted, steady Eamon. A man who had never let her down, never disappointed her. A man who had shown, long before he'd said the words, that he loved her.

She took a deep breath, abandoning the futile fight. From the start, they'd shared a connection. A connection she hadn't let herself feel or contemplate at the time for various reasons; not the least of which was that she was married. Marcus had had his suspicions, but now she had to wonder what his nonchalant, amused reaction had actually meant.

"Stop. Just…stop." Marcus didn't matter anymore. Not the way he used to. How could she mourn someone who had never existed? Instead, she made him the means to an end. An end that if they weren't careful would rob them all not only of their professional futures, but quite possibly their lives.

Lana ducked down, dug out the box of condoms Eden had packed as a "just in case" inclusion. Leaving her bag on the floor of the bathroom, Lana pulled open the door and stepped out.

The cool air from the hotel AC chilled her damp skin. She shivered, but not from cold. From the sight of Eamon Quinn standing in front of her. Alone. In their room.

"I was beginning to think maybe you'd drowned in there." Eamon had his back to her, was busy fiddling with the room service cart and the large silver domes. "When Aiden said we'd be staying in a hotel, I'd have bet most of my savings it would be a hole-in-the-wall hovel. Instead, we've got… this." He took a step back, waved his arm at the large suite they'd been given, decorated in similar gold tones to those in the bathroom. "Makes me sorry we can't enjoy…" His voice trailed off when he faced her.

The fog that crossed over his face, the quick dilation of his pupils, the slow, dazed smile that stretched his lips sent a new wave of energy zinging through her system.

"Confession time," he said.

"Oh?" She arched a brow.

"Yeah." He blew out a breath. "Of all the outfits Eden gave you, I think this one's my favorite."

"I was thinking of you when I put it on."

He didn't move. She thought it a bit strange, that a self-assured man like Eamon Quinn should be frozen in place as if she was Medusa weaving her spell.

"You know what else Eden gave me?" She held up the box.

"I don't think I've ever loved that woman more. Remind me to send her a basket of muffins or…" He stopped when Lana took a step toward him, grabbed hold of the towel knot and twisted it free. "Roses. Yeah, she's definitely earned a basket of roses. Or maybe diamonds."

Lana's lips twitched as she turned and threw the box into the bedroom behind them. "You're overdressed, Special Agent." She could feel the heat of him radiating against her as she moved closer.

"So it would seem." He glanced over his shoulder to the closed curtains at the windows overlooking Boston Harbor. "Hang on. Just…" He held up a finger, darted down the short hallway to the door and flipped the security latch. "Aiden has a key. I'm not taking any chances. Not after waiting this long." He was back at her side and hauling her into his arms in the next moment. "Tell me you're sure." His breath was hot against the side of her neck, sending chills down her spine for an entirely new reason. "Tell me this isn't me asleep on the plane having a dream."

She couldn't help it. She laughed. "Only you would think of something like that."

"Just kind of seems to be the way my luck runs where you're concerned." He straightened, caught her face between his hands and stared so deeply into her eyes she could see the reflection of his soul. "I've wanted you for so long, Lana. So long." He brushed his mouth against hers. "But it's been a really, really rough day. For both of us. If you have any doubt—"

Anger blazed afresh and she embraced it, embraced him. Locking her arms around his neck, she kissed him with every ounce of courage she held and pressed her naked, damp body against him.

Every cell in her body surged to life. Even through the fabric of his clothes the charge between them was enough to set her on fire.

"I should have showered first," he murmured against her lips.

"Later," she promised. "Together." She grinned, pulled back enough to trail a finger down to his lips and tease them apart. She felt him go instantly hard against her. "If you're a good boy."

"Challenge accepted." He bent down as he slid his hands along her bare back, over the curve of her butt. He cupped her, hauled her up, and as he began to walk to the bedroom, she locked her legs around his waist. The pressure and friction of the fabric against her core had her whimpering against his throat. It wouldn't take much, just lowering that zipper of his and…

"Hold on," he urged. "Just hold…on."

They made it as far as the door before he pressed her up against a wall, kissed her and set her entire being on fire.

It was like being caught in the beginning embers of a firestorm. Instant, intense and painfully pleasurable. The heat wove its way through her extremities, stoking in her center as she opened her mouth for him, her tongue dancing with his. She tightened her arms around him to ensure he'd not turn to ash.

She couldn't recall ever being kissed like this, as if his very life depended on his touching her, tasting her. Devouring her.

"Eamon." His name was a drug on her lips, promising ecstasy and escape even as he loosened his hold and let her legs drop to the floor. He backed away, leaving her feeling utterly abandoned and unfulfilled. "What are you—"

"Don't!" He held up a hand, walked over to the bed and pulled the sheets and comforter off the king-size mattress. On his way back to her, he stopped, picked up the box of condoms and had a foil packet out before the smile on her lips could fully form. "You didn't honestly think I was walking away."

She hadn't wanted to. But the doubt was there. Doubt she quickly shoved into the deepest corners of her singed soul. Her body tingled, desperate for his touch, and she pushed away from the wall, joining him at the bed, their bare feet tangling in the sheets that lay forgotten on the floor.

He reached down, grabbed the hem of his T-shirt, but she shook her head and slipped her hands down his arms to do it herself. She had to rise up on her toes to get the T-shirt over his head, but the instant he was free of the fabric, her hands were on his bare chest, reveling in the slight dusting of red hair covering his torso.

Lana pressed her lips against his heart, smiled at the staccato beating she took pride in being responsible for. A wave of sadness threatened to douse the flames of desire. All this time… All this time he'd wanted her and she'd committed herself to a man who had only ever lied to her.

"Lana." Eamon's voice broke through the pain. "Lana, stop thinking. Be with me. Now." He kissed her. Then again, longer, deeper. "Be with me here in this moment. Nowhere else."

She nodded, hating the tears that burned and blurred her vision. Vision she wanted filled only with him. "Yes." She reached up, slipped her hand through his hair as he turned her so her knees hit the back of the mattress. "I'm here with you, Eamon." She gazed up at him, longing for, anticipating the moment when he'd slip inside her body and claim her, heart and soul.

When she'd claim him.

"Only you."

When he let her go this time, it was only long enough to divest himself of his pants, to unwrap the foil package and cover himself. She glanced down and frowned.

"A word of advice?" Eamon said, an unfamiliar waver in his voice. "Don't ever look down at a man in this condition and frown."

She laughed, lifted her head and leaned into him. "I was only thinking how I'd wanted to do that."

"Temptress." His mouth caught hers, drew the kiss out long enough to have her moaning in anticipation and frustration. "Next time," he breathed and slid his hand down between their bodies and cupped her.

She dropped her head back, her mind spinning at the pleasure building inside her. "Not this way," she managed. "I want you inside of me." She held on to his shoulders and in one fluid move toppled both of them onto the mattress.

Before she caught her breath, he rolled onto his back and drew her over him so she straddled his hips.

His back arched as his hands came up, searching for hers. As he filled her, she slid her fingers through his, pressing their hands together while she moved over him. The power she felt, riding this man, pushing him into the same throes of passion she now realized she'd only dreamed about, acted as a quickening, renewing her entire being to one of strength and triumph.

The buildup was slow, but more intense than she could have imagined. She stared down at him, her breathing ragged as he tightened his hold on her and tucked his chin in to meet her gaze.

"Go over," he ordered. "I want to watch you when it happens."

She tried to hold off, to extend the exquisite pleasure between her legs, inside her, but his command was one she couldn't refuse. She rocked herself hard against him, pressing down as she drew him in as deeply as she could as the climax crashed over her and she dragged him with her.

She released his hands and collapsed over him, sobbing.

His arms held her tight and she relished how strong and safe she felt. "Eamon." It was all she could think to say. "Eamon, I—"

"Not now." His lips brushed against her temple.

"But I—"

"Tell me later," he whispered. "Tell me later." He turned her face to his, brushed his lips over hers once more. "After."

"After what?" Even as she asked, she felt him stir inside her. "You're kidding me." Her laughter felt as if it had been bottled up for years, only to flow free and unheeded now.

"Never about this." He slowly skimmed his fingers over her skin. Slick with sweat, it prickled beneath his touch. "Never about you."

He kissed her and started again.

Chapter Thirteen

"Why don't you want me to tell you?"

Lana's quiet question drew Eamon out of a light sleep. For a long moment he reveled in the idea that she was, finally, in his arms. In his bed. It wasn't just a dream his subconscious had cooked up in an effort to quell his seemingly impossible desires.

He could, he thought, draw out her question to the point of teasing. He could distract her—far too easily, he knew. Or...

"Because I want you to be one hundred percent clearheaded when you tell me you love me." He reached down to pull the sheets and blanket more securely around them as he shifted her more fully against him.

Bundled up in bed with her, behind her, being able to bury his face in her hair with a mere turn of his head, knowing she was content being exactly where she was, he couldn't recall a more perfect moment in his entire life.

"What makes you think I'm not clearheaded?" Rather than anger or irritation tingeing her voice, he heard dismay, confusion and perhaps a tad bit of defiance.

"Because I wouldn't be if I was in your position."

She reached back, slid a hand down his hip. "And what position is that?"

He nuzzled her neck, hid his smile in her hair. "You had a lot thrown at you the last few days. I'm betting you can't help thinking that the years you spent with Marcus feel somewhat tainted now. I don't want your feelings for me tangled up in whatever you might be feeling about him."

She sighed. "When you say astute things, I have to wonder if you're altogether real." She drew his arms more tightly around her body, snuggled back against him. "A statement like that really should tick me off. But somehow it manages not to."

"It's a gift." His cell phone buzzed from its spot on the nightstand.

"Aren't you going to answer it? It might be work."

"It could only be work." His main reason for not answering. The night was beginning to fade, turning into what he hoped would be a good day for answers. A good day to take a good chunk out of A&O Solutions' stability and hold them accountable for everything they'd done. What he didn't particularly care to deal with at the moment was what was waiting for him at the Bureau once his leave was over. "I'll call them back. What?"

"What what?"

"I can hear you thinking." He pressed his lips to the back of her head. "What is it?"

"I was considering how hard your job must be. How dark you have to go into the human psyche working the cases that you do. Don't you ever worry about losing yourself? Losing your soul? It has to—"

"It does. But it's tempered by other...interests." His hands began to wander, but they didn't get far before she turned over, lifted a hand to his face. Stroked her fingers down his stubble-covered cheek. It was, he thought, a beautiful way to start any day.

"How does it not consume you? How do you keep the anger, the rage, at bay?"

"Sometimes I don't. Other times I allow myself to get distracted by someone else's demons and ghosts." He kissed the tip of her nose. "Sometimes a damsel in distress allows me to be her defender and slay her dragons instead."

She snort-laughed, smacked him lightly on the shoulder as her smile brightened up the darkness. "You're in quite a vulnerable position to be calling me that."

"I'm a risk-taker, too. You know, if we don't get some sleep—"

Someone knocked on the hotel room door.

They frowned at one another, as if confirming they'd each heard it.

The knock came again.

"What the—" He threw back the covers and climbed out of bed, jumped into his jeans before he grabbed his sidearm and, keeping it low next to him, headed to the door. "Lana, stay—" But it was too late. She was already out of bed and tugging on his T-shirt.

He unhooked the safety latch and opened the door. "Aiden. What's wrong?" He pulled the door open farther and stepped back as Lana switched on the lights.

"What's going on?"

"Did you turn your cell back on?" Aiden asked.

"What? No." Lana picked it up from the coffee table in front of the gray upholstered sofa. "It's still off. See?" She handed it to him. "I haven't turned it on since before we left the bar back in Sacramento."

Aiden barely gave it a glance. "The unit I've had watching Marcus's apartment building just called. They've spotted three surveillance teams staking out the apartment building."

"They know she's on her way?" Eamon asked.

Aiden shook his head. "I don't think so."

"He's right," Lana said. "They checked your phone, Eamon. It's clean. They don't know I'm coming. But they are anticipating my arrival."

"They have a plan," Eamon said.

"Me not answering Felice's messages probably put them on alert," Lana said. "They're tired of waiting." She reached back and slid her fingers through his. "And so am I."

"WHAT?" LANA MUMBLED around a mouth full of French toast and looked across the table at Eamon. It was barely after seven, only a few hours since Aiden had knocked on their hotel room door, and after grabbing a few fitful hours of sleep, she found herself not only energized, but absolutely famished. They'd since moved everything over to Aiden's business suite, which included a delivery of room service breakfast fit for a film crew. "Sue me. I'm hungry and it's mostly your fault."

"If I'd known that's all it would take to get you to eat, we should have slept together days ago." The strained patience in his voice was a reminder Eamon was not, in any way, happy with her and Aiden's plan.

"Have to work off the nervous energy somehow. Since other avenues aren't available to me at the moment." It was as if she had an entire beehive buzzing inside her.

Eamon rolled his eyes.

"You don't get it, do you?" She chewed and swallowed, wiped her mouth and reached for her coffee.

"Pretend I don't."

"I have something they want," Lana explained. Again. "Something they need. And they're desperate to get it." Seriously. What was up with that? "That's all good news, Eamon. It means we have the upper hand."

"Doesn't seem that way from where I'm sitting."

"Then I suggest you switch seats." She hadn't felt this clearheaded, this positive, in ages. Maybe it was the prospect of finally putting the last eighteen months behind her. Or maybe this was the aftereffect of having spent a good portion of the early morning hours exorcising what she hoped were the last of her marriage-related ghosts. It could even be that she was being proactive and productive rather than allowing life to steamroll over her. More than likely, it was a combination of the three.

Whatever the reason, she planned to run full tilt at the situation, even if she ended up smacking headfirst into Felice and A&O Solutions.

"I don't like the idea of using you as bait."

"You forgot the *again*." She arched a brow at him. "You mean you don't like the idea of using me as bait *again*. Funny how it wasn't a problem yesterday when it was your idea."

He blinked, frowned into his coffee. "All right." He paused. "I'll admit you are not altogether incorrect."

She dropped her fork. "You just admitted you were wrong. You really are the perfect man, aren't you?" She considered the smile he offered her a small triumph. "I hear you, Eamon. I do. And I understand where you're coming from, but I know you see this from my perspective, too. This is something I not only have to do, I also need to do it." She had to close the book on the last couple of years, on her marriage, on Marcus's sham of a life, before she had a hope of moving forward with her own. A future she hoped would include Eamon Quinn. "Look at it this way," she added when he didn't appear convinced. "I'm trusting you to make sure I make it through today in one piece. You and your friends. This time last week I'd have considered that an impossibility."

"We're your friends, too." Vince and Slade entered Aiden's suite in time to counter her statement. "We're ready to be brought up to speed."

"And eat," Slade added as he grabbed a plate and piled it high with eggs and bacon. "Definitely ready to eat."

"All right, we're all set with the Boston PD," Aiden said as he clicked off his cell phone. "They'll set up a surveillance perimeter around the public garden near the apartment building. Plenty of cover so they won't be seen as you draw them in. Keep it simple and straightforward from the moment you pick up the car, which is when you turn your phone back on. You'll pick up a tail along the way. Just be ready for that and don't lose them."

"You've got eyes on Felice's teams, right?" Eamon asked.

Aiden nodded. "I brought in three more cars. The watchers are being watched. We'll have eyes and ears on you the entire time, Lana."

"See?" Lana plastered a smile on her face and aimed it directly at Eamon. "Easy peasy." Lana took her last bite as Aiden sat at the head of the table, his own food having gone cold ages ago. She got up to refill her coffee, barely noticing the nervous trembling in her hands. "In case I don't—in case I forget," she quickly amended as she faced the four men seated around the table. "I just want to thank all of you. Not only for stepping up to help with this nightmare of a scenario, but for trusting me with my part in things." She offered them each a shaky smile. "It means a lot."

"You've earned your wings with us, Lana," Slade said. "The only thing we ask is that you trust us. None of this works out without trust."

"Right. Trust will get us through." As she spoke, guilt grabbed hold of her stomach and squeezed. She had every intention of sticking to their plan.

But that didn't mean she didn't have one of her own. One she wouldn't hesitate to put into play if she thought, even for one minute, Eamon and their friends were in trouble.

She'd ask for forgiveness later. If she was still alive.

"YOU'RE A GUY who listens to his gut, right, Aiden?" Eamon couldn't decipher where the unease was coming from as he sat like a stone in the passenger seat of one of Aiden's black SUVs. But it was definitely there. They were parked far enough away to stay clear of any potential countersurveillance, yet close enough they had the building—and Marcus's second-floor apartment in particular—in sight. Aiden's surveillance van was parked where it had been for the past day, directly across the street from the entrance, its plain black color boring enough that it drew no one's attention. Six cars behind sat a more conspicuous cable repair van that rocked enough to betray three or four people were inside. *Amateurs*, Eamon thought. The arrogance of power, thinking they were too good to be caught. "You get the feeling something's not right? With Lana?"

"Yep." Aiden didn't flinch. He rested his head in one hand, his index finger against his mouth, stared at the building as if he could somehow manifest an end to the situation with his mind. "I do indeed."

"How do you...?"

"Being able to read people has kept me alive for most of my life," Aiden said. "That and trusting my instincts." He angled his gaze at Eamon. "Listening to my gut."

"When did you know?"

"As soon as I finished running down the plan," Aiden said. "She thinks my way of approaching Felice is wrong. She didn't say it, she played along, but she disagrees."

"Why didn't you call her on it?"

"Because no amount of research we might have done can come close to what she knows about someone she knows personally," Aiden said. "Add to that she respected me enough not to question me in front of my people." He glanced at Eamon. "She's been conned by the woman for years. In some ways, she has far more at stake than we do. I'm okay giving Lana some leeway if it means she can throw some dirt back in Felice's face. Especially if it helps us get what we want."

"All I want is Lana out of there, safe and sound."

"That's definitely at the top of the list." Aiden pressed a finger against the device in his ear. "Slade? You have eyes on our sparrow?"

"She's headed into the nest now," Slade responded into both their ears. "Just turned the corner into the lot."

"Don't let her hear you call her *sparrow*." Vince's voice echoed next. "She'll fry you both over an open fire."

"Sparrows are hardy creatures," Aiden said. "They can fly through any storm and come out relatively unscathed, sometimes even stronger than before. Mobile one, report in."

Eamon looked out his window into a lush yard in front of a small cottage-style house. It was a quiet neighborhood, far enough outside the main hub of the city to give off suburb vibes. The rotating reports, mobile one, mobile two, mobile three… They all left him feeling slightly disconnected. He didn't like this feeling, sitting out here while she stepped into whatever waited for her inside. "She shouldn't be going in there alone."

"You go in there with her, you risk scaring everyone who's watching." Eamon's phone chimed with Aiden's texted reminder to rotate the broadcasting frequencies to the team. "You want this over, Eamon? Trust her to get the job done. And trust me and my people to make sure she does."

"Right. Yeah." Eamon took a deep breath. "I know. Sorry."

"Stop apologizing for worrying about the woman you love."

"And with that," Slade said, "Vince owes me fifty bucks. I told him this would turn into a therapy session."

"Heads up." Aiden sat up straighter as Lana's rented blue Prius zoomed its way into the parking lot. "Here we go. I know I say this every time, but I need every one of you to hear me. Be ready for anything. And I mean anything. Lana's got the lead on this. Let her have it."

Eamon couldn't help but think Aiden was speaking directly to him.

"She's got this, Eamon," Aiden said.

Eamon nodded. "I know." But that didn't mean he wasn't terrified their first night together may very well have been their last.

LANA PARKED IN one of the two reserved spots for her and Marcus's apartment. The other slot was empty; it had been since the day after Marcus had died. He'd driven a company car, one Felice had been eager to retrieve.

She climbed out, grabbed her duffel bag out of the trunk, her purse out of the back seat, and made her way around to the front entrance, adjusting the oversize button-down dark blue shirt so the button cam Aiden's team had added could have an unobstructed view. She resisted the temptation to adjust the pod in her ear.

"We've got you, Lana." Aiden's voice was loud and clear. "Doing great. We've identified three vehicles in the area, each with at least a two-man team inside. Up to now, no one other than tenants have approached the building, but I'm going to assume that won't last. First hurdle ahead. Let's see if the security system is everything it's touted to be."

It was starting to feel like a dream, being here after all this time, given the obstacles she'd overcome, some of her own making.

The steel-and-glass construction gave the apartment building a cold, almost industrial look. There were no soft angles here, no gentle touches. Everything about the building screamed *stay away*. Even the landscaping came across as a deterrent, with its blackthorn and common holly bushes planted along the perimeter.

It was almost funny, how she could see both sides of Marcus's life reflected in the structure he'd chosen to live in. She should have come here sooner, if only to put those remaining pieces of the puzzle into place. So much made sense given what she knew now. His reticence when it came to talking about his work, his odd fascination with security systems and home protection. The number of books he owned on the topic of toxic plants and substances. The place looked impenetrable, which, given the secrets he'd had, made it the perfect place for him.

She rounded the corner and stopped at the thick glass panel door with a massive brass bar handle. The fingerprint scanner pad was tucked into a discreet alcove, beside a bank of brass mailboxes. She'd thought Marcus was teasing when he'd told her about the various levels of protection. Even the visit from the security system people hadn't convinced her. Obviously he had not been exaggerating. Getting into the lobby was going to be work. She glanced up at the cameras— one on either side of the enormous door. "Okay, boys. Here's where we find out how welcome I really was."

She inserted her key into the slot, twisted it, then held her thumb on the pad, waited for the neon green light to move up and down. When she was prompted, she keyed in her unique eight-digit personal code before removing the key.

"Welcome, Detective Lana Tate." The sultry female voice sounded. "Please, enter and have a nice day."

The lobby door clicked.

"What was that?" Eamon asked in a way that had Lana fighting a laugh.

"The inventor had a thing for new tech," Aiden said. "Can't blame him really. Okay, Lana, remember, once you're upstairs—"

"Disable any signal jammers that might cut us off and

prevent the apartment from being monitored. Yes, Aiden, I know." She pulled open the lobby door and stepped inside. When it closed behind her, there was a gentle *woomph* as if the room had been repressurized.

Her shoes squeaked on the polished tiled floor as she bypassed the elevator for the staircase.

"Mobile one, report," Aiden said.

"Got her in sight," the unfamiliar voice said. "Stairway cameras operational. Elevator cameras check. Button cam clear. Good to go."

Lana took the stairs to the second floor, her hand gripping the rail with more pressure than necessary. The adrenaline surge had gotten her to this point, but now the nerves were setting in. Nerves she needed to get under control if this plan of hers was going to work.

Another keypad awaited her on the second-floor landing. She entered her code again, scanned her thumb again, turned her key again. When she pulled open the door on the second-floor landing, she spotted a middle-aged couple emerging from the door across the hall from Marcus's apartment. They were both tall, slender, and wore enough designer clothes to open their own store. Lana silently swore. Marcus had told her about them, but for the life of her, she couldn't recall their names.

"You're Lana, aren't you?" The surprise on the woman's face was at least friendly as she made her approach, arms open. "Lana Tate? Marcus's wife. I recognize you from Marcus's pictures. How are you? You know, after..."

The dramatic tone, along with the perfectly manicured nails, razor-straight black hair and Botoxed face, triggered the memory. "Veronica. It's nice to meet you. Marcus spoke very highly of both of you." She readjusted the bag on her shoulder to avoid the unwanted hug and air-kiss greeting. "I'm doing okay, I think. Good days and bad. How are you and…?"

"Gordon," Aiden supplied from the van. "He's in finance and she's into spending his money. They also have a Tibetan mastiff named Chanel."

"Of course they do," Eamon muttered.

"Gordon," Lana said, finishing her thought with a glance toward the husband. "And Chanel, of course. Marcus told me all about your beautiful dog."

"Oh, aren't you the sweetest." Veronica rested a hand against her heart and gave her the "I'm sorry your husband is dead" head tilt. "With everything you've been through, you remember our baby. Gordon, isn't she the sweetest?"

Gordon looked as if he couldn't be bothered. "Nice to meet you." He held his thumb on the keypad beside their door to engage the lock before he strode toward them to claim his wife. "We're going to be late."

"Oh, yes, of course." She smiled at Lana as her husband escorted her to the elevator that was waiting for them. "Bye, Lana. Maybe we can get drinks before you…" The rest of her offer faded into the elevator as the doors closed.

Lana gave an absent wave before making her way down the hall to the last apartment on the right. Yet another keypad, only this one had a full hand scanner. She lifted her right hand, flexed her fingers. "This is getting ridiculous. NORAD doesn't have this many levels of protection." She took a deep breath and rested her hand on the plate.

The laser moved up and down, once, twice, three times before she heard the top lock click. The second lock didn't release until she keyed in her code again. The nerves were back, making her hand shake as she twisted the knob and opened the door.

"Well, this is…disappointing." She stepped far enough inside to let the door close behind her. "I was at least expecting—" She yelped and jumped back as a scanner embedded in the ceiling focused on her. She looked up at the bright red light, winced as it moved up and down her body.

"Lana?" Eamon's voice came through loud and clear. Too loud. "What's wrong?"

"I'm being probed." She eyed the comm unit on the wall, saw a video feed of the front lobby on the screen beside an intercom.

"Detective Lana Tate. Primary resident. Entry approved. Welcome home, Detective Lana Tate. My name is Angie. If I can be of assistance, please don't hesitate to ask."

"Uh, thanks, Angie." She dropped her bag on the gray-tinted hardwood floor even as she wondered what on earth she'd ask of a security system. The air smelled slightly floral, and more than a little stale. It made sense. As far as she knew, the only person who had been in this apartment since Marcus's death was the property manager, who'd emptied out the fridge and disposed of any perishable items. As for the rent, that was being paid out of the only account of Marcus's she'd left open. "Guys, can you all hear me?"

"Five by five," Aiden responded. "Ready to make your call to Felice?"

"In a minute." She hadn't anticipated needing to get her bearings. After all, it was just an apartment. She might own it, but it wasn't like it was home. Not her home, at least. No, while her name might be on the deed, this wasn't her space.

The small entry table displayed an old abalone shell with some loose change and a few solitary keys, along with a framed photo of herself: a candid shot Marcus had taken with his cell phone shortly after they'd started dating. She waited for the grief to descend. The sorrow. The regret. Even anger. But none of that came. Instead, all she felt was an unexpected sadness over someone she'd clearly never known.

The short hallway opened up almost immediately into a nicely furnished great room with an angled fireplace. Her sneakered feet were silent on the hardwood floor as she moved around. There was no balcony, only a bank of curtained windows overlooking the wooded area behind the property. There was nothing special about the apartment. It could have easily been a display model with which to tempt potential owners.

The only personal touches she saw, other than the practical furniture choices, were photos. Enough that the number surprised her. She lifted the largest framed one off the mantel, the one that displayed her personal favorite from their very private wedding.

Instead of seeing a happy bride with the beach at her back, her new husband's arms holding her close, Lana only saw a naive woman who'd been fooled into complacency. Who'd been lied to. A woman who just a few short years after this was taken would realize what she'd had then didn't come close to what she had now.

She set the frame facedown on the hearth as an image of Eamon floated through her mind. Despite the anger she felt twisting to life inside her, an unexpected wave of calm washed over her. Eamon had a way of doing that. Bringing her peace, even as he drove the rest of her to distraction.

She made her way toward the kitchen, looked to her left and down the hallway she assumed led to the solitary bedroom. Across the room, on the other side of the kitchen, a half bath, the door slightly ajar, and another secured door beside it.

"Lana?" Aiden asked. "You still with us?"

"I just need...a minute."

She keyed in her code, waited for the click. This time she didn't jump when the laser hit the top of her head and ran far more quickly than the previous scan. After a slight pause, the door opened.

"Granting access, Detective Lana Tate. Welcome, Detective..."

"Oh, shut up." Lana poked her head inside. Once again, nothing special. A simple mahogany desk, matching built-in bookshelves and cabinets. A ridiculously expensive leather chair that looked as if it belonged on a space shuttle. She glanced at her watch, noted the time. She was almost out of it. Lana performed a quick inventory of the cabinets and drawers. The books on the shelves were collectible leather editions that had never had their spines cracked. The file cabinet in the corner? Empty. The only thing she found of interest was a thin laptop in a bottom desk drawer. "Good enough." She snatched it out, held it against her chest as she left the office, pulling out her cell phone. She turned it on and set the laptop on the circular glass coffee table between the sofa and fireplace.

She started to dial when a quick flash caught her attention. Lana looked up, glanced around the room. She must be seeing things. She ducked her head. There it was again. This time, she raised her chin in time to see a thin beam of light flash across the room and hit the back wall of the kitchen.

"What the—"

"Lana? What's going on? You find something?"

"I don't know. Maybe? Hang on." Even with the light gone now, she followed the movement to the fireplace and ran her fingers over a small notch in the wall behind where the picture frame had been. "That's…weird." She stepped back, walked around on one side, then to the other. "The walls are uneven. One side cuts off but not the…other." She returned to the hearth, planted both hands on the mantel and shoved.

Nothing.

The light flashed again. This time when it hit, she saw the odd shape it took. Part circle, part rectangle. Almost like a…

Her stomach dropped.

Almost like a key.

She reached for her necklace, nearly panicked when she found it wasn't there, then remembered she'd taken it off back in Eamon's apartment.

"Lana—"

"I need a few more minutes," she snapped. "Please, Aiden."

"We've got movement out here, Lana. At least two of the cars are pulling in closer to the building and we have four men headed to the building."

"Well, they can't come in unless I let them in. Give me some time."

She ignored Eamon's sigh of frustration. She didn't know what she expected them to do. She certainly didn't want them getting into some kind of shoot-out simply because she'd been distracted by a beam of light.

Except it wasn't just a beam of light. She hurried over to her bag, dug around and into the side pockets until she felt the chain. She yanked it free, dangled it to grab the key and went back to the fireplace.

"Suddenly I know why *National Treasure* was his favorite movie." Lana hesitated only a moment before she slid the key into the recess of the wall. She turned it.

She heard a click and the revving of a motor before the entire panel housing the fireplace slid out and to the side. Behind it sat a safe room door made of solid steel, much like a bank vault door.

"What the...?"

"She really needs to stop saying things like that," Aiden complained. "Especially if she's not going to explain herself."

Another keypad, but she didn't hesitate and inputted her numbers. Zero eight one six eighty-seven. The lock disengaged and she pulled down on the handle and opened the door.

The voices in her ear faded into white noise when she stepped inside, but she barely noticed. Overhead lights blinked on, illuminating the cramped room filled with multiple computers, a personal server and two industrial metal shelves filled with file boxes organized by year. The bulletin board over the desk was covered in pristinely arranged sticky notes with names, dates and various methods of death with question marks beside some of them.

"Recognizing Detective Lana Tate." Angie's voice drifted out of the speakers. "Welcome, Lana Tate. Initiating program Marcus Is Dead."

Lana spun around as the desktop computer blinked to life. She gasped as Marcus stared back at her from the screen.

"Hey, hon." His smile was drawn, tight, his dark eyes shadowed. She could see it now. The weight of what he'd done, in his eyes. His face.

She moved closer, stretched out her hand as if expecting to be able to touch him.

"If you're seeing this, then my plan didn't work and I'm dead. It also means you're in some serious trouble, so I'm going to do what I can to help. Too little, too late, I know. But..." He sighed, and whatever amusement had been in his eyes faded. "I should probably start by saying I'm sorry, but I'm going to assume by now that's the last thing you want to hear from me."

Tears scalded her eyes. "You—"

"I know you're angry," Marcus went on as her knees went weak and she sank into the only chair in the room. "And if I'm honest with myself, I'm glad I'm not there to see it. But before you slam the door and walk away, I need you to do one thing for me. Just listen. Please listen to me for just a few more minutes, Lana. Because I have a story to tell you."

Chapter Fourteen

"We've got no way to get inside," Eamon said as Aiden alternated between teams, telling them to stand down for now while at least one of his people worked on hacking into the apartment's security system through Lana's cell phone. "What is she doing in there?"

"Confronting her past?" Aiden answered without missing a beat. "She's not going to lose the plot, Eamon. She's just gone off course for a bit. She's safe in there, remember. But we might not be."

"Maybe they'll assume we're with them?" Eamon suggested as a pair of dark coverall-clad men wearing even darker knit caps made their way around the perimeter of the apartment building. "How insulated are they from one another? With the way A&O hires local heavies, it's possible none of them have ever met each other before."

"Good point. One that could work in our favor," Aiden said. "Ditch the jacket. Toss it in the back. And the tie." Eamon did as he was told, rolled up his shirtsleeves and unbuttoned the top button on his collar, but when Aiden looked at him, he shook his head. "Doesn't matter what you wear, you still look like a fed. Slade? Keep trying to get through to Lana."

"Just getting static. It's like she's moved into a dead zone."

For the first time since Eamon met Aiden McKenna, the other man flinched. "Okay. Okay, we're going to give it ten minutes. If she isn't back by then, I'm calling in the local PD. We breach that building without them on-site, I'll never hear the end of it." He glanced at Eamon. "Especially from my mother."

"Understood," Slade confirmed, before the rest of the teams did the same.

"Ten minutes." Eamon set his watch, returned his attention to the men patrolling the building. "Let's hope she's back with us by then."

THROUGH THE WAVES of anguish and betrayal, beneath the roar of logic and acceptance, against unmitigated resistance and reluctance, Lana listened. Processed.

Accepted.

She reached over and hit the escape key on the keyboard of the desktop computer, freezing Marcus's handsome face on the screen. His smile came across as part apology, part regret, and all charm. It was the man she remembered, a man she'd never really known.

She stood, surprised her legs actually held her up, and waited until the light on the front of the computer stopped blinking green.

"Download complete," the computer told her. "Please remove flash drive."

Before she pulled the drive free, she opened Marcus's email program, logged out so she could log in to her own, then forwarded the entirety of downloaded information to not one, not two, but three different allies.

Only then did she pull the drive free and, after another glance around the room, stashed it on the top of the highest shelf behind yet another framed photograph of the two of them together.

When it was put away, she zombie-walked back to the door. The instant she stepped out of the room, voices exploded in her ear.

"Three minutes."

"Three minutes to what?" Lana asked as she turned and pushed the door closed, keyed in her code to lock it. Pulling the key free of the notch had the panel sliding back into place. The room settled back into normalcy as if she hadn't just stepped into a portal of clarity.

"Lana. There you are. We thought we'd lost you completely."

"Not completely," she whispered.

"What happened? Are you okay?"

Not yet. But she would be. "I'm sorry I dropped out of range. I... I found something. I'll explain later. I'm calling her now." She retrieved her cell phone, but before she could dial, it rang. Felice's name appeared on-screen. "Felice. Hello. I'm sorry I haven't returned your messages. I was on a plane."

"I'm just glad to hear your voice," Felice said with what Lana could only interpret as false concern. "Where are you?"

Lana caught movement on the security monitor by the door. She walked over, stood in front of it, eyes narrowed as she watched three different teams of men approach the panel in an attempt to find a way in. "You know where I am." She'd never felt quite so calm in her life. And the idea of that terrified her. "You've always known where I am, haven't you? From the very beginning. You've always known."

She heard Eamon swear, but she couldn't think about him now.

"Lana." Felice's voice tightened. "I don't know what—"

"You can drop the act, Felice. Honestly?" She sighed and dropped her head to her chest. "I'm exhausted and I'm too tired to deal with it. I have what you want. The files. The records. All the information about Project Orbana."

Lana winced at Eamon's and Aiden's protests before she ripped the pods out of her ears and tossed them onto the counter behind her.

"You have no idea what you're playing at." Felice's voice was devoid of the affection Lana had always heard until now.

"You slipped, didn't you, Felice? You made the horrific error of caring for one of your vulnerable orphans. The ones you trained to be killers. You cared for Marcus, didn't you? You were blind to him and didn't notice everything he was doing behind your back. All the information he was collecting. You didn't see it until it was too late. That's why he had to die, wasn't it? Because he was going to turn on you and your bosses at A&O."

"You're signing your own death decree," Felice spit. "Stupid woman."

"You were already going to kill me." Lana reached behind her, pulled the gun out from the waistband of her jeans. "The only thing I can do now is make it more difficult for you. Come and get it, Felice. Come and get all the files he kept." She released the safety on the weapon. "I'll be waiting."

Lana hung up and tossed the phone into her bag.

An odd serenity washed over her as she walked over to the window. Feet planted, shoulders straightened, she stared out into the trees and waited.

"SHE'S GONE COMPLETELY off the rails." Eamon dropped his head into his hands. "I was afraid something like this was going to happen." Even as he accepted it, he couldn't find any way to blame her. A switch had been flipped inside her. One that might never be flipped back.

"She does seem to have set her own course. Man, sometimes I really hate being right." Aiden blew out a breath. "Team roundup, prepare to implement contingency plan Lana One, over."

"Confirmed." The responses came as Eamon stared, somewhat dumbfounded.

"You have a plan in place for this?"

"I told you," Aiden said. "I read people. I know them. And I always, *always* have a backup plan. This is when I tell you that if you step foot out of this vehicle you will follow my orders to the letter. Do you understand me, Agent? To. The. Letter." Aiden, cell in one hand, his earpiece still in place, shoved out of the car as Eamon hurried to catch up.

"This probably isn't the right time," Aiden said as they crossed the street and ducked into the foliage cover near the apartment building. "I've been putting together a plan for a dedicated unit specializing in child crimes both here and overseas. I need someone to take the lead. Someone who knows how the law works in this country and elsewhere. Someone who might want a little extra leeway in how a case gets handled but still understands how these kinds of criminals operate. Know anyone who might be interested?"

"Uh—" Eamon blinked. Aiden was either the king of bad timing or a genius. Leaving the Bureau to work for Minotaur could be the best of both worlds. The resources he'd have at his fingertips to do the job he did better than just about anyone else? "I think maybe I do."

"Maybe's good enough for now," Aiden said over his shoulder. "Mobile one in position? Over?"

"Confirmed, over."

Aiden crouched, and Eamon followed suit as a pair of the countersurveillance men headed in their direction. Aiden shifted so Eamon could read his hand signals. Aiden was going after the lead guy, Eamon had the second. Eamon nodded.

They waited until the men were nearly past them before leaping out, locking arms around their necks and dragging them back into the bushes. Eamon's target fought back, kicking and slamming his hands down on Eamon's forearm, but he tightened his hold, twisted ever so slightly until the man passed out. He dumped him and was about to roll him over to secure his hands with a zip tie, but Aiden stopped him.

"Strip him down first. We need those coveralls. And the hats," Aiden added as he pulled his shirt over his head. "Time to make a switch before Felice gets here."

It surprised Lana that it was taking Felice so long to arrive. Considering the woman had known for a good half hour before speaking to Lana where Lana actually was, the delay just seemed... What was the word? Rude.

"Angie?" Lana turned from the window, pulse hammering as the adrenaline began to build once more. Something Marcus had said, something Felice confirmed, had opened up a whole floodgate of ideas. Ideas Lana had finally filtered down to one.

"Yes, Detective Lana Tate?"

Lana rolled her eyes. When this was over, she was going to rip Angie's wiring out by the roots. "Can you show me the schematics to the building?"

"Of course, Detective Lana Tate. Where would you like me to display them?"

She eyed the laptop on the sofa. "Do you have access to electrical devices in this apartment?"

"Yes, Detective…"

"Display on biggest screen, please."

The TV hanging on the wall blinked to life.

"What am I looking at?" Lana asked as she scanned the blueprints of the seven-story structure.

"The schematics you requested, Detective Lana—"

"Show me the staircase and elevator system, please?" Lana stepped closer as the image changed. "Angie, do cell phones work in the elevators?"

"Yes, Detective Lana Tate."

"How?" The steel plating was bound to block the signals.

"Multiple signal boosters have been installed throughout the building, Detective Lana Tate. Including one in each elevator."

"Perfect." She recalled Aiden mentioning the security cameras in the elevators as well. "Angie, do you have access to the operations system of the elevator?"

"I have limited access, Detective Lana Tate. In order to facilitate emergency situations."

Lana inclined her head. "Can I talk to you in the elevator?"

"Yes, Detective Lana Tate. I have vocal interfaces in every part of the building, including the gym, meeting room—"

"Are you able to implement an emergency elevator stop?"

"Yes, Detective Lana Tate. Although it is not recommended."

"What other emergency protocols do you have access to, Angie?"

"I am programmed to assist all residents in various emergency situations. Fire evacuation, flood protection, assault lockdown…"

Bingo! "Do you know how many residents are currently in the building?"

"Yes, Detective Lana Tate. There are currently six apartments occupied. Thirteen other apartments have vacated for the day. Apartment 1C is expected back…"

"Angie, stand by to implement emergency lockdown for all apartments currently occupied. No one in or out until reversed by me or a man named Eamon Quinn. Understand?"

"Yes, Detective Lana Tate. Standing by."

"Thanks."

"Of course, Detective Lana—"

"Just Lana, please." She didn't think she'd ever hear the word *detective* in the same way again. The buzzer by the door sounded. "Stand by, Angie."

"Standing by, Lana."

Even on a screen the size of a tablet computer, Felice Covington made an impression. She wore a tailored suit of the deepest blood red, her jet-dark hair pulled into a knot at the back of her neck. She smoothed a hand down her torso, turned her head toward the men Lana knew were lurking just out of camera range.

Lana hit the intercom button. "Second floor. Use the elevator."

Lana grinned at the flash of irritation on Felice's face. Then she bent down and grabbed her bag to stash in the kitchen. She quickly replaced one of her ear pods, twisted it on to reactivate it. "Aiden? Eamon?"

"Lana?" Eamon whispered. "What the—"

"No time. Aiden, I've got an idea. Is your team still wired into the surveillance system in the elevator? Can you make a recording?"

"Stand by," Aiden said. "Mobile two, please confirm."

"Mobile two confirming. That's a go on the elevators. Recording in progress."

"Okay." Lana felt more confident already. "Okay, good. This is gonna work. We're going to pull this off."

"Pull what off?" Eamon asked.

"I don't want to jinx it." She'd had enough bad luck the last year and a half. She was focused on turning it around, on shutting A&O down once and for all and, hopefully, getting all of them out of this alive.

She heard shouting, voices she didn't recognize coming over her feed. "Where are you?"

"Not something we can explain at the moment," Eamon murmured.

"You and I are due for a discussion at the conclusion of this operation, Detective Tate," Aiden said. "A long one."

"Seconded," Eamon chimed in. Both of their voices had dropped significantly from when she'd first entered the apartment.

"Copy that." Now wasn't the time for second guesses or regrets. On the bright side, she couldn't be fired from a job she'd never had. "Angie, unlock the door, please. Allow my approaching visitor to enter."

"This is not recommended, Lana, as it is against security protocols."

"Understood. Override protocols and unlock the front door."

"Unlocking door." Lana swore she could hear the AI gnash her cyberteeth together.

The click echoed in the empty space. Her heart hammered in her chest as the front door pushed open. The clack of Felice's heels sounded like gunshots as she walked down the hall, turned and stepped inside.

She approached in the same way Lana stood, with her hands behind her back, a disapproving expression on her schoolmarm face. She stopped a few feet away from Lana. "You disappoint me, Lana. I truly believed you were smarter than this."

"No, you didn't." Lana forced herself to relax even as her hand tightened around the butt of her gun. "You tolerated me because I was married to your favorite orphan. The terrified little boy you programmed and trained to do your bidding. Yours and that of A&O Solutions."

"Where are the files?" Felice sounded bored.

"Safe. Where's your backup? You didn't come alone."

"They're in the hall." Felice glanced over her shoulder. "They're armed. All of them. In case you were curious. Even if you did get past me, they wouldn't let you take two steps before firing."

"Well, at least I'm prepared." Lana's smile was quick and

cursory. A few weeks ago, even a few days ago, she might not have worried so much about dying, but now? She held strong to the image of Eamon, to what it felt like to be so completely loved. It was, quite simply, the best thing to live for. "I have a few questions for you. Before we conclude whatever this business is between us."

"Stalling before I end your life." Felice sighed. "How predictable."

"Do you plan to kill me yourself or will you be outsourcing this to one of your minions?" Felice's eyes narrowed in a way that bolstered Lana's confidence. "Project Orbana. You know it needs to end. You've ruined hundreds of lives. And that's just the children you manipulated. I told you," Lana said at the flash of disbelief across Felice's face. "I know everything."

"You're the only one who will." Felice reached into her pocket and withdrew a small hypodermic needle. "Just to build the anticipation. It'll be a lot more tidy than a bullet wound. Blood makes such a mess."

"Always planning ahead." Lana's gaze caught the shift of shadows out in the hall. The men who had been circling in and around the lobby cameras. She checked the monitor. No one there. They must all be inside.

"I plan and I watch," Felice confirmed. "For instance, your little stunt at the coffee shop. You confirmed what I always believed to be your weakness. You care too much. Collateral damage, it's unspeakable for you." Her lips flickered. "It's why I've ordered my men to go door-to-door and fire on every single person inside should you refuse to come with me."

"Come with you?" Lana frowned and her heart skipped a beat. "Why would—"

"As fitting as it might be to have you die of an overdose in your late husband's home, I can't take the chance of leaving something behind for the authorities to find. My sweeper team is on the way. This is what I meant about disappointing, Lana. You see, they can only be let in by someone on the inside. You've removed a significant obstacle. Now…" She stepped closer. "Where are the files?"

Lana swallowed hard, let her arm drop to her side, weapon tight against her thigh.

Felice scoffed. "You aren't going to use that."

"Why not?" Lana aimed it at Felice's chest. "The apartment is soundproofed. No one will hear."

"You kill me, you'll never make it out of this apartment, let alone this building, and neither will anyone else. The files, Lana. I tire of asking."

Lana hesitated, did her best not to look to the sofa, where the laptop sat.

"Ah. You are off your game." Felice spotted the computer and brushed past Lana to claim it. "Now come." She stepped forward, held out her hand. "Give me your weapon and we'll leave together. Peacefully. Let everyone else be safe."

Lana's hand trembled. It made a grotesque kind of sense that she'd walked right into a trap after being so careful about creating her own. She knew without a doubt that if she did what Felice wanted, if she left this building with her, she'd never make it back to Eamon alive.

But there were others to worry about besides herself. Others she had sworn to protect. She wouldn't allow any more innocents to die.

"All right." She raised her hand, let the gun slip free and spin in her hold, the muzzle rotating until it pointed at the ceiling. "All right. I'm putting it down." She walked over to the small dining table and left it there. "You lead, I'll follow."

"I don't think so." Felice, needle still in hand, stepped aside. Every muscle in Lana's body tensed as she moved on. She counted her steps, keeping an eye on the shadows that shifted into solid forms as she reached the door. On the bright side, there were only two men in the hall.

On the other hand, they were two men armed with semi-automatic pistols.

She could feel Felice behind her, drawing closer with every step. Just let her get a little bit...

Lana spun, grabbed Felice's hand and yanked her forward before she quickly let go. As Felice plowed into one of her men, Lana dived for the door handle and before she pulled it closed yelled, "Angie, lockdown mode, now!"

She heard every lock on the second floor slide into place as the door to Marcus's apartment clicked shut.

A masculine hand caught her shoulder and jerked her back. She ducked and turned in one quick motion, pivoted and drove her foot directly into the nearest man's solar plexus. He slammed against the wall.

She didn't stop to think. She ran. Full out. Eyes locked on those sliding metal doors. "Angie," she yelled. "Open elevator A."

She didn't have time to contemplate the fear that had plagued her most of her life as the elevator doors slid open and she dived inside. She hit the floor, immediately pushing herself over and into the corner as heavy-booted footfalls echoed toward her.

"Angie, close doors!"

A hand slammed into the door opening, shoved the nearly closed doors open once more as one of Felice's guards stepped in, gun in hand, and aimed the muzzle directly at her head. Lana blinked, unable to see anything beyond that black, dark barrel.

"Enough!" Felice's voice snapped and she clipped along the hall toward them. She shoved her foot soldier inside before joining them, her injured hand clutched against her chest, the hypodermic needle still in her grip.

Lana's breaths came in short gasps as she pushed farther into the corner, shoving the terror aside as she stared up at the woman responsible for turning her husband into a monster. For robbing him of whomever he'd been meant to be.

The doors slid closed. Lana's vision cleared as she looked at the now lowered gun. "Angie, sixth floor." The elevator took off, its whine a symphony of gears and ingenuity as Lana grabbed hold of the railing above her head. "Angie, emergency stop!"

The car stopped abruptly. Felice shrieked, stumbled against the wall, only to be righted by the man in black. Lana raised determined eyes first to Felice, then to the man who had retrained his gun on Lana.

A man with beautiful, familiar hazel eyes. And the faintest hint of red hair escaping the hem of his cap.

Love so powerful she almost whimpered draped over her as her confidence surged. "He trusted you. He was a child, a lost little boy, and you made him believe you cared about him."

"He was useful," Felice said. "Until he wasn't. My only regret is that I wasn't the one driving the car that ended him." Felice crouched, wobbling on her bladelike heels as she stared into Lana's eyes. "But I heard you scream for him." She touched a finger to Lana's face. "And that brought me more pleasure than anything has in a very, very long time."

"You betrayed him," Lana whispered, her voice breaking. "He trusted you more than he ever trusted anyone. He loved you and you betrayed him. You killed him."

"He betrayed me first. Betrayed all of us. After everything we'd done for him, everything we made him, everything we gave him, he was going to walk away. For you. For you and whatever brat offspring you hoped to give him." She seemed to catch herself, as if she'd admitted too much. "We simply couldn't allow it. He was ours. He was never yours."

"You didn't have to kill him. He was trying to do the right thing."

"Oh, don't be so melodramatic. Marcus Tate wasn't a victim," Felice spit. "And he certainly wasn't a hero. He wasn't going to turn that information over to the authorities. He was holding it over our heads. He wanted money. Enough for the two of you to start over. To disappear. Did you know that Marcus Tate wasn't even his real name? He was made up. I made him up. I created him. He knew the price for betraying the syndicate and he did it anyway. The second he did that, he forfeited both your lives."

"You turned him into a killer." Lana stared. "How many people did he kill for you?" she asked on a whisper. "How many deaths is he, are you, are they, responsible for? Murders. Bombings. Shootings. Poisonings."

"More than you'll ever know," Felice boasted as she stood. "And they're all up here." She tapped a finger against her temple. "I am the human record of our success. And now that I have the only other record—"

"Do you think that's enough?" Lana glanced up at Eamon as he pulled the black knit cap off his head and holstered his weapon.

"Should do it." He glanced up at the camera. "Aiden? Did it come through?"

"Loud and clear and in full Technicolor."

Felice blinked, her confusion obvious. "I don't—"

"That's okay." Lana pulled herself up and brushed herself off. "After you take some time to replay this all in your head, you will."

Felice's eyes darkened and sharpened as she turned on Lana. Her hand came up, the needle poised to plunge. "Angie, first floor. Express!"

The elevator plummeted. Felice lost her balance but stumbled toward Lana, who grabbed her hand and whipped it behind her. The needle clattered to the floor as Lana pressed Felice up against the wall of the elevator as it came to a sudden stop on the first floor.

"Lana." Eamon moved in behind her, rested a hand on her shoulder. "Aiden, cut the feed."

"Here's what's going to happen, Felice." Lana released the woman, although she didn't turn around. "You have a choice to make. You can testify against A&O Solutions and help put them out of business once and for all, or you can take full responsibility for every single crime your orphans committed. Not that you'd live long enough in prison for that to happen. I'm sure there's another Marcus out there who would like to take you out. You know, because it's his or her job."

"I think she gets the point," Eamon said.

"Speaking of points."

Lana turned at the sound of Aiden's voice. He stepped into the open elevator, bent down and picked up the hypodermic needle. "I'm betting this is oleander."

"I should have poisoned your Scotch when I had the chance," Felice said. She strode past Lana and into the custody of two of Aiden's men waiting just outside the elevator. "I certainly had plenty of chances, didn't I. You're a disgrace, Lana. A drunken, pathetic disgrace who never deserved Marcus."

"Only one of us is a disgrace," Lana said calmly. "And it isn't me. Aiden, I'd recommend keeping her in one of your vans until the feds can get here. There's sensitive information upstairs in the apartment we wouldn't want her to see." She looked at Eamon as Felice was led away. Sirens blared in the distance, a sound that brought her such comfort she felt as if she could breathe again. "You should call it in."

He shook his head. "Not my call to make." He looked to Aiden.

"I think it would make a pretty big last call," Aiden said. "Earn yourself some serious DOJ goodwill on your way out the door?"

Lana caught Eamon's arm. "Out the door? Where are you going?"

"We have some details to work out." Eamon glared at Aiden. "Suffice it to say, I've been made an offer I'm not entirely sure I can refuse."

"You Godfathered him?" Lana straightened as a cacophony of emotions battled for control. "Aiden McKenna, you really are one smart cookie. Speaking of cookies, I'm starving."

"We can fix that," Aiden said. "Vince? Slade?"

"On our way," Vince said amid the rustle of food packages.

"Meet us upstairs at the apartment," Lana said as she stepped back into the elevator. "There's something I think you all might want to see. Coming?" She held out her hand to Eamon, who looked surprised.

"You hate elevators."

"I do." She nodded and sighed, tugged him in as Aiden followed. "But I'm just not up to tackling another flight of stairs right now."

Chapter Fifteen

"I need to get to the airport." Eamon eased his arm out from around Lana's shoulders and sat up. But he wasn't without her for long as she shifted her legs under her and scooted up behind him, pressed her lips against his bare shoulder. "If I'm lucky, I'll get back just in time to get Jason to his tuxedo fitting. Sure you don't want to come back with me?" He reached back, found her hand and squeezed.

"Not yet." Lana sighed, a big smile on her face. Aiden had been gracious enough to extend their room reservation for a few days, and they'd made very good use of both the bed and room service. A bonus incentive, he'd told them, to sweeten his job offer.

"To be honest," Lana continued, "I'm really not in any rush to get back on a private jet. I'm good with commercial for the foreseeable future."

It had been two days since Felice Covington's arrest by federal authorities. A little over thirty-six hours since the story broke on the truth about A&O Solutions. And twenty-four hours ago the first round of arrest warrants had been issued.

Aiden had been right. It was the perfect case for Eamon

to end his FBI career on. Among other information found in the files Marcus Tate had left in the care of his wife had been countless evidence trails that would shut down multiple child trafficking and exploitation sites around the world.

"I can come up to Seattle this weekend, help you decide what you're going to do." He drew her arms around him, resisted the temptation to press her back into the mattress and lose himself in her.

"If you come up to Seattle, I won't be capable of thinking about anything other than you. No. I need to do some serious self-examination," she said. "I need to figure out where I go from here. Although I'm thinking there might be room for me with you in Sacramento? I heard through the grapevine those final two apartments in Greta's building are finally finished. Not entirely sure I can afford it—"

"I have an in with the landlord," Eamon said. "But it would be awfully greedy of us to take both of them." Eamon grinned. "Plenty of space for both of us in one."

"Yeah?" She shifted around and straddled him, wound her arms around his neck and kissed him. "You want me to move in with you?"

"Yes." He kissed her again. Her body stiffened, and for a moment, he thought he'd spoken too soon.

"Wow."

"Is that a wow as in yes or a wow as in I don't think—"

"Eamon." She clasped his face in her hands, stared into his eyes. "I'm not in the right frame of mind to answer that question right now. How about…three weeks. Give me three weeks."

"Three weeks as in Kyla and Jason's wedding?" His initial flood of disappointment vanished.

"Is it?" She mock-gasped. "Well, so it is. What a coincidence. Three weeks." She lowered her mouth to his. "How about we take a shower before you head off to the airport?"

"You heard about the water shortage in Boston, didn't you?" He shifted around, held on to her as he stood up. "We need to double up to conserve."

"Whatever you say, Special Agent Quinn." She buried her face in his neck. "Whatever you say."

It HAD BEEN far too long since Lana had felt anything close to excitement about the future. But as she slid the "Offer pending" plaque on the top of the For Sale sign in front of her house, that was precisely what she felt. Excited. For whatever this new life of hers was going to bring. She was two days shy of the three weeks she'd promised Eamon. Her rented trailer was mostly packed, her resignation with the Seattle PD processed, and, thanks to a stellar real-estate agent, she was just a few days from entering escrow.

She turned to walk back into the house when a dark SUV pulled into her driveway. Her heart leaped, as she assumed at first it was Eamon surprising her, but then she remembered he was neck-deep in wedding festivities, so she tempered her disappointment until she saw who it was.

"Aiden." She stopped, pushed her hands into the back pockets of her jeans and smiled as he approached. He was business casual today, dressed in dark slacks, blazer, no tie. With his black hair, he looked far more intimidating than she knew him to be. "This is a nice surprise. Everything okay?"

"I was in town for a meeting. Thought I'd stop by, give you an update on the Covington case."

"Oh. Sure." She shrugged. To be honest, she didn't want

to give another thought to Felice Covington, A&O Solutions, or the crimes they were responsible for. "Come on in. I haven't packed the coffee machine yet. You want some?"

"That'd be great, thanks."

She had a pot brewing before he joined her in the kitchen. "Place is a mess, I know. I'm selling most everything with the house. The rest that I want to keep is already packed. It's a little sad, but it all fits in the smallest trailer they rent."

"You're smiling, so I think that means it's the right move."

She laughed, pulled two mugs out of the dish dryer. "You've spoken to Eamon."

"Didn't have to. The man is broadcasting on every platform available. I'm kidding," he added. "But I have been talking to him. It's going to be an adjustment for him, moving from the Bureau to the private sector."

"You couldn't have found a better man for the job. I know he'll still be working in the field some, but it's important that he knows he's making a difference."

"The Bureau's giving him a lot of credit for the A&O Solutions indictments. He's going out on a high. That's good for him."

"And for you." She took the filled pot and poured. "I've done some checking up on you, Aiden McKenna. You pride yourself on hiring the best of the best. That goodwill he's earned is going to rub off on your firm."

"You think?" He sipped, but not before she saw his grin. "Never crossed my mind. So. Felice."

She rolled her eyes. "Don't tell me. Someone shanked her in the prison yard."

"Hardly. She took the government's offer and is singing like the biggest canary in the coal mine."

Lana frowned. "I think you're mixing your metaphors."

He shrugged. "The deal she's getting only takes the death penalty off the table. She's in for life. Hard time, too."

She nodded. "Couldn't happen to a worse person."

"So, how are you doing?" His gaze drifted to the ninety-day chip she'd left on the counter. "Dealing with the fallout about Marcus."

"It is what it is. He was what he was. I loved him. Who he pretended to be." She searched her cabinet for the last package of sandwich cookies. "I've stopped blaming myself for that. The video he left, it helped me see that at least he hadn't married me because of my job. He loved me, too. Enough to try to break away from Felice and A&O. That means something."

"I think it does," Aiden agreed. "And work?"

"That is the big question. I put a call in to Lieutenant Santos in Sacramento. Asked if he had any openings for a detective." She hesitated. "I haven't heard back yet."

"Might be a reason for that."

"Ya think?" She couldn't blame the lieutenant. She hadn't gone out in a blaze of glory like Eamon had. She'd done serious damage to her career. It was going to take a lot to earn the trust of people she hadn't yet worked with. Even though she had. Kind of. "So, what was this meeting you had out here?"

"Funny you should ask. It was with Captain Davis."

"My Captain Davis? Or rather my former—"

"One and the same. I had some questions about you, thought maybe she'd be a good one to ask."

"And yet here you are." Butterflies the size of bats took flight in her stomach.

"Taking all things into consideration, she confirmed what I already know. You're a good detective with excellent instincts and a talent for thinking out of the box. You knew my plan for Felice Covington wasn't right. The only thing you did wrong was keep it to yourself and left us to play catch-up."

"Sorry about that." She shoved a cookie in her mouth. "At the time," she said after she swallowed, "I was thinking if I was wrong, at least the only person that would get hurt would be me. Hindsight's a...well, it's something."

"Things could have gone very wrong, but they didn't. You saw all the angles. And now that you know me better, I'm guessing you wouldn't have any issues telling me I'm wrong."

She narrowed her eyes. "Where is this going?"

"I'm on my way down to Sacramento before I head back to DC. I'm going to suggest a partnership with Vince Sutton, make Sutton Investigations a part of Minotaur. Expand our reach to the West Coast. He's got good people around him, a lot of excellent resources. And it'll allow Eamon and maybe his future wife to stay put. Close to their family."

"I think that's great." But she still didn't see what it had to do with her.

"Vince isn't manager material. I want someone heading up the office I can talk to honestly, be told what works and what doesn't. Someone who knows how local law enforcement works and to liaise when needed. Starting salary would be double what you were making with Seattle PD. And there would be benefits, of course."

"Of course." She blinked, swallowed hard. "I, uh, don't really know what to say. Would I still...? I really like being a cop." The idea of abandoning a career she'd worked so hard to build on didn't completely sit right with her.

"You're always going to be a cop, Lana. It's in your blood. It's who you are. I'm just asking you to think about expanding your horizons a bit. You'll get to travel. Flexible schedule. And best of all, you'll get to shoot me down on occasion."

"Well, when you put it like that." She felt that zing of excitement shoot through her system. The same zing that struck whenever she heard Eamon's voice, felt the touch of his hand. Imagined his face. "When do you want me to start?"

"We can talk details on the plane." He folded his arms over his chest. "I am on a roll. We're wheels up in an hour. You can hitch a ride to Sacramento with me."

"An hour?" She shook her head. "I've still got packing to do—"

"Make a list of what needs doing and I'll get it taken care of. You didn't want to make that drive down by yourself, did you? I've got friends in the moving business. Consider it done."

She hesitated. She didn't want to disappoint him right out of the gate, but this was one of those times when she had to put herself first. "I'm sorry, Aiden. I've got something in about a half hour that I can't reschedule or miss."

"You're acting as if you think that's a deal breaker." He pulled out his phone and texted someone, got almost an immediate answer. "My pilot's looking into a later window. In the meantime, I'll call my moving contact. Will after seven tonight work?"

"Sure." She smiled, imagining Eamon's face when she showed up two days early. "After seven is perfect."

"Okay, then. I'll be back to pick you up later." He finished his coffee and headed out.

Lana glanced at her watch, gathering her jacket and purse before she locked up the house. Aiden was driving down the street as she pulled out of the driveway and headed in the opposite direction.

Twenty minutes later she parked in the lot of the nearby community center, made her way inside and through the double swinging doors into the meeting room. She forwent the coffee for a change, ignored the doughnuts and surrendered to the pull of the homemade brownies that frequently made an appearance.

"Evening, Lana."

Lana looked up and smiled at the young woman taking a seat next to her. The folding metal chair was hard against her back, but she draped her coat over her knees and settled in as the other attendees joined them.

"Hello, everyone." Marsha, the leader of their group, welcomed the two dozen people sitting in a circle. "It's good to see everyone here. Let's just jump into it, shall we? Who would like to start?"

Lana fisted her hands in her jacket before unclenching one of them and raising it. "I'll go."

"Okay," Marsha said with an encouraging nod. "The floor is yours."

Lana took a deep breath. "Hi. My name is Lana. And I'm an alcoholic."

EVER SINCE HE was a little kid, Eamon Quinn had detested surprises. He was a nightmare at Christmas, and the kid who secretly searched the house for his gifts weeks before the big day. Birthdays? Forget about it. He'd been given one surprise party and it had traumatized him for years.

So hearing from his new boss that he'd be making an unexpected stop in Sacramento and bringing Eamon a surprise did not make his evening of frivolities more enjoyable.

Instead, as he mingled with his friends on the private patio of the Brass Eagle, he found himself constantly looking toward the door, hoping he'd soon be put out of his misery. He looked at his watch. It was already after ten. If Aiden didn't get here soon, the party was going to be over.

"You do know this is a celebration, right?" Jason Sutton, the groom-to-be, slung an arm over Eamon's shoulders and futilely attempted to put him in a headlock.

"Don't mess with the fed," Vince warned him.

"Ex-fed," Eamon corrected him. "Or I will be in another forty-eight hours." He'd put in for his pension a little over two weeks ago, about twenty-four hours before Aiden sent him a list of possible contenders for his child crime task force. Needless to say, he'd pretty much been working two jobs ever since. Add to that moving into the empty two-bedroom apartment in Greta's building and counting the hours until Lana arrived, hopefully with an answer to his proposal, and he'd kept busy.

The music was constant, the drinks flowing and the food grilling as the bride and groom and their close family and friends dived into the pre-wedding celebration full bore. Eden and Greta were holding court in the back corner of the patio, away from the smoke of the grill, and toasting one another with various nonalcoholic concoctions. Allie and her husband, Max, along with Riordan and Darcy Malloy, were having some kind of comical dance competition that could have made them a small fortune on social media.

Simone waved Vince over so she could hand off baby Caleb in order to go grab a plate of food while Kyla and Jason drifted toward one another in a dreamy waltz that made even Eamon a bit misty-eyed.

"Up!"

Eamon glanced down at little Chloe Ann, dressed in an adorable white-and-red polka-dot dress, her arms stretched toward him. "Up, Amu." Her tiny fingers wiggled as she did a little shimmy.

He set his beer aside, bent down and lifted her, settling her into the crook of his arm as she grabbed hold of his neck. "You do like your parties, don't you, Chloe Ann."

"Party!" She lifted both arms up and squealed, grabbed hold of him again and planted a wet kiss on his cheek. "Love Amu."

His throat tightened and he touched a finger to her cheek. "I love you, too, Chloe."

"Hey! Look who's here." Jason abandoned his bride-to-be and made his way toward Aiden McKenna. "Welcome to the party."

"I don't want to intrude," Aiden insisted as he looked pointedly at Eamon. "Eamon didn't tell me there was a party when I said I wanted to stop by."

"Well, it's too late to leave now," Jason insisted. "Kyla, this is—"

"Aiden McKenna." Kyla, her tropical-flowered dress flowing around her lithe figure, approached with her hand out. "I've heard a lot about you. Welcome. Please. Join us."

"Happy to, thanks."

"I'll get you a drink. Beer?" Kyla offered.

"Ah, sure."

Eamon grinned at his new boss's discomfort. "It's your own fault," Eamon told him once he was within earshot. "You're in the circle now."

"Not that I need to earn any more goodwill, but I've got that surprise for you around here somewhere. Hello, there." He inclined his head at Chloe Ann. "And who might you be?"

"This is Chloe Ann. Chloe Ann, this is Aiden."

"Den!" Never leery of strangers, she pitched herself forward. "Hi, Den!" She grabbed hold as he lifted her free.

"Look at that. Got me an instant friend at the party. Now, let's see who your mom and dad might be."

As he held Chloe Ann securely in his arms, Eamon turned, his heart swelling. "Lana."

"Hey." She moved toward him and didn't stop until they embraced. "Surprise."

He folded her into him, his hands sliding down her back as he felt every nerve in his body settle. "I'm so glad you're here."

"Me, too." She stepped back, looked down at her simple black dress. "I hope this is okay. I packed most of my clothes in the trailer already."

"You look beautiful." He bent his head and kissed her.

"Sorry we're late. I had a meeting." She snuggled against his side, rested her head on his shoulder. "Have I got news for you."

"Yeah?"

"Oh, yeah." She beamed up at him. "But I think I'll start with saying I love you, Eamon Quinn. I am so, so grateful you didn't give up on me. That you were waiting, however far in the wings. I love you for now and always."

He didn't have any doubt. But hearing the words, seeing the absolute certainty on her face, he could feel those wounds on his heart finally begin to heal. Eamon slid his hand into the pocket of his jacket, pulled out the ring he'd been carrying around for the past two and a half weeks. It was a simple band, nothing fancy and flashy. Gold with a rounded diamond that caught the twinkling lights of the strands strung across the patio.

"Pretty!" Chloe Ann yelled as she reached up to try to catch the reflection in her fingers. "Amu and Lala pretty."

The crowd quieted, all eyes turning on them.

He didn't have to ask. He only had to look into her eyes as she smiled. And nodded.

"She said yes?" Eden yelled from across the patio.

Eamon nodded. "She said yes."

Lana chuckled as the cheering exploded and Vince hurried inside and returned with two bottles of sparkling cider. As he poured, the whole group moved closer, everyone encircling them.

"This is Kyla and Jason's night," Lana said as she wiped tears of happiness off her cheeks. "I don't want to—"

"You're part of the family now, Lana." Greta reached out and slipped an arm through hers. "I'm afraid you're stuck with all of us now. Congratulations."

"Thanks." Lana smiled up at Eamon, tears glistening in her eyes. "I love you."

"I love you, too." He drew her close and smiled.

Above the laughter, and the whoops and hollers and congratulations, there was the familiar memory of the sound of a little girl's laughter. He squeezed his eyes shut. "I miss you, little sister."

When he opened his eyes again and looked up, a star shot across the sky.

"She's here," Lana whispered. "She always will be. And so will I."

He kissed Lana, and he knew, without hesitation, that he was finally where he belonged.

He was home.

* * * * *

COMING SOON!

We really hope you enjoyed reading this book.
If you're looking for more romance
be sure to head to the shops when
new books are available on

Thursday 4th January

To see which titles are coming soon, please visit
millsandboon.co.uk/nextmonth

Introducing our newest series, Afterglow.

From showing up to glowing up, Afterglow characters are on the path to leading their best lives and finding romance along the way – with a dash of sizzling spice!

Follow characters from all walks of life as they chase their dreams and find that true love is only the beginning...

Two stories published every month. Launching January 2024

millsandboon.co.uk

OUT NOW!